Honestly, I'm Totally Faking It

a novel

Amanda Gambill

Amanda Gambill

Copyright © 2022 Amanda Gambill

IBSN: 9798789069905

All rights reserved.

No part of this book may be reproduced in any form, stored in any retrieval system, or transmitted in any form by any means—electronic, mechanical, photocopy, recording, or otherwise—without prior written permission of the copyright owner, except as provided by United States of America copyright law.

This book is a work of fiction. Any references to historical events, real people, or real places are used fictitiously. Other names, characters, places, and events are products of the author's imagination, and any resemblances to actual events or places or persons, living or dead, is entirely coincidental.

Cover design by Mary Scarlett LaBerge
Author headshot by Allison Hammond

Printed in USA

amandagambill.com

Dedication

To my Bookstagram friends who are always just a comment, Story, or message away. Thank you for being my cheerleaders, my hype women, my devoted readers, and my friends. Love y'all!

To Robert, you're the reason I can write about love — always and forever

HONESTLY i'm TOTALLY faking it

CHAPTER ONE

Honestly, crashing on your ex-boyfriend's couch has tons of positives.

Like JD couldn't really change the Netflix password with me parked right in front of the television.

And he always made too much coffee so I could sneak a cup once he left for work. Who cared if it was leftover from when he went to work at night and I didn't start my day until the next morning? It was still coffee.

The leftovers he'd leave in the fridge from his fancy chef job were fair game, and the empty apartment after a long day of work gave me plenty of time to meditate. Once I had an entire weekend to binge HGTV shows, not even knowing where he was.

And he was offering me super cheap rent while my tiny basement apartment was being fumigated for mold and creepy critters I didn't like to think about since I'd be moving back any day now.

Sure, having the whole relationship and future thing would have been nice. But my mom always taught me to think optimistically.

And all signs pointed to us getting back together anyway. Small romantic gestures like cute notes left with his leftovers. The sappy movies in his recently watched list on Netflix. Obviously, he missed me.

And when I woke up on my birthday, sitting right on

the bathroom counter was lacy, emerald lingerie.

I may have wanted to believe in horoscopes and signs, but *this* was solid evidence.

It was make-up sex lingerie.

A totally-getting-back-together bra paired with sorry-I-dumped-you-and-said-you-were-going-nowhere panties.

Our-breakup-was-a-mistake sexy time set.

I slipped it on and smiled in the mirror. Even if it didn't fit perfectly, it was the nicest thing I owned.

The emerald matched my eyes and contrasted with my raven hair. I stood on my tippy toes, pretending I was in heels. At five-foot-ten, I'd gotten used to ditching them, but just this once, I felt like at the right angle with the right lighting in the right outfit, I looked like I could be a woman who had it all.

I wasn't too tall with too straight, too black, too thick hair that I couldn't possibly manage except to tie back in a ponytail. My two front teeth that never seemed to be covered with my too big top lip was maybe even cute. *Cupid's bow*, my mom had called it when she'd seen me grow self-conscious, a name for what I'd thought had been a flaw so pretty and so whimsical.

I felt pretty and whimsical now when I imagined the future. Knowing JD missed me, wanted me again, saw me, chose me, picked me, believed I was enough.

His bedroom door was locked, sleeping in from his string of late nights, so I kept the set on as a reminder of something to look forward to after work.

Knowing all the signs pointed to things looking up, I beamed on the cramped bus, not even minding when someone splashed coffee on me.

"No worries, it's like a natural perfume," I said brightly to their mumbled apology, but they'd kept walking, not noticing I'd spoken.

I didn't mind, too happy that JD had remembered my birthday.

Last year, when we'd been more off than on, he'd accidentally scheduled a guys' trip during it. When he'd come back, he'd given me a rock he'd said reminded him of me. I'd appreciated it, grateful he'd been thinking of me, but the lingerie did seem like a slight step up.

My horoscope this morning had said, *"A wonderful illusion is in play and change is extremely likely."* I hadn't had a chance to check JD's, but it was clear.

Change *was* on the horizon. Good things were to come.

Nothing could damper my spirit. Not even the somber conference room where the personal assistants who worked in the office gathered for an all-hands meeting. As I juggled everyone's coffees, I also got to catch the latest gossip.

"He's a monster," Kelsey whispered to Carolyn.

"That was his fourth assistant in two months," she replied, taking her coffee from me without a glance.

The morning chatter was always interesting, as jolting as the caffeine itself, so I never minded being mostly ignored as I passed out coffees.

Being a personal assistant to personal assistants may have seemed like a sucky job. But really, it meant all I had to do was get through this day — run errands no one else wanted, pick up coffees, make copies, answer inquiry emails and calls, and keep everyone generally happy — and then JD and I could reunite.

"Thanks, Rebecca," Kelsey said over her shoulder as I sat down her coffee before turning back to Carolyn.

"It's actually Rach, sounds like Rachel, but it's just Rach. Not Rebec—"

Not hearing my attempt at a correction, she continued, "Melinda was panicking. She said if he fires someone else, he'll probably switch firms. Apparently he's looking to expand his needs so it'd be an even bigger loss."

Carolyn rolled her eyes. "Old dudes are the worst."

"Old *rich* dudes," Kelsey added under her breath.

I held back a laugh and continued handing out orders.

"Hey, Rita, this coffee isn't right. I said chai."

"*Chai* am so sorry," I said with a laugh and made my way back to Carolyn. "The shop must've gotten mixed up. You're in luck, I also ordered chai. It was a birthday freebie, so it's probably good luck, too. You can have it."

Giving me a weird look, she took it and turned back to her conversation.

"I just hope I'm not placed with him," she whined. "I have my hands full with four lawyers. I don't want to have to housesit for some geezer."

"Housesitting?" I asked. "He's a virtual client?"

Our firm had virtual clients, but none ever made the internal gossip circuit. They mostly just needed our services to walk dogs and water plants while they remained enigmas.

Both women looked at me like they hadn't realized I was still there.

"Basically. He's never home," Kelsey answered. "He's in DC like twenty days out of the month."

"Yet he manages to be an asshole all thirty days of the month," Carolyn grumbled.

"Hey, at least you have one good day every other month."

They both blinked at me.

I kind of laughed, shaking my head at my stupid joke.

"I'm just kidding. I meant because there are some

months with thirty-one days and you said he was mean thirty … never mind."

She turned to Kelsey. "He made Emma cry. He emailed her and said that he considered her a subpar assistant, so she should consider herself fired. Who just puts that in writing? At least be nice and sugarcoat it."

Before I could ask more questions, our agency's owner, Melinda, hurried in, and I settled in my chair against the wall to take notes.

"First order of business, the St. Clair situation."

Just the mention of this man's name made everyone sit up a little straighter and inhale a little sharper.

Yet another reason I was grateful I was basically just another plain yogurt in the fridge — forgotten in the back and not expected to do more than sit quietly.

"I'll put it bluntly. He's unhappy. You know this. He knows this. I am very aware of this. I'm also aware he is a pain. I'm not positive *he's* aware of that fact. But Prestige Staffing provides top-tier service to luxury clients. He fits the bill. He also helps pay the bills. So I'm doing something unorthodox. I'm asking for a volunteer."

I peeked up from my notes when no one broke the silence, not even with an inhale or body shift.

Wealthy, busy clients meant perks: connections, exclusive experiences, and even travel. I'd personally been knocked down three times by assistants racing to Melinda's office when coveted clients needed extra help.

Melinda cleared her throat at the lack of excitement.

"You'd be assigned to just him, so you won't have to come into the office anymore. Consider it like having your own personal penthouse to work out of."

Other than Carolyn bravely sipping my chai, no one budged.

My eyes widened, shocked by how many faces were still cast downward. If they managed his schedule, they'd know when he'd be there. Which meant they'd know when he wasn't — meaning unsupervised access to a *penthouse*. I bet this St. Clair man had a nice kitchen and a huge television. Instantly, I imagined JD and I in it — it could be a great thing to surprise him with and show him I had plenty to bring to the table.

In this new lingerie, I felt like I could be a different person. Someone new entirely. Someone better.

Melinda sighed.

"It comes with a bonus. Ten percent of your salary."

My heart quickened. This was a sign.

I could save a little money. I could advance in my stalled career. I could prove to JD I was better than he thought, that I was worth being with. Once he believed in me, he'd ask me to be with him for real.

A future. A home. Somewhere to belong.

This could be life changing.

There were so many possibilities, and all I had to do was not kill this old man's plants?

"I'll do it," I blurted out, nearly dropping my notebook. Good thing I'd given my coffee away because I would've spilled it on the ground in my haste.

For once in my life, everyone was acutely aware of my presence in a room. And they all looked shocked.

"Uh, I mean, I'd be honored to take one for the team," I said and brushed my hair off my face and straightened up, trying my best to look poised and confident. "Maybe a nontraditional solution could be the fix? I'd be honored to try … if no one else wants to."

"Rose," Kelsey whispered, "were you not listening? You'd be the fifth assistant he'd fire in two months."

"Yes, I was actually taking notes." I turned to Melinda with my best poker face. "But I tend to have good luck."

She looked around for another volunteer.

Just like their coffee orders, everyone was content to let me take care of it.

"How about you fill in for a few weeks until we find a suitable replacement?" she said after a long, awkward silence. "If he thinks we're going out of our way to find someone special in a dedicated search, maybe we can appease him. Until then, it can be you, Rach."

My smile never faltered. I didn't need to be special, I was just happy someone remembered my name.

. . .

"JD, I have exciting news," I called out, sitting down appetizers I'd picked up at a nice restaurant between errands since he hadn't mentioned us getting dinner.

I'd studied its menu throughout the day, carefully Googling the words I didn't know during a lull in the line at the dry cleaners. *Foie gras*, to my surprise, was not pronounced how I'd imagined or remotely similar to being fooey grass. So I'd gone with something less sad and hoped JD wouldn't mind.

I slipped off my dress pants and blouse and walked to his bedroom where his shower was running.

"I'm pretty sure I got promoted. You won't believe it, the man I'm going to work for is a sixty-year-old, four-term senator. Super wealthy, super in DC. It literally couldn't be a better situation. I've had a *great* birthday."

Melinda had given me a quick run-down.

"James St. Clair. Works in politics," she'd said, waving her hand vaguely as if I should already know. I'd nodded, pretending I did. "I introduced you via email, and I sent you his file. According to Emma's schedule, he's in DC for two weeks, so just do whatever he asks over email. He has lots of notes and is very detailed, so you'll probably be able to manage."

I'd nodded, hastily Googling "James St. Clair, politics."

"Just do what he asks, and stay out of the way. Even virtually," she'd added. "No offense, but I don't think he'd like someone like you."

Before I could ask what she meant or tell her his file hadn't come through, she'd left for another meeting.

After skimming the first two pages of Google, I'd felt like I needed a political science degree to understand how woven he was in politics.

I tried not to judge, especially not the man who'd be responsible for my employment, but my stomach sank as I learned more. For decades, he was behind nearly every bill that disenfranchised those who needed help the most.

Entire Twitter threads dissected why he was one of the most disliked politicians in modern history. His name dominated the news tab, headlines and opinion articles — *James St. Clair is worse than the Grim Reaper, Sen. St. Clair is the apex predator of US politics, St. Clair embraces his dark side, St. Clair holds up budget talks, millions may lose benefits, Senate Majority Leader stalls reconciliation, Senator James St. Clair: The Man Who Sold America For Himself* — making it clear he was influential, well-connected, wealthy, and didn't quite care if he was as hated as he was powerful.

I couldn't even imagine him having plants or caring if they stayed alive. Maybe that would be a plus, I hoped, one less thing to do. Unless he cared more about plants than people, which was possible.

But, he was kind of my only chance.

So I just had to stay positive.

Instead of worrying, I paused to double-check my

reflection in the mirror in JD's hallway.

The birthday lingerie really did look great.

I stood a little bit taller and opened his door.

He was sitting up in his bed, the sheets rumpled, his hair disheveled, looking totally hot. And totally naked.

"Rach!" he said, startled. The lingerie must have looked better than I'd thought. "Oh shit."

"Happy birthday to me! And I guess in some ways, you," I singsonged. "I loved the present. Now it's my turn to return the romantic gesture."

I started to step forward when I suddenly stopped.

I was an optimist.

But I wasn't an idiot.

The shower.

The shower was still on. And his hair wasn't wet.

"JD," I said slowly, glancing around. His clothes were on the floor ... next to a dress that didn't belong to me. "Please tell me there's a small leak in the bathroom. Nothing too bad, but enough to make that sound."

"I can explain," he said, scrambling for his clothes. I just stood there, glancing between the dress and the bathroom. "We broke up weeks ago, so this isn't even cheating. And you're leaving soon anyway. How long was I supposed to wait before I brought her back here? I've been waiting weeks."

I barely heard him. Because a very beautiful, nearly naked woman stepped out of the bathroom. She was a hostess from his work, and suddenly those cute notes paired with leftovers in the fridge made a lot more sense.

She gasped, tightening her grip on her towel.

Well, I couldn't have gotten this more wrong.

"Oh no," I stuttered, squeezing my eyes shut. The images of them next to each other, her dripping wet, him tousled, burned in my brain. And yet somehow, *I* was the most naked. "Oh fu—dge brownies. I'm *sofa*-king sorry. Ha, get it, because I sleep on the couch. But not now, now I'm going to go. Oh my gosh."

I banged into the doorframe as I turned to run away, my shoulder already stinging.

It couldn't get worse, I reminded myself as I tried to gather my pride, bearings, and clothes from the floor.

Rock bottom hurt, but at least it couldn't get worse.

"Wait," the woman said, appearing in her dress as I tugged my blouse over my head. I got stuck, trapped in a silk cocoon of eternal embarrassment, trying and failing to wriggle my way free. She stepped closer, and I stopped wriggling to squeeze my eyes shut, hoping if I just stayed still I'd eventually disappear.

Because I was wrong.

It definitely could get worse.

And when she spoke next, I was grateful I couldn't see her face.

"I'm pretty sure you're wearing my lingerie."

CHAPTER TWO

"You aren't on the list."

"Yep, we've established that," I said with as much brightness as I could muster. "I'm not trying to attend. I just need to drop off this dress. One of the people *on* the list spilled wine on her dress."

The doorman at Hotel Chanceux looked skeptical even as I held up the bagged dress. "Why are *you* dressed up then? Looks like you're trying to sneak in."

When Kelsey had called — just as I'd curled up on the lobby couch with the unopened file on James St. Clair I'd finally managed to track down, cheeks still red from embarrassment — she'd said her client was having a meltdown so she needed three things.

One, a new dress for her client. Two, that *I* needed to look the part in order to step inside the Mayor's Charity Ball. Thankfully, I'd befriended our firm's go-to dry cleaner, so I was able to get a dress of the client's after-hours and borrow one for myself. All I had to do was return it in the same condition as I got it in.

And that was easy since I'd bought underwear from the corner store across the street.

The third thing Kelsey had demanded was that I hurry the eff up. And, well, that wasn't going too great.

"Look, helper to helper, can we make a deal?" I asked the doorman. "I'll sneak out appetizers or something."

He scoffed. "So you are up to no good."

I shook my head as a sleek car pulled up to the valet.

"I just need to deliver this dress and move on," I said, keeping my voice down as the guy from the car made his way to us, wearing an expensive-looking navy suit and a crisp white button up.

Even without the right clothes, it was clear he belonged here. It was in his walk, the way he looked so assured, a whole confident aura he carried.

The doorman shrugged. "The people in there have more power over my job than you. Can't risk it. Go around the back and through the kitchen if you really want in. Sorry, Ruth."

Ruth or Rach, it didn't matter, I wasn't getting in.

Behind me, I heard the guy shift, signaling an impatient glance at his watch.

To make his impatience clearer, he sighed.

Arguing with the doorman was one thing, but annoying a guest was not okay. I just needed to get inside and get out.

"I can't risk this dress in a *kitchen*," I scoffed.

A quiet huff came behind me, possibly a laugh, but I ignored it, not wanting to draw more attention to myself.

"I promise, I don't even want to attend this event. I just need to go inside, play my part, and leave. And then I can go to bed. That's what I really want — eight hours of uninterrupted sleep, not whatever schmoozing is going on in there."

I was almost certain the sound behind me was a laugh.

As I turned to apologize and let him go ahead of me, he stepped forward.

"I'm on the list. Pres, right there," he said, flashing his ID and tapping the list in one smooth motion of unquestioned confidence and a dash of impatience. "She's with me. Let her in."

Then he walked inside without waiting on an answer.

I glanced at the doorman, uncertain.

"You should've led with that," he grumbled, waving toward the entrance.

Careful not to drag the bagged dress on the floor, I scrambled inside behind the guy.

"Hey, thanks," I called out. "I owe you one, Pres."

I replayed his name in my head, having never heard it before. He'd said it like the verb, *press*, crisp and clipped. A distinct, definitive end, sharp and swift.

He glanced over his shoulder — his blue eyes striking even in the dim hallway — and shrugged.

"I feel the same way about coming to these, Ruth."

I opened my mouth to explain I wasn't a guest and the doorman had gotten my name wrong, but he didn't linger, headed to the ballroom with an assured stride I still hadn't managed to mimic to perfection.

He paused at the door, smoothing a hand over his perfectly styled golden hair, and adjusted his suit, his long, elegant fingers effortlessly fastening a button on his jacket. It was tailored just right to his tall, lean body.

He looked to be just a bit older than me, but he seemed so far ahead.

I had the urge to stare, curious by how he moved, the motions practiced like he could easily see a reflection of himself. But he disappeared inside before I had a chance to catalog the movements.

Then my phone buzzed, reminding me of my place.

"Took you long enough," Kelsey said once I'd met her in a coat closet. She hastily unzipped the dress bag. "Shit, this is green. She's wearing Louboutins."

I blinked at her. "Shoes?"

"With red soles," she said, barely holding back her *duh*. "It'd clash. You have to go back."

"Once I get across town and back, this will be over. And I don't think I can convince the doorman to let me in again. I just had, like, really good luck to get in. Maybe no one will notice the bottom of her shoes?"

"Give me your shoes."

I stared at the coats behind her, wishing I could disappear between wool and cashmere. This was not an exchange where I'd end up with designer shoes.

"Kelsey, even Cinderella got to keep her shoes in the end, and I'm pretty sure she was a chimney maid."

"Well, your job is to help people even if you don't want to," she snapped. "But you could try sweeping chimneys instead if this is too much for you?"

And that's how I ended up in the hotel lobby barefoot, asking for shoes from the lost and found.

I'd already worn someone's underwear and was in a borrowed dress. What was another stranger's shoes?

Afterward, I decided to capitalize on the universe helping me get inside and made my way to the bar in the ballroom for a little mood lift.

The Mayor's Charity Ball was a convenient way for people who wanted to donate to charity without ever having to come face-to-face with actual charity cases.

As I skimmed the glittering silent auction, I realized this was quite literally a bidding war for luxuries I didn't even know existed let alone knew I needed to desire. And I'd yet to see a listing for less than my annual salary.

If I didn't need a drink before, I definitely did now.

On the plus side, there was an open bar.

It was there I learned the main benefit of this event.

Networking.

"Everyone who matters," a woman said intensely, leaning close to her confidante as I stood invisible at the bar, "is in this room."

I really needed to get out of this room.

With a gin and tonic in hand, I slipped out a side door, knowing I'd been pressing my luck, and leaned my head against the cold brick wall, exhaling slowly.

I just wanted one drink — a present to myself to cap off this not-so-great birthday — then I'd spend a night in the office to give JD space. Surely manila folders made great pillows.

I'd just taken my first sip, closing my eyes against the dumpster in my field of vision to savor this moment, when the door I'd slipped out of snapped open.

I straightened up, certain I was being kicked out and probably charged for the drink. I turned, right as the dim light hit him in just the right way, cutting across his strong jaw line, splashing across his perfect cheekbones, making his eyes even brighter.

It was Pres, with a cigarette between his lips.

"Oh," he said, catching the door before it closed. "I didn't think anyone would be out here."

"Me too," I said with a small laugh.

He took the cigarette from his mouth and glanced at it and then back at me, as if trying to decide if my company was worth the nicotine. He let the door close and stood several paces beside me.

Out of the corner of my eye, I watched him pat down his jacket pockets and a flicker of annoyance cross his face. Then he sighed and turned to me.

"Do you have a light?"

"Actually, I do," I said, amazed. From my clutch, I

plucked out a little souvenir matchbook I'd snagged from a dish at the front desk. "How lucky! It's like a sign."

He gave me a strange look, not understanding.

"I told you I'd owe you one," I explained with a laugh, handing it over. "Quickest debt I've ever repaid."

"Hmm," he said, not quite smiling.

He lit the match with a crisp scrape and held it to his cigarette, the warm, flickering glow casting across his chiseled face. He was gorgeous, the perfect blend of sharp lines, fine features, and full, heart-shaped lips, almost pouty, even if his face remained guarded.

He offered a cigarette from his pack with a flick of his wrist. "I guess it's my turn to owe you."

I smiled. "No, thanks, I don't smoke."

He lifted his chin, exhaling a stream into the balmy September sky. "Yeah, me either."

I laughed, almost positive he was joking.

"Are you enjoying the night so far? It looks much nicer in there than outside with the doorman. Thanks again for letting me in. I'm probably the lowest maintenance date you've ever had, huh? You didn't even have to get me this drink," I said with a smile, tipping my gin toward him.

"Oh, I don't know about that," he said in a dry, serious tone. "Bringing two dresses to an event. Seems like I got more than I bargained for."

I paused, thinking this over, and then laughed.

"Oh wow, wait, that was funny. You're funny, Pres."

He smirked, giving me another "who-are-you" look.

"So why did I have to help you get in? Usually people who come with an outfit change are on the list, Ruth."

He still thought I was a guest. That I was a woman named Ruth who belonged.

I took a measured sip of my half-full drink to buy

myself some time. Because when I hit the bottom of this glass, it'd all be over — this golden-studded event, the nice dress, the open bar, this attractive guy thinking I was like him — and I'd be on my way back to the office in an Uber, the next morning a promise of a bad boss.

So maybe I didn't have Cinderella's shoes, but I could still play pretend until midnight.

"Oh, my assistant messed it up, of course," I said, mimicking the woman at the bar's voice, like I was sharing a scandalous secret. "My schedule is a *travesty*."

He nodded, rubbing his forehead with his thumb, looking like he couldn't agree more.

"And she completely messed up my chai tea latte this morning," I said, grinning at how he rolled his eyes like he completely understood. "Sometimes I wonder if *she* should be paying *me* for correcting her."

His short laugh was dotted by cigarette smoke, pillowy clouds drifting to the sky, another sign he got it.

"I'm glad you're not my boss."

I tossed my hair back, nailing a perfect haughty laugh. "Oh, yes, I'm notorious for strictness. Shall I punish her by making her wear white even though it's after Labor Day? A labor day punishment feels very on brand for my employees, yeah?"

Amusement crossed his face. "People do say branding is everything."

"Of course. And I'm so busy firing all my assistants, I just don't have enough time to ponder life's biggest questions," I said dramatically, "like the ones in this event. Chicken or beef? Simply *exhausting*."

And then he actually laughed. A great, strong, rich laugh deep and warm from his chest. He had a brilliant smile, one that lit up his entire face, making his eyes sparkle and shine, smoothing out all the seriousness and sharpness his features carried.

I thought of how my mom would say you could read someone by their smile. I wondered what it meant when they seemed to hide theirs, when it only appeared if they were caught off guard.

Regardless, his smile spread the giddiness from this silly situation to the rest of my body.

"So I can safely assume you've had a terrible week then?" he asked, slightly shifting so we faced. "Personal branding notwithstanding."

"What makes you say that?"

"You've clearly experienced assistant drama. You weren't on the list. Something else negative must have happened for you to go the front desk." He held up the matchbook as proof. "And your shoes are … an interesting choice." I glanced down at the grungy tennis shoes peeking underneath my dress. "All signs point to slight distress, no?"

He may have been beautiful, but his voice gave his looks a run for his money.

Every syllable was punctuated with confidence, each sentence sounding like it ended in a smile even if he wasn't. His voice was rich, smooth, and demanded attention.

It was the voice of someone who had a lot of practice speaking, who knew their exact place in the world, and we'd just be lucky to have a peek.

It was the exact voice of someone not at all like me.

"It's nothing I can't handle," I said with a shrug. The past few hours flashed through my mind, and I held back a cringe. "I've definitely had worse days. Are you a lawyer? That was a lot of evidence presented pretty quickly."

"No, I'm not a lawyer."

"If you're a lawyer, I think you have to tell me."

He laughed. "I think that misconception is typically correlated with police officers. It's also not true. I'm neither..." He paused, glancing at me with a half-confused, half-expectant expression.

I knew that look. It was the face of a person who was used to being recognized without introduction. He was probably in our agency's "Important Person" binder, his headshot among other power players who always attended these sort of events.

If I were an actual assistant, I would've had the binder memorized to whisper his name in the ear of one of my clients, spouting off helpful facts so they could make appropriate small talk.

Pres Something Another.

Late twenties.

Absolutely gorgeous.

Obviously works in a field that requires no-nonsense. Seems very thrown off by nonsense.

"I'm just a consultant," he said lightly. I nodded, knowing that was one of those secret-coded careers that could really mean anything. It also probably explained why he spoke so factually and even-toned. "Nothing to get excited over. What about you?"

There wasn't a world where a woman named Ruth in this dress at this event turned out to be an assistant.

So I waved my hand flippantly at his question, remaining in character. "Same, something like that. Did you also have a terrible week? Is that why you're not smoking?"

He smirked, taking a drag on his cigarette, and rolled

his eyes toward the ballroom. "Once you get past the menu philosophy, the conversation becomes drier than the aforementioned chicken."

I smiled. "Maybe next time you should get the beef."

He laughed again, startled by my joke.

"You're funny."

He hadn't said it with overt affection, but I beamed anyway. I could tell he wasn't someone who handed out compliments lightly, even if he said them nonchalantly.

"How have I never run into you at one of these events before? I'd remember meeting you."

I smiled and squinted, still trying to play it coy.

"Is that a compliment?"

"I'm not sure yet." A smile played on his lips. "I guess that depends on who you are."

I let out a breath, wondering if I should fess up before he figured me out and called security.

"Honestly, I don't really belong here."

He raised an eyebrow, exhaling a stream of smoke to the side. "So what brought you here then?"

"I feel like my answer should be a tornado."

He looked at me with such a taken aback expression, breaking his stoic demeanor, I couldn't help but laugh.

"I mean, like Dorothy in *The Wizard of Oz*. It's like she woke up and, bam, nothing made sense. Surrounded by strange people..." I said, gesturing to the hotel behind us, my hand swooping over him too. I paused, thinking of JD. "And the wizard ends up just being a crummy dude behind a dumb curtain."

Pres laughed. "Good thing it was all a dream. Maybe the moral of the story was that she just needed a good night's sleep, Ruth."

Ruth, I repeated silently, turning the identity over in

my head, wanting so badly to be her, this well-to-do woman who made a beautiful guy smile, who could be anyone, ask for anything.

"It's kind of sad, isn't it, though?" I pressed at his nonchalance. "She experienced a whole new world then she woke up at home and nothing had changed."

"It wasn't real." He shrugged. "It'd never been real."

"That's the saddest part. I feel sorry for her."

"She's not real either." He flicked ash to the side, more emotionally invested in his dwindling cigarette. "Didn't she keep the dog though? She seemed attached to it."

I laughed at his deadpan voice. "Whoa, hey now, don't be such a bleeding heart. People might mistake you for a poet instead of a consultant."

He laughed and shook his head like he still didn't understand how he'd ended up out here with me.

"Sorry Emerald City isn't doing it for you," he said, playfulness hidden in his eyes, and lifted his chin toward the door. "Maybe next time. You'll be on the list, and I'll get you a drink."

As he turned his head to exhale, I quickly studied him.

His cigarette was almost finished, and my glass was almost empty. Just like Dorothy or all the other leading ladies of fairytales and fables, my time was almost up, and I'd be sent back to where I started.

But as the smoke curled up like ribbons, grazing and disappearing in the glittering night sky, a soft white glow washing over us, everything seemed dreamy. It was as if I were in a completely different universe.

And for just for one night, it could feel so good to be someone else, someone without baggage, who just selfishly took whatever she wanted. Be in total control of the situation and its outcome.

I was definitely single. No one had to know. Heck, it was my birthday. I was foolishly starting a new job tomorrow that would basically exile me to a lonely penthouse. And based on what I'd learned, Pres wasn't the type to run in the same circles as personal assistants with only a bus pass and bad credit to their names, so it was unlikely I'd run into him again. It would be so easy.

And even though he was only a hand's distance away, he still seemed just as distant as when he'd first walked in the hotel — untouchable, unable to be pinpointed on any sort of map, maybe from another world altogether.

I smiled, lingering two seconds too long on his lips as he turned back to me.

"There won't be a next time," I said definitively.

"Oh—"

When I sat my glass down on the concrete and stepped closer, he stopped speaking.

Instead, he watched me, blue eyes cataloging my every move: how I stood close enough to feel the warmth from his body, to make out the impeccable stitching of this stranger's suit, to breathe in hints of his cologne, amber and oak, and of his skin, smoky and warm, reminiscent of burning timber and cold nights cradled in comfort.

I could even see his tiredness, the faintest fine lines around his eyes, as if he spent a lot of time squinting in concentration. I wondered what consulting even meant, what he did when he wasn't at ritzy events, but alone with no one watching.

And I was close enough that he could hear how my dress rustled when I plucked the cigarette from his lips.

"I'm not very good at sharing," he said lowly, running his teeth over his bottom lip where his cigarette had rested. That motion alone sent shivers down my spine.

His tone was still so steady, radiating a calm intensity, a stark contrast to how hard my heart was beating. "Did you want a light? It's still my turn to owe you, yes?"

I grinned. He was much funnier than he let on.

"No, not a light."

"Not a light and not a drink," he said with a smirk, his eyes playful. "Then what do you want from me, Ruth?"

"Can I kiss you?" I blurted out before I lost my nerve. Except Ruth wouldn't even ask. She'd demand it. She'd get what she wanted. I tried again, "Then let's get out of here. A one-time thing."

His eyes flashed — with surprise and I could've sworn intrigue — and just when I thought he was going to lean in, say yes, sweep me off of my feet, push me against the wall and cover his mouth and body over mine, kiss me hard, the door banged open.

"Pres, there you are," said a harried man.

Startled, Pres moved away, and I braced for yet another embarrassing moment. At least this time I'd be in a stranger's shoes instead of just lingerie.

Except the man wore a suit instead of a towel, and didn't appear to have romantic interest in Pres.

The man glanced at me, took one look at my shoes, my empty drink on the ground, and the cigarette in my hand, and made a face.

"I'm sorry I didn't find you earlier. Did this door lock behind you? I'll speak to someone about that." His subtext was clear: *Sorry I couldn't rescue you from this company.* Then for good measure, he frowned at me and said, "You know smoking is bad for you."

Pres sighed. "Did you need something, Ethan?"

"Your presence is missed. The people inside are the sort you need to network with. They're the most influential for what you're doing. Are you prepared?"

"Of course I'm prepared." The stern coldness in his tone made Ethan hurriedly nod and squeak out "four minutes" before disappearing.

We were left alone in the silence as the clouds moved over the moon, silver shadows shielding the details between us. And that moment, that one tiny perfect slice of spontaneity, was gone.

"Next time maybe, Ruth," he said with a slight smile.

I kind of smiled and nodded, not bothering to admit I had been being honest when I'd said there'd be no next time. Being Ruth really was a one-time thing. The stars wouldn't align like this again.

He reached out to return the matchbook.

I shook my head, wondering how many times a woman could feel utterly embarrassed until she just crumbled and disappeared.

"Keep it." I smiled. "For good luck. Or for your next sneaky smoke break. Your secret is safe with me, Pres."

He kind of laughed and plucked his cigarette from my fingers. With one last long drag, he stepped away.

He paused at the door, not to look back, but to smooth his jacket, roll his shoulders back, tuck the matchbook away, every piece of him properly in place. Then he took a barely detectable breath and walked inside.

I turned to walk the other direction, far, far away from here in stranger's shoes, any hope of being someone else, someone special, disappearing like a trace of smoke in the nighttime sky.

CHAPTER THREE

There were no signs of life in James St. Clair's penthouse.

He had floor-to-ceiling windows overlooking the city, a pristine marble kitchen with a sleek, stainless steel, complicated espresso and coffee maker, a speckless living room with a barren stiff gray couch and a massive mounted television, and an untouched dining room. But no plants, photos, trinkets, mementos, or any little clues about who he was.

After letting myself in his place using the private elevator code, I reread the email he'd sent at 2 a.m., not quite sure what to make of it.

Melinda, thanks for the handoff. Rach, nice to meet you. I've given you access to my inbox and calendar. See if you can make sense of it. My last assistant couldn't, and that's why I'm on a redeye to DC at this hour. She was incompetent; at the very least, I hope you're marginally better. I've attached a list of action items I need completed correctly. -jps

So for the next several days, I walked on eggshells like the color of his walls and tried to fix his schedule. Emma really had made it a mess, using a color-coded labeling system that had no basis in reality. I also picked up dry cleaning, set up his travel for the few months, restocked his pantry with bland foods, and vetted house cleaners because his last one was "unacceptable."

I was beginning to think the reason James was dissatisfied was because there was nothing to clean.

Everything appeared untouched. The only difference between his guest bedroom and his bedroom was the size. His bed was so perfectly made that even brushing my hand over it felt like a violation. His closet, filled with designer suits, seemed unreal, like clothes waiting at an abandoned movie set. Even the televisions in his living room, bedroom, and office seemed to have never been programmed, defaulting to CSPAN or the news.

His office, the only place I could imagine someone with his stature spending time in, was equally bare with a minimalist black desk and white leather chair. One guest chair sat positioned quite far from the desk, and it looked like it'd never been used. No photos. No books with personality. Nothing.

"I'm starting to think I'm being pranked," I said to JD one morning before I left for work.

"If anyone was going to be, it'd be you."

He brushed past me to continue cooking breakfast for his new fling, Blair.

Since we'd broken the ice — shattered it, really — she'd been staying over nightly. JD hoped "we could be chill about it," he'd said in what I'd considered an apology text after my birthday.

Three more days. My landlord had said my place would be ready in three days. So until then, I was playing the role of Supportive Ex-Girlfriend Rach.

"I have sympathy for him," I sighed. "He's an old, bitter man, and he has nothing to show for it."

JD rolled his eyes. "Isn't he rich?"

"Money doesn't buy happiness."

He laughed. "Spoken by someone who's never had

money."

"Yeah, maybe you're right," I said, turning back to my email, focused on finding where James had said exactly what he didn't like about his past cleaner in preparation for an interview I'd scheduled.

Between the hundreds of emails he got daily — requests for meetings, calls, lunches, dinners, favors, *so many favors*, and interview requests — my inbox was almost as big of a mess as his calendar.

"Hey, even though you're busy with this dude, you're still good to do my laundry, right? It's not a conflict of interest, is it," JD joked. "I'm so busy, and I kind of let you crash here, you know, for super cheap. Doing one more load isn't a big deal, right?"

"Yeah, sure," I mumbled, distracted.

JD gave me a light punch on the arm and turned to the stove. "I love how chill you are. Most girls can't handle being friends after being dumped, but you're different."

I smiled tightly, choosing to believe that was a compliment.

"Morning," Blair said, yawning as she shuffled into the kitchen. "Oh, hey, Rach. JD said I could give you some of my laundry? Are you sure that's cool?"

"Sure, fine," I said, finally finding the email.

It was worse than I'd remembered — *I've fired the cleaning company my old assistant hired because they insist on using an artificial lemon disinfectant that gives me a headache.*

This poor old man.

"Told you she was chill," JD said to Blair. She fit under his arm perfectly, and if I hadn't been sitting there like an old bowl of cereal, it would've been a really cute moment for them. "Rach is like an assistant, so she's used to doing stuff. She loves helping people."

My email pinged, making me jump. James. Again.

I took a deep breath and headed to the door. "I've got to catch the bus. I'm pretty sure James is a ghost because he's never home, but he's always awake and on email. A very productive, available ghost. It's barely seven, and I already feel late."

"You ride the bus?" Blair said. "That's so retro."

My morning horoscope had told me to have patience. It must have been referring to this moment. Honestly, I didn't really have time to explain I rode the bus because JD had broken my axel when I'd let him borrow my car and I couldn't afford to fix it yet.

"You meet tons of interesting people on the bus," I said with a smile. "Every morning is an adventure."

"Hey, have fun with your ghost," JD said. "Maybe try meeting a human and staying at his place tonight?"

I paused at the door. The last man I'd interacted with had been Pres, and that had gone *great*.

"If I find any interested human males, I'll be sure to let you know," I said with a light laugh. "Wish me luck."

Then I glanced at my phone, already behind.

Rach — if I sort through my own emails then I don't really need an assistant, do I? Also, my calendar is still incorrect.

I groaned, stopping myself from responding if he'd just let me do my job, then he wouldn't have to deal with his own emails. Instead, I typed back, *On it! No worries. Hope you have a great day. (If I knew your birthday, I could just check your horoscope to know and not have to waste your precious time with these sort of pleasantries, ha!)*

I hit send before it dawned on me how incredibly stupid of a joke that was and that he certainly wouldn't find my humor endearing.

While I desperately scrambled to recall the email, I

missed my bus.

I exhaled slowly, trying to stay calm. My mom always said bad things happened in threes — this morning with JD, being a total idiot via email with my scary boss, and missing my bus. So the rest of the day would be fine.

I just had to run to catch the next bus that ended a stop early, walk in the pouring rain, get splashed with mud by a biker, and try not to ruin James' white stone floors when I finally stumbled inside.

Dripping and breathing heavily, I checked my phone, sure I'd been fired by now, and blinked at his response.

Well, that's quite personal, isn't it.

I looked at it again and kind of smiled, not positive if he was joking or scolding me. Needing the win, I chose to view it as humor and pressed my luck, responding: *Well, I am your personal assistant. :)*

I hurriedly tucked my phone away and scrambled to wipe up his floors before the cleaner arrived for her interview.

"Oh shoot!" I gasped when I saw my reflection in the guest bathroom mirror. My top was splattered with mud, and my hair was basically a wet mop. "This is not a good impression for the most sought-after cleaner."

I didn't know much about James, but I knew if I blew this and didn't get the best cleaner, his maybe-joking-maybe-scolding would become a full firing.

So I tore off my shirt, scrubbed it in the sink, and searched for a hair dryer. The bathroom was stocked with luxury soaps and shampoos, plush Turkish cotton towels, and every moisturizer and serum I could imagine.

On the vanity sat an untouched Dior candle and an accompanying matchbook placed just-so, like out of a magazine.

I turned the matchbook over in my palm and smiled, thinking of my alter-ego, Ruth.

Then I glanced at the shower behind me.

I *was* already half-naked...

Surely this was a sign.

She'd never really gotten what she wanted. I glanced at the shower again. Ruth would do it. She wouldn't even ask. In some ways, a glorious shower was as nice as a one-night stand.

"Honestly, sometimes better," I mumbled and shimmied off the rest of my clothes.

It was just a simple, quick shower so I could make a good impression. Easy peasy.

I stepped inside the ceiling-mounted rain shower with seven different spray settings and individual body jets, moaning as the water rushed over my body and cascaded to the black mosaic tiled floor.

It was the best shower I'd ever had.

Honestly, it was the best I'd ever felt naked.

And definitely the best decision I'd ever made.

Feeling like a new woman, I wrapped up in a plush towel and resumed my search for a hair dryer for my hair and shirt.

Nothing.

"That's the problem with hiring someone to design your home like a magazine. They forget human needs like hair dryers," I said to myself as I made my way to James' en suite. "I wonder if ghosts blow dry their hair..."

I paused in the hallway when I heard the television.

I'd been in his office yesterday to put up his mail — a catalog for luxury bedding, an offer for a point-reward credit card, *The New York Times*, and a copy of *The Annual Review of Political Science*, proving rich old people truly had the least interesting mail. In my haze of boredom, I must have left the television on.

I swung open the door, still talking to myself, "Someone has to shut up the old men—"

And that's when I knew my mom had been terribly wrong.

Bad things didn't happen in threes.

It was fours.

Definitely fours.

He didn't notice at first. Because he was busy saying something in the video call, his voice perfect and rich, and not at all old-man-like. My heart stopped.

"Uh, Mr. St. Clair, uh, sorry, I'm going to have to interrupt, it seems like, uh," stumbled the reporter on the other end, "you have a, um, visitor."

Interestingly, this was the second time I was basically naked in front of a stranger.

But the first time in front of what was clearly a news broadcast. Or, you know, the entire CNN viewership.

And not quite a stranger.

The blonde hair, blue eyes, beautiful bone structure, and tailored suit was all too familiar.

"Oh fu—dge nuggets," I gasped, instinctively covering my mouth with both my hands as the reality of the situation hit me.

Pres whirled around in his chair, his mouth falling open when he saw me.

"Oh," he said. "*Oh.*"

Nope. Not basically naked.

Fully naked, I realized, falling down to the floor where my towel had slipped.

Yep, bad things happened in fours.

And I was definitely getting fired.

CHAPTER FOUR

Breathing, it seemed, was difficult when you were cowering in a towel under your boss's desk, the same boss you'd propositioned for sex a few days ago, the same boss who you had thought was a 60-year-old man notorious for firing people at the job you desperately needed, and the desk was in the very room where you'd shown off your kibble *and bits* and really the whole shebang before falling to your knees and crawling to said desk, the only place that offered the least bit of solace as your boss wrapped up his video call with millions of viewers, who, yes, had seen it *all*.

Breathing was absolutely the least of my concerns.

"Hey, hey," Pres snapped as he crouched in front of me. Somewhere in the distance, a phone was ringing and a laptop was pinging, and I still really wasn't breathing.

"Oh my gosh," I wheezed, "I think I'm dying."

"You aren't dying," he said so sternly that I immediately nodded.

"Okay."

"Why are you in my home, Ruth?"

I squeezed my eyes shut. *Ruth*. I wasn't her biggest fan at the moment. It was possible that shower-loving, alter-ego Ruth was actually the worst.

"*Your* home? *You're* James St. Clair? How are you sixty? What is your name? Your mail says James. They all said your name was James."

"Yes, my name is James *Prescott* St. Clair." Alarmed, he scooted back and spoke slowly. "What is going on? Who is they? My mail ... are you ... stalking me? Should I call the police? Are you mentally well?"

"Don't call the police," I gasped, sitting up on my knees with a near death-grip on my towel. "You're a four-term senator?"

He frowned. "You've been Googling my father. Are you stalking my father?"

"No! I'm sorry. I'm not a stalker. I'm not Ruth. I'm Rach. Rach Montgomery. I'm supposed to be here. I got caught in the rain so I took a shower here, which was *such* a stupid mistake. I'm—"

"Rach," he repeated, his eyes widening. "As in, Rach my personal assistant?"

I covered my face with my hand. "Oh no, this is so bad. Your schedule ... it didn't show you were here—"

"Because my previous personal assistant messed it up," he said shortly. "Which I made very clear. I didn't think her replacement could possibly make it worse."

His phone rang again, and he shrugged off his suit jacket. "Here. I need to answer this. I'm sure my inbox has hit catastrophic levels—"

"I can check—"

"Don't do anything," he said, frustration buzzing off his skin, his features sharp and serious. "I may need to talk to my lawyer."

I swallowed hard. The last time I was around lawyers, my mother was in tears and handcuffs.

"Um, can you not do that—" I started, but he'd already answered his phone on speaker.

He nodded toward the jacket he'd given me and

moved to the other side of the desk. I carefully slipped it on and buttoned it, wrapping the towel around my waist.

When I stood, his icy blue eyes swept over me quickly — sending cold shivers down my spine — and then he looked away, focused on his phone.

"Sable, I have Rach on the line. She was the … interrupter. Rach, Sable is my PR person in DC."

"Oh my god, Pres," she shouted. "Give me some warning before you unveil your girlfriend like that."

"Girlfriend?" I repeated.

"I made a mistake," he said firmly, as if the very words pained him. He defended himself to Sable, "There was no other way to explain it without damaging my reputation. Would you have preferred I said on national television I had no idea who she was or why she was in my place without clothes on? How would that have looked?"

"What did you say?" I whispered. "I'm pretty sure I blacked out."

"Pres, you don't know her?" Sable gasped. "Was she a … one-night stand?"

We glanced at each other, and it was clear, even in a fraction of a second, that he definitely remembered when I'd propositioned him for exactly that days ago.

"She's my assistant," he said flatly.

"You had a one-night stand with your assistant?" Sable asked incredulously. "Or your assistant is your girlfriend?"

He scoffed at both possibilities. "No, of course not."

"But you're sleeping with her? Oh no."

"No, I haven't slept with her."

"Because she's your assistant or because she's not your girlfriend?"

"Sable," Pres snapped, his patience running thin. "I'm

not sleeping with anyone regardless of their employment status. Draft a statement. We amicably parted ways, I wish her the best. You get the drift."

"Okay, but I do think—"

Ignoring her, he muted the phone and looked at me. "Who are your people?"

I blinked. Lawyers, PR, and people, oh my.

"I don't have people. I have, like, an ex-boyfriend, and I'm friendly with the receptionist at work. Please, please, don't tell Melinda. I'll do anything."

"I'd actually prefer if you did nothing," he said firmly and unmuted the phone with a harsh jab, interrupting Sable, "Just do your job and stop asking questions."

"We should discuss this because you've … gone viral."

The following silence was long and uncomfortable. I shifted, cursing that stupid, incredible shower, and studied Pres who somehow still looked powerful and in control. Except he kept rubbing his thumb against the knuckle on his index finger.

"Hi, sorry. Sable?" I said in the phone when I couldn't bear the silence. "What does viral mean?"

"It means don't check Twitter," she said with a hesitant laugh. "And maybe turn off your phone for the next 48 hours. Pres, are you still there?"

"Viral?" he said, his voice coming out jagged.

"They're calling it Boobgate."

"Boobgate," he repeated. "*Boobgate?*"

Then he moved quickly, grabbing his laptop to open Twitter. He already had at least 200 notifications.

"Just let me handle it," Sable said loudly. "You pay me to do my job, so if you just stay chill and let me handle—"

He muted her and played the first clip that appeared, a recording of a TV playing CNN. He was perfect in his office, the chyron reading *Pres St. Clair, Political Analyst & Commentator* as he spoke about aggregated data from a recent public poll on infrastructure. Then his door swung open.

"Someone has to shut up the old men—" I watched myself say before I froze, eyes wide. The anchor stumbled to interrupt Pres, and then there it was. I slapped my hands over my mouth, right on cue with "*Oh fu—dge nuggets!*" Everything. My gazongas and a hint of hot pocket. And then I dropped to the floor out of frame, and Pres turned back to the camera and exhaled slowly.

"Uh, sorry about that," he said with a light laugh, kind of shaking his head, bouncing back nearly effortlessly. "My girlfriend and I are still figuring out each other's schedules."

The anchor laughed, recovering just as nicely, like there wasn't a naked woman crawling on the floor at the exact moment, "Well, best of luck with your new beau, and let's go ahead and move back to that data, shall we?"

The tweet had hundreds of retweets. Ironically, the number was ticking up in sync with my blood pressure.

Pres closed his laptop with a hard snap.

I covered my mouth, but it was too late.

He narrowed his eyes. "Are you laughing?"

I shook my head, covering my mouth with both hands.

"No, I'm sorry," I said through my giggles.

My eyes were watering, and I carefully tried to wipe them without rustling the jacket.

"No, it's just the second worst possible moment of my entire life and it's called…" I inhaled sharply, a horrible string of laughter bursting out of my mouth. I could barely breathe. "It's called *Boobgate*. My life is officially over, and I guess I'm lucky because now I'll have video proof and a spiffy name to commemorate it by."

He stared at me, his mouth a firm line and his brows furrowed, like nothing I was saying made any sense.

"The statement is in your inbox," Sable's voice broke through our silence. "We can distribute it asap, and sync up with Rach's people. Rach, who's your PR person?"

"I don't have a person," I said to Pres, inhaling a shaky breath, my laughter fading. "I just have ... me."

He exhaled shortly and opened a desk drawer. Perfectly parallel to a notepad sat a pack of cigarettes and a silver lighter. He grabbed them both and addressed his phone.

"Sable, I'll review the statement. Don't do anything until I tell you. No interviews, no media. Do *not* tweet on my behalf."

"I think if you'd consider my expertise—"

He hung up before she could finish and walked off. I blinked in confusion at the empty room then raced out.

"Wait!" I quickly darted into the bathroom, chucked the towel and jacket, and tugged on my still-damp clothes. I glanced at my reflection ... randomly dirty, wet clothes, messy hair, chest rising and falling in a deathly fashion, a confused but hopeful expression on my face.

Hopefully, Pres was the pitying type.

He stood on the terrace, cigarette in hand.

"You aren't firing me?"

Now it was his turn to look confused. "Of course I'm going to fire you. You should already have assumed you'd be fired. In fact, you are."

I inhaled sharply.

Pres was not the pitying type.

"Please give me a second chance."

"Why?"

His question didn't sound hateful or demanding. It was just a point-blank, very intimidating question that hinged on me saying the *exact* right thing.

"I wasn't even supposed to be permanent here. They're going to give you someone special because, you know, you're so difficult—"

"I'm difficult?"

I opened my mouth and closed it, cursing myself internally.

"No, I didn't mean, like, difficult. I meant ... extra special," I said unconvincingly. "I mean *I'm* not special. *I'm* not good enough to be *your* assistant. You require someone who ... gets you. And I'm no one important."

He frowned.

"I'm sorry, I didn't mean to hurt your feelings—"

"You didn't hurt my feelings," he said sharply. "*Feelings* aren't involved in this. This is my *reputation*."

I took another shot when he paused to light his cigarette, still frowning.

Maybe sucking up would work.

"I *want* to be your assistant. That's it. It'd be an *honor*."

He looked at me flatly. "No."

"Let me change your mind."

He shook his head. "That won't be necessary."

"Look, if you fire me, I'll be fired from the whole agency. I *need* this job. My basement isn't ready, so I'm on a couch with a very thin wall and a very sexually active ex next to it. And having a job equals money and then I can fix my car and credit, I don't know, and get a place with a nice mattress. I can figure out my life."

When he faced me, I could tell he hadn't understood any of that.

"Pres, come on, you owe me."

His expression was unreadable, but based on how my pulse had quickened, I knew that hadn't been the right thing to say.

"I didn't mean how that came out—"

"What do you want from me?" he asked, exhausted, like he'd been posing this question his whole life.

"I meant it playfully," I said, shaking my head. "That night at the mayor's ball, you said that—"

"So what do you want? I have things to do, and I'm not interested in negotiating with my personal assistant."

"You've fired all your assistants before me, but at least they had a chance. Let me lose this job on my own merit. Let me have a fighting chance?"

He stared at me, his brows furrowed, then shook his head. He didn't sound harsh, and if I listened closely, I could've believed I heard a tinge of understanding buried inside his precise words when he said, "I *have* to let you go. Think of the optics. To the public, I'm in a relationship with you then we break up, but you still work for me as an assistant? It's messy, it's chaotic, it's complicated. Those are all characteristics I do *not* associate with. Do you understand?"

I tried to think of a different angle to keep my job.

Because the guy behind the cold blue eyes and set jaw was unreadable, dealt in facts, even tones, and measured movements, every aspect of his presence considered and calculated. His playful glints and barely-there smiles were so gone I wondered if I'd imagined them.

But I smiled anyway, hoping that first tiny spark we'd had the night we'd met had the ability to put out this dumpster-fire of a mess.

"You're dumping me right after you introduce me to the world? Talk about a tough crowd."

He squinted at me.

I tried to laugh. "Sorry, it was a silly joke—"

"You're right," he said suddenly. "It doesn't look good if I break up with you right after this."

I kind of laughed. "Yeah, and we've really only had one drink. Take a girl out to dinner first before breaking her heart, am I right?"

He didn't seem to hear me, talking to his cigarette more than me.

"We need to determine the best timeframe. There's probably some simulations I can run based on the average breakup time for fairly new couples with an additional factor on how that number fluctuates based on the overall notoriety or popularity of the couple. I can find the exact right date and announce it then."

"Um, what?"

He faced me and repeated himself, saying the exact same words only slower like that made it clearer.

I shook my head. "No, I think I understand you ... mostly. I'm just confused, so you aren't firing me?"

"No, not yet. Not until I know the date."

"So it's like a countdown," I said, not exactly *thrilled* at how this was all playing out. "Okay, cool, yeah, I guess that's one way to make it fun."

He rubbed his temple and sighed. "Right. Well, I'll let you know. In the meantime, let's keep the truth between us."

I nodded, and he turned away from me.

"Did you..." I stepped forward and then backward, unsure, "want me to leave?"

"You're still my personal assistant, aren't you? My schedule is still unacceptable. And the floors look terrible. What happened out there? Where is my cleaner?"

I broke out in a huge smile. Sure, I was eventually getting fired, but having extra time to prepare was more than I could have asked for.

"Oh my gosh, thank you. I promise, I'll be such a good assistant. You won't even know I'm here. And then this whole Boobgate thing can just be a blip. If you think about it, I bet there's a silver lining. Like, this can just be a funny story you tell at parties. Or a fun fact when you introduce yourself."

He looked to the sky, like he was evaluating if being materialized into a cloud was the only way to remove himself from this conversation.

"A fun fact," he repeated dryly, shaking his head. He took a final, deep drag on his cigarette and stubbed it out, already walking back inside. "Facts cannot be fun."

Then he shut his office door, the lock clicking in sync with my exhale of relief.

CHAPTER FIVE

My mom had been big on signs, constantly seeking outer forces to guide her life. While I'd check the weather, she'd check our horoscopes. While I'd scan everyday items at the Food Mart, she'd scan fortune cookie numbers for good luck.

When I was a kid, my favorite game was to unfold a crumpled map from a gas station to see how I fit into the world.

"This is us," she'd point to the smallest dot, so inconsequential that it could have been a misprint, a dot of ink dropped by mistake.

I'd trace my finger over the roads, the veins of my hometown, trying to find a heartbeat.

"But there's so much more," she'd remind me with a smile as bright as the stars. She'd spread it out until it covered the folding card table that functioned as our dining table. "You'll get there, Rach. The universe has already chosen, you just have to follow the signs."

I'd study the map, wondering about the other towns, memorizing their names, too, just in case. Middletown was the biggest, the most important, marked by a star. *A sign*, I'd thought.

I'd imagine my future twisting and turning in multiple directions. With each line, I could imagine a different me with a different life.

She'd tell me to just believe everything would change one day. Just stay positive.

She brought that same upbeat energy to her business "adventures." My life ran parallel to hers, neatly spliced by these phases.

Elementary school was plastic containers that promised to store food like no other. All she had to do was sell them to others, and then we'd hit it big.

The sound of my packed lunches rattling in my backpack no matter how slowly I'd walk — a melted ham sandwich container clunking against a plastic bowl of off-brand chips knocking against discounted "ugly" vegetables in a separate compartment — announced my presence down the long school hallways, punctuated by snickering classmates.

Middle school was makeup. Everyone has a beauty queen inside them, she'd say, letting me test out products, smoothing my skin with soft brushes and buttery palettes until I felt brand new.

"You should tell you friends about it," she'd say excitedly. "Then you can help me grow my business!"

I wore gobs of makeup for a year, trying to mimic the models in the glossy magazines she'd pull out of other people's recycling bins.

It wasn't until I showed up with bright red lipstick — thinking a beauty queen *really* was inside me and all queens had friends — that I realized I'd been mistaken.

"Is that the makeup your mom always tries to get my mom to buy?" Sara A. sneered as I sat at her lunch table. They all wore makeup, so I'd thought I could belong at their table, too.

"It looks *awful* on you," Sara H. added.

When I got home that day, lips rubbed raw from the

tissues I used to scrape it off, redder than the lipstick had been, my mom hugged me tight and hard.

"In some ways, this is a good thing," she'd said, smoothing her hand over my hair. "Because now you know they wouldn't be real friends. Real friends would see you as you are, Rach. They'd like you just like that."

That night, she made us paper crowns with extra glitter. We ate ice cream under a blanket fort, pretending we were royals in a castle, laughing with brain freezes until I'd forgotten all about the incident.

High school was split between an exercise-and-shake venture and selling candles she swore smelled better than any other in existence. Gesturing to the countless boxes of product we'd store in my room, she'd promised, "These are going to be a hit."

They were.

Boys and boxes would keep me company as she worked late or drove around town to sell more products.

I'd light three for good luck, turn off the lights, and let the boys — the ones who now paid attention to me because I'd figured out the makeup, because the exercise and shakes worked wonders, too, and maybe because the Saras had moved away — do whatever, hoping they'd stay, pick me, choose me.

Instead, they'd leave, mumbling a confession that they really preferred another girl. They wanted someone less complicated with less baggage, someone poised, someone who said and wore the right thing.

One without a mom who asked their parents to buy candles, essential oils, or weight-loss shakes, wore out-of-date thrift store clothes and flowers from the park in her hair, cleaned their houses and their parents' offices, held up grocery stores lines to count change made from lucky pennies, attended PTO meetings to meet men, slipped annotated fortunes between my books just for them to fall out in English class, and had no qualms about plucking busted furniture out of dumpsters, saying it just needed a little extra love.

But even if the boys would ignore me the next day, my room always smelled like candles. The best candles in the world, just like my mom had promised.

She'd been my best friend, my compass, someone to believe in.

And by the time she was sentenced, I'd learned enough to know my place in the world and where I'd absolutely never belong.

Like being Pres' girlfriend.

He spent the whole day in his office with his door closed. I kept my head down and focused on my tasks — showing the cleaner around, setting up lunch in his office as he smoked outside, removing his untouched lunch, trying to sort through his emails from people who had no idea what'd happened and ones who were flabbergasted. I'd remained generally unsure of what I needed to do until he emailed, *Have a good evening, Rach. Please leave.*

As I fell asleep that night, a small part of me thought maybe it would all be a dream.

Maybe I'd wake up before I'd shown up in this town — driven by a childhood dream to live in the star — before I'd felt like I needed to start over, to build a life with meaning, before my mom had gone to prison. Maybe I'd wake up to the times she'd promise things would work out if I just believed.

I closed my eyes, almost certain that when I opened them again, I'd be home and Pres wouldn't be real.

"Boobgate," JD's laughter woke me up. "Oh my god,

Rach, you gotta see this. Your tits are famous."

"She does have pretty good boobs," Blair agreed. I cracked open my eyes to see them watching the TV with wide-eyed expressions.

"Fudge nuggets," JD continued with another loud laugh. "Who says that? How embarrassing. I can't believe you're able to show your face in public anymore, Rach."

A major morning daytime show had picked it up, blurring out my only claim to fame, and focused on Pres.

And that's how I learned James Prescott "Pres" St. Clair IV was a 28-year-old well-known political analyst turned commentator, regularly appearing on CNN, MSNBC, and Fox News. He was also the son of Senator St. Clair III and MacKenzie Meyers-St. Clair, one of *Time*'s most influential people as a New York hedge fund manager. Unsurprisingly, Pres had two master degrees in political science and data policy statistics, was verified on Instagram and Twitter, and, oh, was the heir to the nation's largest healthcare provider.

And that yesterday he smoked half a pack of cigarettes on the terrace and doom-scrolled on his phone before locking himself in his office without a word.

That last part Good Morning America hadn't covered.

"Holy shit," Blair said. "*You* know him?"

I nodded, shocked by what I'd learned. The b-roll was also really great — Pres looking gorgeous in suits at fancy events, astute during news segments, powerful at political events next to his father, and one they kept replaying of him doing an incredible squinty secret smile in an all-black matte suit from some magazine event.

"And you're *with* him?" Blair asked through a mouthful of cereal. "But you live on a couch."

I opened and closed my mouth. The only thing Pres

had asked of me in exchange for not firing me on the spot had been to keep our secret between us.

JD laughed harder. "There's no world where that guy is her boyfriend. What could he possibly gain by that?"

"He said so himself," Blair said, pointing to the TV.

"Rach is an assistant to assistants." JD rolled his eyes. "She's not pulling dudes like that. Clearly there's been a miscommunication."

"Boobs out like that only have one message," Blair said with a laugh. "And did you see his face? He was *into* it. Good for you, Rach."

JD faced me. "When did you get together?"

"Shortly after you and I broke up. He…" I thought about the night we'd met. How he'd laughed at my jokes. How for just one split second, I'd thought he had been going to kiss me. "Consoled me."

"Bullshit. You thought he was an old dude."

I nodded solemnly. "He is older than me."

He shook his head. "This is sad. You can't actually believe this. Horoscopes are one thing, but this is another level. Guys like that don't date girls with no money and no connections. What'd you do, lie about who you were?"

"Of course not," I bluffed. "He knows me."

"Then he's using you more than you're using him."

"The beauty of relationships is that it doesn't matter where someone comes from or who they are to the world," I said, not sure why I was so determined to make JD believe me when this was going to end in like two days anyway. "When you truly care about someone, nothing else matters—"

Thankfully, my email pinging interrupted me because I really didn't know where I was going with that.

I opened up my phone, grateful I'd deleted all social

media years ago, and ignored the few texts from people at work who'd learned my name well enough now to use it to ask why I had kept Pres a secret and we should totally double-date sometime!

"Oh look, this is him now. He asked me for coffee. Morning dates are the best, right?" I said cheerfully, hopping off the couch to bolt.

Sure, the message was a little drier than my translation and fell more on the assistant side of things, but it was the thought that counted, right?

My place — 9:30 a.m. Coffee. Don't be late.

"I don't believe you," JD said, following me to the door. "One conversation with you, and people will know you don't belong with him. He won't stick around. You're not worth it."

I turned and looked him right in the eyes. "Why? Why is it so hard to believe?"

He laughed, giving me a pitying look that I'd used to see as adoration. "Because when someone asks where you're from, no one recognizes it. When someone asks about your family, you don't answer. When someone asks about your future, you have nothing to say. And when someone asks who you are, no one cares enough to listen."

I took a deep breath and smiled brightly.

And then I made a mental note to write a letter to my mom to ask what it's a sign of if a Libra slams a door so hard she nearly crushes her Virgo ex's fingers.

. . .

Morning coffee actually meant a staff meeting of four.

As I set up his dining room to function as a conference room with scones and coffee, I couldn't shake the segment from my mind.

Honestly, I didn't need JD to remind me that I didn't belong in Pres' world. Not when that segment existed, when I stood in this pristine penthouse, when the only reason he'd given me the time of day at the mayor's ball was because he'd thought I'd been Ruth, someone who mattered.

But I couldn't help feeling bad for the chaos I'd created. Because he was someone, and I was nobody, the segment had focused solely on him.

He'd just been trying to talk about data. There was no way he could have predicted a naked woman blowing up his life. Sure, I was going to be fired, but I couldn't just leave without actually saying sorry.

I knocked on his closed office door and rehearsed what I'd say once again.

"Come in."

I smiled to bury my sudden nervousness at seeing him behind his desk. Even in his own home on the weekend, he still dressed smartly in suit pants and a cashmere sweater, every thread in place.

"Do you like our new system?"

He looked up from frowning at his laptop, transferring the look to me. "Excuse me?"

"I knock, you say 'come in.' Pretty fool-proof, yeah?"

A barely-there smile flashed across his face. "That's pretty funny."

I smiled and stepped closer to place a scone on his desk. "This was the last one of this flavor in the shop, which I took as a sign."

"What, that no one else wanted it? Something's wrong with it?"

I laughed. "No, either it's the best flavor so it sells

quickly or it was meant for me to find to give to you."

He looked at it then me, a trace of confusion crossing his brows. "Oh, I didn't ask for this."

"Well, it's an apology scone. So you can't ask for it, it's given. I hope we can at least end things on good terms. I shouldn't have used your shower or burst in your office. It was wildly unprofessional. You don't have to forgive me, but I hope you can believe me when I say I am sorry."

"I've never heard of apology scones before."

I shrugged. "They may or may not be real things. Like fun facts."

"Right." He studied the scone, almost suspiciously. "Well, this wasn't expected or necessary, but thank you nonetheless."

I laughed. "That's not exactly how you accept a gift or an apology."

He smiled faintly. "Noted." Then he glanced at his computer, his frown reappearing.

"Anything I can help with?"

"No. It's personal."

"Well, I am your personal assistant."

He laughed shortly and closed his laptop. "It's fine."

For a brief second I saw his screen, and whatever he was reading looked like a report full of charts and graphs. Clearly, his personal life was very different from mine.

"I'm sure whatever it is will work out. I genuinely believe everything will go back to the way it was for you. Your life before Boobgate."

"Right. And you mentioned something about a couch or basement." I was surprised he actually recalled my blabber. "About needing to keep your job."

"Oh, yeah, it's fine." I shrugged, positive he didn't care to hear about my problems. "I'll figure it out. Nothing for you to worry about."

He frowned and shook his head, a look I was recognizing as him not enjoying being misunderstood.

"I'm not worried. I don't know anything about the situation to feel concerned, and I'd rather not. Your personal life is personal." He glanced at the scone, his frown deepening. "However, I did speak with your boss yesterday."

My pulse picked up.

"I thought not hearing from Melinda had just been good luck," I said with a nervous laugh, trying to remain upbeat.

"No, it was because I called her." He nodded to his guest chair. "You can sit."

Well, that was fast. At least he'd end it quickly, unemotionally, and with clarity.

"I'm not sure how much she'll fill you in because she's your boss, and I'm your client. She asked if I was firing you for ruining my appearance. I told her for the time being, we are … infatuated with each other."

I pretended not to hear how it pained him to say it, and he pretended I didn't look pathetically hopeful.

"You … saved my job?"

"I'm still going to let you go," he said quickly, as if the kindness I felt made him uncomfortable. "But the models say it would reflect negatively on me unless I wait four weeks and two days. Roughly sixteen hours, give or take. Breakups are tricky to calculate."

"So I have four weeks to find a new job?"

Four weeks to secure some income, move back into my place, and finally settle down. I'd done more in less time.

Pres frowned. "I said four weeks, two days, and roughly sixteen hours."

I laughed. "Sure, sure. I get it. The point is, you're saying I have a guaranteed paycheck for a month and you managed to get my boss to not flip out. And you get to go back to your life the way it was in just a few weeks. This is all great news."

"Actually, I need to talk to you about that. You and I are in a delicate position," he began.

I nodded. "That's one way to put it."

He looked like he wanted to laugh, but instead he shook his head. "Yes, well, the circumstances have been quite odd. You heard I was meeting with people influential to the mayoral office—"

"I'm so sorry about pretending to be Ruth…" I paused, trying to figure out how to say to someone like him that I'd just wanted to pretend to be someone else for a night.

He kind of smiled. No. Smirked. Definitely smirked.

"It's fine. In politics, the most likely outcome is someone misleading you."

I shook my head. "That's terrible."

He laughed dryly. "No, that's life. That's facts. But that's not why I bring it up. With that knowledge, your access to my email, and the brief Ethan sent around last night, I'm sure you have your suspicions. As I consider your post-employment here, I want to be able to control the message."

I nodded slowly, not exactly sure what he was saying other than that he definitely had trust issues.

"I would never use your emails against you or whatever you're thinking. And I signed an NDA with the agency that covers all clients. So I don't even know what you're really asking me, to be honest."

He blinked. "You didn't read the brief?"

I shook my head. By the time I'd seen it, he'd already

responded and moved everyone to bcc, so there had been nothing else for me to do.

"Should I have? I didn't think I should read reports marked confidential."

He exhaled and kind of laughed. "Well, then, the smart thing I should do is lie. But I can't seem to bring myself to do that. So I'll just say it simply, I'm preparing to run for mayor."

I nodded. Maybe I should've been surprised, but it made perfect sense he'd follow in his dad's footsteps. He was smart, attractive, wealthy, already in politics, and came from a line of successful people. Of course he'd run.

I thought of my mom then, wondering if we were all destined to become our parents. If the maps of our futures were already drawn, determined, and destined, and there was nothing we could do to end up differently.

"Oh, okay. That's really cool. Congrats."

"On what? I haven't won."

I laughed at his genuine confusion. "Yeah, but I'm sure making the decision was a big deal. Hopefully you celebrated that at least."

He kind of smiled, his blue eyes sparkling just a little brighter. "With scones?"

I laughed. "Scones for apologies. Cakes for celebrating. But seriously, Pres, I won't tell anyone if it's a secret."

He didn't look convinced, but he nodded anyway.

"It's not public knowledge. Campaign finance laws are pretty specific, so I can't say I'm running yet. I'll continue my work as a political consultant, commentator, and analyst until I can announce my candidacy. I'm more in the research phase. That's what today's meeting is about."

He hadn't let me make the agenda, shortly emailing that he could handle it.

"So I'd appreciate your discretion when you leave. When I let you go," he said, and for a split second, he seemed to trip over his words, "When we break up."

"That's one way to get a girl's vote."

He blinked, that same bemused expression crossing his face nearly every time I was around, then he laughed. It was a real laugh, the one I'd heard the night we'd met.

Quickly composing himself, he shook his head and turned back to his laptop.

I smiled and turned to head back to the dining room to finish setting up for the meeting.

When I reached to close the door, he said my name.

"Thank you," he said, pulling the scone closer, still looking like he couldn't believe I'd given him something.

I didn't ask what he was thanking me for. Instead I nodded to the door.

"Do you want to keep this open?"

And somehow, without knowing him much at all, I knew that I'd experienced something special, something just between us, another shared secret, when he returned my smile.

"Yeah, you can keep it open."

CHAPTER SIX

The first staffer to arrive was Ethan, Pres' right-hand man, campaign manager, and the one who'd interrupted us at the mayor's ball.

"This is a disaster," he said, tossing his coat at me. "Months of planning out the window. I hope you're happy. Google Pres St. Clair and it's all about Boobgate. What sort of politician has Boobgate next to their name and people think, 'that's the one I'll vote for'? *So much SEO work gone…*"

I opened my mouth to apologize, but he didn't break his stride to help himself to the coffee I'd sat out.

As he read headlines angrily in my direction, two more staffers arrived. They introduced themselves — Jamar and Olivia, a post-grad research assistant — wrung their hands, and debated stepping off the elevator.

"How is he?" Jamar asked with the sort of dramatic severity reserved for the set of a medical drama.

"It's been very touch and go," I said somberly. "But I think he'll pull through."

They both stared at me, wide-eyed, and I shook my head. "Sorry, I was trying to make light of the situation. He's fine. All limbs intact, but it's possible his head will pop off. I'm really sorry about all of this … can I get you some water?"

"Do you work here?" Jamar asked, glancing around

suspiciously. Then he scanned me in the same way. "Are you actually Pres' girlfriend?"

"No way," Olivia breathed, her eyes growing even wider. Then both of their gazes fell to my chest. I guess it was nice to finally have a claim to fame.

I adjusted my top and went into the kitchen, deciding they'd need water anyway if they kept their mouths hanging open in shock.

"Um, we're still figuring out labels. In the meantime, I'm just here to help," I said hesitantly, wondering if I should add that I wasn't sticking around for long.

They looked at each other, puzzled.

I was baffled by the only way they'd know if their boss had a girlfriend was if she went viral.

"What's he like?" Olivia asked, nodding toward the office like she was too frightened to say his name. I wondered what would happen if I said "Pres" three times in the mirror.

"He's pretty nice," I said with a shrug.

"Nice," she repeated incredulously, dazed by the very idea. "The last meeting we had, he said he'd save us both time by reprinting the report I'd written in red ink rather than notating every place he'd change."

"You think that's bad?" Jamar whispered. "When I first started, he did my work in addition to his for weeks. Then he gave me a calculator and said I should familiarize myself with it."

"That's kind of ... giving?" I suggested.

"I'm his campaign treasurer."

"Are you having a tea party," Ethan shouted from the dining room, "or do you want to be useful?"

As everyone settled, I took my rightful place against the wall when Pres walked in.

It was fascinating to witness how his team sat up straighter, shifted in their seats, and tidied their area, their expressions clearly wanting to please him while their body language hoped he didn't acknowledge them. Their intimidation was palpable, but he didn't seem to notice.

He sat, reading his iPad as everyone held their breaths.

The conference phone crackled as Sable spoke, "Am I muted? Is he there yet? Are you guys freaking out that he's pissed—"

"You aren't muted, and I'm here," Pres said without looking up. "To be determined if I'm pissed, I suppose."

"Oh, whoops," Sable laughed nervously. "I was just reading the brief about the poll you all had done, and I'm sure you're unhappy—"

"The poll has valuable insights," Ethan jumped in. "I wouldn't characterize it as something Pres should be unhappy about."

I glanced at where Pres sat impassively.

"It was an expensive poll, it better be valuable," Jamar said with a skittish laugh.

"Why doesn't someone tell me what it says?" Pres said evenly.

Another silence washed over the room.

Until Olivia made an eep sound and sank lower in her chair.

"Walk me through it," Pres said, squinting at his iPad. It was impressive — without even changing his tone, he'd made it clear he was displeased. "Spare no details."

The agenda listed this portion as *Discuss Campaign Viability.* Methodology, percentages, and margins dominated the conversation. They discussed voting data, previous nonpartisan mayoral elections, and attitudes toward various past candidates. Pres followed it easily, mostly looking bored.

Then it took an interesting turn when we moved to *Discuss Candidate Support.*

"So that brings us to when we tried to determine the variability we can expect around your potential level of support," Jamar said slowly. "Well, I'd argue that the results were inconclusive. The margin of error—"

"The margin of error is in line with what I'd expect based on how the data was weighted to match the city's population. That increase in variability is explained," Pres said so factually it came out cold.

I leaned forward in my seat to sneak a peek at his iPad. It was the same thing he'd been reading in his office.

"Jamar, are you implying he doesn't understand design effect?" Ethan interjected. "He's not an idiot."

"No, of course not. I definitely think Pres understands design effect. Probably better than anyone in this room."

Pres' expression remained flat at the heavy-handed compliments. The men exchanged nervous glances.

"I meant we have to take this sort of thing with a grain of salt," Jamar said quickly.

"I don't remember the salt factor from when I ran these sort of polls myself," Pres responded.

No one laughed even though it was kind of funny.

"Olivia, what do you make of the results?"

"Um, well, people have so many thoughts in their heads, and maybe this poll was a little off? But I'm appreciative of this job," she said, buckling under his scrutiny. "And people on your Instagram seem to like you, so maybe it doesn't matter what a poll says?"

"That's the headline, isn't it?" Pres said shortly. "I'm unlikable." He glanced down at the brief. "By a vast majority it seems."

"People are intimidated by you," Ethan jumped in. "You're too powerful. Too smart. Too good."

I was glad I was sitting in the back because I hadn't been able to stop my eye roll in time.

"Of course," Pres said dryly. "However, respondents gravitated toward descriptions closer to 'too dull,' 'too cold,' 'too stuck-up,' and 'too stiff.'"

I held back a wince. I'd never want a piece of paper to tell me what people thought about me. And I'd really never be able to make a joke out of it out loud.

"What does *likable* even mean?" Jamar supposed. "The whole have-a-beer-with-'em is a myth. The salt of the earth stuff is bullshit. It has no real standing in politics."

"Myths and bullshit," Pres repeated flatly. "We should have polled that instead. Unicorns. Rainbows. Moon magic. Maybe I'm likable on Mars."

His team whirled around to stare at me when I snorted with laughter.

"Oh gosh, whoops," I said, covering my mouth with my hand. "I thought you were being funny on purpose."

Pres glanced over his shoulder. "I was. I guess not being funny is right up there with not being likable.

"What about you, Rach, do you think I'm likable?"

"Oh, I don't know," I said quickly, trying to fit in with the rest of his team. "It's not my place."

"Difficult, I recall, was the word you used."

His team gasped in almost perfect tandem. I was about to apologize, but paused when I saw a spark of amusement in his eyes. It was the same barely-there playful look begging to be challenged that I'd seen the night we'd met.

I smiled, figuring if I was getting fired in a few weeks anyway, I could at least be honest.

"I guess I think you're a prickly pear. The problem is, most people only like that flavor in margaritas. Some people just go best with tequila."

Ignoring his staff's horror, a devastatingly attractive look crossed his face, somewhere between a secret smile and a smirk. Then he laughed, shook his head, and turned back to his bewildered team.

"Does anyone else have a beverage they'd like to compare to me?"

"Maybe sparkling water. Sophisticated, elevated," Ethan said, scowling in my direction. "A cheap, kitschy margarita doesn't seem right at all."

"Maybe espresso," Olivia added. "Strong. Powerful."

I was proud of myself for holding back from saying, *And super hot!* My honesty did need *some* boundaries.

"Right, well, unless Jamar or Sable have a drink they'd like to throw in the mix, this meeting is over," Pres said.

"Wait," Sable called out. "I need to discuss Boobgate."

I sunk lower in my chair.

"I'd rather not," Pres said dryly. "It'll blow over in a few days, and I'm not dignifying it with interviews. We need to focus on this poll. On the future."

"Have any of you even looked at what everyone is saying about it?" Sable pressed.

"People are so stupid. It's horrible how much attention this has gotten," Ethan said with an eye roll.

"A travesty," Jamar added seriously.

I hadn't thought it had been *that* bad.

I mean, my boobs alone made it at least *interesting*.

Pres sighed, rubbing his forehead with his thumb.

"Well, that's the thing, it's actually not negative," Sable said. "Most people actually … loved it. I just emailed around a report. I agree no one will be talking about this in a week because viral things like this fade. And it's being taken down as soon as it goes up because, well, it's of a sensitive nature—"

Okay, my boobs really weren't that bad.

"—But I do think there's a takeaway. An intern read through every response, and we evaluated sentiment."

Everyone scrambled for their phones as Pres calmly clicked open her report. Since I was supposed to take notes and my boobs were technically part of the conversation, I stood and peered over his shoulder.

QUEEN.

How I feel when I watch CNN. #letsshutuptheolddudes #MoreBoobsLessBoys

Who's this girl? Finally someone tells the truth on the news.

I've spent 30 minutes trying to find this woman. I need more of her hot takes.

I will now refer to all embarrassing situations as "fudge nuggets."

That dude is f$%@^&g lucky

A reason to start watching CNN:

Literally me anytime I walk into a room unprepared

Behind every man stands a woman who tells it like it is.

Boob Girl for President

"These are actual tweets?" I asked, pointing to a screenshot of one that had hundreds of likes: *Who here feels this deep in their soul? We're all Boob Girl.*

"Yes. Rach, people are loving you," Sable said. "And by association, you, Pres. Your followers have doubled, your search volume has increased significantly, and sentiment on social media is mostly positive. People like that you're with someone so relatable, so *regular*—"

Pres turned to me, our faces close. And for the first time since this meeting started, he didn't look bored. He looked intrigued.

"—someone special."

I laughed.

Out of all the things that had happened to me over the past couple weeks, this was the absolute most ridiculous.

"What are you suggesting?" Ethan asked. "Interview Rach and post it? Get her to apologize on CNN?"

"No, she has nothing to apologize for."

We all paused, surprised by Pres' swift interjection.

He shrugged. "Even if she were to apologize, it wouldn't be to those who shared the video of her without her consent. She didn't do anything wrong."

"Thank you," I said softly, taken aback by his quick protection. "That's really kind of you."

He glanced at me with a slightly confused expression, as if no one had ever called him kind before.

"We need to leverage this," Sable interrupted. "Keep the momentum. It's actually pretty common. Tons of my clients do this sort of thing. And you've already set it up so perfectly. It could be seamless."

"What are you talking about?" Pres asked.

"I'm confident Rach can be useful. She's liked across the board by almost all demographics."

"I'm not showing off my boobs again," I joked.

The only laugh came from Pres, and he turned it into a cough when he realized he'd been the only one.

"I meant more the whole package. Body and brain. Your salt-of-the-earth thing. I'm sure we can reach an agreement for the appropriate compensation."

"Sable, what are you talking about?" Pres asked again.

"This poll is clear. You struggle with being relatable. It says it right there, Middletown views you as an outsider."

"That just proves the people in this town are oblivious.

He's from here," Ethan snapped. "He went to undergrad here."

"Yeah, then he spent the past seven years networking in DC," Sable scoffed. "And he's from Pecunia, which is two hours away. People from Pecunia are not the same as people from Middletown."

Pres glanced at me. Our confusion matched.

"Rach, where are you from?" Sable asked, ignoring Ethan's sputtering.

"Um, a really small town," I said tentatively. So small that, thankfully, no one watched CNN and they certainly wouldn't have recognized me since I'd left. "I've lived in Middletown for several years though."

"Exactly. Pres, a huge portion of your voters aren't fawning over your face on CNN. You're in Middletown to build a base of supporters not just wealthy donors before you announce your candidacy. With Rach, it makes perfect sense."

He exhaled slowly. "I don't like to repeat myself. For a third, final time, what are you talking about?"

"*Date*, Pres. Like, fake it. With Rach. People already think you're together. So take her to events, fundraisers, interviews. Show you care about Middletown and that you're relatable to regular people. So much so that you're in love with one of them. Rach can help you boost your profile and get these numbers up before you're official."

I almost laughed.

"No," Ethan said immediately. "When we need Tinder advice, we'll ask you, Sable. But this idea is ridiculous."

"No one would believe it," Jamar added. "The future mayor dating his personal assistant? Who comes up with this stuff?"

"We won't say she's his personal assistant. She'd act

like his girlfriend not an employee. No one knows anything about her, so she can be whoever we want," Sable said. "Pres, you know better than anyone a politician in a relationship polls better than one who isn't. We already know people like her. And you need someone on your arm for these events. It's great PR. So why not?"

My heart was racing, and my cheeks were flushed. Sable and Ethan started arguing, but Pres ignored them, turning around to face me.

He wasn't saying yes.

He also wasn't saying no.

It was reminiscent of how he'd looked at me that night at Hotel Chanceux. When we'd been inches apart, and I'd always wonder if he'd been about to kiss me, to take me up on my offer to get out of there for a one-time thing.

I'd been playing pretend then, trying to belong, to find a new place in the world, desperately wanting to be someone else, and he'd almost been able to take me there.

"Two conditions," I said slowly, keeping this between us as his staff continued their uproar, "I keep my job longer than four weeks, two days, and roughly sixteen hours. And when we're done, let me quit. Don't fire me and give me a job reference."

"To where?"

I shrugged. I'd never had options before. With Pres' connections, the possibilities were limitless. And I'd certainly never experienced what leverage felt like.

It was nice.

"Anywhere I want."

"Okay," he said with a smile just for me, and that was just as nice, too. "I told you I'd owe you one."

CHAPTER SEVEN

As it turned out, Pres also had conditions.

At 2 a.m., my email pinged: *Just events. You can leave as soon as you're seen. No interviews. No gimmicky press events that Sable will want to set up. -jps*

When I woke up at 5:30, my inbox was filled.

3:03 a.m. — We can discuss work when we're at these sort of events, so it's not a waste of your time. I would assume my assistant would be there anyway, so as long as you don't mind confirming in a few sentences or less that we're in a relationship and I'm likable that would be ideal.

I laughed, wondering how he'd write an anniversary card if this was him asking someone out.

3:45 a.m. — I've attached a list of all the events I'm considering over the next three months. Let me know what dates work for you. And then confirm these with the hosts and add to my calendar, thanks.

I got started immediately.

While he may not have wanted me as his girlfriend, his need for an assistant was genuine. He spent a majority of his time juggling consulting phone calls, requests for commentary for various outlets, and managing his future campaign.

As a boss, he was, to put it nicely, a challenge.

In an effort to be accurate, he alienated people.

I'd seen it earlier this week when I'd been researching

gifts for Pres to approve for, as he put it, "someone I don't remotely care about, but am obligated to send a present."

Olivia had been pacing in front of the dining table as he reviewed a report she'd worked on. Finally, he spoke, his tone flat, "This is wrong. You need to redo it all."

"I worked really hard—"

"Not hard enough," he said, already walking away.

Before he'd left for DC, he'd dropped two binders in front of where Jamar and Ethan had turned his dining room into a command center. Pres had ripped the pages in half, rearranging them how they should have been organized in the first place.

"If you can't do something correctly," he'd said sternly, "then let me know, and I'll do it myself."

Pres, I'd learned, was unique in that he had very specific thoughts on how reports should be organized, tabbed, and collated. Actually, he had very specific thoughts on mostly everything.

Even on calls where I took notes, he'd cut through the small talk — calling it "mindless chatter" — to get directly to the point, quick to correct.

He saw the world in black and white. Questions were to be answered, not danced around. Directions were meant to be followed. Chaos could be rationalized and avoided. Every problem had a solution.

I believed in the universe.

He believed he could predict the universe.

And in doing so, his straightforward manner came across as intimidating and cold. I didn't need a poll to figure that out. I just had to talk to him for five minutes.

So I was glad the boundaries were clear. I'd play date for few minutes at fancy dinners and fundraisers and the rest of the time, I'd just be his assistant.

Job security and an accurate job description were some of the best things a girl could ask for.

6:07 a.m. — Do you need shoes?

I laughed. He must've been freaking out about agreeing to being stuck with me. Tennis shoes on Ruth was cute and quirky, tennis shoes on a personal assistant who'd snuck in an event was quite another thing.

6:09 a.m. — As you know, I'm in DC until Friday. Coordinate several items from my DC apartment arriving today; movers at 2 p.m. I've attached a spreadsheet of items you should expect; please check, confirm, and put away.

In between errands, research, travel coordination, copious copies, and more, I unpacked and organized his things, wondering when I'd find the buried treasure, little clues to who he was when he wasn't being Pres St. Clair. Because it was mostly dress clothes and old reports.

If I asked, I was sure he'd equate commitment with clutter. Memories were messy. Trinkets were trash.

He could leave town without a trace, and his penthouse wouldn't look any different.

His moving to Middletown full-time wasn't surprising if he wanted to build a base of supporters here. And the post-script in his final email had been even less surprising:

Also, I want to be clear that I'm committed to keeping this "relationship" between us professional and courteous. You'll be my "girlfriend" in name and public events only — I have no expectations for you outside of that. Essentially, the label has no meaning in reality as we know and define it. -p

I allowed myself to feel powerful for a moment knowing I wouldn't be fired, teasing: *You've swept me off my feet with that declaration. Yours in name only, Rach.*

And so, for the first time in my 24 years of life, even if

it was closer to dream than reality, I had it all — a guy, a job, and future to plan for.

...

"When life gives you lemons," I said to myself as I brushed my teeth, "use it to polish off your gin and then depuff your eyes."

I rinsed my toothbrush and tossed the lemons I'd used in the trash, feeling pretty good.

Unless someone was actually paying attention, it was impossible to tell that, in between doing things for Pres who was still out of town, I'd spent all afternoon moving back into my basement apartment.

JD had said he'd help out, but then he'd texted if my boyfriend liked me so much, *he* should help instead. And the thought of asking Pres to move dusty boxes or even catching a glimpse of my place was out of the question.

Putting my place back together after the exterminators had torn through it had been a good workout anyway.

My phone pinged, signaling that the car I'd organized for everyone was outside.

My horoscope had said to allow myself to embrace a serious, future-oriented mindset.

I glanced at the email Pres had sent me this evening to confirm the details for the charity dinner, adding, *Consider this a trial run to see how we connect in public as two people in a committed relationship.*

Serious? Check.

Future-oriented? Could have been Pres' nickname.

I was as ready as I could be for our first fake date.

As an SUV pulled up to my block, I paused to examine my reflection in the window. I'd wanted to completely transform into a new person, erase my imperfections, get rid of my past. Surely dollar store foundation and lemons could handle the task.

But as I stared at my distorted reflection, I wondered if looking different was enough to *feel* different.

The window cracked open.

"Are you getting in?" Pres' impatient voice carried from the darkened backseat. "Is this not the car you arranged?"

I slipped in, said a quick hello to his team, and glanced where he sat alone in the very back.

I knew it wasn't a real date, but my body hadn't gotten the memo to suppress first-date jitters. Especially when he was wearing a tailored suit, his hair styled perfectly, his lips set in a perfect pout.

He glanced from his phone to my building. "I thought you said you lived in a basement."

Yeah, not exactly a real date.

"It's down those stairs. I just moved back after it was…" I paused, trying to think of a nicer way to say 'recently fumigated,' "…remodeled."

He nodded and looked back at his phone.

"How was DC?" I asked, unable to handle the silence. "All your travel arrangements go well? Were you able to rest on the plane a bit?"

He shrugged, rubbing his temple. "It was fine."

"I watched your segment. You did great."

Wow, I bet he'd never heard that before.

I was killing this date.

Literally.

It was dying a slow, stoic death before it even had a chance.

He smiled tightly. "Thanks."

I tried to remember how I'd done this so well when I'd been Ruth. I'd even had a little gin for liquid courage like that night, but it hadn't soothed my nerves.

"It was kind of boring though," I added with a stupid laugh.

Oh, there was the gin, right behind schedule.

His team collectively sucked in a breath.

Pres glanced up from his phone, his blue eyes icy, jaw set. His tone was pleasant, but had an edge, "Was it?"

I had a feeling not a lot of people told Pres the truth. And even less people teased him.

I smiled and cocked my head playfully. "Well, no one even asked about my boobs. Did you even go viral?"

Instantly, he smirked.

"A shame really," he said. "Though I can't believe you aren't enthralled by the critical evaluation of theoretical claims and the reasoning of policy makers."

I laughed as the rest of his team tried to one-up each other on how great he'd been. Ignoring them, Pres looked back at his phone, the hint of his amused smirk not disappearing.

But as soon as the car stopped, nervousness washed over me again. Because between just us, we could joke around, but when we stepped out of this bubble and into the real world, it was serious. We were going to date.

"Did you review your talking points, Pres?" Ethan asked. "You're connected, you could make any favor come to life with one phone call, your father is…"

He trailed off when Pres gave him a flat look.

"Right, of course you have. So just stick to them. These men love your father, so they'll love you, too."

Pres rolled his eyes and glanced at where I was gripping the seat a bit too hard.

"Don't be nervous. Be yourself," he said. "Or a version of yourself that polls well. Preferably that version."

Yep, definitely not a real date.

I smiled weakly. "Are you joking?"

He laughed and stepped out of the car, adjusting his suit jacket, and waited for me.

"I am. But enough time has passed since Boobgate that I don't anticipate anyone mentioning it. Most of these attendees aren't even aware of what viral means. You probably won't have to speak at all."

"Oh good. Great. Right?"

"Right. If we have any luck, I won't either," he said lowly, taking index cards from Ethan. Without a glance, he slipped them in his suit pocket.

Ethan briefed Pres, telling him about all the important people who knew his father, while Jamar filled him in on the ones who had the biggest checkbook.

As soon as we stepped inside, Pres was pulled away by Ethan, and I was left behind to check everyone's coats.

I stood at the edge of the crowd, years' worth of self-doubt washing over me, hyperaware of how my dress didn't fit quite right, my makeup was shades from last season, and I had absolutely nothing to say to anyone.

"Ethan," I said as he quickly walked by. "What should I be doing? How can I be the most helpful?"

"I think Pres would prefer if you stayed out of the way," he responded. He glanced to where Pres stood with his arms crossed, nodding every so often, as an animated circle of older men surrounded him. "He needs to make the exact right impression tonight."

"So he just wants me to … stand here?"

Absolutely definitely not a real date.

"If someone approaches, feel free to talk. Network. Mention how great Pres is. Your choice."

"Cool, awesome options," I said, holding my smile

until he walked away to shake hands with Pres' men.

So I did just that — stood until someone approached.

"Excuse me, ma'am, can I clear this high top?"

I nodded, scooting over to let the server take away the drinks a group had left behind.

"Having a good night?" I asked as I helped pick up stray napkins. "These events are something else. I used to be a server, and I always thought it'd be nice if people left tips around as much as they did napkins, am I right?"

She cocked her head, a look I'd been receiving my whole life, unsure of who I was or where I belonged.

"Are you ready to go?"

I jumped at Pres' voice behind me.

"It's over?"

"I'm done," he said, glancing at the server. He smiled politely then glanced at me. I could see him trying to work through if I knew this person.

She looked equally unsure by his role in my life.

He'd already turned, heading to the door. I glanced at the server, but she was gone, the table cleared.

I did a final sweep of the room, but it looked like it had when I'd first arrived, just as it should — as if I'd never even been there at all.

CHAPTER EIGHT

The next event went about the same.

Ethan swept Pres away to introduce him to people who were too important to risk me messing it up.

"It's what he wants," Ethan assured me at a networking dinner as he led me to the back of the room. "We'll get a photo of you two together later. Nobody really cares. You're just a social media stunt."

But once it was over and everyone filed out, Pres appeared, frustrated. "Where were you? Someone asked where my girlfriend was, and I said the bathroom."

"The dinner lasted two hours."

He shot me an exasperated look. "I know. Now I look like I'm dating someone with major digestive issues or am so unlikable my own girlfriend can't stand to sit next to me for one dinner. Neither of which would poll well."

"I thought you wanted me to sit back here. I can go introduce myself—"

"It's fine. Next time," he said, walking to the door.

"Wait." It was a good thing I was almost as tall as him so I could keep up with his strides. He turned a corner, opposite of where everyone gathered for the valet. "We need a photo of us."

He paused. "What for?"

"Because we're dating."

He kept walking until we were tucked away with only

moonlight to show our features. It was the first time we'd had a real chance to talk since Boobgate.

"I don't want to post a photo of us."

"The whole point of me is so you seem relatable," I said with a confused laugh. "The photo is so you'll seem like yourself instead of a politician."

He sighed and cupped his lighter against the wind, not seeming like he necessarily wanted to respond.

"I am being myself," he said through a plume of cigarette smoke, his expression masked. "I wouldn't post a photo of my girlfriend publicly. That's my private life."

"Okay, but this is pretend. So what would Pretend Pres do if he were pretending to date me?"

He exhaled slowly and watched the smoke fade before speaking, "You want me to determine what I'd do if I wasn't myself but pretending to be myself but a public version of that self who isn't reflective of who I am currently? With a fake girlfriend? I'm excellent at future modeling, but this may be too advanced even for me."

I laughed. Out of all the wealthy, powerful, cocky politicians I could have flashed, I'd found the nerdy one. I wasn't sure if that was good or bad luck.

"Let's just take a selfie. Please? Sable asked for it."

Her email had been clear: *Get the photo, Rach. People want to see more from Boob Girl. REAL people. Not the people Ethan keeps networking with. I've cc'ed Ethan here so he understands this is more than a social media stunt.*

"How about if you do this, I'll move your upcoming dentist appointment so you'll have an excuse to skip the children's choir show Sable wants you to attend?"

"Are you attempting to barter with me using my own schedule as leverage?"

"I think so, yes." I paused, smiling. "…Is it working?"

He sighed. "I'd rather have a root canal than listen to children attempt to sing, so I guess so."

"Good for you, it's just a regular cleaning," I said with a smile. "You know, I actually love going to the dentist."

"Do you?"

"Of course! A fresh smile *and* a goodie bag at the end? What more could you ask for?"

Pres shook his head and took a deep drag on his cigarette before stubbing it out and sliding it in his pack.

"I don't have a response to that. You can take a photo."

"We have to be in it together."

He smirked. "I figured that one out, babe."

I laughed, but it came out all wrong, high-pitched and weird, and my cheeks instantly felt hot. "Babe?"

"How about Pretend Pres calls his pretend girlfriend pet names? It matches how ridiculous this whole thing is. Maybe darling. Honeycakes. Cookie doll. Sugarlump—"

I laughed for real that time.

Then I jumped, surprised when he slipped his arm around my shoulders. I held my breath steady, not wanting him to detect my heart cartwheeling in my chest.

"Ready?" he asked, holding out his phone.

It was too dark.

He shrugged, pulled his arm away, and slipped his phone back in his pocket.

"Damn," he said, not at all upset. His rare bright smile was infectious. He'd known the photo would never work. I'd bet he was an incredible chess player. He was always two steps ahead. And two steps ahead felt pretty dang far. "Next time."

. . .

It didn't go any better.

I'd spent the first half of the night at the coat check,

having been mistaken for staff and unable to bring myself to bail when I saw how slammed the worker was.

While I tagged coats and wrangled gloves, Pres was in the ballroom surrounded by people who wanted to connect with a St. Clair. When I'd finally finished, telling the real worker to keep the tips, and scrambled over, someone from security asked me to please back up.

By the time we'd managed to connect, I was outwardly frazzled, and he was inwardly frustrated.

He and Ethan were talking to an educator — a rare sight at these events — and he'd asked Pres what he thought about the latest report on the city's education.

I stood there, unsure of what to do, while Pres went on a high-level explanation about how the data was actually inaccurately done, so it was impossible to determine what the problems really were.

"Right … but what do you believe?" the man asked.

"I'm not saying I believe anything at the moment," Pres said. "I'm just stating factual truths."

The educator nodded, exchanged an equally lost look with me, and made an excuse to exit the conversation.

"That was great," Ethan said immediately. "Excellent. You were much smarter than him."

"I need fresh air," Pres said and walked off.

I turned to Ethan. "I think he wanted empathy."

"Who? Pres?" He scoffed. "You're mistaken."

"No, the educator. I think he wanted Pres to say he heard him and that his struggles were valid. And, like, they'd connect, you know? Bond?"

"Where'd you get your master's in political science?"

I shook my head.

"So Communications?"

"I have an associates in general studies."

"So maybe leave interpersonal analysis to the experts."

My mom taught me if I didn't have something nice to say, not to say anything. So I remained silent while Ethan and Jamar strategized on the most important people Pres should talk to — weighing connections over capital — until Pres reappeared, not smelling quite like fresh air.

We tried our hands at our ruse again when someone asked how long we'd been together.

Unable to keep the dryness out of his voice, he said, "It's felt like forever," while I chirped, "Oh, who really counts those things?"

And when someone asked me what I thought of his father, Pres changed the subject swiftly and with such finesse, I'd almost missed it. When they asked if he'd met my family, I tried to do the same. But instead I made a silly joke, threw my hands up, and immediately dumped my wine all over Pres.

He tensed, took a deep breath, then excused us, his smile so perfect that it was definitely fake.

"I'm sorry. It really was an accident," I said, following him to the bathroom.

"It's fine."

"Don't cry over spilled milk, right?" I called through the door as he ran the faucet. "Spilled wine is similar, don't you think? Good thing my glass was only half-full."

"I'm not crying," he replied flatly. "And milk and wine are inherently different substances."

I leaned against the wall, feeling guilty and stupid. I'd never be the girl who could explain her parents, have the guy over for intros and appetizers, make small talk in a ballroom, or be charming on demand. These past two weeks had proven I wasn't good at faking it. And being around him made that even clearer.

I was all about being positive, but I couldn't shake the feeling that I didn't belong, that being here was worse than being fired, that I was bad luck.

He came out of the bathroom, not looking any better because he'd probably never needed to know how to remove stains, and asked if I'd call him a car.

As we headed to the exit and I grabbed his coat, we ran into Olivia.

"Can I get a photo of you two?"

"No," Pres said firmly.

"Sorry," I said gently. "Pres' car is on the way. Maybe next time."

"But Sable said you have to capitalize on Boobgate," she said, barely able to meet Pres' disgruntled expression.

He sighed. This really wasn't part of his social media brand. He didn't even post on his own Instagram. Instead, he'd approve a pre-drafted content calendar, a task he'd put off until Sable's emails became threats.

He was active on Twitter, but his threads were specific to polls, analyzing and contextualizing politics across the country. It was fascinating, but it was a far cry from smiling with his girlfriend.

"Fine. One photo," he said, adjusting his coat so the wine I'd spilled was barely visible.

Even as an optimist, I could tell the photo wouldn't work. We looked stiff, strangers with fake smiles and distant stances.

"This turned out great," Olivia said brightly.

I half-expected Ethan to pop up and agree, saying, *"Absolutely fantastic, no one takes a better photo than Pres."*

Pres walked away without a word.

I waved bye to Olivia and caught up with him to make sure his car arrived and because I really didn't know who

I was supposed to be or where I was going anyway.

Here I was again, outside another ballroom, in another borrowed dress, once again pretending to be someone I wasn't, and I was having trouble seeing the silver lining.

And even though Pres was next to me, I still felt alone.

"It was half-empty."

He spoke like we were in the middle of a conversation. I cocked my head, confused.

"The glass of wine you spilled on me." He said it like it was indisputable. "It was half-empty, not half-full."

"Are you joking?"

"No. You were drinking it, so you were in the process of emptying it. Half-empty. If you'd been pouring it, then you would've been in the process of filling it. Half-full."

I crossed my arms over my chest and shook my head. "I don't believe that."

"You can't argue facts."

Unable to stop myself, I groaned. "It's not *facts*. It's perspective."

"Well, you're wrong."

And then, after three bad fake dates, I realized we were finally going to do what real couples did — argue.

"Well, *you* wouldn't know. No one is honest with you. So I'm not sure you have the luxury of perspective."

"Excuse me?"

"This is the third event where I've been told to stand against a wall to just watch you, and it goes the same way. Ethan introduces you to five variations of the same man, and you talk about the same thing. He tells you it went great, and Jamar backs him up. Because when your team isn't busy sucking up to you, they're terrified of you, do you realize that? Do you even care? And on the off-chance you speak to a regular person, you don't connect. I know that because *I'm* that person," I said, pressing my hand over my chest. "We don't connect. We aren't even trying. And I think I'm supposed to be some litmus test for the regular Joe?"

"We're supposed to be dating. I wouldn't date a constituent."

I was almost certain he rolled his eyes.

So I did roll mine. "I *am* a constituent. But it's clear you're only going to do what you want to do. Which is great, really, I do admire your tenacity—"

He let out a frustrated breath, a deviation from his usual stony demeanor. "Why do you do that? What is that strange twist you do, turning bad things into half-hearted positives? You seem delusional."

"I'd rather be delusional than a grump," I snapped. "Someone would have to be delusional to believe we're dating. Or believe that I make a difference."

I held up my hands, defenseless, but I couldn't stop.

"You want the truth, Pres? I guess I don't understand the point. Are you going to be just another politician who cares more about themselves than the people they're supposed to serve? Because if you're going to be like all those men in that room, what makes you special enough for someone who *isn't* them to vote for you?"

He stared at me.

I'd never had someone look at me like that.

An icy fire behind bright blue eyes.

Like he was taking in every part of me, cataloging and accessing, rolling over the words I'd said in his head to commit them to memory. It was a look that meant he'd remember this forever.

A look like this was the first time someone had spoken to him this way. Knowing him, it probably was.

His look made me shift, nervous, and a blush creeped up my neck. Sure, he'd seen me naked before, but this felt much more intimate.

I exhaled sharply, realizing this was the first time in years *I'd* been truly honest with how I felt.

I broke eye contact, equal parts exhilarated and terrified. I knew he could be more scathing and direct in his factual, no-nonsense way. I didn't want to know what he thought, what facts he'd gathered about me these past weeks, how quickly he'd learned the character Ruth I'd so desperately wanted to be was just a facade, that I was nothing like the woman he'd believed I was.

"I'm sorr—"

He turned away from my apology.

Then his car arrived, and he stepped forward, not looking back until he was about to close the door.

"Why don't you take tomorrow off?" he said evenly, the suggestion really a statement.

So I watched him leave, hoping I hadn't messed this all up. My heart was pounding, and I didn't know if it was because I chose to be honest when I knew I was right at the wrong time or because the guy who held my future in his hands could decide to toss it over his shoulder without a second glance.

CHAPTER NINE

I had done enough research on Pres to not only be able to imagine him in several scenarios, but also to have actually seen them play out.

Poised and eloquent on television, wearing shades of blue that made his eyes brighter and icier.

Dry and deadpan at the head of tables.

Focused and frowning behind a desk.

Intelligent and intimating in crowds.

Secretly smoking against brick walls.

I'd thought I'd seen it all.

But early on Saturday morning, when I'd answered the knock at my door, thinking my landlord was coming to fix my leaky shower, I realized I had been wrong.

Because on the small, dingy stairs that led to my place, dressed like he belonged anywhere else but here, in slim fit suit pants, Louboutin beaded loafers, and a white Saint Laurent button-up, Pres stood.

I slammed the door in his face.

"Oh my gosh," I gasped. "What are you doing here?"

"I came to talk to you." His voice was clear and calm through the door. "May I come in?"

I hastily glanced around my messy apartment.

Last night's dinner, a bowl of cereal, sat next to this morning's breakfast, a frozen breakfast burrito, on the disorganized coffee table. Before he'd appeared, I'd been attempting to sort out my budget, planning the loss of the extra ten percent I'd been given to be his assistant, paper and receipts scattered across the living room.

The mysterious stain on my thrifted couch was somehow worse after I'd scrubbed it, and the potted plant I'd rescued from the curb was wilting rapidly.

"Uh, just a sec," I called out and ran into my bedroom.

I scrambled to pick up last night's dress off the floor — a perfect, melted outline of a nonexistent woman — and make my bed, shoving the photo of my mom and me on my bedside table in the drawer. It wouldn't fit.

Because the drawer was ridiculously small and my *vibrator* was in the way.

I groaned, trying to decide which would lead to the least questions if he came into my bedroom. He wouldn't though, I reminded myself. People who fire assistants didn't do it in the *bedroom*.

Pres knocked again, so I shoved the vibrator under my pillow and closed the drawer on my mom's smiling face. Then I shut the curtain separating my living space and bedroom and hoped for the best.

"Sorry," I said through the door, trying to catch my breath. Maybe if I kept my eyes closed, the mess and Pres would magically disappear. "Um, you can't be here."

"Why not? You know where I live. In fact, you're quite familiar with all aspects of my place. Shower included."

I opened the door. "That's not funny."

And there it was, a startling scene I could have never imagined: Pres grinned. A charming, teasing boyish smile that made my knees weak.

"I thought it was pretty funny."

"I just moved back here. That's why it's messy," I said quickly when he glanced over my shoulder. "What are the chances of you showing up right after I moved back?"

He opened his mouth, and I shook my head. "Wait, don't actually answer that. I was asking the universe. Also, I thought you fired me."

He moved his gaze from the pile of laundry I'd been planning to get to today and frowned. "I never said that."

"You told me to take the day off and left."

"You needed a break. My car had arrived. It made sense," he said with a shrug. "When I fire someone, it's not open to interpretation."

I'd seen him give enough direct commands to his team that imagining someone asking him to clarify or explain further did seem impossible.

"We have an agreement, Rach. You said this was over when you quit. Have you quit?"

I looked down at my bare feet, cringing at my chipped nail polish. No matter how hard I tried, he always saw my worst side.

"I can't be your girlfriend. I'm messing it up."

"We."

His voice was gentle then, deep and quiet, and when I met his eyes, his smile was softer than I'd thought it'd be.

"*We're* messing it up. You were right. I haven't been trying. It's the first thing I haven't tried to succeed at. So last night, I skimmed a couple books and two podcasts and read some blogs on fake dating, and I'd like to talk."

I hesitantly stepped aside, expecting an aghast comment about my place. Instead, he faced me, studying me more closely than the tiny basement.

"Did you know nothing comes up when you Google your name? Other Rach and even Rachel Montgomerys exist, but none are you," he said, sitting on my couch's edge as I scrambled to pluck away a receipt for five frozen dinners that had plopped into my coffee cup. "One mention on Prestige Staffings' website, but no photo."

As many times as I'd Googled him, I'd never thought he'd do the same.

"Other than this moment," he continued, and I braced myself for a cold analysis, "there would have been no way for me to know you're someone who enjoys breakfast burritos."

I burst out laughing and shook my head in disbelief. "Oh my gosh, are you teasing me?"

"Isn't that what boyfriends do, honey bear?"

I laughed again. "Well, I've found the one thing you're bad at. You're terrible at pet names."

He rolled his eyes and shuffled a few scattered receipts until they lined up. He didn't look at me when he asked, "Have you ever Googled me?"

I bit my lip. It was one thing to look him up because he was my client and was already well-known.

But admitting I'd typed his name in my search bar on sleepless nights, when I wondered if this was all a dream, squinting at my glowing phone to commit facts and smiles to memory … that seemed like admitting to something deeper than innocent curiosity.

"Are you supposed to ask people that?" I teased instead with a smile. "It feels personal."

"I think it's a fair question for my girlfriend."

I laughed again. "You're really hammering 'girlfriend' into your vocabulary, aren't you?"

He formed another neat pile of receipts on the coffee table. "A fatal fake dating flaw is that the couples aren't authentic. They don't fully commit. It's not something we can slip off and on. I read about it last night."

I nodded slowly.

"I've determined that you being my personal assistant is actually perfect. You know enough about me. You're around me enough that it can feel natural."

"Right," I said with a slight laugh, "but you're forgetting that you don't know me."

"Yes, and that's why I'm here." His expression was serious, and I suddenly felt very nervous. "I want to spend time with you. I'll just watch and listen. And then, if anyone has any questions about you, I'll use today as a reference point."

I glanced around my apartment, wishing I had access to the notes he was keeping in his head. Well, if I had multiple wishes, I'd probably wish my place was cleaner.

"What if someone asks something you don't know?"

He didn't look fazed. "All day, every day, I take small pieces of information and apply them holistically to make accurate predictions. I question hypotheticals and focus on proving if they have real viability." He shrugged. "Just show me a typical day in your world. I can do the rest."

When he put it that way, it sounded easy. And it involved way less of my personal baggage. All I had to do was be a version of a perfect girlfriend who looked like me but wasn't really, and we'd be set.

I smiled. "I'm worried you might be too emotional for a job like this."

He laughed. "Oh yes, that's always the feedback I receive. I'm such a bleeding heart. I've been told I have to be careful or I'll be mistaken for a poet."

It was the first time he'd ever referenced specifics from the night we'd met. If the universe was listening, it would have heard me begging not to blush.

"But seriously," he said, not lingering on the memory. Maybe he'd forgotten I'd said that … pretty much right before I'd asked him to sleep with me. "Do you realize what it means that you have no SEO, nothing pops up when someone types in your name, and the Boobgate Internet detectives couldn't find you? That to the world at large, you don't exist?"

I flinched at the evidence that I was nothing.

"I'm not sure if you realize this, but you saying that didn't make me feel great," I said with a slight laugh. "People feel things, you know. You can't talk about us like you do statistics in a report."

He shook his head. "No, that's not what I meant."

"This won't work if you keep insulting me. I'm happy to be your assistant because I need the money, but maybe I can find someone better suited to be your girlfriend."

He gave me a flat look. "I don't need help getting a girlfriend. I've had plenty of girlfriends, and *none* of them have been like you."

I groaned, trying to tame my budding embarrassment and frustration. "Again, that feels like an insult."

"It's not," he said, positively annoyed. "I meant—"

He paused to straighten a coaster parallel to the table. Then he met my eyes with a deep, searching gaze that sent shivers straight to my core.

"No one speaks to me the way you did last night."

I opened my mouth to defend myself, but his expression stopped me. He wasn't mad. Instead, he looked serious, maybe even pensive, close to confused.

"You were," he paused again, and I realized I'd never seen him struggle to find a word, "truthful. I liked it."

I smiled, touched.

He cleared his throat and busied himself with adjusting a throw pillow. "By *like*, I mean I appreciate your honesty. It's a valuable resource."

"A valuable resource," I repeated, amused by how he turned something sweet into something technical.

He smiled wryly. "I think you could be an asset. And I could do the same. That's all I'm saying."

"Pres, the romance is overwhelming me."

He rolled his eyes, the blues sparkling like they had the first night we'd met. Seeing him truly smile, one that wasn't hidden or perfected, and laugh because of me made my chest feel a little bit looser, a little lighter.

"I mean it though, Rach. My research shows we both need to be properly invested in order for this to work. So I can help you outside of just giving you a job reference. Depending on the ask. And if my schedule permits," he added quickly.

"Which I'm in charge of," I teased, unable to resist the urge to poke the little control freak bear inside him.

He smirked. "Of course. Also, what I meant about you not being online and unsearchable…"

I shook my head. "It's okay—"

"You can be anything you want, is what I meant. Nothing has to define you. You get to make it all for yourself." He glanced at the receipts he'd stacked neatly and then back at me. I shifted under his intense gaze. "And I can help you. I can help you be anything. You just have to answer the question, who do you want to be?"

It wasn't that easy.

I was my mother's daughter. Even if no one knew about her and what she'd done, her legacy would always stick with me. And as much as I didn't like to believe it, I was destined for bad luck. I was broke with bad credit, scraping by on a job that hung in the air to everyone's whims but my own.

I was an ex-girlfriend to a guy who thought I was a

joke.

And I was a fake girlfriend to a guy who definitely didn't care about me. I didn't need a sign from the universe to tell me that this was tit for tat. Literally, if we were counting Boobgate.

I didn't know how to respond.

"Just think about it," Pres said gently. "And let me know when you've figured it out. I can make it happen."

I felt like he'd taken the breath from me.

"How can you be so sure?"

I glanced around, realizing where he sat was now spotless. Throughout these past few weeks, I'd found myself noticing he had a tendency to straighten things as he went, tidying the world around him, leaving it in a better place than before.

And now I looked at him, sitting up straight in my space without touching anything at all, still an arm's distance away while we shared the same couch.

"It's my job to be sure," he said with a small smile.

I nodded, my heart banging in my chest.

And he nodded, the agenda item crossed off in his head. "Excellent. Now we should discuss one more thing. Our sex lives."

CHAPTER TEN

"I don't mean I want to sleep with you," he clarified as I nodded like hearing that said directly to my face was totally cool. "But we should look like we're sleeping together."

"Do you want coffee?" I popped off the couch to my straight-line kitchen without waiting on an answer.

"Do you mind if I look around your place?"

I shrugged. "Go ahead."

If we were talking about sex, it hardly mattered if he also saw my dirty laundry.

He slowly walked around, hands cusped behind his back like he was evaluating an art exhibit, and explained we needed to pull off our physical chemistry.

He'd never mentioned when I'd asked for a one-night stand. I wondered if he'd bring it up now. I wondered if he would've said yes.

If he had, we definitely wouldn't be here today.

He would've been just a guy, a one-time thing.

Easy peasy.

He stepped into my kitchen and close to me.

I'd never even seen him in *his* kitchen, but here he was in mine, a hand's distance away, watching me with bright blue eyes, toned arms crossed, tall and powerful, asking if I wanted to pretend to sleep with him.

This was not easy peasy.

"Do you agree? I want you to feel comfortable. Meaningless gestures is all I mean."

"Meaningless?"

He shrugged. "We hold hands. I put my arm around you. I touch you—" I jumped at a splash of water fizzling on the stovetop, having forgotten what I'd been doing. "—Just in public to make it believable."

"Did your research tell you to do this?"

He laughed, the faintest smirk crossing his lips. "No. I told you, I've had girlfriends. I know what's involved."

"Have you pretended to date someone before?"

He shook his head, his displeasure at the idea blatant. "Absolutely not. But most relationships are pretty fake anyway, aren't they?"

"Gosh, what a terrible take. How many girlfriends have you had?"

Some things weren't easily found on Google.

"Enough to know the rules of the game."

I laughed. "So it's all a game to you?"

"We're working together toward a common goal." He shrugged again. "We're even practicing to be the best. That's pretty close to playing a game, no?"

"Right, well, then," I cleared my throat, trying to stay composed, "you can touch me in public. That's fine."

The smile that crossed his face was bright and teasing and made me feel very unfocused.

"Rach, the romance is killing me," he said, tipping his head back with a dramatic tortured groan.

I laughed, knowing he'd be horrified at how quickly my mind went to a very unprofessional place with that look, all sexy with groans and teasing smirks.

He glanced at the cup I'd handed him. "What is this?"

"Green tea. I just realized I'm out of coffee. Silver

lining, you can reduce your caffeine intake. I'm concerned you don't sleep."

"I meant the mug. What is *this*?"

He held it up, his brows furrowed at the pattern of various cats spelling out the words *Good Meowning*.

Out of all the flaws in my place this was the one he'd chosen to see.

"I know it's not one of the white mugs you prefer—"

"This also isn't coffee."

"I just said that. Drink it anyway. It won't kill you."

He frowned at being told what to do, but it was more of a pout, a face I didn't think he realized he made. If he knew his lips formed a perfect, disgruntled heart, with the purity of a sleepy child and a tiredness that softened his eyes, he probably would have been even grumpier.

"So what did you think?" I dared to ask, sweeping my hands across my apartment. "Did you get all the data you needed? Can you prove that a tour of my apartment is equal to dating me? Who is Rach if someone asks?"

His face lit up at showing off his skills. "For starters, you put others ahead of your own needs, which ties in perfectly to your career—"

"How do you suppose that?"

"My laundry is clean and put away. Yours is on your floor. You had a hand in both, yes?"

I rolled my eyes. "That's easy, you know my job."

"Fair," he said with a nod. "You also have a few plants, upcycled items, and recycle which denotes a greater appreciation for the world around you—"

"You are such a politician—"

"You don't have many books, but what you have is fantasy. That and the horoscopes taped on your fridge suggests you toe a fine line between seeking guidance and forging your own path. It's an interesting dichotomy. Conflicted, possibly. Most likely confused."

I laughed, hoping my cheeks didn't give me away. "This is pretty unfair, you know. Since you have nothing in your apartment. What's the greater meaning there?"

He shrugged. "A realtor chose my place, and an interior designer put furniture in it."

"And let me guess, you like to control the message and your reputation so you like that it's empty. Am I doing this right?"

He just smirked.

I laughed and returned it. "Please, continue."

"Based on how disorganized this place is, I'd suppose you're in a period of transition. Who you want to be and who you are seems to be in misalignment. You also seem to overweight sentiment over practicality."

I nodded slowly. "Why do you think that?"

"Scones for apologies. Rocks as decor?" he said flatly.

I laughed. "One of those was a birthday gift from my ex-boyfriend."

"Then you make poor choices in who you choose to be in relationships with."

"I guess I'm on a hot streak."

He laughed. "Somewhere in this apartment, I'm sure I could find evidence that you have a very strange sense of humor. But thankfully for me, you choose to demonstrate that outwardly at all times."

I rolled my eyes and grinned, refusing to admit I was pretty impressed for his ego's sake. "So that's it? I could have told you all that."

"Okay, last one," he said, clearly enjoying this little game, "you're hiding something."

I gawked. "Excuse me?"

"There's nothing here that denotes you have close relationships. You're clearly single," he said with a curt nod to the frozen meal containers in my recycling, "and you keep to yourself. There's nothing to truly tell me who matters to you and who you are at your core."

I thought of the photo of my mom, carefully hidden.

"But you said all those accurate things," I sputtered.

"People believe what they want to believe," he said calmly. "It's called the Barnum effect. It's a common psychological phenomenon. People think personality profiles are tailored to them, but they're actually vague and generalized enough to apply to a wide range."

I made a face. "You tricked me?"

He shook his head. "Not at all. What I said is accurate enough to fold into small talk. But for this to really work, I have to actually get to know you, Rach. Honesty is key here. And that's why who you were last night, straightforward, strange, and truthful, will always get you further. We could be good at this."

I laughed, wondering how he was charming, tricky, smart, and frustrating all wrapped up in one. Before I could respond, he looked at me, determined.

"Now I'd like to touch you. A practice run."

I opened my mouth and closed it then straightened my shoulders and nodded.

He stepped closer until our bodies were only a fraction of an inch apart.

With his smirk and playful eyes, I believed him when he said this was just a game, something he had to pretend until his numbers went up. I *knew* it wasn't real.

He probably was doing this so he could get the green tea out of his hands. He was calculating, steps ahead of everyone at all times, I *knew* this. But my mind wasn't communicating with my body, which was currently humming and buzzing and stepping just a little bit closer.

"Meaningless," I said, cringing at how I sounded breathless.

"Exactly," he agreed, leaning closer, his hand falling on my waist, sliding to my hip. His grip was firm, not at all the delicate way he held his cigarettes, and I gave myself permission to inhale just a little bit sharper, a little deeper, as his fingertips pressed down and our bodies met.

Being his assistant meant I knew the cologne he wore, bought the shaving cream, shampoo, and body wash he used, made sure he had the ridiculously expensive hair products he preferred. I was partially responsible for how soft his shirts were. Gosh, I even knew his measurements, could've told his tailor exactly how broad his shoulders were to the centimeter.

But all of those abstract concepts coming together in one very real form of Pres St. Clair against my body was startling. I tightened my hold on him on accident, biting back the smallest of gasps.

He shifted slightly against me, trailing his hand up my back, an incredibly lightly sensual touch that made me dig my teeth into my bottom lip, and then his fingers flitted with the ends of my hair.

His heartbeat was subtle under his white button-up, and finally, my mind caught up with the realization that we were hugging. Just hugging. Easy. I leaned my head against his shoulder, closing my eyes and taking in the warm amber and oak smell of his skin.

When he spoke, his lips close to my ear, his voice deep and low, shivers cascaded down my spine. I had a mortifying thought of wondering what his skin would taste like against my tongue. So it took a minute for me to hear what he'd said.

"That mug really is atrocious."

"Wait, what?" I said with a laugh, pulling back and blinking a few times. "You were thinking about a cup?"

He grinned and stepped back, pulling his cigarette pack from his pocket, completely unaffected by that hug.

Of course he wasn't. He was a functional adult who had a solid grip on reality. I could only be so lucky.

"Truthfully, I was thinking about the effect peppermint has on headaches. I read a study about it a few years ago, but I couldn't quite remember the details," he said, placing a cigarette between his lips. "Then I saw the mug, and it really took me out of the moment."

"Okay, sure, that makes perfect sense. Yeah, I was thinking something similar."

His gaze swept over me then he stepped back again. He couldn't get away from me fast enough.

"That was a good practice. Good work."

I nodded, leaning against the counter and groaning into my palms once he'd slipped outside.

I half-expected him to email that he was halfway down the street because me getting so hot and bothered and wriggly over a hug was super weird.

It was obvious that — outside of his typical triggers of coffee and eating — he smoked when he was stressed. I clearly stressed him out. And he was too busy and too important to be stressed by someone who had punny cat mugs and swooned at his touch.

I was actually surprised when he came back, washed his hands, neatly folded my hand towel, and picked up his mug, studying it as intensely as he studied reports.

"So you drink this on weekends?" he asked, taking a tentative sip, and looked at me curiously. "My girlfriend drinks herbal tea. Huh, I would have never imagined."

Laughing, I shook my head. "I ran out of coffee. I was going to go to the store this morning."

"The store," he echoed. "The grocery store?"

I grinned at his confusion. "Yeah, to buy things."

"Food?"

"That's typically the goal of the errand."

He nodded. "Okay, I'll go with you. You can tell a lot about someone by their purchases at the grocery store. Preferences, decision-making approach, etcetera."

Pres ate virtually the same lunch every day — protein and steamed vegetables from the place around the corner — and he'd either leave for dinner meetings or worked so late I'd never witnessed him eat in the evenings.

His pantry and fridge, which I kept stocked, was full of healthy, easy-to-throw-together foods. They were as put-together and tightly wound as he was. Left to his own devices, I could easily picture him surviving solely on avocados, rice cakes, and cashews, snacking in a suit. He'd never asked for chocolate, ice cream, wine, or even cheese — nothing indulgent in the slightest.

I raised an eyebrow. "So what does it mean if someone else gets you things from the grocery store?"

He laughed, his eyes flashing, surprised by being teased and not used to laughing at himself.

Then he stepped forward, put his arm around me, and pulled me to his side. He pressed his mouth against my temple, his lips brushing my hair as I reminded myself this was just a game, one he was very good at, as he said, "It means your boyfriend owes his girlfriend a couple grocery trips. So let's go, sugarkins."

CHAPTER ELEVEN

When I was a kid, I would play a game with my mom.

"Ready, Rach?" she'd say as we walked in the grocery store, gearing up for our version of I Spy.

The goal was to find the cheapest item. I knew every aisle inside and out, moving faster than her to grab off-brand items, cheering when I'd find one with a bright yellow sticker. That meant it was on sale, making it less than the week before, scoring me extra points in our game. She'd always smile at my joy, telling me I was an all-star.

The trickier part of the game was adding everything up with the small calculator she kept in her purse. The goal was to stay under the price she'd whisper in my ear before we'd walk through the sliding doors.

If we went over, I'd flip through coupons she kept in a plastic baggy to find a way to bring the number down. I almost always did, scouring coupon after coupon before we'd go shopping, determined to win the game.

On the rare occasions I couldn't get the total down, she'd tell me it was okay, I still won because I got to be the one to choose the items we'd put back.

"Anything you want, Rach," she'd say with a smile. "You can choose whatever you want."

It took me years to realize winning and losing could sometimes feel the same.

And now, years later, I was in a different grocery store, playing a very different game, one where I didn't quite know the rules. It was the most bizarre 20 Questions I'd ever played.

Pres had been analytical the whole trip, asking why I chose one brand over the other, did I enjoy cooking, what was my favorite dish, what spices did I use, did I have any allergies, what was my typical meal.

"How do you know how to cook?" he asked, bouncing on the balls of his feet impatiently and rubbing his temple. For someone who could sit in his office for hours without interruption, this errand seemed to be too much.

I shrugged. "You just pick it up over time."

"You went to cooking school?"

I laughed. "No, like, from life. How'd you learn how to cook? Your mom teach you how to make pancakes? Let me guess, your dad is a big cookout kind of guy?"

Pres looked bewildered by this assessment until he realized I was joking.

"But seriously, my ex is a chef, so I probably learned a few things from him."

He stopped bouncing. "Your ex is a chef?"

I nodded.

"Officially? He's paid to do it or has an inflated ego?"

I laughed. "No, he's a real chef at a real restaurant."

"Where?"

I just laughed and headed to another aisle. He quickly followed me.

"He cooked for you or taught you? Both?"

"What is it with the questions?"

"I'm trying to get to know you. Why did your relationship end?"

I paused.

How do you tell your fake boyfriend that your ex-boyfriend dumped you because he was tired of being with someone who had no prospects, money, or future? And part of the reason was the secret that your mom was in prison? That when he'd ask, frustrated, why couldn't I just *be better*, it was impossible to explain my future had already been determined by my mom and her mistakes? That the cards had already been dealt, and I was just trying to keep up? Pres would have 40 questions if I answered that, none I wanted to answer.

I shook my head. "That's personal."

"Well, you are my personal assistant."

I laughed at his teasing, and he nodded.

"But I understand. You don't have to tell me. I respect your privacy," he said quickly, massaging his eyebrow with his thumb. "I want to buy some things."

I glanced over my shoulder where he studied the aisle markers.

"I got you everything you asked for this week. Did I forget something?"

"No. You're actually a pretty decent assistant most of the time," he said as he pulled out his phone. He looked absolutely startled when a box of tea bags bounced off his chest. "*Ouch*. You just hit me with that."

"Excellent observation," I said, scooping up the box and placing it in my hand basket. "Now I see why people beg you to explain things on TV."

"Were you aware you threw that? Do you have a hand tremor or some sort of spontaneous—"

"If you want my help to be more likable, you gotta be open to feedback. In an effort to be accurate, you were kinda a jerk, Pres. I'm a *great* assistant—"

"Well, you did walk in on me during an interview and

show millions of people your—"

"I'm at least better than decent," I huffed. "Most assistants would have already quit by now."

"They would have already been fired."

My mouth dropped open, and he threw his head back and laughed. His laugh was loud, this really great delighted sound, and for once, I didn't care that people stared at me in the grocery store.

As he headed to a different aisle, I noticed that he had the faintest trace of confusion on his face. The whole time he'd been going down the wrong aisles, seeming very lost. An errand that should have taken 15 minutes was already taking more than double.

"Where do you think aspirin is?" he asked after we found ourselves in the aisle with energy drinks.

"Probably with the medicine. Definitely not with the caffeinated drinks."

"Oh," he said, nodding. "Right, yeah."

"Have you ever been in a grocery store?" I teased as he started to turn down another wrong aisle, clearly having no idea where the medicine was located.

Without thinking, I grabbed his hand to pull him in the right direction. He looked at our laced fingers, then my face, and grinned.

"That's perfect, shmoopie."

Shmoopie.

His commitment to this act was going to kill me.

"Of course I've been in a store. It's just been a while."

"Wait, so you actually have no idea where you're supposed to go right now?" I said with a laugh. "You know, you almost had me fooled, James St. Clair."

He squeezed my hand and ignored me, biting his lower lip to stop from smiling. I couldn't help but beam even wider, which only deepened his frown.

"I am familiar with the concept."

I laughed, watching as he squinted at the pain relievers, like this decision was as important as the news.

"While you do that, I'm going to grab one last thing," I said, slipping my hand from his and stepping back.

"Wait, no. I won't be able to find you."

I rolled my eyes before turning the corner. "It'll just take two seconds."

"We're supposed to do this together," he huffed, his tone so bossy, and grabbed a random bottle of aspirin before catching up with me. "I'm learning about you."

"I'm really not that interesting."

"Strangers on the Internet disagree."

I sighed, trying to think of a way to get rid of him, but his determination was too strong.

His expression changed when I stopped in the aisle I needed.

"Oh."

"I guess this is the dark side of being my boyfriend," I said with a laugh, rewarded with a sheepish smile.

He seemed more confused than affected, working over the concept of "wings" and "applicator" over in his head.

"Let me guess, you've never run out to the store to get your girlfriend's tampons? It's a classic boyfriend move."

"Definitely not."

"You won't turn to stone if you touch them. You won't get cooties," I teased, tossing the box at him.

He instinctively stepped back — just as I was about to quip that if calling me "shmoopie" was part of the ruse, so were these — and expertly kneed the box into my basket like a soccer ball.

"Goal," he said, laughing at my surprise.

I rolled my eyes and smiled. "Lucky shot."

He laughed, brightness splashing across his features. When he smiled, he seemed so much lighter, a weight easing off his chest, sunshine alighting his blue eyes.

"Sure, but I don't believe in luck," he said simply.

"Seriously?"

"Everything can be predicted," he said definitively. "To believe in luck would be to give up total control."

"So you don't believe things happen for a reason? You don't believe in signs?"

He looked skeptical, the concept impossible to understand. "Signs? I don't know what that means. I do believe things happen for a reason. But more importantly, that you can always discern what that reason is. And if you can get ahead of the outcome, predict it before it happens, you'll never be surprised. You'll always be able to know what will happen. The future completely founded. That's not luck."

"So you don't think there's any sort of greater meaning to us meeting? Once as strangers and then again, paths already intertwined before we knew it? You don't believe there's a reason for all this? For you to know me?"

My voice came out soft like a secret, and I realized this was the most honest I'd been about who I was, no smoke screens to hide behind, no way to pretend.

He faced me, and, suddenly, I felt like we were the only two people in the store. With our eyes locked like this, just a step away from each other, it felt much more intimate than I'd intended. I couldn't look away, loving how he looked at me. Like he'd never seen me before, his eyes this gorgeous bright, hopeful blue, like he'd never thought of the world this way.

Then he looked away, letting out a breath, saying

nothing, the brightness falling from his face, the sun disappearing behind a cloud. I realized I was blushing, and I touched my face, brushing back my hair.

It smelled like peppermint.

"To get what we want in the end," he said, taking a step back and studying the aspirin in his hand. The moment, real or not, had passed, neat, tidily packaged and filed away. "We're focused on a singular goal. For me, that's winning. For you, it's a job reference from a St. Clair, right?"

"Right," I said and cleared my throat. "A better job."

Once we stood in line, he put his arm around me. It was a casual touch, like he'd done it every day for years, his hand brushing my shoulder, his fingertips tracing small circles against my sleeve. I leaned into his touch, knowing I needed the practice to be as good at this as him.

"To be clear, the dark side of having you as my fake-girlfriend-slash-real-assistant isn't your period."

"It's that I used your shower and you can't get over it because you're a closet germaphobe?"

He rolled his eyes. "No. It's your hair." He flipped a chunk of my hair with his fingers. "It's everywhere. You shed."

I gasped, laughing and covering my face with my hands. "No, I do not! That's so weird. Don't say that. That's like telling someone they snore."

He laughed, squeezing my shoulder, and pulled me closer. "I bet you do that, too."

"Well, I bet you take up the whole bed," I said with an eye roll, poking him in the side. The way he squirmed was adorable. "I bet you're the type of guy who thinks he's too cool to cuddle."

He laughed, returning my smile. "You just lie there. What are you supposed to do? What's the point?"

"To talk?"

"About what?"

"Secrets? Hopes and dreams?" I teased as he laughed once more, shaking his head.

It was all too lofty for someone like him. The idea that he'd slow down long enough to even do so, that he had secrets to share, that he'd ever whisper a weakness, that he even had fears was comical.

The idea that he'd need to suppose his hopes and dreams, toss them up to the world to see what would fall down and stick — as if he didn't already have all those things decided, neatly planned and coordinated, just as organized as his kitchen drawers or closet.

It was his birthright, James Prescott St. Clair IV, to already know his place in the world, a firm future ahead of him, a past written in the history books, a birthright to have anything he'd want and need.

It was impossible to imagine him vulnerable, lying in bed next to someone, bare from clothes that defined his wealth or status, admitting a tear in his heart, a desire he couldn't achieve or attain. That he was someone who felt lost or lonely. That he was anything like the rest of us, that I had even been close to thinking it was possible.

I'd be a fool to believe otherwise.

Those concepts were just as unfounded as wings and plastic applicators.

CHAPTER TWELVE

I was covered in syrup, and it was all Pres' fault.

In just fourteen short days, he'd changed the trajectory of his pre-campaign plan.

The Monday after we'd gone to the grocery store, he'd handed his team several papers covered in pen marks.

"This is the new plan. On-the-ground events and grassroots functions centered around people who effect real change in this community. Regular people. People who don't know my last name."

He'd plotted out everything. The entire next three months, dates, locations, all the events' backgrounds, research on everyone who was expected to attend, and the probability of each event leading to an uptick in his likability and viability as a candidate.

"Are you sure?" Ethan had asked, taken aback by the crossed out fancy dinners and ritzy networking events. "But these people love you. They love your father."

"How many campaigns have you won, Ethan?"

"You know my credentials—"

"All of you, how many campaigns have you consulted on and won? Dominated in the polls?"

Ethan had opened his mouth then closed it, and Olivia and Jamar kept their eyes on the papers in front of them.

"Unless your answer is 'more than you, Pres,' then I'm not interested."

"Your father won with the very plan we're using—"

"I am not," Pres had said evenly, "my father. Change the plans or I'll do it without you. Remember, I'm the unlikeable one, and *I'm* in control."

Then he'd walked out, leaving his team wide-eyed and slack-jawed.

My email had pinged two minutes later. In addition to his renewed focus on being likable to regular people, he was determined to nail being a boyfriend. To him, that meant coming up with pet names throughout the day.

Honeycakes. Muffinbear. Little Booty Ham Sandwich. Partial to LBHS, but willing to consider being flexible.

I'd snorted with laughter, switching from adding the new events to his calendar to respond, *Did you come up with Little Booty Ham Sandwich on your own?*

In true Pres fashion, he'd replied almost immediately even though he was preparing for a policy data call and probably doing four other things.

It's incredible what can be found online. Would you bring me a sparkling water? If I come back now, it'll mess up the scary-I'm-your-boss vibe, and I'm thirsty. -James Prescott "Choosing LBHS" St. Clair

p.s. I liked how you organized my call notes.

That, I was almost certain, was Pres' version of flirting.

And now, less than 12 hours after I'd left his penthouse, waving bye as I sat yet another cup of coffee on his desk while he'd been finishing an analysis, we were at a pancake breakfast in a community center.

The goal, as Ethan had put it, was to "network with influential community leaders for maximum leverage."

But the handmade sign on the door said it was to raise money for the center's after-school programming.

As soon as we'd walked in, Pres had been pulled away

by Ethan, and I'd gotten lost on the way to find him coffee and ended up recruited to work a pancake maker that had seen better days.

"It's tricky, so watch it closely," the volunteer coordinator demanded. "The last person who operated it burned their hand. It ruined the whole breakfast."

I nodded, unable to come up with a polite way to get out of this, as she shoved a bag of pancake mix in my arms, sending dry puffs over my face and sweater. Smiling, I decided to go with it and hope it worked out.

"Are you hoping to meet a nice man today?"

"Oh no, I'm single—ly happy with one person," I fumbled, glancing across the room where Pres wore his perfect practiced smile that appeared on Google Images.

If his team was confused by the change in plans, I guess it was nice to finally be part of a team. Because I couldn't shake when, right as we'd walked out of the grocery store and back to my place around the corner, he'd said he needed to go.

"Your calendar is free," I'd reminded him, hoping I sounded light and casual.

"My schedule being free means I have time to catch up on work. I need to go," he'd said, rubbing his eyebrow with his fingers and squinting against the sun. He'd seemed physically pained by being near me.

By the time I'd put away my groceries, rinsing out his barely touched green tea, I was convinced that no matter how many signs and clues I looked for to understand Pres, he was dead-set on being untouchable.

Even though he looked so dang touchable sometimes.

"That's Senator St. Clair's son," the volunteer coordinator said skeptically, following my gaze. "You might want to set your sights elsewhere, dear."

"I actually have twenty-twenty vision, so who knows, maybe I have a shot," I said with a laugh.

She gave me a puzzled look, and I just nodded, pretty much used to people thinking I wasn't very funny.

She pointed to the pancake maker. "Do you know how to work this?"

"Yeah, my ex is a chef. I spent many mornings trying to surprise him with breakfast, and he was pretty good about telling me how I could improve."

"Well, don't mess it up this time. And do be a dear and clean up the kitchen after."

I tried again to clarify that I wasn't actually supposed to be volunteering, but she'd already walked away.

I glanced around unsurely, but I was alone and the machine was already heating up. I couldn't abandon it, so I tied back my hair and reminded myself why I was here.

I needed this job.

I needed money. I needed to fix my credit. I was supposed to be making my life less messy.

I glanced back at Pres, watching how he laughed and smiled at all the right times, how he seemed to listen closer than anyone else, cataloging everyone's moves until they became natural to him, until he was a perfect reflection of what everyone wanted.

Laugh, smile, nod, say something serious, nod, smile.

The strive for perfection was dizzying.

The only crack in his exterior was so subtle, I doubted anyone basking in the glow of a St. Clair noticed. It was how his fingers were poised just so where a cigarette should've rested between them. How they rubbed together ever so slightly, a sign of an unsatisfied craving.

He wanted a cigarette.

He was stressed.

"What are you doing?"

Ethan's sudden frustrated voice startled me so much that I dropped a jar of homemade syrup I'd been struggling to open. Shattering glass made everyone stop and stare.

I gasped and ducked to the floor to pick it up. "Oh gosh, I'm so sorry."

"You're embarrassing everyone," he hissed. "Pres needs his coffee. You've been gone for twenty minutes. Are you also pretending to be his assistant?"

"Sorry, I got roped into a pancake predicament. If you watch this, I can grab a paper towel and his coffee? I think this last batch is really good."

"Of course not. I have important things to do. This event is ridiculous. Why did you tell him to do this?"

I glanced up from where I crouched to look at Ethan in disbelief. "I didn't tell him to do anything. Do you think anyone has the ability to control Pres?"

"He was fine with networking events and nice dinners then you come along. Now, he's changing the whole plan. You aren't his adviser," Ethan warned. "If you keep recommending stupid stuff, he'll lose focus."

I smiled tightly. "I hardly believe he's the type to lose focus on anything."

"The plan we were using is the same his father uses to win elections. Wine and dine the biggest donors, make deals, and move on. This on-the-ground, salt-of-the-earth stuff is bullshit. And your whole act is mediocre at best. Handing out pancakes?"

"People don't like pancakes?"

"Voters don't care about pancakes."

"That's a pretty sweeping generalization. And we both know Pres does not like generalizations that aren't based on valid data points."

He rolled his eyes. "Great, now he's coming over. I hope you're happy. He was having a productive conversation—"

"Are you okay?" Pres asked, giving us both a strange look. His confusion settled on me. "Why are you on the floor on the wrong side of this table?"

I stood and tried my best to brush flour off my clothes as syrup slowly covered my shoes.

"It's a long story. I'll get you coffee as soon as I flip this. If I do it too early, I'll ruin it. I'm sorry, but I care about the integrity of these pancakes. I can't leave them."

He looked even more confused.

"What is this?" he asked, reaching out to touch the top of the metal pancake maker.

Ethan gasped when I slapped Pres' hand away.

Pres looked shocked.

"It's hot," I said quickly, pretty sure slapping my boss-slash-boyfriend's hand in public wasn't part of the ruse. "I didn't want you to get hurt. You use the handle."

"He knows how to use it. He doesn't need you to explain it," Ethan snapped. "Pres, let's go, there's someone I think you should meet—"

"Why don't you get me coffee?"

Ethan and I did a double take, but Pres' icy gaze on Ethan never faltered.

"Rach is busy," he said coolly. "Now my hand hurts. So get me coffee then maybe I'll meet the next person."

Once Ethan scurried off, nine different shades of red, Pres turned to me. "He's kind of annoying, isn't he?"

"Your hand hurts?"

He shrugged and smirked.

Pres in a tailored gray suit smirking in my direction

made my insides feel similar to the puddle of syrup pooling at my feet. He may have been a tough cookie, but he really was so nice to look at.

"I needed a break," he said, scanning the crowd, looking more tired than he let on. "And I can hardly smoke outside of a community center. How are you?"

I shrugged, the truth spilling out before I could stop myself, "Honestly, if I'm going to be sticky and covered in whipped cream, I'd prefer to get something more thrilling out of it than a pancake, if you know what I mean."

His gaze snapped back to me, surprise flashing in his eyes, and quickly cleared his throat.

"Yes, well, you're correct. You do look very messy," he said, his tone cool and professional.

I brushed a lock of hair off my forehead, accidentally coating it with syrup. Hopefully syrup was good serum for hair. "Yeah, it's been a weird morning."

"You're also standing in syrup and shards of glass."

"Yep, welcome to a typical day in the life of Rach."

At least in a place like this, I fit in better than in a dress surrounded by hors d'oeuvres and cocktail ingredients I couldn't pronounce.

A lady walking up to my station interrupted us before Pres could probably tell me how one day in my life was enough for eternity.

I smiled brightly. "Let me get you a pancake! What's your favorite topping? You can tell a lot about someone's favorite."

She smiled. "Chocolate chips?"

"So I bet you're really fun. Classic with a twist," I said, sprinkling chips on her pancakes. "And you make everyone's day just a little sweeter. Here you go. Enjoy!"

"What are you doing?" Pres asked lowly once she'd

walked off. "Why are you doing that?"

"Small talk?"

"Do you actually care what her favorite topping is?"

I laughed and shrugged. "It's nice to connect with people. If you never get to know people, how will they become your friends? Plus, you're the one who told me about Barnum and Bailey statements."

"The Barnum effect," he corrected. "It's not a circus."

"This feels like a circus," I countered, laughing. "I don't know, Pres. I'm just trying to have fun."

Somehow, this seemed to confuse him even more.

By the time I'd come up with six more topping personalities, joking with the small group that had gathered at my station, I actually was having fun.

"Do you want to try?" I asked Pres quietly as I flipped the pancake maker. He stood next to me, arms crossed, watching the machine I'd slapped him over skeptically.

"Just say something fun."

"I can't think of anything fun. I can't accurately extract someone's personality based on this one data point—"

"Let's practice, what's *your* favorite topping?"

"None. I find pancakes unappetizing."

"Oookay, what do you think about people who like cereal sprinkled on their pancakes?"

"I think that's disgusting."

I laughed loudly, genuinely amused by his bluntness, and he looked at me, surprised.

"Has anyone ever told you that you're charming in your own very specific way?"

He shook his head. "No."

I laughed again. "Just try. There are no wrong answers. Just try not to insult the person."

We were hit with a slight rush, the pancake personality

tests making a little wave throughout the crowd, so I lost track of Pres for a moment.

When I turned back to him, he was asking a confused-looking gentleman, "Do you enjoy high sugar content in the mornings?"

I slapped my hand over his forearm to shut him up. "You're so silly! Pres really cares about the health of this community," I said to the man with a laugh.

If this wasn't challenging enough, in an even worse twist of fate, the assistant center director stepped up to offer Pres a pancake.

"Who has you working this event?" she asked, shocked. "I've never seen a St. Clair get their hands dirty."

"Technically, I'm sticky," Pres said, sounding slightly overwhelmed. I failed to cover my mouth with my hand in time, laughing loudly.

My laugh made the woman smile, hearing Pres' dry statement as a joke instead of just his horrified truth.

"The center director and I noticed you haven't had a pancake yet, so I brought you one."

"No, thank you, I don't like pancakes," he said, trying to step away as she pushed the plate in his hands.

Even I had trouble seeing the good in this one. It was smothered in syrup, clotted sprinkles, melted whipped cream, and congealed butter, but she was insistent.

An event photographer had wandered over, and the center director was a few people back in line, surrounded by several community leaders we needed to impress. Being a personal assistant did have some advantages — I'd managed to snag and study the guest list in advance.

I nudged Pres, noticing the center director watching him with a skeptical expression. "You should try it."

He shot me a desperate look.

"People love people who love pancakes," I added helpfully. "Be a team player. Come on … honeybun."

"Actually, I care about the health of the comm—"

"How about we share?" I scrambled since he wasn't picking up on my signals. There was no way he could eat this whole thing without throwing up anyway. I took the plate and beamed at the assistant director. "Thanks so much. You get the first bite, Pres."

He glanced at the fork I offered. This close, I could see the pain in his expression at the dripping, chunky butter and the now-muddy sprinkle blobs.

I looked at him seriously.

"Trust me."

A camera clicked.

So he smiled, this incredible, great, photogenic smile, and leaned forward, taking the bite I offered.

Another camera clicked.

My heart was thumping hard, realizing we were finally doing this. We were actually faking it. And there was a good chance we were good at it.

"Wow," he said, projecting just enough to be heard without being obvious. "This is *indescribable.*"

He licked his plush, heart-shaped lips, and I was certain I'd passed out, melted on the floor, and would have to be mopped up alongside the syrup.

I tore my gaze away from his lips to see the center director smiling over his shoulder. Relief washed over me.

We'd done it.

It was over.

"Can we get that shot again?" the photographer asked. "The lighting was a little off."

Pres silently signaled his displeasure with one look to me as I held back a laugh and cut off another bite.

When I started to hand him the fork, the photographer interrupted.

"No, do it the same way. That was great."

I dug my teeth into my bottom lip and nodded as Pres took a deep, silent breath. I wasn't sure what was worse for him — eating this pancake or being fed it by me.

He stepped closer.

I was pretty sure the pancake maker had gotten hotter.

As he leaned forward again, he dropped his hand to my waist. I was grateful we'd practiced this, because instead of jumping like my heart in my chest, I leaned into his touch. If I was going to go through this level of torture, I was determined to get a stellar photo out of it.

"Mmm," he said, his eyes flashing with amusement as we locked eyes.

Pres was a lot of things.

Difficult. Nerdy. Sarcastic. Particular.

When he was in a good mood, he was even playful.

But I would have never pegged him as a tease.

"So good," he said, running his tongue over the trace of syrup on his lower lip. I refused to follow the motion as he kept his gaze on me. "Don't you think, Rach?"

Then he stepped back, smiling to the crowd, his voice professional and goodnatured, "The only thing better than this pancake is the incredible work this community center does for our town. I hope you'll all join me in helping keep it thriving for years to come. Plus, it feels wrong not to pay for a pancake this good. Who do I write the check out to?"

The crowd tittered with laughter at the same time Jamar introduced himself to the center's bookkeeper, slipping a donation Pres had determined well in advance.

"I have to say," the center director said once she'd approached us, "you didn't seem that enthused about this event a moment ago, Pres. To be honest, we were concerned you were just showing up for brownie points."

"You mean pancake points."

When they faced me, I realized I'd said that out loud.

"Oh gosh, sorry, that was, um, unprofessional. I was just making a joke."

She smiled, bemused. Everyone looked at me that way these days.

"I don't believe we've met," she said, offering her hand. "Are you a new volunteer?"

Pres interjected. "Mrs. Klein, this is my…" he paused, and I held my breath, "girlfriend, Rach Montgomery."

I exhaled, but that didn't help calm me down since Pres had placed his arm around my shoulders.

"In addition to her pancake-making skills, she has an interesting sense of humor," he said with a slight laugh.

"It's a pleasure to meet you," I said not missing a beat even as my nerves skipped all over the place. "I really do think this is so invigorating. Community centers played a big role in my life."

She glanced at me then Pres, surprised. "How so?"

"My mom worked a lot when I was growing up, so I spent most days after school at our community center. I could make crafts or read or play Solitaire. It felt like a home away from home. Even on bad days, it gave me hope for limitless possibilities."

I finally managed to look at Pres. He was staring at me, his expression unreadable. The only glimmer that maybe I hadn't totally screwed up was how bright his blue eyes were.

"That's exactly what we strive for here," she replied. "So it's a shame that Senator St. Clair promised us years ago he'd take care of this place. Then he endorsed the current mayor who is cutting our funding."

In any other scenario, I would've thought Pres was completely unfazed. He looked fine, pleasant, poised even. If I hadn't been under his arm, I doubted I would have noticed the slightest ripple of tension in his body.

"Pres isn't like his dad."

Everyone around us fell silent.

That was my first clue they'd all actually been listening.

It was also a clue that I needed to shut up.

"Uh, never mind," I said quickly, glancing at Jamar who was shaking his head behind the director. "Sorry."

"No, go ahead," Pres said. "There's no wrong answer."

I did a double take, but he just smiled.

"Well, Pres spent the whole ride over here talking about the impact of these sort of hyperlocal, community-based centers have on the overall wellbeing of cities—"

In fact, he'd snapped a version of it after Ethan had grumbled this would be a waste of time then no one spoke the rest of the ride.

"—He said they're one of the most important metrics of long-term prosperity for all. Coming together as a community for the greater good. So I dunno, that doesn't sound like what I've heard Senator St. Clair say. Maybe Pres being here is the first step, him believing that is the second, and the third is giving him his own chance to prove it?"

I couldn't bring myself to meet Pres' gaze, hopeful it didn't mirror Jamar's shocked and horrified one.

"Sorry, I've totally rambled and probably haven't

articulated him well," I said quickly. "If you want specifics, I'm sure Pres would be happy to talk about it. You were just reading a comparative analysis on how Middletown's community centers stack up to other mid-tier cities, right?"

He gave me a little surprised smile. "Yeah, I was. It was fascinating," he said, turning to Mrs. Klein. "There were a lot of takeaways Middletown could implement with the right leader supporting the effort."

She and the smaller crowd listened, riveted by his recall and details on a plan that had just come out this week, realizing Pres wasn't phoning it in.

As he spoke, confident and calm, I felt the tension in his body melt a little, his fingers relaxing on my shoulder to play with the ends of my hair.

I was equally impressed, coming to the conclusion that he demanded an online and printed version as soon as these sort of reports came out because he actually cared.

He may have been faking us — glancing at me with a smile, biting his lower lip when I returned it — but this sort of passion, this sort of obsession, his drive for perfection, for something better, was nothing but real.

"What did I miss?" Ethan asked, pushing his way next to me. "What's this crowd for?"

I smiled. "Maybe you were wrong. Voters may not care about pancakes, but Pres does. He just ate one."

He scowled, not understanding.

After Mrs. Klein walked off with a satisfied smile and a one-on-one lunch booked with Pres to discuss things further, Ethan handed him a coffee. "Sorry, it took me a while to figure out the coffee pot."

Pres took a sip and instinctively gagged.

"This is terrible. I don't want this," he snapped,

pushing the cup back into Ethan's hands, and walked off.

Ethan glared at me. "*You* should have made the coffee. It's your job."

I glanced across the room where Pres had moved on, still feeling my flushed face and wild heartbeat.

He was surrounded by people, but his eyes locked with mine.

He wasn't smiling, but he wasn't frowning. In some ways, he looked unsure, hesitant, maybe even a little lost.

We'd done it. We'd pulled it off once, and I was confident I could do it again.

So I just smiled and shrugged.

He returned it, and it was such a startlingly warm smile that I felt my cheeks heat up. I quickly looked away, knowing that appreciating his attractiveness was one thing, but actually *blushing* at his smiles was quite another. That was a direct contradiction to our promise to stay professional.

I turned back to Ethan. "You know, I think my job just became way more complicated than coffee."

CHAPTER THIRTEEN

We had fallen into an incredible rhythm.

After the pancake breakfast, Pres had pulled me aside, demanding, "Who taught you how to be like that?"

"Like what?"

"Charming," he'd snapped suspiciously. "Relatable. You wooed everyone effortlessly. How do you know how to be like that?"

"Um, I guess my mom?"

"Is she in politics? Does she work in the media?"

I'd laughed, hoping it hadn't sounded nervous, and quickly shook my head. "Definitely not."

He'd squinted at me and then nodded, satisfied.

"That was excellent." He'd leaned closer as people walked by, his low and serious voice sending shivers down my spine. "We must do that again."

When he'd said practice makes perfect, I hadn't realized just how much he'd meant it.

Our mornings and afternoons were normal, meetings for him, errands for me, coffee in between. The only deviation was when he'd drop a silly pet name into casual conversation, making his team falter and me laugh.

To get back at him, I'd started serving him coffee in my *Good Meowning* mug, making him shout my name when he'd notice in a frustrated, adorable way. I'd just laugh and ignore him, further confusing his team.

But before any events, we'd go over our game plan.

Sometimes, I'd explain how he'd talked about a poll didn't translate to how he actually felt so people would get the wrong idea. He'd patiently explain his actual thoughts so I could boil it down into laymen's terms to whomever we'd meet before he'd swoop in as an expert.

I'd tell him when I'd zone out, when he'd lost me, or if he'd come across as snobby or snarky when he'd answer a practice question.

I kept the parts where he came across as devastatingly gorgeous to myself — when he'd bite his lower lip in concentration, when a lock of his perfectly coifed hair would fall over his forehead and he'd run his fingers through it, lifting his chin to expose his neck, or when he'd smile that sexy squinty secret look.

I'd also create and update a Very Important People binder of who'd be at whatever event we were attending.

"We just gotta butter them up, and then the rest is baked bread," I'd said cheerfully the first time I'd slapped the binder down on his desk.

He'd looked at it then me, and if a man could've fallen in love with an organized binder, that was the moment.

We'd pour over it, dissecting who we needed to impress, then develop a plan to corner and charm them.

Like when he pointed to a severe-looking woman in the binder, explaining she essentially controlled the entire 40-year-old-plus vote.

"She'll hate me because my father endorsed the head of Public Works years ago, and he consistently refuses to even listen to her sidewalk and mobility concerns," he said. "She's denied meeting requests with me from Ethan for weeks."

"She volunteers at the animal shelter on Saturdays."

He narrowed his eyes. "How do you know that?"

I held up her Instagram. "Some people actually show their personality online," I teased as he rolled his eyes. "How do you feel about dogs?"

"Unsanitary," he answered without hesitation.

I sighed heavily. "Try again."

He acquiesced slightly. "I'm operating mostly under an assumption. I've never had a pet."

"Well, get ready," I said with a grin, making his eyes flash with intrigue. If there was one thing I'd learned, Pres loved a challenge.

And that weekend, as she stood in listening distance of the shelter's puppy play area, I could barely remember how grave he'd looked when we'd agreed on this plan.

"Oh, I love him," I crooned, burying my face against the puppy.

I glanced up at Pres — tall, gorgeous, and just a little bit stiff in a crisp button-up and Burberry wool trousers, the most casual he could manage — and quickly pushed away the thought that I wouldn't mind burying my face against him either. See if I could break his composure and make him growl.

"Can we get him, Pres?"

"No."

"But look at his floppy ears. He's so doggone cute."

Pres' lips twitched at my improvised pun, and I was certain he almost laughed.

"We don't have anywhere to walk him, snookums."

"Please tell me you aren't talking about sidewalks again," I sighed. "I don't care about Public Works."

The puppy jumped, accidentally tugging down my neckline with his paw. I laughed, wondering if I was destined for all our plans to end in a Boobgate situation.

Pres inhaled sharply, something we hadn't practiced. I repeated my line, hoping he hadn't forgotten the whole script, as the woman inched closer.

"You don't *care* about Public Works?" he asked incredulously.

"I care about Puppy Works," I said, sneaking a glance at the woman. She was smiling.

"The sidewalks in this city aren't up to par," he said, huffing. "Do you really want Fluffy to have to navigate dangerous crosswalks and sidewalks that just drop off?"

"Fluffy is a cat's name," I whispered.

"Oh," he said, the cute startled look crossing his face unplanned. "Well, I care about *all* animals' wellbeing."

Pres knelt, tentatively petting the pup. I smiled encouragingly as the woman dropped the pretense of being absorbed in kittens to fully eavesdrop.

I did my best pout, which weirdly made Pres bite his lower lip and look away. "But you said that the five-year mobility plan had promise."

"You two are adorable," the woman said, stepping over to introduce herself. She nodded to Pres. "You look familiar."

"Pres," he said, standing to firmly shake her hand.

"Ah," she said, nodding at the unspoken St. Clair lingering in the air. "And who's this?"

"I'm Rach," I said with a wave as the puppy took over my lap. "Pres' girlfriend. We're new volunteers. Maybe you can help me convince Pres that I *need* this dog."

She laughed. "Well, I hate to say it, but he's right about the sidewalk issue. I'm surprised *you* feel this way, Pres."

He glanced my way, making me realize I did play a vital role in these moments. Sure, he needed a girlfriend for ploys and to seem more approachable and friendly.

But he also needed someone to say what he couldn't. And I was just enough of an outsider and insider to the St. Clair family that my words carried weight.

"He's not like his dad," I said definitively. "He may surprise you."

She looked at us closely — an innocent, puppy-loving couple passionate about sidewalks — then smiled.

"So tell me, what's the five-year plan you mentioned?"

Twenty minutes later, Pres had an invite to meet with her women's group of activists and community members.

"Unbelievable," he said as we walked out after actually volunteering. It'd been my only nonnegotiable. "Absolutely unbelievable."

I grinned. "Maybe you should work on believing a bit more."

He caught my hand as I stepped away. I was startled, still not used to his touch, but melted against his chest anyway as he pulled me into a hug.

One delicious moment later, he stepped back and lit a cigarette in one quick, smooth motion. "She's gone now."

I glanced over my shoulder where the woman was getting into her car and then back to him, cheeks flaming.

"I didn't want her to think we weren't really together, muffin," he explained, turning his head to exhale slowly, a cloud of smoke masking his expression.

"Right, yeah, totally. Good call."

"Great work. You're excellent, Rach," he said seriously, his unshakeable words warming me straight to my toes.

"Are you okay?" he asked, placing a gentle hand on my shoulder. And then because he was Pres, and he was honest to a fault, he said, "Your face looks weird."

I nodded, pretending I didn't still feel the warmth from his touch once I was in my apartment alone.

Because being with Pres meant faking a lot.

Smiles at events when I didn't feel like I belonged.

Outfits I pieced together from thrift stores.

Stories about myself focused on positive highlights, having learned anyone's life could sound glamorous with the right tone and shiny moments plucked from reality.

Normalcy at his arm around my shoulders at a Rotary luncheon, his hand on the small of my back at a tour of a new food bank, his hand laced with mine at a prayer breakfast, his fingers twirling the ends of my hair at an LGBTQ+ fundraising art show.

It's fake, just a game, I'd remind myself every time he'd laugh loudly at my unpracticed jokes, introduce me as his girlfriend, catch my gaze across the room and smile, stop what he was saying in a crowd to ask for my input.

I'd remind my overeager imagination — the one that wanted to read into every smile, every lingering touch, every glance as a sign — to refocus, turning away from his smile, and channel my energy on whoever I was chatting up, careful to stick to facts.

...

At the actual events, we were inseparable.

"The board chair loved us," he said as we left a library foundation fundraiser. He laced his fingers with mine — *practice, practice, practice* — as we dodged the crowd for the valet. "When you said you believed your city is only as strong as your library? Incredible. And your story about spending most of your weekends at the library? Amazing."

I'd shared how my mom had excitedly framed the seat in the back of the library and the stack of fantasy books she'd leave me as "a magical portal to other worlds." I'd conveniently left out it was also "free daycare" so she could go door-to-door to sell essential oils and knife sets.

"How about when you said no matter where you've lived a library always felt like home? Totally melt-worthy," I said, squeezing his hand.

He grinned and dropped his arm across my shoulders as we made our way to the shadowy side of the building.

His post-event smoke breaks were also part of our routine, and one of my favorite moments. It was one of the few times Pres was himself because he was alone.

And of course, he'd turned it into a game as well.

A few weeks ago, I'd been served an ice cream cone at an event celebrating bicyclists. Just as I'd started to eat it, Pres knocked it out of my hands where it landed with a splat on the concrete, startling me and making the group we'd been networking with fall silent.

"That has walnuts in it. You're allergic," he'd said, aghast. I'd never seen him so unsettled in public.

I'd blinked at him, shocked he'd known that.

"I'll get you something else," he'd said quickly. "Don't cry over sweetened, frozen milk, right?"

He'd won over two people with that humanizing act.

After we'd networked our hearts out, I'd exhausted all my knowledge on bikes — not having a car in high school had paid off — and had gotten a replacement cone, he still hadn't taken his eyes off of me.

"You don't have to monitor me," I'd laughed, carefully swiping my tongue against the cream to not make a mess.

"What?" he'd said, sounding dazed.

"I'm not allergic to anything in this," I'd clarified, lapping up dripping cream from the side of the cone. "Oh wow, this is *so* good."

He'd stepped back suddenly, fumbling for a cigarette.

"Are you okay?" I'd asked, sucking a drop of cream

from the tip of my finger, and Pres groaned.

"This is messy," he'd snapped and took it, "and a mistake. I'll get you ice cream that comes in a box. *Spoons*, Rach. People use spoons. We need to leave. This is over."

"*Come on*, don't be a bossy clean freak. You were just becoming chill. Get it, it's an ice cream joke!"

He'd already walked off to a trash can, refusing to look at me.

True to his word, though, the next day I buzzed up a delivery, surprised to receive a pint of ice cream.

When I went in his office to thank him, I'd also asked how he'd known I was allergic to walnuts anyway.

He'd said I'd mentioned it in the grocery store.

"I told you my method would work," he'd said, back to being cocky.

I'd nodded, impressed, and popped a spoonful of ice cream in my mouth.

"Oh, sorry, am I not allowed to eat in here?" I'd asked, noticing he'd stopped studying his computer and was staring at me. "I can go."

"No, it's good." He'd frowned quickly and shook his head. "I mean, fine. It's fine."

It had been clear he didn't want me standing there with a spoon in my mouth, so I'd turned to walk away.

"Rach, wait," he'd called out. "I was thinking, if we keep learning about each other, we could dominate this."

"How about we can ask each other any question, and we have to answer? Kind of like 20 Questions and Emotional Chicken. Ooh, let's call it Truth Chicken!"

"Yeah, okay, Truth Chicken. If you agree, we can dedicate more time before or after events with each other to hone it in."

I'd nodded. "Sounds fun. I don't have anything else

going on anyway."

He'd smiled then frowned then settled on neutral.

"Yes, well, I'm glad you're excited to spend time with me when compared to literally no other options."

I'd laughed, thinking if he had to spend more time with me, I could find a way to make work more fun for him. "Hey, we can keep score. One point every time you pass on a question. Whoever has the least points wins."

We played for bragging rights, which carried a lot of weight for a competitive perfectionist like Pres.

And over the past few weeks, I'd learned little things: his favorite color was blue, he loved soccer, he listened to old presidential speeches when he went on daily morning runs, and he had a slight phobia of blood.

I'd also unearthed lesser known, more important facts that made who Pres was a little clearer.

Like he'd been sent to boarding school at just five years old — until he had to move back to Pecunia to be a part of his father's reelection campaign.

"You were eleven," I'd asked, confused. "How would you have contributed?"

"He's a family man, Rach," had been his dry response. "Politicians with a family unit are much more likely to be elected to higher office than those without."

He'd gotten a point when he hadn't answered how he'd actually felt about moving back.

I'd also learned that he detested one-on-one events, overthinking anything that intimate, and preferred TV appearances. But really, he'd said, he preferred working instead of talking about work that could be done.

In return, he'd learned simple stuff about me: my favorite book, my fascination with astrology, and my inability to resist DIY-fix-it projects.

I'd also revealed more than I'd planned, confessing I'd always wanted to be a guidance counselor. I'd received a point when he'd asked why I wasn't. When he'd asked about my parents' careers, to avoid a point and answering fully, I'd found myself admitting I didn't know my dad. He'd nodded, gently ending family follow-up questions.

"Okay," he said now, lighting a cigarette and leaning against the brick wall. "Favorite food."

"Pizza. Classic."

He made a face. "Cliche."

"Has anyone ever told you that disliking things most people like isn't a personality trait?"

He laughed and shook his head. "Just you, love bug. Your turn."

"Do you ever Google yourself?"

He smiled, only slightly sheepish. "All the time."

I laughed and whacked his arm as he laughed, smoke coming out in little cotton candy puffs.

"I know," he groaned. "My turn. Same question."

"I'm not ... Googleable? I'm a social nobody."

He shook his head.

"You'd poll quite nicely, you know. If you ever wanted to become a true public figure."

I rolled my eyes. "Right, I'm sure."

"I'm serious. We know qualitatively your likability is well within acceptable metrics. Another favorable factor is your attractiveness level, which skews quite high."

"Quite high ... Wait, are you calling me attractive?"

"Speaking as a pollster," he said, looking where he flicked ash to the side, "that's probably what I would interpret."

I grinned and poked him in the side. He squirmed away and tried to scowl.

"You think I'm cute?"

"As someone whose job is to look at data objectively, the facts in front of me," he said, his gaze meeting mine, "would lead me to that absolute conclusion."

I burst out laughing as he rolled his eyes at himself, unable to hide his smile.

"You're such a nerd! Why are people afraid of you? You really are like a prickly pear margarita. Sugary sweet."

He laughed, bumping my shoulder with his. "You say the strangest things. I've never been able to predict your responses. It's fascinating. You're fascinating."

My face flushed, ignoring my heart banging in my chest at the sparkle in his eyes.

We'd become great at touching, playing our boyfriend and girlfriend roles so nicely, but we hadn't practiced this: secret laughter, direct compliments, playful pushes.

He loosened his tie, and I followed the motion, unable to shake a vision of him taking it off completely. And if I were making wishes, I'd also take his long, delicate fingers undoing a button or two from his crisp white shirt so I could run my tongue over his sexy throat.

"Your turn," he said lowly.

I tore my gaze away to meet his eyes. "Huh?"

"Did you still want to play the game?"

"Oh, yeah," I said, clearing my throat and pushing off the wall. I decided to ask what I'd been wondering for a while and to recenter us to our goal, let the reality of our arrangement douse me like cold water.

"Why do you want to be mayor? Why open yourself up to judgement, criticism, just all negative things?"

He gave me a flat look. "I asked your favorite food, and you're asking for my stump speech?"

"I thought you'd appreciate my upping the ante."

He smiled. "I've been around politics my whole life. Negativity is just a part of it. A fact," he said with a shrug, turning his head to exhale. "It's who I am. We can't stand here and pretend you aren't aware of who my family is. What my last name is."

"Yeah, I guess that makes sense. You get a point."

He faced me, indignant. "What? No, I answered."

"You did not. I asked *why*. According to the running score, I'm winning."

"No, we're tied. Take away that point."

"Nope. Gosh, winning feels good," I said dramatically. "I get why you like it so much."

He frowned, but it looked more like a pout. "I'll stay out here all night to argue with you, if I have to. I'm not losing due to a technicality."

I laughed. "I don't make the rules, Pres. I think you do, actually. And it's your turn."

"Okay, how about I've planned my whole life for it?"

I smiled and shrugged. "Eh. Doesn't feel real."

He rolled his eyes and huffed out a puff of smoke.

"Campaigns, polls, statistics are all pieces to a game that you can control. Whoever can minimize the chaos has a better chance of winning. The only way to do that is to have a metric-driven plan. And then all you have to do is stick to the plan as much as possible."

I shrugged again. "Still not convinced."

He shot me another disgruntled look. "Doesn't that sound nice? To be able to control every aspect of your life without chaos or confusion? To be able to get to the real truth? Predicting the future by understanding the past?" He inhaled and rubbed his temple with his thumb. "How's that?"

"You must hate surprise parties."

He laughed, that great laugh again, and smiled. "Yeah, I'm not big on surprises. I'm too analytical for that sort of thing. Now give me my point back."

"But it still doesn't answer why mayor. Why not stick to campaign consulting or what you already do? Why do *you* want to be the one to change things?"

"It's personal."

I laughed. "Well, then I guess you still get a point."

He frowned. "No, I meant, it's *personal* for me. I'm so tired of the same people calling the same shots to benefit the same people. I'm so tired of bureaucrats blaming bureaucracy for why they can't get shit done. They don't want to put in the work. They don't want to push themselves harder to create something equitable and equal. They don't want to look at themselves and think, can *I* do better? What can I do to effect real, meaningful change? How can I be different from those who came before me? I'm tired of the excuses. I'm so tired of how fake it all is. People pretending they care when they really just want to get ahead for themselves. I get it, I grew up with it, I know how the game is played. And I have an advantage because of who I am. It'd be a shame to not use that to do more. I want to push myself and this town to be the best version for the greater good," he said with such passion, I wondered just how personal this was for James St. Clair IV.

He took a drag on his cigarette, keeping his eyes on it as he exhaled.

"People always think because I want to do what my father does, I'm like him. I want to do it because I'm *not* like him," he said, a trace of bitterness in his voice. "I want to create my own legacy. I actually want to help people. Even if no one likes me by the end."

I was stunned. I wondered if it was possible to believe in something like that — that you could be someone better, create a new path, especially if it looked so similar to those who'd already done it.

I watched the smoke drift away, reminding myself that this was just temporary as I tried, and failed, to pretend his words hadn't unsettled something in my chest.

"Well, that certainly doesn't come up on Google."

He laughed and shook his head, the smile he tried to keep hidden splashing across his face.

I leaned against the wall, so close I could feel the tension he carried. "I like your passion."

"And I don't like playing games with you," he said, flipping a chunk of my hair. "I'm not used to losing."

"Okay, okay, I take back the point."

"Now it's my turn." He squinted at me, clearly wanting to play harder. "Why are you my assistant?"

I laughed, surprised by his question. "Excuse me?"

"Why are you here?" He kept his gaze steady with mine. "Is this the life you wanted?"

I opened my mouth and closed it, unable to come up with an upbeat answer. Unable to return the sort of honesty he'd just given me.

There was no monologue to explain that my mother went to prison for stealing from the wealthy.

I couldn't eloquently explain the life I wanted and the life I had would never be one and the same. I didn't have a choice, having already spent so much of my life trying to prove I was worthy.

Reading signs and believing in everything I could get my hands on was nice as long as I didn't admit it was because believing in myself wasn't enough. How could I say to this beautiful, confident guy that I was absolutely terrified? Fearful of the unknown, of being destined for something out of my control when I just wanted better?

There wasn't a positive spin to say I paid for other people's mistakes, that every decision I made was always for someone else.

That I would spend my life trying to honor where I'd come from and to understand the person who made me, while trying to balance my own plans and my own future to become my own person.

That my whole life was pretending to be someone different, someone better, someone without a complicated past and a bleak future, and I was so, so tired of faking it.

Instead, I stepped back and looked away, reminding myself the better we got at this, the more I needed to focus on the end goal. Money. A better job. A *real* future. Something to prove I could reverse my luck.

"I don't think that'll come up at networking events," I said with a forced laugh. "Most people just ask if I prefer chicken or beef."

He nodded, the faintest touch of disappointment crossing his features.

"You get a point," he said and straightened his tie. "Could you call the car?"

As we waited, he closed his eyes and rested his head back against the wall, streetlights hitting his cheekbones in just the right way. Even in a dingy alley, he looked perfect, untouchable, from another world.

I was reminded of when I'd first seen him this way, how he'd taken my breath away. How I knew, even then, that being Just Rach would never be enough.

Somehow, things hadn't changed.

CHAPTER FOURTEEN

"Team meeting," Pres demanded, making us jump when he appeared suddenly in the dining room. "Now."

He turned and walked away, leaving us to scramble.

Ethan turned to me. "What did you do?"

"Why do you think I did something? I just learned about this meeting like everyone else."

"Exactly. Clearly you've missed something and now we all have to pay the price," he snapped.

We filed into Pres' office where he sat with a stony expression. It was a good thing he was wearing a sweater because I could *feel* the chill in the air.

"What is this?" he asked in a deep, commanding tone that was honestly pretty sexy and distracting so I'd almost missed him sliding his phone across the desk.

"Your Instagram," Ethan answered swiftly. "Those notifications mean you're very popular—"

"Do you think I'm an idiot?" Pres said flatly. "I'm referring to the *photo*. I did not approve this."

The good thing about being taller than everyone around me was I could peek over their heads.

He'd finally relented to allowing photos of us on his Instagram — Sable called the practice "#BoobGirlLifts." They were always carefully curated of us being productive, charitable, and wholesome in the community. Even the cheeky one where I'd fed him a pancake had been the do-over, flirty and faked.

This one was different.

Two days ago, I'd been making his fourth cup of coffee when he'd appeared. I was startled, not used to seeing him in his kitchen.

"It's almost ready. The machine was programmed wrong, but I got it back the way you like."

When he didn't answer, I glanced back, assuming he was annoyed. Instead, he held up a colorful knitted potholder between two pinched fingers.

"What is *this*?"

"It's a potholder."

He looked at it again, unsure.

"I made it," I added.

"You made it," he repeated, studying it closer, his confusion deepening. "With string?"

"Yarn. I knitted it. I can actually knit lots of things—"

"Why did you knit a tiny blanket for a pot? Why is it on my counter?"

"I use it when I'm in here. I brought it from home."

"I'm certain whoever I hired to put this place together included oven mitts."

"You can have oven mitts and potholders. It's called harmony. You're really trying to outlaw potholders?"

He still looked skeptical.

"If you shelve more cans than me at the food bank tonight, I'll get rid of it," I offered.

"I assume you know where the trash can is?"

I laughed. "So you aren't serious about being likable?"

He sat it down and crossed his arms, considering its place. The well-worn, colorful potholder did seem wildly out of place in his sterile kitchen.

"Can we at least keep it in a drawer?"

"Sure," I said, dropping it in the drawer with the oven mitts. "Look, see, they're friends. Cozy and happy."

He looked at where I smiled at them side-by-side then back at me. "Did you just say they're friends? The two inanimate objects?"

"When I was little, my mom would pretend our appliances and stuff were alive. Not in a concerning way, and I knew they weren't. But it was fun. It teaches you compassion and flexibility. Mr. Toaster doesn't feel well today so we can't have toast for breakfast. Let's see if Mrs. Can Opener can rally and open this tuna."

He looked at me blankly. "You eat tuna for breakfast?"

I laughed. I'd expected him to be more concerned that I'd accidentally revealed we had secondhand appliances that often went on the fritz. But, of course, he was more caught up with the practicality of my food choices.

"People eat salmon on bagels. Tuna on bread is pretty similar, don't you think?"

Rather than responding, he took a deep breath and exhaled slowly before busying himself at his pantry.

"Sometimes I think *you're* an inanimate object," I grumbled as I poured his coffee.

He laughed, another one of those rare startled ones.

"Hey, Rach," he said suddenly. I looked up, expecting him to have changed his mind about keeping the potholder. "Who was Mrs. Can Opener married to?"

I laughed, my own surprised laugh, and squinted skeptically. "Do you actually care?"

"I really do. It'll bother me all day," he said seriously.

I smiled and gave him a little shrug. "I honestly don't remember. It was a long time ago."

He thought this over before speaking again, "Maybe the next time you see your mom you can ask."

I forced a smile as my chest tightened.

Hearing someone mention her, having no idea what she was like or what she'd done, assuming I had a regular mom I could call up to ask silly questions, gutted me.

"Yeah, I can ask," I said, avoiding his gaze as I passed him his coffee.

"*Can* ask, get it?"

I looked up from the cup to meet his eyes, sure I'd misheard him. But the playful glint in his eyes and the way the corner of his mouth tipped said otherwise.

I laughed, completely startled — and elated — by his pun. "Oh my gosh, that was so … dorky."

A smile splashed across his features. "I know. I did it on purpose."

The photo had captured that moment.

His immaculate kitchen, spotless counters, white mugs balanced on top of the coffee machine, the tiniest trace of steam coming from it.

And us: mid-laugh, standing much closer than I'd remembered, his hand meeting mine halfway, the beautiful smile on his face startlingly bright. I was laughing, my head thrown back.

I hadn't even known anyone had seen us, that we should have been pretending, acting on display.

The caption read, *So lucky to spend mornings with her.*

"Who posted this?" Pres demanded, that smile a thing of the past. "This has *nothing* to do with my campaign."

"It's authentic," Olivia stammered. "Posts of you two together get the highest engagement, and everyone says to make you relatable. That moment was just so—"

"That was a private moment," he snapped.

We all stared at him.

"What I mean is, I'm in control of the message. Not

you, not Sable, no one but me. *This* isn't the message."

"But it's about you," she stumbled to explain. "I thought you two looked—"

"You went behind my back to post this. You knew I wouldn't approve."

"I just thought—"

"I don't want to surround myself around people who hide things from me. If I can't accurately grasp the situation and its players, what's the point of any of this? Why don't I just end my campaign now if I can't trust my own team? Is that what you want, Olivia?"

"Pres," I said gently. "It's just a photo."

"It is not *just* a photo."

My silly heart jumped at his words, but saying that out loud seemed to make him more frustrated.

"It's personal." He shook his head. "I mean, this was between us. To clarify, I didn't even know we looked like *that* ... I wasn't ready. We don't even look that great."

I rolled my eyes, making someone next to me gasp.

"I'm sorry," Olivia sniffled.

I patted her shoulder. "It's okay. You made an honest mistake. Next time, just ask."

Pres was unconvinced. "There is no such thing as an honest mistake, and apologies aren't effective if you intentionally deceived me. You need to gather your things and leave, Olivia."

"What," I gasped. "You can't fire her."

He frowned. "Yes, I can."

"No," I said, shaking my head. "That would be wrong. You say you want to help others, and then you fire someone who made a mistake?"

"You're overstepping, Rach," Ethan snapped. "This isn't your business. An example needs to be made."

"An example of what?" I said, my face growing hot. "She did what she thought was right. She was trying to *help*, and you're punishing her? Why would anyone ever trust you or come to you for help if this is your reaction? Geez, what an incredible politician you'll make. I can't wait to fill out my ballot. Does the 'P' in James P. St. Clair stand for 'pretty mean'?"

Something flickered in Pres' eyes. "You know what it stands for. It's my name."

"Well, now I think it's pretty mean," I said, determined to continue with my example even though it had quickly become really stupid.

I crossed my arms and performed my best scowl.

The same look crossed his face again, and his jaw tightened. I realized he was trying not to laugh. I bit the inside of my cheek because now *I* was trying not to laugh.

We stood at a standstill, attempting to scowl at the other without breaking into grins.

"Get out," he said eventually to his team. "I don't have time for this. Leave the photo up. And next time you have a question about what to post, ask Rach."

Ethan inhaled sharply. "That's not her job—"

"Get out," he repeated, standing to usher us away. As we all left, his hand fell gently on my shoulder. His expression was genuine when he said, "I'm sorry. I'll apologize to Olivia, too."

I placed my hand over his and smiled, wondering what a photo of this would look like. If it'd look as real as it felt.

. . .

Middletown University was breathtaking.

The historic campus had a lush quad, a massive library, ornate academic buildings, and even a cool coffee shop with hot, artsy baristas.

I zoomed in on its website, imagining myself there.

Clearly, playing pretend had gone too far.

The chiming bell on the shop door interrupted my daydreams, so I told myself to get a grip and focus on the Chinese food in front of me.

"Rach?"

I glanced up, horrified to see JD with takeout.

The universe had a twisted sense of humor.

"Are you here alone?"

I wanted to ask where he'd been when I'd been in a cocktail dress with Pres' arm around me the other day at the opening of a mental health facility, but instead, I cleared my throat and evaluated my current outfit.

Yoga pants. A sweatshirt I'd definitely dropped a noodle on. Untamed hair.

Eating alone in a Chinese food place.

Any other day, it would have been fine.

Embarrassing, but fine.

But today was Thanksgiving.

It had snuck up on all of us, Pres especially. As someone who'd interviewed with NPR on how Americans felt about talking about politics at the dinner table, he hadn't seemed to realize being around a family dinner table on Thanksgiving wasn't just a concept.

So when he'd walked into the dining room yesterday, he'd stopped short when he saw just me, working on setting up his appointments for the next month.

"Where is my team?"

"Olivia had an early flight, Jamar hit the road about an hour ago, and Ethan lives a life of secrecy. He was here all morning, though. You told him to leave."

"I meant it more like, 'get out of my office.'" He

sighed. "What are they all doing?"

I wasn't sure if he was joking.

"They're going to see their families for Thanksgiving."

He nodded. "Right, of course. Well, if fifty-eight percent of Americans dread having to talk politics on the holiday, I suppose my team isn't exempt from that either."

"I guess you talk politics at your dinner table with or without the presence of a turkey," I said with a laugh.

He smiled, but it didn't reach his eyes.

"Could you send me the details about volunteering at the food bank tomorrow? Where I'm supposed to check-in, details like that, please?"

"Yeah, of course," I said, pulling up the email where I'd registered us. "I've actually always wanted to—"

"And then you can take off."

It was such a casual expression from such a stoic guy, I almost wondered if he was dropping the whole client act and was giving me actual direction for what he wanted. Like, take off my shirt. Take off my pants. Lay on this table and let's figure out how to do an interpretative Thanksgiving dance that involved stuffing.

"Rach?"

"Yes, sorry, I was distracted by…" I said, my face burning, "…my inbox. Classic business things."

"Okay … Send me the email, and you can leave. Head off to see your mother early."

I tried not to look too stunned. "You don't want me to be with you tomorrow? What about our plan? I can be impressive over creamed corn."

He kind of laughed and turned to walk away, sliding his hands in his slacks' pockets. "We can pause pretending for one day. And even my worst assistants would get holidays off. I'll see you on Monday."

"But—" I cut myself short. If he assumed I was going to see my mom, he'd probably wonder why I wasn't. I didn't want to burst the bubble. So instead, I thanked him, blinking at my reflection in the elevator door when I left, unsure of how I'd ended up here. Then I realized I hadn't coordinated any travel for him either.

He was alone.

And I was alone.

Yet somehow, we were still pretending.

"Must be some relationship if you're sitting here," JD said with a laugh, pulling me out of my memory. He noticed my phone. "Middletown University again?"

I quickly locked it and shook my head.

Ever since Pres had asked who I wanted to be and what I'd wanted, I'd found myself drawn to the school's website, a long-forgotten idea now unsettled in my mind.

"I'm not applying. I was just … daydreaming. "

"You really think you'd get in?" he asked skeptically. "Don't you think it'd be weird for you to go back so late? You'd be so far behind."

I shrugged. "Plenty of adults go back to school, right?"

"They'd probably interview you. Can you qualify for the loans? Doesn't your credit history factor into that?"

JD didn't know me well, certainly none of my secrets, but he'd seen when I'd searched for an apartment when the rent increased at my old place. He'd noticed I only looked at cheap places that didn't require a credit score check. The look of disgust on his face had been hard to forget. I'd told myself then that it was because he was angered by the system. I chose to ignore when he refused to stay in my basement.

"I don't know, I haven't researched it. I'm busy."

"Oh, right, *dating*. Looks like that's working out for

you." He laughed, nodding to the sad scene.

"It is. We're very happy. Pres and me. My boyfriend."

"Yeah, sure, I believe you," he said flippantly, spinning my fortune cookie on the table. "So where is he?"

"Working," I said with a shrug. "He's important."

I knew days off were rare, and that I should've really taken advantage of an uninterrupted day, but instead, I hadn't been able to stop myself from checking my inbox.

Pres had emailed me four times.

I hope you're having a good holiday.

Quickly followed up by, *I should add, we should debrief about the food bank. There was no creamed corn as you'd mentioned, so I looked foolish when I asked about it.*

And then another an hour later, *To be clear, I'm not upset about the creamed corn. I looked it up later, and I can see why you'd assume it would be there. I'm certain had it been, and you had been there, too, you would have made an incredible impression over it. Maybe next time? Apologies for this email. But I felt if I didn't send a clarification, it's possible you would have the wrong impression. Irony at its finest, I suppose.*

Best -jps

P.S. Do you normally add milk to vegetables when cooking?

And then a fourth, right as I'd started to reply, *Please don't respond to these. I've reread them, and they all seem a little unhinged. Let's never discuss these. Enjoy your time with your family. Thanks.*

Even though I hadn't been entirely sure why he'd sent me rambling messages about corn, I couldn't help but smile, reading and rereading the messages, thinking at the very least they meant I'd been on his mind.

"I still don't understand what he's getting from you," JD said, cracking open my fortune cookie and tossing its paper aside. "Is it more convenient for him to sleep with his assistant or what? Does he get a discounted rate?"

He laughed, a loud laugh that didn't sound anything like Pres' startled, delighted, room-filling ones.

I grabbed the crumbled fortune, reading, *If you look back, you'll soon be going that way.*

I stared at JD, seeing him clearly for the first time.

I used to see him as a jokester.

Now I realized he was just a jerk.

"You know, I forgot how funny you can be, JD."

He smiled, and it didn't looked like Pres' bright smiles either. I must've been losing my mind because I was almost certain my fake boyfriend treated me better than my actual boyfriend had when we'd been together.

"We should catch up properly," he said. "What do you say we grab a drink soon?"

The whole reason I'd taken the job with Pres, when I'd thought he was a cranky old man, was to impress JD. To show him I had my life in order, that I was more than his complicated girlfriend, that I was worthy of his respect.

Maybe this wasn't the universe playing jokes, but to give me a second chance, a way to recover from the original Boobgate: Wearing-A-Stranger's-Lingerie-Gate. A double date was the perfect way to prove it. Pretending to be awesome was literally my job at this point.

"Yeah, we should," I blurted out eagerly. "How's Monday?"

He looked surprised, but nodded. "Yeah … I'm down. Who knows, maybe it'll end with us feeling lucky."

I agreed, and once he'd left, I sat up straighter. It was a rush I'd never felt before — in control, accepted, powerful — and, for once, it wasn't something I had to fake.

Now I just had to get Pres to agree.

CHAPTER FIFTEEN

"I already confirmed with Rach that you're free then. It's good PR," Sable said as the look Pres shot in my direction attempted to melt off the side of my face.

I smiled innocently, not looking up from taking notes.

"What *is* a fall festival?" Pres groaned. "Are we celebrating dead leaves and an abundance of moss? How do ceremonious rotting pumpkins relate to the issues Middletown faces? Why do I need to go to that?"

I held back a laugh as Ethan scrambled to jump in to list reasons why fall was so bad.

"Abundance of moss?" Sable echoed, her confusion coming through clear over the phone.

"Yes, moss thrives in autumn and winter," Pres explained flatly. "Some grow in six weeks, others take up to two years to flourish. It depends on the type—"

My laughter escaped me. His team stared, shocked I'd interrupted him.

"Sorry, but how is no one questioning you?" I said with another laugh. "How do you know moss facts?"

"You'd be surprised what you stumble upon when you can't sleep at night."

"Was this before or after you discovered creamed corn?"

He laughed and leaned back in his chair, both casual and relaxed actions startling everyone. "Very funny. Are you putting this in your notes?"

I beamed. "Of course. I'm being very professional. So should I arrange for you to go to the festival?"

"I detest attending events unrelated to issues I care or know about. I want to be mayor, not pumpkin king. Will anyone want to discuss myriad ways to support our public school system while maintaining a balanced budget? How about public transportation—"

"Hayrides are transportation."

He laughed again, so loud his team jumped.

"But seriously, people can talk about those things anywhere," I said with a shrug. "It's probably more enjoyable over apple cider. For what it's worth, I love fall festivals. Everyone is in a good mood, and the weather is great. Would you be opposed to wearing flannel?"

His heavy sigh covered up his smile, and he pressed the heel of his palm against his forehead. "Fine. Yes to the festival, absolutely not to flannel. Ethan, draft talking points. Find a way to connect the dots between hayrides and how the current mayor's transportation plan leaves out our most vulnerable populations. Jamar, let me know of donors who may be in attendance."

"I'll wear flannel," I said, jotting down his instructions. "Ooh, let's enter the pie baking contest. I don't mind to bake one. That's super relatable, right? *Pie* am so excited."

He smiled, rolling his eyes, then looked at his frozen-in-disbelief team. "What?" he said flatly. "Clearly, this meeting is over. Please leave my office. I'm busy."

He hung up on Sable and turned to his laptop.

"That was the weirdest meeting we've ever had," Olivia whispered to Jamar as they passed.

I hesitated at the door. "Hey, um, do you have a sec?"

He glanced up and smiled. "Of course. How was your

holiday?"

"Great, amazing. You?"

"I should apologize again about my emails. I was unprofessional, and I don't want to make you feel—"

I had to do this quickly or I'd lose my nerve.

"Are you free tonight?"

He looked at me strangely. "Yes. You manage my calendar."

"Right, and I noticed you're free. Would you want to, um, get a drink?"

He glanced at his inbox, as if my request was in an overlooked email. "With whom? I'd be pretty unprepared if it's someone important. I don't typically prefer same-day meetings."

"I know. It's not someone important," I laughed. "Because, uh, I meant me. Would you want to get a drink with me?"

Surprise flashed across his face.

"Oh."

"It'd be a favor," I said quickly before he rejected me. "Remember, you said that you'd help me sometimes if your calendar was open and it was a reasonable request?"

He smiled. "Well, a drink doesn't seem unreasonable."

"And the favor is that it's drinks with my ex-boyfriend and the woman he's seeing."

His expression flattened. "Oh."

"He just kind of thinks I'm a mess," I said with a light shrug. "You get it. You think the same thing, right?"

"Why do you care what he thinks?"

"You care what everyone thinks," I teased. "Surely you can relate."

He crossed his arms over his chest and shrugged.

"I'm not sure I can. I don't care what my exes think."

I knew he would dig his heels in on this — doing something where he saw no benefit or clear reason. This was the fall festival argument all over again.

"When I ran into him, he made a joke about us dating. Out of everyone, he's the only one who believes we're faking it. It could be good practice with a skeptic."

"People believe what they want to believe. Does he want to believe you're single?"

I laughed. "No, that's silly. JD doesn't get jealous."

"Wow, amazing," Pres said dryly. "How did you ever let him go?"

"He actually dumped me—"

"He dumped *you*?" Pres almost looked indignant. "Well, you don't have to worry about him figuring us out. He's clearly stupid. Where did you run into him?"

"Just this little Chinese food place near me. It was so random—"

"It's not random if you two used to go there on dates," Pres said evenly. "That's not at all what random means."

I laughed. He didn't.

"Well, I wasn't doing a scientific study. I was eating Chinese food and fortune cookies. And I don't know, I got caught up in the idea of proving him wrong. Pres, please? I pretend to be your girlfriend all the time. Can't you do it for me for one night? A one-time thing?"

A cocky expression flashed across his face. In that moment, he didn't look like a politician or my client. He just looked like a hot guy who I'd offered a "one-time thing" to once before.

"Fine, sugarcakes," he said, smirking. "I'll be your boyfriend. I'll be the best boyfriend you've ever had."

. . .

I shifted as I watched the door of the brewery JD and I

had settled on, suddenly aware this would be the closest to a real date Pres and I would ever have.

Even though we'd been to dozens of events, worked across from each other consistently in his office, and had even grocery shopped together, this felt different.

We'd never ended the work day by trading glances as his team left and planned to meet up an hour later.

He'd never texted me when he was leaving his place, saying he'd see me soon.

I'd never prepared for one of our dates by spending double the time in the shower, feeling more like a soft-boiled egg than sexy when I emerged, before groaning in a pillow that this wasn't a real date so *what was I even doing*.

I checked the door again, wondering if it was too late to bail on JD. But Pres hadn't wanted to do this in the first place, so I doubted he'd stick around if he didn't feel obligated to do me a favor.

Then he walked inside, and I inhaled sharply.

He wasn't wearing a suit.

He was gorgeous in a Fendi gray wool overcoat layered over a fitted cream cashmere sweater, slim fit jeans, and cream calfskin Givenchy lock boots. And his hair was styled differently, layered blonde locks perfectly pushed back, falling just slightly and sexily in his face.

Seeing him casual, cool, and so *date-like*, broke me. I was hit with the overwhelming urge to peel it all off, see what more layers I could get to, unravel him completely.

"Hi," he said, slipping off his coat. His sweater clung to him, accentuating muscles that made my mind go blank. I wanted to reach out, press my palm against his chest, feel if it felt as nice as I imagined.

He sat next to me, his leg bumping into mine. I knew a

lot about Pres — being his assistant meant I probably even knew he owned these jeans — but I did not know how fit he really was until I glanced down at his leg.

"Parking was terrible," he said, totally unaffected by his toned thigh just being right *there* and his bicep basically at eye level as he rested his elbows on the table.

Just how much did he work out?

And should his assistant be there?

"I hope I didn't keep you waiting long."

I blinked, reminding myself to slip into pretend date mode — cool, calm, collected. We had a goal, and it wasn't to drool over his body. I'd do that in my own time.

"Sorry, what? Should I have called you a car?"

"No, that's not what I meant. I can drive, you know. I'd never ask you to arrange a car for me to our date."

"Right, our date." I glanced around, trying to see it how he probably did. "You're probably used to nicer places. Less laminated menus, more three-course meals."

He grinned. "Beer cheese accounts for at least two courses, right? And when you inevitably spill your half-full drink, the laminated menus come in handy."

When I laughed, his eyes flicked down to my lips. I hastily covered my mouth, hoping I didn't have something in my teeth.

But he just smiled and shrugged. "But no, I don't go on a lot of dates. Before our … arrangement, I mean."

"No super attractive, accomplished women in DC?"

He laughed. "I was busy with school or work. I dated around but," he shrugged, "most girlfriends I've had wanted to date James Prescott St. Clair IV. It didn't really matter to them who that actually was."

"What about here?"

He glanced at me, uncertainty crossing his face.

"Not everyone in Middletown knows you. You could be just Pres."

"Last time I didn't tell a woman my last name, she burst into my apartment unclothed."

"In most cases, that's not an entirely terrible outcome."

He smirked. "I'm not so sure I could get that lucky twice in a row though."

I grinned at what had to be sarcasm. "But seriously, you could do better than a fake girlfriend."

"No, I'm trying to be mayor. It's complicated."

"You're a great problem solver. I'm sure it doesn't *have* to be complicated if you set your mind to it."

He shook his head. "I'm busy. I don't have time."

I shrugged. "You have nights like tonight—"

"I have you," he said, straightening the plastic menu in front of us. I cringed at the table, thinking it was probably sticky and driving him up the wall.

"Well, yeah, you're stuck with me now. But after—"

"I'm not stuck with you. You know what I want. In meetings. In conversations. Or, like, this. So I have a hard time following why I need someone else. When I have … you."

I flushed at his words. Other than the creamed corned emails, this was the first time I couldn't figure out what Pres, who was always blunt and direct, really meant.

Before I could respond, he glanced at the door then faced me. His eyes glimmered playfully as he took my hand resting on the table.

"Are you nervous?"

"We're good at this," I said, ignoring how my voice had dipped lower at his touch. "A total power couple."

He laughed and ducked his head, his mouth suddenly close to my neck. He gently brushed my hair away with his free hand, and I officially stopped breathing.

"You look incredible, Rach. I don't say that enough."

"You're wearing jeans," I said because I was an idiot.

He laughed softly. His tone was steady when he whispered, "Do you want me to kiss you?"

There was no faking how I nodded, my body having a mind of its own, *yes, yes, of course, please, duh.*

He dragged his teeth over his lower lip, a deeply attractive move I wasn't sure he was even aware he did, and leaned close.

I closed my eyes, lifting my mouth to his, taking in his cologne, his aftershave, the softness of his sweater where my hand had found its way to his hard chest.

His breath ghosted my lips, and then I felt the softest pressure of his lips against mine—

A heavy clunk interrupted us. I jumped, nearly knocking my water over. Pres laughed, unfazed, as we turned to see JD standing there.

"Sorry to interrupt," JD said gruffly, sitting in the chair he'd knocked against the table. "Looks like you beat me."

"You're absolutely correct. We do win. Hi," Pres said, standing to offer his hand. "I'm James St. Clair the fourth. Call me Pres. Or Rach's boyfriend. I prefer the latter."

I pressed my fingers over my tingling lips, heart hammering, realizing Pres had seen JD approach. Holy smokes, he was good.

"Where is your partner?" Pres asked, glancing around the brewery.

"We broke up. I thought I'd made that clear, Rach."

Then both men turned to look at me, frowning.

Oh no.

I'd just invited my fake boyfriend on a real date with my ex-boyfriend.

CHAPTER SIXTEEN

A few weeks ago, Pres had asked me to read the report on his likability. He'd called it research, saying if I knew his shortcomings, we'd make a better team.

"Best to get it all out in the open," he'd said flatly. "I'm the worst."

"I don't care what people who don't know you think," I'd protested, sliding his iPad back across his desk.

He'd pushed it back. "Some of us have to be the ones to boss people around, say no, and make enemies to get things done. Not all of us can light up a room when they walk in and instantly have people on their side."

At my confusion, he'd sighed in his usual overly dramatic way. "I'm referring to you."

I'd beamed. "You think I light up a room?"

He'd sighed again, somehow even deeper. "Not literally. It's an expression. I should have been more clear. What I meant was—"

I'd laughed, taking his iPad and ignoring when he called after me. The report was basically what I already knew. It wasn't necessarily inaccurate. But it was definitely an oversimplification.

Except ... James St. Clair was good at being unlikable.

And he was playing his role perfectly tonight.

"So the fourth, huh," JD said as they both sat. I guess we were all going to pretend this wasn't the most awkward moment of our lives. "Your parents couldn't come up with anything original?"

Pres smiled sardonically. "I've found it works well whenever I want something. What is it that you do? I don't recognize your name."

"I'm a chef. Surely Rach has told you."

I didn't answer, too busy eyeing the door for an escape route.

Pres shrugged, looking absolutely bored by JD's confusion. "I suppose you're not worth the name drop."

As JD told him about the restaurant, Pres wore a flat, uninterested expression.

"Huh," he replied dryly. "I've never heard of it. I prefer to take Rach to upscale restaurants." A cocky expression crossed his face. "Do you serve a lot of people with roman numeral suffixes? We're usually excellent tippers."

I covered my mouth, officially a terrible person because I found his ridiculousness funny. As Pres slipped his arm around my shoulders, the Rolex he never wore, not even at fancy events, glinted next to me, perfectly placed at JD's eye level.

Pres continued, "Have you ever heard of Michelin-rated restaurants? James Beard Awards?"

JD scoffed. "Of course. I work at a pretty nice place—"

"And you're the executive chef?" he asked skeptically.

JD flushed. "Well, no, I'm a junior chef—"

Pres nodded dismissively. "Yeah, I don't really need your resume, JP."

"JD," he said tensely. "I'm kind of shocked you're real, to be honest. When I saw Rach on Thanksgiving, she seemed pretty lonely. It was sad."

My cheeks flushed, hoping Pres didn't question why I

hadn't been with my mom, but he remained unfazed, too focused on besting JD.

"Yeah, the Chinese food place near hers," Pres said easily. "One of our favorites. Rach has me hooked on fortune cookies. What did yours say, 'Egotism is the anesthetic that dulls the pain of stupidity'?"

JD didn't get it, but I had to bite my lip to hold back from laughing.

"Or is that more of a proverb than a fortune?" Pres mused sarcastically. "I'd say thanks for keeping her company, but company is usually welcomed." He said this with a disarming smile before turning to me, his expression all sexy smirks. "And we caught up later that night, didn't we, darling?"

He pulled me closer, his grip perfectly practiced possessive, and dropped his mouth to my neck. It was the softest press of his lips, just enough to toe the line, the worst kind of teasing that took all my strength to not scream and climb on his lap.

Regardless of how the night ended for them, I knew I'd be Googling if it was normal to be attracted to a pair of jeans.

"So you just skipped the whole dinner part of Thanksgiving?" JD asked skeptically.

"I was volunteering," Pres said, the cutest grin appearing on his face. "I was being a good, likable person. Have you ever tried it?"

"Maybe we should get some drinks," JD said, clearing his throat as Pres trailed his fingers up my neck, sending an involuntary shudder through my body. Maybe I should've been bringing JD along to all our fake dates. "Rach, wanna dust off your old waitressing skills?"

Pres placed a firm hand on my arm. "Let me. What do

you all want?"

JD watched him walk away before facing me, bewildered and fuming.

"What the hell, Rach? I asked you out and you bring him along? That's so not cool."

"You asked me out when I have a *boyfriend*," I said slowly. "*That's* not cool."

He shook his head. "I didn't think you were serious."

"Yeah, we are," I said softly, glancing to where he stood at the bar.

Our eyes locked, and Pres smiled. It was such a warm smile, so opposite of who everyone thought he was, that my heart ached. I was tempted to go over to him and tell him to be himself instead, forget the plan. That I wished I was on a date with Pres, the nerdy, sarcastic perfectionist who made me laugh.

I turned back to JD who looked at me like I was a puzzle he couldn't quite figure out.

"So you're actually ... happy," he said slowly, noticing our smiles. "Not that fake positive bullshit you always do, but actually happy? With *him*?"

I nodded.

"And you don't want to hook up?"

"Not with you," I answered honestly.

He shook his head. "Why would he actually be interested in you? He could get anyone. Have you ever Googled him? He's everything you're not."

"Are these supposed to be pickup lines?"

"That's exactly why I like her," Pres interrupted, his voice icy and even, nearly spilling JD's drink in his lap. "I've never had a better teammate. She makes me better." He paused for a beat and then added, "Which is hard to do because I'm generally quite incredible."

I almost choked on holding back a laugh. He was absurd, and JD actually thought Pres was serious.

"What do you mean, teammate? I thought Rach just brought people coffee."

Pres set his cold blue eyes on JD. "You're incorrect. Rach is invaluable."

I laughed. "Okay, well, that's—"

"The absolute truth. I was lost before you," Pres said, pulling me closer. "You're incredible, sweetheart."

I flushed, reminding the butterflies in my stomach that if he was using silly pet names, he was fully in character.

Pres faced JD. "If you have additional questions on how I feel about Rach, you can ask me directly. I'm an open book."

Then he placed a drink in front of me, his voice low and just for me, "Told you I'd owe you a drink one day."

I sipped it, breaking into a smile. "Prickly pear."

He grinned, slipping his arm around me again. "Anything for you, Rach."

"This beer isn't what I asked for," JD interrupted.

Pres shrugged. "I forgot what you'd said."

I snorted, trying to hold back laughter. The same guy who could recite moss growth statistics had forgotten a simple beer order.

When JD got up to get the right drink, huffing under his breath, I turned to Pres.

"I'm really sorry. I had no idea he was asking me out."

He narrowed his eyes in JD's direction. "I told you he wanted you to be single."

"Are you seriously spending time saying 'I told you so' when we should be planning our escape?"

He laughed and settled back against his seat. "Oh, I'm not going anywhere. We have a goal tonight, Rach. I cleared my schedule for this."

I laughed. "You did not. Your schedule was clear—"

"Ladies and gentlemen, it's time for trivia night," an emcee interrupted. I groaned. This weird twisted reality couldn't possibly get any stranger. "Winner takes all. A gift card to—"

"You in?" JD asked Pres with a smirk when he sat back down. "A little friendly competition never hurt anyone."

Seeing how Pres looked at JD, the expression "if looks could kill" finally made sense.

"You have to put your phone away," JD said.

Pres looked at him evenly. "I'm not going to do that."

I laughed, gently placing my hand over his. "Pres, it's the rules. They'll think you're looking up the answers."

He made a face but slipped his phone in his coat pocket. "Why would I do that? It defeats the purpose."

JD scoffed. "You really think you just know all the answers?"

Pres flashed a cocky smile. "I think you're very lucky to be on the same team as me."

I pressed my face against his shoulder, burying my laugh against his sweater. He reached up and gently ran his fingers through my hair.

"Don't hide your talent, honeybee. I love when you show off how smart you are."

"You're killing me," I whispered, grinning up at him.

"I'm crazy about you, too, snuggluffagus," he said, raising his voice. "I'm never letting you go. I'd be a massive *idiot* to let you out of my life."

JD cleared his throat loudly, but Pres just smirked.

Naturally, we took the game seriously. Well, Pres and JD did. I mostly sipped my margarita and decided if I was going to be on an outrageous faux date with my ex and fake boyfriend, I was at least going to enjoy it. And what better entertainment was there than two guys nerding out over history, science, and sports trivia?

And I didn't hate how Pres' arm still hadn't left my shoulders, his fingers twirling the strands of my hair.

"Round two, question four," the emcee said. "This saleswoman is known for the success of Tupperware?"

Our table fell silent, the guys frowning at each other until Pres snapped, "You're a chef, shouldn't you know?"

JD glowered. "I don't work in a restaurant with Tupperware—"

"Brownie," I gasped. "Wise. Brownie Wise."

JD shook his head. "That's not a name."

"Yes, it is," I said with a laugh.

"Come on, Rach, can't you take this seriously? Now isn't the time for jokes."

"My mom used to sell—" I stopped myself, glancing at Pres. "Never mind. I'm probably wrong."

"What about Karen?" JD suggested. "She probably named the stuff after herself."

"Karen Tupperware?" Pres repeated flatly. "You're seriously going with Karen Tupperware?"

JD glared at him. "I don't see you coming up with anything better. It's better than Brownie. At least Karen is a name."

I felt Pres tense next to me, clearly frustrated.

"It's just a game," I whispered, nudging him with my knee. "No biggie if we win or lose."

An unreadable expression crossed his face. "No, Rach, it's not just a game."

"And the answer is," the emcee announced, "Brownie Mae Humphrey."

"Close." JD smirked at me. "But not good enough.

Good thing we didn't listen to you."

"Right. Sorry. Karen wasn't a terrible guess either," I said, feeling like an idiot when Pres glanced at me, his expression still unreadable.

The game continued, Pres growing even more restless. Halfway through, his hand fell to my knee, curving to my thigh, tracing small circles on my jeans. I glanced at him to signal that JD couldn't see the gesture, but he seemed focused on the emcee.

"Last question before we see if we need a tie breaker," the emcee said. Tensions in the bar ran high as he read out the current scores. If we got this right, we could win. "This is the third sign of the Zodiac."

"Easy. Pisces," JD said, already writing it down.

"Wait," I said quickly, "that's not right."

"Yes, it is. It's the sign in March, which is the third month. It's obvious."

"Yeah, but that's not—"

"You haven't gotten any right so far."

"But I'm pretty sure—"

"Rach," JD sighed. "How many times in your life do you have to be wrong before you get the message to give up?"

"Are you kidding?" Pres interrupted. His voice was loud and serious, making us all jump.

"Pres." I shook my head. "I'm probably wrong."

"No, you're not," he snapped and faced JD. "She reads her horoscope every morning. If you're lucky enough, she'll read yours, too, even if you never asked. Even if you have no idea why she started doing it in the first place or why you look forward to it. Even when she tells you you're a fucking sea goat, and you have no idea what that means except that pretty much everyone on the

Internet agrees that sea goats don't pair well with scales. But it doesn't matter because it's imperative to your morning because it makes *her* happy. So if anyone at this table is going to know, it's her. Listen to her. She's always right. She knows best!"

Our table and a few surrounding ones had fallen silent.

I still hadn't managed to close my mouth from where it hung open in shock.

Pres glanced around the bar, cleared his throat, and smoothed his hand through his hair.

"And that would be my, uh, professional opinion."

"Okay, okay," JD said, his face flushed. "Sorry, whatever, fine. What's the answer, Rach?"

"Um, I thought it was Gemini, but I could be wron—"

"Write Gemini," Pres demanded, tapping the paper in front of JD. "And turn it in."

"Hey," I said softly as JD walked off. "Thank you."

He shook his head. "I'm mortified. I'm sorry I lost control. I just really like…" he glanced at me and then at a few strangers who hadn't stopped staring, "…winning. It's very important to my reputation. You know this."

Before I could read into *any* of that, the emcee said, "Alright, folks, we have a winner. We only had one team get this right—"

"It's you," Pres said, meeting my gaze with bright eyes. It was a look that took my breath, made me feel like a winner, like anything was possible. "It's you, Rach."

"And the correct answer was … Gemini."

"Fuck yes!" Pres shouted, slamming his hand down on the table, jarring the drinks, and then turned to me, cupped my cheeks and pulled me to him.

His lips were on mine before I could respond.

I scrambled to kiss him back with a gasp, pressing my mouth hard against his, parting my lips to let him in deeper. At the same time, I tried to grab his sweater to pull him closer, but my hands came up empty.

Because it ended as quickly as it happened.

He'd jerked away.

So fast I would've questioned if it'd really happened except my lips were begging for more, my body felt like it'd been shocked, and my brain was properly mush.

"Man, you must really love winning," JD grumbled as he sat back down.

Pres looked, for once in his life, at a loss for words.

A trace of panic crossed his face, probably worried we'd blown our cover by seeming so stunned by such a chaste kiss.

"It's fine," I whispered. "It was just adrenaline."

"Congrats, Rach. You win," JD said flatly. "Any chance one of you has a light? I left mine in my car."

On autopilot, Pres slid his lighter across the table.

"She hasn't managed to stop you either, huh? Rach was always asking me to quit," JD said as he pulled out his cigarettes. "We must not be that different after all."

Pres didn't respond, still dazed.

I pressed my fingers over my tingling lips.

Maybe I wasn't actually great at reading signs, but I could figure this one out pretty clear.

I was totally screwed.

CHAPTER SEVENTEEN

"*Gemin-I*'m so sorry," I practiced as I stepped off Pres' elevator, determined to get things back on track.

He'd be in his office, and I'd bring him coffee, say last night got out of hand, and promise to never drag him into my personal life again.

We'd forget how after JD collected the winning gift card and left, Pres basically bolted without a word, and I went home alone, lust-drunk, margarita-tipsy, and absolutely confused.

"Let's *be-rownie wise* and move on—"

His office was empty.

I double-checked his calendar, confident I hadn't forgotten something. It was 7 a.m., which meant he'd already be two hours deep into work, the morning news playing as he frowned at his computer.

"Pres?" I called out.

"I'm in my bedroom."

I exhaled, relieved to avoid another Boobgate. Then I inhaled sharply when I walked in his bedroom. It was dimly lit, and he was laying against the pillows on his king bed. Suddenly, every fantasy I'd been suppressing flashed in my mind.

So it took me a second to notice he was in joggers and a fitted pullover, his left ankle wrapped and propped on a pillow.

"Oh my gosh," I gasped, "what happened?"

He waved away my concern. "It's just a sprain. Could you bring me my laptop and phone charger?"

I rushed to his side and sat down on the bed's edge. "Tell me exactly what happened."

"I went on a run, sprained my ankle, had it checked out, and am applying the RICE method—"

"All before seven in the morning?"

"Yes, I decided to sprain my ankle because of the convenient timing," he deadpanned. "So because of the rest and elevate aspects of RICE, I'm asking my personal assistant to get my laptop and phone charger. Per usual, she's pushing back—"

I laughed at his teasing then ran my hands over my face, embarrassed. "I'm *such* an idiot. I've been freaking out since I haven't gotten any testy work emails from you. I thought you were mad at me."

He looked confused. "I thought my work emails were coming across nicer lately."

I shook my head. He wasn't panicked about last night's barely-there kiss. He probably hadn't given it another thought.

Because he'd been *acting*. That had been the whole point: making our relationship seem believable, proving we were a real couple, pretending I was someone he'd want to be with.

And how was a fake kiss any different from the other fake touches we'd been exchanging?

I stood. "I'm glad we're on the same page. I'll get your stuff and some water and coffee. Let me get the light—"

"No, don't," he said quickly, wincing when he tried to move. His ankle was pretty swollen, and I realized that he wasn't just asking me to do these things because I was his assistant. He genuinely couldn't move. "Lights make it worse."

I slowly sat back down. "I'm not getting your charger until you tell me the truth. Lights make what worse?"

He gave me a flat look. "I am your boss, you know."

I shrugged. "Not really. You can't even really fire me."

"My phone is at three percent, Rach."

I shrugged again, determined to win this.

He frowned then sighed. "I experience migraines."

"Migraines," I repeated slowly.

I had a flash of all the times he'd seemed short and irritable, rubbing his temple or forehead, his office door shut, demanding silence. Or when he'd ditched me after the grocery store, frowning at the sunlight.

"Yeah, it adds to my bubbly, fun personality. Everyone likes someone who avoids red wine, chocolate, most dairy, baked goods with yeast—"

"But not cigarettes and caffeine?"

He glowered. "It turns out, I'm not perfect. Anyway, I don't tell people so it doesn't matter."

"Why not?"

"No one wants to hear that I have a headache," he said, rolling his eyes.

I gestured to his position in bed. "Clearly, it's not just a headache."

"*I* know that. But it's not a good enough reason. It wouldn't poll well. Someone like me doesn't get to play the sympathy card."

I made a face. "It's not a sympathy card if you just want people to understand you a little better. Migraines are a real—"

"Rach," he sighed. "It's easier to leave it."

I frowned, disliking that he felt he had to hide

something that was part of him, something that brought him pain, just because most people wouldn't understand.

"Anyway, sometimes migraines make me dizzy," he added. "I shouldn't have ignored the signs of an impending one and gone on a run, but I needed to blow off steam."

I held back a sigh. Clearly, he'd been upset about last night. Once again, the second he came into contact with my life, it was a chaotic whirlwind.

"I'm fine now. This migraine attack didn't last very long. My doctor told me to rest, so I'll work from bed today. Could you push my conference call and schedule a meeting with my old public policy firm? They want to loop me in on a project."

"No." I stood. "I'll check on you in a few hours."

He narrowed his eyes. "What do you mean 'no'?"

"Uh, I mean no. As in that's a negative."

"What? Bring me my computer and my charger."

"No can do. I control your schedule, remember?"

"At least give me my iPad."

"You don't have urgent meetings today. You just said your doctor said to relax."

"He said rest, not *relax*," Pres called after me as I shut the door to his bedroom. "Rach!"

An hour later when his team showed up, I'd told them Pres was taking a personal day. Thankfully, he'd stopped calling for me after about five minutes of me leaving his room. And after three more minutes of him throwing his pillows at the door, he'd run out of ammunition.

"What does that mean?" Ethan demanded. "He doesn't take personal days."

"I'm his personal assistant so I'd think I'd know. He's in bed right now. Are you going to disturb him?"

Ethan glared and glanced behind me, considering it.

"We need to prep for DC in a couple weeks to discuss Phase Two of his campaign. He has client meetings then, too. Do you think this is just a game for him?"

"I can make sure he's prepared."

"Really, *you*?"

I smiled and gently placed my hand on his shoulder.

"I'll tell him you were concerned," I said, steering him to the elevator. Jamar and Olivia hadn't even bothered to step off. "Come back tomorrow."

I waved, pressing the close button as Ethan sputtered in confusion.

"What are you doing?" Pres asked a few hours later when I dragged his desk chair to the foot of his bed. He was really pulling off that sexy grumpy look. "Did you bring my stuff? I'm relaxed. I'm so relaxed."

"I printed some reports for your DC meetings so you can avoid screens. Let me know if I can help. Otherwise, I'll work on my stuff, and you work on yours."

"Fine," he said, his mouth set in a very kissable pout. He opened his bedside drawer and pulled out a pair of glasses, closing it with a snap that was supposed to be intimidating.

But I was too busy realizing that a man laying in bed in black-rimmed reading glasses was really, incredibly, surprisingly hot.

I took a measured breath and tried to avoid staring, opening my laptop and sinking down in his chair.

He watched me, his expression smoldering.

We remained in a standstill for the rest of the day. I worked, managing his emails, deferring all the people who wanted to use him, ask for favors, cozy up with a St. Clair. And he read quietly, sometimes putting his papers down to close his eyes.

In those moments, he looked exhausted, and I resisted the urge to sit by his side. I wanted to hold him, smooth out the tension in his body, ask him why he put all this pressure on himself.

I'd never worked so hard or been so sure that if I just kept going, I'd eventually get what I wanted. I'd never believed in something as much as he believed in the ability to control his destiny. It was admirable, cracking open a feeling in my chest I refused to indulge.

By the end of the day, I'd promised myself 10 times I'd close my laptop and say bye without looking back. As I started to do just that, Pres spoke.

"It was Brownie Wise," he said, keeping his gaze on a report on childhood literacy. "I looked it up last night. She went by a different name professionally. So you were right. You're right more than you give yourself credit for, Rach."

"You looked it up?"

He nodded, looking just as frustrated as he had last night. "You'd think someone named *JD* would know that. Is that even his real name?"

"That's an interesting question, James."

He rolled his eyes. "He and I are nothing alike."

"Don't take him too seriously. He'll probably vote for you anyway."

"I don't care who he votes for."

"You care how everyone votes," I said with a laugh, which earned me another eye roll. I shrugged, not sure what he wanted and definitely not wanting to dissect last night. "Are you good for the night? I'll grab you dinner at the place around the corner. Want your usual?"

"I want pizza."

I laughed.

"I'm serious."

"There's an upscale pizza place across town. I can call ahead and pick it up and be back in probably an hour?"

"Do the delivery thing from one of the regular places. They bring it in a cardboard box. It's quite convenient."

I laughed. "Okay, what sort of pizza do you like?"

"I want what you like," he said, sitting down his report to look at me seriously. "And I want you to stay."

My heart lurched, but I smiled tightly, reminding myself that he was literally confined to a bed and I was paid to coordinate things exactly like this.

This was not a romance unfolding.

I had to stop reading into signs that weren't there.

Like after the pizza was delivered, he sat up in his bed, motioning for me to come closer. I rolled his chair to his side, keeping a pizza box barrier between us.

Or when we chatted the entire time, talking about nothing, no agenda, just trading stories that didn't lead to an ultimate goal or to impress someone else.

After I'd cleared away the box, he turned on the television, asking what channels were the most relaxing.

So I tentatively sat back down, and we somehow got sucked into an HGTV *House Hunters* marathon. Pres had *a lot* of thoughts. Watching him watch people buy houses might have been more entertaining than the actual show.

A small laugh escaped me as he scowled at someone's carpet choices. He glanced my way, his fingers on his cheekbone, the bedroom's shadowed light highlighting just how gorgeous he was. I looked away and tried to play it cool by kicking up my feet on the edge of his bed and leaning back in his chair.

He shifted, his hand bushing against my calf.

Practice. His hand on me was just practice for our next public event. Every slow inhale I took as each of his fingers pressed down, an individual spot of heat against my leg, was just practice.

"My chair isn't really that comfortable," he said after our third episode.

"I can order you a new one."

"That's not what I meant."

His voice was even, but when I stole a glance at him, his eyes were bright blue, playful, and breathtaking. I couldn't look away. He smiled and cocked his chin to the spot next to him.

My stomach flipped, and my body fully overpowered my brain as I gently lowered next to him on his bed. I was hyperaware of his warmth, how soft his workout clothes were when his arm brushed mine.

If we were playing a game, I officially couldn't quit.

He sighed. "I really want a cigarette."

I nodded to the window. "Did you want me to get your pack? Does that open—"

"Could you do me a different favor? In my bathroom, second left drawer, there's a box of nicotine patches."

I was surprised, having never been tasked to buy these, but nodded. When I resumed my spot next to him, he focused on opening the box, squinting to read it.

"Why don't you just always wear reading glasses?"

He smirked. "Because I'm vain. Those are a secret."

I laughed at his blunt honesty.

"My turn," he said, transitioning into Truth Chicken. "Why didn't you tell me you don't like that I smoke?"

I faced him, surprised by the question and even more surprised he looked frustrated.

"You get a point then," he said.

"Surely I wouldn't have been the first person to tell you that smoking is bad for you. Your family owns a national hospital network. Would it have mattered?"

"Point," he said stubbornly. "I asked why *you* didn't tell me it *bothered* you, not if I'm aware of the health effects."

I laughed, thinking he was pretty testy to be winning. "Honestly, I guess I don't think it's my place to tell you something like that—"

"You told JD."

I laughed, confused. "Well, JD wasn't my boss."

"I'm not your boss. You even said that earlier today."

"Client, whatever. Same diff—"

"It's not same diff," he scoffed. "Not *same diff* at all."

"JD was my boyfriend."

"I'm your boyfriend."

I laughed, rolling my eyes. "You know what I mean."

"Fine." His frown hadn't disappeared. "Your turn."

I nodded to the patches. "When did you buy those?"

"Last night."

"You can't let JD get to you like that. He's a nobody."

"He was someone to you. The way he treats and talks to you makes me so—" Pres gave up on opening the box correctly and just ripped it open. "Why did he ever get to be yours? *He's* fundamentally unlikeable. I could do a poll right now and prove it—"

I laughed again, cutting him off. "He wasn't enough, Pres. He was just someone at the time. I thought he liked me, and he did until he didn't. Believe me, I'm starting to realize I could stand to accept a little bit more than I'm given. And he certainly didn't make me feel like enough."

In response, he struggled to peel the backing off a patch, his irritation palpable. I sat up on my knees next to him. "Let me help you."

"I can do it on my own."

I shushed him, slipping the patch out of his fingers.

"I don't let people tell me what to do," he said after a moment. He grumbled with absolutely no bite in his voice at all, "I should have fired you when I had the chance. Before I knew you."

I laughed and read the instructions for the patch. "It says the best place to put it is on the inside of your bicep."

I glanced at his pullover. His sleeve was definitely not going up over his toned upper arm.

"Oh, um, if you don't care, I don't care," I said, trying my hardest to sound casual, maybe even professional.

He raised an eyebrow.

"I mean, you've seen me without a shirt, so I guess in a way, it's fair. You owe me one," I joked.

He smirked, sat up, and pulled off his shirt in one swift motion. Vaguely, I knew Pres worked out in the mornings. But what that resulted in *tangibly* was a whole other ball game.

I dug my teeth in my bottom lip, trying not to stare at the light dusting of blonde hair on his pecs, trailing down to his defined abs, disappearing below his waistband—

"Give it to me," he said, firm and demanding. All at once, my heartbeat quickened, my cheeks heated up, and my knees weakened. "Rach, you know I want it."

Sucking in a sharp breath, I quickly stuck it on his arm. Experiencing his first hit of nicotine all day, he inhaled deeply, closed his eyes, and leaned against the pillows.

It was the most erotic thing I'd ever witnessed.

Now I just needed to move.

"Your turn," he reminded me, his voice low, daring.

The room was dim with only moonlight spilling across

the bed. It felt like all those nights we'd stood against brick walls as he smoked, just us and our shadows in our own world.

And just like that first night, I thought maybe we could keep playing pretend. Pretend we were in another life. That we weren't client and assistant, fake boyfriend and girlfriend, that he wasn't him, and I wasn't me, and he could grab me, use his deep, bossy voice to tell me what to do, what he wanted, and say what he wanted was what I wanted, too.

"When we first met, if Ethan hadn't interrupted when I asked to kiss you, for a one-time thing..." I said, the words already tumbling out before I could stop myself.

Pres opened his eyes, electric burning blue, waiting.

I took a measured breath.

Every word in my head said get out of this bed and go home, do not make this mistake, you know better, you know how it's going to end. The banging from my heart did a pretty good job of almost drowning them out.

"...What would you have said?"

"Fucking *finally*," he said, sitting up and pulling me to him before I could take it back and play it off as a joke.

And without a second's hesitation, our lips met.

CHAPTER EIGHTEEN

He moved the same way he spoke. Confident. Steady. Powerful. Slightly demanding, definitely in control.

And just like he'd been keeping score in our game, he seemed to want to win this, too.

He kissed me deeply, taking it from one to hundred with a desire equally matched to mine.

As I straddled his lap, he touched me urgently — cupping my jaw, running his hands through my hair, trailing his fingers down my back, and grabbing my hips to tug me closer.

And just like real life, he didn't hold back, saying exactly what he thought as he slipped his hands under my shirt, undoing my bra in one swift motion.

"Yes," he said, cupping my boobs with both hands. "You have no idea how long I've wanted to do this."

He pulled me forward, one arm around my waist, and pushed up my shirt, dropping his mouth to my collarbone, kissing and licking down to my chest. With fierce determination, he sucked and bit my nipples, devouring me, until I moaned his name, overwhelmed by how good this felt. Better than I'd ever imagined.

"God," he groaned, his tongue soothing his bites as his fingers found their way to my dress pants, "*yes*. You're incredible."

He kissed me, committed to learn every pulse point,

draw out every shiver of my skin, wring out every place that made me moan. He didn't stop when he unbuttoned my pants, pushing them down to my knees as I struggled to keep my mouth on his.

I fumbled with his joggers, gasping at how hard and thick he felt, but he pushed my hand away.

I groaned, my turn to be pouty. "Pres."

"Patience is a virtue," he said, laughing as I glared at his smug, delicious, stupid smirk.

"Not if we only have one night," I said, hastily tugging off my pants and tossing them over my shoulder. "Just a one-time thing, yeah?"

He nodded, watching me with a heated gaze, scraping his bottom lip with his teeth as I stripped off my shirt.

"More," I demanded, grinding against his dick, making him laugh again and raise an eyebrow.

"That's not how this works," he said, cocky and firm. To further his point that he was in control, he traced his tongue over my hammering pulse, lightly biting my neck until I moaned. "If this is a one-time thing, I'm taking my time. I want to savor you."

I shivered at the low desire in his voice, and he pushed my legs apart and stripped off my underwear.

"Say you're wet for me," he said, trailing his fingers up my inner thigh as I shuddered. He held my shoulder tightly, keeping me in place as I tried to buck against his thumb gently pressed against my clit.

"Oh god, Pres, yes. Please."

I didn't know what I was begging for, but I knew I wanted it. I wanted all of it, as much as I could take.

"Is that what gets you off? Making me want you so bad it hurts? Is this what you want, Rach?"

Without breaking my gaze, he brought the pad of his

thumb to his mouth and licked it, the languid motion of his tongue wet and sensual and *god*—I moaned again, fully falling into a fog of arousal.

Who knew he was such a *tease*.

I nodded hastily, whimpering as he rubbed me in slow, firm strokes. I begged for more, running my nails through his perfect hair and down his muscled back.

He tightened his arm around my torso as I gasped, pressing my face in the crook of his neck. His skin was hot to the touch, his pulse jumping as I kissed and sucked any skin I could make contact with, needing to soak in as much as possible before this ended.

Never letting up the pressure on my clit, he slid a finger inside me, making me cry out. Any semblance of control I'd managed to hold on to was dissolving rapidly.

"Oh god, Pres," I said, arching my back to meet his skilled hand. "*Yes*. Holy cow."

He laughed, the sound deep and warm in his chest, and pressed his lips against my flushed throat.

I couldn't believe the same guy who stoically analyzed politics on TV and charmed wealthy donors in expensive suits was the same guy who got lost in grocery stores, hid from crowds, and took deep drags on cigarettes was the same guy now.

A guy who was laughing, hair mussed, eyes bright but a shade darker as his gaze roved my naked body in his bed, lips full and reddened from my kisses.

Our eyes locked, and he smiled, one reserved for very few. It was bright, genuine, a little raw, meeting his eyes in a way none of the others I'd been able to discover. It cut through the ice of his blue eyes and the sharpness of his features, unguarded to reveal a deep warmth.

My heart ached at that smile.

That smile made me want this — *him* — over and over. It made me want him to be *mine,* meant to be, just for me.

So I closed my eyes and leaned back, sliding my hand under his waistband. Before I could make contact, he thrust another finger inside me, pressing deeper and harder against the sensitive spot inside, making me cry out. His other hand twisted in my hair, pulling just enough that I moaned, heat shooting through my body.

"If I only get this once, I have to taste you," he said roughly, lifting my hips and scooting down the bed to lay.

I was certain I'd misheard. "But your ankle—"

"Ride my face," he demanded, jerking me forward so I straddled his chest. "Fuck, Rach, yes."

I inhaled sharply. "I've never—"

"Do it," he said, tightening his grip on my hips. "You're gorgeous like this. Give me your pussy. Let me do this for you. You want it. Take it, Rach."

He was so right. I wanted it.

I wanted to take all the pleasure I could get in this moment.

Who was I kidding, I'd wanted him since we first met.

He grinned, reading my mind, and rested his head back against the sheets. Biting my lip, so incredibly turned on, nearly drunk on lust, I shifted until my knees hit the bed on either side of his head.

He didn't wait for me to hesitate. He yanked me down by the hips, his mouth on me before I even had a chance to gasp.

"Oh my god," I shouted, slapping my palms against his headboard, barely able to keep myself upright as he opened me up with his tongue. "Pres, holy, *oh*, ah—"

I closed my eyes and rested my forehead against my arms, trying to catch my breath, my heart hammering.

And then I remembered he'd told me what to do. What he wanted. And that Pres liked being listened to.

I rolled my hips, following the motion of his firm tongue. I could hear and *feel* him moan, the sensation making me shudder and shivers run down my spine.

He roughly slid two fingers inside me from behind, not at all gentle like that smile had been. The feeling of his mouth and his fingers was overwhelming.

I threw my head back to ride him in earnest, bracing a hand on the headboard as his tongue flicked me in every direction and our bodies worked in tandem.

His bedroom filled with dirty, needy sounds — his tongue making me wetter, my moans, my fist banging against the headboard, his muffled, dark, and delicious, moans — and the heady realization washed over me that being treated like I wouldn't break, like I was just as strong and powerful as Pres, was intoxicating.

That thought, paired with his thrusting fingers and him circling and sucking on my clit, made my orgasm build. A fire deep in my belly grew, my whole body tensing and tightening, higher and higher.

He became even more determined, sloppy, wet, hard, rough, unrelenting. He wanted me to let go, lose control, completely unravel, let him be the one to bring me to my knees, let me take exactly what I wanted.

Pure pleasure crashed over me, and the only words I could manage was his name over and over until I fell off of him, writhing in aftershocks.

"Oh my gosh, Pres, *wow*. How are you so good at everything? Holy cats and kitten and caboodle."

He laughed, and I fought the urge to tug him closer and press his head against my heart so he could hear how it beat wildly for him.

Instead, I reached for where he was still hard, but he gently pushed my hand away. "Tonight was about you."

He sat up, smoothing his hands through his hair, and grabbed his pullover to run it over his face. Even that was hot, so unlike him, that I had to close my eyes, positive I'd say something stupid if I kept watching him.

"Well," he said, his voice deep and serious. I glanced at him, worried he was going to confirm even just a one-time thing was a mistake. "Now I really want a cigarette."

I sat up to say I should leave when my hand brushed against something plasticky stuck to the bedsheets.

"Oops," I said, holding up his fallen nicotine patch. "I'm the worst assistant in the world."

We looked at each other, disheveled, breathless, and maybe a little nervous. Then he started to laugh. A great, rich, genuine laugh. I began to giggle, too, overcome by emotion. Then we couldn't stop, dissolving into a fit of laughter until tears filled our eyes and our stomaches hurt, unable to speak without laughing even harder.

CHAPTER NINETEEN

I took a deep breath, reminding myself to be cool. Chill. Professional. Or at least something similar to that.

When I walked into his bedroom, Pres was already awake, reading a report from yesterday.

"Good morning," he said, slipping off his reading glasses. "Sleep well? Was the guest bedroom up to par?"

"That bed is amazing. My commute was even better."

"Look at that, not even mayor yet, and I've already solved traffic."

I laughed at his playful, cocky grin. "You should make that one of your campaign promises. Orgasms and arrivals in under five minutes."

He laughed again, loud and big-hearted, his smile soothing any worries that things would be awkward.

Last night, I'd slipped out of his bed and tugged on what few scattered clothes I could find, saying I'd crash in his guest bedroom.

"To be clear, you'd rather sleep in my *guest* bedroom?"

"That's what it's for, right? Guests."

He'd gestured to his disheveled bed. "You're hardly a guest."

Not quite a guest, not quite a girlfriend.

I'd smiled. "If you need me for any ankle-related situations, just call out."

He'd rolled his eyes so hard I'd thought he'd injure

himself again. "I'll be fine."

"But seriously, tonight was amazing, and, you know, I'm glad you were able to relax."

"I didn't go down on you to relax. I went down on you because I'm attracted to you. Was that not clear?"

And that's when I knew I really did have a thing for blunt dirty talk. In true Rach fashion, I'd stuttered something about how he was super hot, cringed after I said thanks for the o, then left the room before I asked for more, more, more.

He stood now, careful to keep his weight off his injured ankle, saying, "I've been in bed for way too long. I need a shower, and I have at least twenty items that need my immediate attention. Feel free to do whatever you please until the day starts."

I laughed, realizing he'd need a total personality transplant for things to be weird between us.

Pres assessed risks. He wouldn't have kissed me, done anything with me, unless he'd already analyzed and determined it would result in minimal chaos. Which meant sticking to the facts.

We were friends, I was confident of that.

Professionally, we worked well together.

And, sure, yeah, we pretended to be in a relationship.

So if I were pretending to be Pres right now, I could even rationalize it made perfect sense this had happened.

And if I were being me, I didn't expect more.

Anything more was impossible.

So rather than worrying, I surveyed his room. Sunlight tumbled onto the nearly spotless floor, and the only thing amiss about his neat, orderly life was scattered pieces of my clothes that had been out of reach last night.

Signs of me, out of place, once again somewhere I

didn't belong.

Proof of disruption.

As I tidied up, the same possessive streak that had washed over me last night bolted through my body again. I wanted to stake claim in something — some*one* — I didn't have. I wanted to take more than I'd been given, be totally selfish. I wanted more even though I knew it'd only lead to disaster.

He'd said I should do whatever I pleased.

And well, I hadn't gotten this far by making great decisions anyway. In some ways, my bad decisions had actually led me here. I chose not to read too much into that either.

Instead, I stepped into his en suite.

"You know," I said, deciding the real world didn't start until 7 a.m., "you never really experienced the full circumstances of Boobgate."

His laugh came around the tucked away stone shower.

"I think I got a sense of it last night," he deadpanned.

"I meant the origin story. It all started because I couldn't resist your amazing shower," I said, breathing in the heated steam as I slipped off my clothes and turned the corner to step inside.

He looked incredible, slick from the waterfall shower, droplets cascading down the hard muscles of his body.

"Oh," he said, inhaling sharply, "you're serious."

"I owe you one for using it then."

"Wouldn't the true repayment be my using *your* shower, not you using another of mine?" he said, focused on accuracy like we weren't standing naked in front of each other. So I tossed my hair over my shoulders and off my chest to give him a helpful reminder.

"What was I saying?" he said, running a hand through

his damp hair. It was darker wet, lightly messy like it'd been when we'd made out, a slight curl at the ends where it rested against his neck. So imperfectly unlike him, another side of him just for me, I thought, as a water droplet rolled down his collarbone.

I leaned forward and licked it.

"Oh shit," he said with a laugh, reaching out a hand to the wall. Because of his ankle, he couldn't put too much weight on his left foot, keeping him slightly off balance.

Ironically, that was a positive in this situation.

"I thought you said this was a one-time thing."

I lifted a shoulder in a shrug and smiled. I knew he needed rules and boundaries to operate in the world, and maybe this was one of them — maybe he thought he could walk back to the line we'd dangerously toed if he remained partially clothed or if he hadn't come.

But I decided to change the rules.

"I choose to believe if all events occur within twenty-four hours, it still falls under the category of a one-time thing."

He opened his mouth to protest, but no words followed. I'd never seen Pres speechless. I liked it.

"Plus, I thought I could return the favor," I said, skating my tongue down his chest and sinking to my knees as the shower sprayed down his shoulders.

"This isn't how it works," he groaned. His eyes flashed when I pressed my lips against his toned torso. Despite all his teasing, he wanted me.

"Yeah, what was that about you being in control?" I asked with a laugh, taking him in my hands. He was hard, heavy, and thick.

Yep, Pres had a perfect dick.

Finally, something I'd accurately predicted.

So I licked that, too.

His head fell back, a moan in the back of his throat. "Oh my god."

"I want to make this good for you," I said, swirling my tongue over the tip. "It's your turn to lose control."

He didn't respond, his fingers trying to grip the slick stoned wall as I slowly followed a water droplet from his crown to his base with my tongue.

"Tease," he ground out as I traced a line up the other side and lingered, gently using my lips to take the head into my mouth. I looked up at him through the mist, elated at how restless he looked, his teeth digging into his bottom lip.

"Just let go, Pres."

He didn't respond, clenching his jaw and watching me with a dark, heated gaze.

I wanted him to completely unravel. I wanted to bring James Prescott St. Clair IV to his breaking point. I wanted him to be consumed by me.

So I smirked, wrapped my hands around his toned thighs, and leaned forward, taking him down all at once, reveling in how he filled my mouth.

"Oh sh-fu-god," he gasped, slapping his other hand against the wall to keep from falling.

I'd never felt more powerful on my knees.

Just as I was getting into it — moaning around him which only made him groan louder, the sounds barely covered by the shower's roar — a voice interrupted us.

"Dude, are you okay?"

"Oh shit," Pres inhaled sharply, hitting the wall with a loud, wet smack. I gasped and pulled off of him, my heart pounding, frozen on my knees. "What the fu—?"

"It's Roe," the voice said from the other side. "Are you

okay? I just got here and thought I heard groaning."

"Why are you here? Get out. Leave me alone," Pres said, his chest rising and falling rapidly.

"Apparently I'm still the person you've allowed doctors or whatever to call," Roe replied, seeming unfazed. "I think it's from your soccer days—"

Of course Pres had played collegiate soccer. It explained a lot: his discipline, obsession with winning, analytical, game-playing nature, and, well, his body…

"—'Member when you broke your wrist, kept playing then had to be sedated your junior year? Anyway, your pharmacist, nurse, somebody called me last night saying your crutch and migraine pills are ready for pick up? You fell and hurt your ankle? Gotta be honest, dude, I got a lil freaked you weren't answering your phone."

"My assistant let my phone die," Pres replied, glaring at me. I covered my mouth to hold back a laugh. "Can you leave, Roe?"

"Maybe your assistant should be the contact person since I don't live around here anymore? You being alone worries—"

Pres took a deep breath and ran his hands through his wet hair, clearly trying to compose himself. So I leaned forward and wrapped my mouth around his dick again.

"Ooooh," Pres groaned, palming the wall to keep himself upright. "Ohkaay, thanks so much, Roe, that's great. See you later."

"No prob." I faintly heard him fiddling in the vanity. "Hey, do you have eye drops? My contacts are killin' me."

I released Pres, his glare heating my face, and smiled innocently. I'd just found my new favorite game.

"Stop it," he mouthed.

I cocked my head, miming confusion.

He gave me a dark look, but, as it turned out, sexy bossy scowls were hot.

I nodded obediently anyway, placing my palms on my thighs, my hair cascading over my breasts, water droplets rolling down my body. I didn't move, just blinked, licked my lips, and opened my mouth, letting him choose what he really wanted.

Something about the visual must have broken him. His eyes never left my mouth as he ran a thumb across my lips, blue eyes glittering, mesmerized, and gently guided me forward.

"Eye drops in the second drawer," Pres gritted out as I licked a bead of arousal off of him, making him tip his head back and hold back a groan. "Third. Left. Right. I don't know. *Please* get out of here."

It wasn't exactly the begging I'd been looking for, but I'd take it. I hadn't thought he could get harder, but one glance down, and I could tell wherever his brain stored eye drop location knowledge was a thing of the past.

"First drawer, left side," I whispered against his skin with a smirk, then licked up and down his shaft, pressing the head with my tongue.

Pres repeated me, every syllable strained.

"Are you sure you're good?" Roe asked.

I took him deep again while using my hand to jerk him in fast, shallow strokes to match his breathing.

"So good," Pres choked out.

"Found 'em," Roe said with a laugh. "I'm starving, dude. I can make breakfast for ya. Eggs? Bacon? Bagels?"

His legs tensed, muscles flexing under my palms, as he held back another moan. Letting him catch his breath, I slowly glided my tongue to circle around his width.

"Yeah, that's good," Pres struggled to say, leaning back

against the wall. His wet body was taut and hard, his chest flushed, his eyes flashing as he watched me.

"Do you like pancakes?" Roe asked.

I thanked the universe for oblivious men and loud showers as I worked my way down until Pres hit the back of my throat.

He was lost in it now, a ragged shudder rolling over him as he closed his eyes and thrusted gently. The heady feeling of lust, secrets, and the taste of him made me want to lose control right with him.

"Pres, pancakes or nah?"

"Yes," Pres said, biting his knuckles as he tried to keep himself upright. "Yes, fuck, *yes*."

Roe laughed. "Okay, dude, pancakes it is. On it."

The bathroom door closed, and I paused to make sure he'd disappeared.

"*Rach*," Pres groaned, sounding and looking wrecked. His voice was raw, sending a little thrill to my heart.

He was so close, his abs tightening and his hand tensing in my hair, so I sped up, squeezing him harder and tighter with my hand, working him over with my lips and tongue, determined to make him lose control.

As he rocked his hips and warned me breathlessly, I took him as far as I could, all the way to the base, to deep-throat him. That was it for him — he shattered, coming as he cursed my name on a moan.

He slumped against the wall, the muscles in his arm jumping as he held himself up off his left leg.

"Oh my god," he breathed, water droplets trickling down his flushed, dazed face. "Oh my god."

I stood, smiling victoriously. He glanced at me, his scowl holding no heat.

"Well, I have a pretty busy day," I said with a laugh.

"At least twenty action items and apparently a phone to charge. My client is really *hard* on me, so I better go—"

He laughed and pulled me under the stream, pressing his body against mine. I gasped, laughing, as he kissed me, warning me he was going to get me back, his hand already sliding lower.

By the time we slipped out of the shower, we were soaked, and Pres now wore the triumphant grin.

"Oh, by the way," I said over my shoulder after quickly drying my hair. "Your friend definitely thinks you love pancakes. I'm pretty sure you have to eat one."

Blue eyes snapped to mine, slightly horrified. "*What?*"

I laughed and left him to get ready for the day.

By the time I'd set up his office — charging his things, returning his chair, pulling up call links and his DC itinerary for review — Pres was in the kitchen, poised and coifed, like he hadn't just been moaning my name.

I hesitated at the threshold, unsure of who I was supposed to be. Because being his assistant pretending to be his girlfriend who just did some very real sex acts was just a little complicated to explain over pancakes.

So instead, I caught his eyes and motioned I was heading out to run errands.

He frowned. But before he could say what had crossed his mind, the pancakes were served, Roe was chattering, Pres' phone turned back on, pinging at an alarming rate, and his team was filing off the elevator, asking for waters and coffees.

I hadn't needed to decide who I was.

The universe already had.

"Get this on index cards," Ethan snapped, handing me a stack of papers as he passed me. "Pres' speech for the fall festival. And grab me a coffee. We have a long day ahead of us. Your personal day is over."

And just like that, everything was back to normal, the world back exactly where it belonged.

Our one-time thing had ended.

Except as I stepped on the elevator, Pres slipped inside before the door closed, undetected. Without a word, I placed my hand where his nicotine patch was hidden under his sleeve, drawn to him against my will, even when I knew no matter what happened between us, we already knew the ending — he'd always be him, with a future burning bright, and I'd always be stuck being me.

"Before our time is up," he said with a playful smile, "one more for a one-time thing?"

I laughed, and he kissed me, tasting like sugar, syrup, and secrets.

CHAPTER TWENTY

I kept waiting for things to get weird, proof we'd pushed a boundary too far, for our ruse to overwhelm our reality, but, like most things in Pres' life, our casual one-time thing had fit nice and tidy into his already determined life.

But I hadn't expected to step foot on Middletown University's campus with him on my arm — my silly little dream and my fake boyfriend colliding.

We'd ended up here when I'd been going over his social requests in his office.

"A recital at Pecunia Academy? It raises money for music programs in the community."

"Just send a check," Pres had said flatly. "I'm not driving two hours to watch kids attempt to play piano."

"Alumni networking event Wednesday? Grad school."

"Pass. Do I need to send them a donation too?"

"I don't think so. The ticket was like twenty bucks."

"That's fine. Send whatever. Probably more, right?"

I'd laughed and crossed it off my list.

"Middletown University award dinner tomorrow?"

He'd looked up from flipping through a deck I'd made him for a client presentation, intrigued. "Am I winning an award?"

"It's like lifetime achievements. I think the youngest recipient is sixty-five."

He'd rolled his eyes, flashing his devastatingly secret smirky smile. "Fine. If you think we should go, I will. It's probably good to network with lifetime achievers."

"Do you want me to ask Ethan for his input?"

Biting down on the nicotine gum he constantly had in his mouth — a really confident, sexy move that accentuated his lips and distracted me without fail — he'd somehow managed to roll his eyes harder.

I'd laughed. "True, Ethan would somehow try to find a way to get you an award better than everyone else."

Pres had laughed, nodding. "Exactly. Let's keep this one between us."

"It could be fun. I've always wondered if campus looks the same as it does in photos."

It didn't. It looked even better.

Pres knew I had an associates degree, but I'd never gotten around to telling him "campus" had been community college online attended between any job I could get and waiting outside the hallway of my mom's public defender.

So I'd been trying to mask my awe as we crossed campus, sneaking glances at all the places I wanted to explore in another life.

Under the moon's hazy glow, campus was beautiful. Low fog filtered through soft lamp lights to make it seem mystical, and it was quiet, a sense of calm hanging in the crisp air. I felt surrounded by opportunity, like everything I could learn about the world was right at my fingertips.

"Wow," I breathed when we paused in front of an ornate building with tall, thick white columns flanking grand marble steps. "This is gorgeous. It's the oldest building on campus, right?"

Pres looked up from where he was scanning my email

on the award winners and nodded. "Legend says if you kiss on the steps, you marry that person."

"The website doesn't say that online! Good thing steps are out for you," I joked, gently patting the crutch he was using until his ankle healed.

"I've read that only about fifteen percent of people marry their college sweethearts. So I'd say the steps are cursed."

I laughed. "Well, if someone is kissing on the steps, they probably believe in the idea though. So what's the percentage of people who kiss on the steps getting married? I bet it's higher. I bet the legend is true."

He shook his head. "I can't possibly determine that. That's not how statistics work."

"But it's nice to believe," I said with a smile.

He grinned, giving me one of those looks like he just wasn't quite sure how I existed in front of him. "So you don't remotely care if it's true or not?"

"I guess I think feelings and truth can get all jumbled. Feelings can be stronger than facts—"

"You're a statistician's nightmare."

"Good thing you're a politician, huh?" I quipped, making him laugh. "We should go in so you can network. I read up on the winners, and they've all been married for decades and are all alumni. I'll be the odd one out, but I know a good amount about the campus, so I feel pretty confident I can nail the small talk. Oh, maybe they all kissed on the steps! We should ask them."

"Yeah, we can ask them," he said with a soft smile.

"Okay," I said, turning to reach out my hand. "Ready? I can help you if you need a hand. There's also a ramp to the side. I looked it up earlier to be sure."

He looked at my hand, and I had a flash of when I'd

given him a scone months ago. He looked just as baffled now, like no one had ever offered him a hand before.

"Have you been here before?" he asked with a squint.

"What do you mean?"

"You've been … very intrigued by this walk. You know things about this place, but you don't know it. You remind me of me in a grocery store."

I laughed, hoping the blush crawling up my neck wasn't visible.

"It's important to be prepared. I am your assistant."

Pres didn't look convinced. "You don't have to tell me the truth, but I can't stand here and pretend I don't notice you, Rach."

I was one step above him, putting us right at eye level. The moonlight splashed across his steady gaze in a way that made my heart lurch. And his words made a little breath of air escape me and a warm buzz zing right in my chest. I believed in him so much it hurt. But it would hurt way worse to hear he didn't believe in me.

I shook my head. "It's silly. Like, majorly stupid."

A corner of his mouth lifted. "As silly as wearing tennis shoes with a ballgown? Because I noticed that and we still managed to talk that first night."

I laughed and rolled my eyes. Pres' stubbornness had no bounds. "Have you ever pretended you could have a different future? Like, genuinely imagined it, put yourself in the scenario, tried to role-play it or whatever?"

"I'd be down to role-play," he said so easily I almost choked. Okay, so *almost* everything was back to normal.

"Wait, really? That's not what I meant. Although—"

He laughed. "What did you mean? We're pretending with our whole thing, so I suppose I can understand what you mean outside of a sexual context."

"Right. Well, I've just always wanted to go here. But I've only looked at the website and photos and stuff. I guess you picked up on that. It just feels surreal to be somewhere I've always imagined. It's different in reality."

"You live ten minutes from campus."

I laughed. Of course, his first question was logistical.

"It's not a transportation issue."

"Rach, I know you're smart. Are you a poor test taker? There are a lot of tips to get better at that sort of thing."

"That's not the issue."

"You've applied and didn't get in?"

"No. There's no point."

I shifted as he thought this over, a small frown crossing his face. People were hurrying up and down the steps, students leaving classes and people in dresses and suits heading inside to the awards dinner. I couldn't help but feel like I didn't belong in either direction.

"We should go inside," I said, regretting admitting yet another reason we didn't fit. Another proof point I was a mess. "The networking—"

"I don't care about networking," he said shortly. "Well, to be clear, I do. But not at this exact moment. You can't tell me you've dreamed of something then follow it up with there's no point in trying to get it. I'm supposed to be the negative one, not you."

"Being realistic isn't being negative. I'm pretty sure you taught me that. We don't have to talk about this. It's complicated, and you…" I gestured to him in a designer suit, perfect and assured, so far beyond where I'd ever get, "…have way more important things to focus on. I don't think you'd understand."

If he could have, I was certain he would've crossed his arms. Instead, he shifted on his crutch and frowned. "I'm *highly* efficient at understanding complex problems."

I had to laugh at how formal he could get when he was pouty. "Sure, but have you ever wanted something and didn't get it? Have you ever wanted something so badly but you knew, no matter what, the cards had already been dealt?"

"Of course I have."

"My job is to know you, and, honestly, I have a hard time believing that."

"Come here," he said, nodding to the space in front of him. "Let's go."

"But the—"

"If you say networking one more time," he said, giving me a very stern, very sexy look, "I'm going to kiss you on these steps."

I burst out laughing. "Is that such a bad thing?"

"Yes, because then you'll be stuck with me, and I'm very unlikable, haven't you heard?" He reached out his free hand. "Let's ditch. These things last hours, we'll be back in time for dessert. I want to show you something."

My eyes widened. "Ditch? You?"

He nodded, flashing a melt-worthy smile that proved he was more daring than he let on. "A one-time thing."

I smiled, ignoring the giddiness bubbling in my stomach.

We hadn't spoken about our little tryst since his shower. Emails, meetings, and everything else had gotten in the way, and we'd fallen right back into place.

But flirting? Well, there was never any harm in flirting.

It was basically our job at this point.

. . .

He led me in the opposite direction.

The walk was completely different than before. Instead

of going over our talking points for the dinner, he pointed out the buildings dotting campus, giving me a run-down of their history and the majors they housed.

We popped into the campus coffee shop, an effortlessly cool little place where the staff seemed to have a penchant for tattoos and piercings. While we waited on our orders, he told me Roe used to work here before becoming a tattoo artist.

"Roe doesn't seem like … someone you'd have as your emergency contact."

I'd snuck a peek at him before I'd slipped out of the penthouse the other day, surprised to see a man with tattoos of various symbols and drawings scattered across his arms and a lip ring, a nose ring, and several hoops snaking up his ear standing in Pres' kitchen.

Pres laughed. "Yeah, but he's surprisingly reliable."

"How do you know him?"

"College. He needed a place to live. I had one to offer."

"Wait, you had a roommate and didn't spontaneously combust?"

"We had a very strict the-sponge-goes-here rule," Pres laughed. "You should be even more impressed by me because I actually had *two* roommates."

I laughed, shaking my head as he explained his family had an investment property here.

"Roe's a good guy, and he balanced out my other roommate, Derek, who is arguably the loudest roommate in history. He never stopped playing music. Ever."

I could barely imagine any of this except for Pres' family having an "investment property."

"It made sense to share," he said simply.

Once we got our drinks, he nodded to the grand library lit up by stately white lights and told me all about it and all the other learning resources on campus.

Then we lost track of time just talking, trading stories and jokes, until our cups grew cold.

"Did you like your time here?" I asked after we'd paused in front of the political science building.

He shrugged. "I was focused on getting my degree and preparing for grad school. I was pretty busy with soccer and then being SGA president."

I wanted to say that sounded more lonely than busy. Instead, I teased, "So you haven't changed at all then?"

He grinned. "Well, I didn't have an assistant then."

By the time we hit the edge of campus, I realized there were no other buildings to see. He'd taken me on a full campus tour.

"You didn't have to do this," I said softly, almost feeling guilty. Because it didn't matter if I saw the place.

It wasn't real. It would never be real.

"One more thing," he said firmly.

We kept walking, making twists and turns I'd never be able to replicate on a map, until he stopped in front of a chainlink fence next to a dumpster.

"Okay…" I said slowly. "This is nice, too. It's probably good you started the tour back there though—"

He laughed, his breath little puffs of joy dotting the night sky. "Get over here. This is what I wanted to show you."

He tossed his crutch over the fence.

I gasped.

Then, using a ridiculous amount of upper body strength and one leg, he hauled himself over the fence and slowly climbed down until he was on the other side.

"Oh wow," he said with a laugh, coughing as he caught his breath, "that was harder than I remembered.

Your turn. I'll catch you if you fall."

I stared at him. "You're injured."

"I promise, I'll catch you."

"What if I tear my dress?"

He waved away my concern. "I'll buy you a new one. You won't fall. It's easy with two functioning ankles."

This believe-in-everything Pres was alarming.

And thrilling.

How could I say no to this beautiful guy who was smiling at me with bright blue eyes, asking me to believe, making promises, saying he'd catch me if I fell?

Plus, I'd done about a hundred other embarrassing things in front of him. Falling off a fence and ripping my dress would barely scratch the surface.

So I kicked off my heels, tossed them over, and then, by the grace of the universe only, dropped down next to him, my dress swishing right back into place, laughing as he placed a steady hand on my shoulder.

"Told you so. I'm very rarely wrong, Rach."

I rolled my eyes at his playful cockiness and glanced around where we stood behind bleachers.

"Are we supposed to be here?"

"We won't get in trouble if we're caught."

"How can you be so sure?"

He shrugged. "I did this all the time in school. It's unlikely they changed their security patrol."

I grabbed my shoes and followed him until we came around the bleachers, greeted with a massive soccer field.

"Whoa." It felt surreal to be in front of a deserted stadium, bright white lights washing over the perfect green grass. "This is bigger than it looks in photos."

He laughed. "Yeah. It's a beast."

"You used to sneak in here? Why?"

"When I couldn't sleep, I'd come here to practice."

We sat on the first row in silence. I tried to predict what he'd tell me. Maybe something inspiring, like the stats on how many times you had to pick yourself up after falling before you would accomplish your goals.

"So," he said, pointing to the halfway line, "that's where I threw up during my first championship game."

CHAPTER TWENTY-ONE

I couldn't help but laugh, startled by this confession.

He grimaced. "It was gross, Rach."

"It probably wasn't *that* bad."

"It was televised."

"I've experienced worse," I said with another laugh, nudging him in the side and sticking out my chest. He grinned, quickly looking away before his gaze dropped.

"Well, you asked what I wanted. I'd like to have never experienced that. It's on page twelve of Google. It took years to bury it. Actually, it's probably deeper now because of Boobgate. I should check."

I laughed again, truly unable to believe it. "Did you throw up because you were nervous?"

He shook his head. "I'd had a migraine. I'd thought I could play through it, but apparently I was wrong."

I nodded slowly. "I'm not sure what the moral of this story is though?"

"Oh, I wasn't telling an allegory. I'm presenting facts."

I laughed, certain I'd always wonder how he was so charming by being the exact opposite of charming.

"I was recruited to play here. When the coach and scouts met with me, they said I could go pro. I just had to keep doing what I was doing. Practice, train, eat, breathe, sleep soccer."

"Oh, wow. That's incredible."

"For the first time in my life, I was offered something and my last name didn't have anything to do with it. My father wasn't involved at all. He'd never even come to one of my games. St. Clair on my jersey meant me. It was all me. Just me. Someone wanted me."

If throwing up was buried past page 12, I was positive a quote like this could never be found online.

"I don't understand then," I said, knowing if Pres was that close to getting something, he would have. There was no question in his dedication, resources, or ability to succeed. "What happened?"

He exhaled and rubbed his hands together against the cold. I could tell he was craving a cigarette by the way he shifted restlessly. So I reached out and took his hand.

"I was in a car accident when I was eighteen."

I blinked, not expecting his answer, and nodded. "Okay, tell me about it."

"That's not a question."

I smiled. "We aren't playing Truth Chicken. Tell me anyway."

He laughed, keeping his gaze on the immaculate field.

"My best friend and I were in a car accident the summer after graduation. Someone ran a neighborhood stop sign at forty-seven miles per hour."

He stated the facts like it was something he'd practiced to himself until he got it just right, every syllable taut and unshakeable.

But I could feel his hand against mine, how his grip tightened by a fraction, so subtle I wasn't sure if he'd even noticed.

"You were hurt."

He looked at me then. I thought of all the times he'd looked right at me, like he wanted to study and memorize me, awed, see all of me. I wondered if he saw I looked at him the same way.

"Yeah. I had a pretty bad concussion. I broke a couple ribs and had to have surgery on a torn meniscus," he said in the same factual way. "It hurt to breathe for months."

His tone shifted then, the slightest crack in his perfect, practiced exterior.

"I'm so sorry. That's terrible. It must've been so hard."

He shrugged, but it hardly felt light. "I was lucky."

I was surprised by this sentiment. But when I met his gaze, I understood. "Oh, no. Pres. Your friend didn't…"

He nodded. "We were supposed to be roommates and play soccer here. We had everything planned. My back-up plan was to work at a policy and polling firm. I've never lied to you about liking politics and data. That part of me is integral to who I am. But I *wanted* soccer."

He nodded to the expansive field. "I wanted this. Soccer was the only place I've ever felt I belonged. I've never really fit in. I know I'm unlikable. I know how I come across sometimes, and it's very difficult for me to be a different person. But on this field, no one cared. No one cared about my father. No one cared if my family made it on a *Forbes*' list. No one cared if my last name was splashed on headlines or hospital buildings. St. Clair just meant that guy can kick and run. I *wanted* that, Rach. I wanted that life so badly."

I squeezed his hand harder, knowing *this* was a one-time thing. No one would ever see James Prescott St. Clair IV like this. I was special. I was lucky.

"The fact is, my freshman year and every year after, I pushed myself harder and harder because I thought I could change the outcome. But it was over before it started. I just couldn't reach where I'd been before my accident. I couldn't get it back. One random, life-changing occurrence rearranged all the cards. So, yes, I do know what you mean and how you feel. You aren't alone, Rach. I may not be like you, but that doesn't mean I don't understand."

He exhaled slowly, his breath coming out white. It was the only time I'd ever seen him look self-conscious when he glanced at me.

"And to answer your question, if I could really have what I want, it would be to bring my best friend back."

His tone was more than factual. This was *truth*.

I'd never be able to put into words how I felt about him, how he made me feel, how touched I was that he'd trusted me to tell me this, how I wanted to keep feeling this way, free of secrets.

"Thank you for sharing those ... facts with me," I said with a soft smile. "I know it wasn't easy to tell me this."

"Well, I'm very good at facts," he said with a grin, instantly cocky.

"Just not fun facts."

He laughed and nodded, slipping his arm around my shoulders to pull me into a side hug. It was something we did all the time in front of others, so surely it was okay to do alone, too.

"Why do you want to be a guidance counselor?" he asked, giving me a little squeeze. "Just thinking about doing that stresses me out."

I burst out laughing. "Says the guy running for mayor."

He grinned. "Yeah, I want to help people and this city, but what you want is much closer to martyrdom."

I smiled. "When I was in high school, my guidance counselor was really helpful. I felt ... lost a lot," I said hesitantly. "I wasn't well-liked, and I wasn't sure what options I had for the future. I wasn't very … well off."

Pres looked confused.

"I mean, you know," I said with a laugh, "monetarily inclined."

He shook his head. "No, I'm confused by you not being well-liked? How?"

I laughed again, wondering just how the most realistic, negative guy I knew only saw the best in me. "I was kind of a loser, Pres. You were popular, weren't you?"

He shrugged. "Everyone knowing you isn't the same as being liked. I'd stayed in Pecunia when I was eleven for my father's campaign, but was sent back to boarding school after he won. So when I moved back permanently at fifteen, I already had a reputation before I'd even met anyone. Everyone already had their mind made up about how I'd be. Sometimes, it felt harder to be myself than whatever they wanted."

I nodded. "I get that. Sometimes it's easier to just meet people's assumptions."

"Yeah," he said, looking right at me, "exactly, Rach. See, if I'd had a guidance counselor like you in school, maybe I would be different now."

I rolled my eyes at his silly flirting.

"I'm serious," he protested. "I probably would've had more actual friends, opened up more, and laughed more. I probably would have been more likable. And honestly, I probably would have liked myself a lot more, too."

A shiver crossed my skin, and I wasn't entirely sure I could blame the winter chill.

"I think you could be life-changing."

"I really would love that life," I said softly. "If I could help others feel less alone. Everyone is special, and I'd love to help people believe that."

He nodded. "You can, Rach. You don't have to tell me why you feel like you can't apply here. But don't let your silence be because of me. I may be unlikable, stubborn, stiff, not funny, and stuck-up … but I understand what it feels like to want something out of reach, Rach."

I scooted closer, warm and comforted by his side.

There was something about being in a place I'd only dreamed of on a ditched fake date under bright lights with just him, that I had to believe we could say anything.

"I have a really bad credit score and no savings. So if I applied here, and on the off-chance I got in, I'd have to go into a lot of debt. I can't afford to do that. I can't put my life on hold to pursue something that isn't guaranteed."

"What about grants or scholarships?"

"Pres, I'm *busy*. I wake up early every morning and don't stop until you stop. And you never stop," I said with a laugh. "I'm not blaming you, because if it wasn't you, it'd be someone else. Say I got in, when am I supposed to actually go to class? Do the work? You really think my future employer won't hold that against me?"

He shook his head. "You can negotiate."

I laughed, burying my face against his shoulder. "I have no leverage. I only got this job because no one else wanted it. And I only kept it because I flashed my boobs."

He didn't respond.

I turned his frowning face to me and smiled. "I already told you, it's okay. Sure, I used to want to be a guidance counselor, but I can kind of do a version of that now. I mean, come on, being a personal assistant is like being the ultimate counselor. You need me, right?"

"Yes, but—"

I pressed my fingers over his lips, and he cocked an

eyebrow, not used to being shushed and definitely not in that way.

"So let me believe that I'm doing good. I'm not asking you for help. This isn't a favor I'm cashing in. I'm just telling you this because…"

I stopped myself from saying something too revealing, too foolish. Instead, I stood, in a nice dress in front of a guy that I was quickly feeling too strongly for, and shook my head.

"You're wrong."

"No, I'm not," he said, muffled behind my hand. "About what?"

I laughed. "You aren't unlikable. I think it's possible that you're the most likable guy I've ever met—"

He rolled his eyes.

"If we're being honest, I like you a lot," I continued even if he didn't believe me. "More than I should."

He mumbled something, his eyes glinting playfully.

I moved my hand off his mouth.

"I find you preferable to networking."

I laughed, smacking my hand back over his lips as he laughed loudly.

Then we returned where we belonged, laughs, dreams, and secrets bouncing over a lone soccer field together.

"You ready, Rach?" he asked, pausing on the steps of the networking event.

He reached out, tucking a strand of my hair behind my ear, his fingers delicately brushing my cheek, and smiled. It wasn't a touch to fix me, to right me into place, but a tender caress, like I was something to be admired, someone worth remembering.

He didn't look like someone who'd jumped a fence moments ago, who'd made nerdy jokes and had hopes and dreams he'd never accomplish, who'd taken me on a campus tour because he'd wanted me to believe in something I didn't think was possible.

"Rach," he repeated. "Are you ready?"

"Pres," I started, my pulse racing as I looked at him, tall and powerful in a suit, the lights cutting across his beautiful face. He looked just like the guy I'd first met, from another world, only in a dream. But I knew now, he was so much more. And I wanted so, so much more. "I need to do something."

He gave me a strange look. "Okay … did you not want to go inside at all? Networking actually is importa—"

I didn't know what the rest of his sentence was, and I really didn't care. Because I'd already grabbed him, his crutch clattering down a step, pulled him down by the lapels, and crashed his lips against mine.

At first he was startled, giving me the upper hand, so I kissed him harder, biting his lower lip and deepened the kiss with my tongue.

A groan of pleasure and surprise came deep from his throat, a sound that shot heat from my heart to between my legs. Then he was all in, too, one firm hand pressed against my back, dragging me up so my chest was flush against his, our mouths connected, his tongue taking over the bruising kiss, teeth sinking into flesh, fingers grazing skin, our breathless gasps disappearing white and hot in the night sky.

It was a wild kiss, unpolished and hurried, heated and slick and fierce.

"Just casual," I gasped, still frantically kissing him. "To get it out of our system before our time's up. Then we stop. You become mayor, I disappear, everyone lives happily ever after."

I was a woman born from bad decisions. Some people inherited fortune or class or fame. If they were lucky, they got all three with roman numerals suffixes as proof. I'd inherited always getting it wrong because of the innate desire to make the best out of nothing — unable to accept that sometimes nothing is just a sign of nothing.

So in the interest of staying positive, I'd already made enough bad decisions in my life, what was one more?

I didn't care if this was a mistake. I didn't care that all signs pointed to the fact that, yes, this would end, duh, hooking up didn't magically make this a real relationship, and, no, we'd never *truly* be together because our futures were too misaligned to even entertain the idea.

But I wanted to be selfish, I wanted something I couldn't have, and all that added up to Pres.

I'd thought maybe he'd reject me after we'd run out of breath and pulled away, say this was a bad idea. After all, he was the responsible, controlled, calculated one.

He was the Capricorn.

Instead, he ran his thumb over his flushed lower lip and nodded.

"No one has to know," I added. "I'll still be your fake girlfriend. People believe what we want them to—"

He kissed me again.

And just like that, we had a new game to play.

CHAPTER TWENTY-TWO

It takes roughly two weeks for a sprained ankle to heal. I preferred to count the days by orgasms.

Because when life gives you lemons, you make lemonade. And when life gives you Pres St. Clair's mouth at your whim, you say yes, thank you, I'll take seconds.

Our ruse became a balanced whirlwind of work, attending events where we acted like nothing had changed, and getting each other off with our mouths and hands in between.

It was amazing how controlling a man's calendar could lead to several mid-day excursions.

"God," Pres breathed three days ago, slumping against the dry cleaning I'd just hung up in his closet. He smiled wryly as I laughed and rose from my knees, handing him his crutch. "And now I really want a cigarette. This is all your fault, Rach."

He got me back two days later. I'd been in the kitchen making coffee after his team had left for lunch when he'd pressed against me, balancing his weight with his palm on the counter as his other fingers sank into me.

His timing had been perfect, stepping away with a smirk just as I'd buttoned my pants, caught my breath, and his elevator door had opened.

And just yesterday, when I'd tried to even the score, blocking off his schedule and locking his office door behind me, we'd realized he had a thing for me sitting on his desk and I had a thing for him kneeling for me.

It was dirty, secret fun that only made us *better* and more believable at events.

We'd even nailed it the night after kissing on the steps.

"How's your ankle?" I'd whispered after we'd righted ourselves, grabbed his crutch off the maybe-lucky-maybe-cursed stairs, and found our seats at the alumni dinner.

"When it heals completely," he'd said lowly, "I want to fuck you like you deserve."

Full body chills rushed my skin.

"Yes, please, I'd like that, thanks."

"It's a date, angel pudding pie," he'd joked with a smirk, the pet name bringing us right back to reality. Then he'd smiled, offering his hand to one of the alumni award winners who had approached us. "Pres St. Clair, so lovely to meet you. My darling date hasn't stopped telling me about you."

Through a fog of not-fast-enough dissipating lust and a hastily gulped wine, cheeks still pink, I'd beamed, launching into what I'd researched, Pres chiming in at the parts we'd practiced, playing our roles perfectly.

...

I hadn't necessarily expected my phone to buzz at 11:57 p.m., but I really should have considering Pres was still my client.

Some things really hadn't changed.

What's that channel with all the houses?

I laughed, texting "HGTV" like a good assistant, and turned back to trying and failing to fill out a Middletown University application.

Seeing campus weeks ago felt as hazy as a dream, except for the very real lingering feeling that maybe applying was something I *could* do.

But trying to wrangle my transcripts seemed like a whole second job, and by the time I'd finally gotten all my paperwork together, I was stumped by the application's essay prompts. I'd expected common questions, like to explain ways I've grown or what I'd been doing for the past few years. But the first one had already stumped me: "Why is now the right time?"

How much time do you have, I wanted to write.

The second was even worse: "Who are you and who do you want to be?"

Enrolled in college, please, I scribbled as my phone buzzed again.

No, that isn't right. The one where couples look for houses?

I laughed. *It is HGTV. Promise.*

This is some sort of construction show.

"Are you for real?" I asked, laughing when I answered his FaceTime call.

He nodded seriously. The motion was really driven home because he sat in his office in a suit, having not changed from a client dinner.

"I wanted to judge couples judging houses," he said, frowning in the direction of his television. He sighed deeply. "What are you doing up?"

"I think that's a better question for you."

He shrugged. "Reading city department master plans. I finished sidewalks and am moving onto public parks. It's fascinating information. I might dig into the history of property taxes next."

I nodded, knowing he wasn't joking. "And are you planning to go to bed soon?"

He flashed a smile. "Are you inviting me over?"

I laughed. "I didn't remotely do that."

"So I can't come over?"

"Are you requesting a booty call?" I joked.

He laughed. "Is it a booty call if I'll see you in the morning, afternoon, evening, and for the foreseeable future? We do have a deal, bunny-bear. I'm all yours until you quit."

I rolled my eyes. "Do you need me to call you a car?"

"No," he said, already standing. "But turn on the house searching channel. See you soon."

"It's the *same* channel—"

He'd already hung up, and I shot up, realizing he was being serious. He was coming over to *my* place.

He'd ditched the crutch and had gotten the all clear from his doctor today.

Pres was nothing if not an efficient man who stuck to his word. His promise of what he'd do to me once he was healed flashed in my mind.

By the time I opened the door, I was out of breath, having hastily picked up my apartment, tossed a throw pillow on my bed to function as a second pillow, realized he hadn't said he was staying over, threw the pillow back, ran back to grab it, carefully placed it, picked it back up to scream in it, and then got the door.

He looked like an actual model in his suit, leaning against my doorframe, a candy in his mouth.

Another thing we were pretending was that Pres wasn't overcompensating his nicotine cravings by eating hard candies at a nearly constant rate. And personally, I pretended that I didn't stare at his mouth when he did, reminded of his talented tongue and plush lips on my body with each sugar swirl.

And now, his smile looked absolutely delicious.

Then his expression changed to give me a weird look.

"What are you wearing?"

"Dang it," I groaned. Too caught up in my pillow debate, I'd managed to skip over changing out my oversized bedshirt with Nicolas Cage's face all over it.

"This is horrifying," he said, settling his hand on my hip to draw me closer. Just when I thought he was going to kiss me, he said, "New dress code. Email the team."

"You really want to see Ethan in this?" I asked, spinning away with a laugh. "Also pantsless or no?"

He groaned and followed me inside.

"So that's my couch," I said as if he couldn't possibly identify it.

"Okay."

"And that's my bed," I said, continuing the world's worst home tour of a place he'd already been.

He nodded. "Ah, yes. So that's what that is."

"And that's the television—"

"How about you take off your shirt?"

My pulse picked up, and heat flooded my cheeks.

This *was* a booty call. This was happening.

"Oh."

He smiled. "No?"

"No, I mean, yes, yeah, totally," I said, stripping it off as he reached for me, kissing me earnestly.

Like most things, if Pres committed to it, he did it intensely, slightly impatiently, and oh-so-right.

So our kiss went from sweet to hot, hard, and overwhelming in seconds. We stumbled back against the wall, which he took as an opportunity to pin my wrists above me and strip off my underwear. I rocked against him, his suit against my bare skin a delightful, dirty feeling, and moaned as he kissed his way down my body until he was on his knees.

"Oh my gosh, you're strong," I moan-mumbled when he tossed my leg over his shoulder and pushed me up.

My brain couldn't keep up with the indulgent, incredible feeling of his mouth between my legs. *Everything* felt good.

I closed my eyes and tipped my head back against the wall, twisting a hand in his hair, a rush washing over me, heat building, body tensing, right on the edge—

He pulled away.

Then he actually *laughed* at my bewildered expression.

"Not yet," he said, licking my inner thigh because he was a tease. "I want you to come with me inside you."

"The poll was right," I said breathlessly, "you are a jerk."

He laughed again and stood, kissing my neck until I was melting again, and we stumbled to my bedroom.

"On the bed, Rach."

I laid down, but he remained standing. As he unbuttoned his shirt, his eyes roved over my body like he couldn't decide what he wanted to devour first. I'd never felt so desired, and he hadn't even *touched* me yet.

"I want to see what you do when I'm not here," he said evenly.

I faltered. Just like when I'd ridden his face, I'd never done this in front of anyone before.

"Touch yourself," he said, flashing his secret, sexy smirk. I'd never look at a picture of him smiling that way with an innocent mind again.

It was also at that moment I realized how little Pres bossed me around in real life. I knew if I said no, he'd do what I wanted or asked instead. In fact, the past few months crossing my mind, Pres actually did whatever *I* said most of the time already.

"And what do you plan to do?"

He raised an eyebrow and crossed his arms, the hard lines of his chest and abs teasing me. "Watch. Enjoy. Maybe learn a thing or two."

I grinned, liking this little game. Not breaking eye contact, I slowly grazed my hand down my oversensitive body, slipping lower between my thighs, holding back a gasp at how wet I already was for him.

He looked composed, except for how his throat worked as he swallowed just a bit harder, his eyes just a bit darker, his breath deepening.

I touched myself languidly, drifting one slow hand up to cup my boobs, really grateful for my claim to fame in this moment.

I wanted him to lose control just as much as me, and that meant going head to head. Holding back a moan, I spread my legs wider and inhaled a shaky breath, having never felt this way. So turned on, so out of control, so wild. So *wanted*.

My heart raced and my skin pinpricked with desire as he watched me with a heated gaze, looking at me like I was the only person in the world.

"Tell me how it feels, Rach."

"It feels lonely," I said, biting my lip. "I want you."

"Soon," he said lowly. Just the sound of his voice made me want to crawl across the bed, peel off the rest of his suit, take him in my mouth and then deep, deep inside.

This waiting game, this feeling of being so close, made my whole body vibrate.

"Pres," I moaned. My face flushed at how needy I sounded until I saw how much he liked it. It was the faintest of movements, his jaw clenching, how he sucked in a silent breath.

Satisfaction rolled off of me as I realized he was barely staying in control. I wasn't the only desperate one here.

So I circled my clit, waves of pleasure and deep warmth rolling over me, and slipped a finger inside myself. "*Please.*"

He made an appreciative sound, and I threw my head back at it, thrilled I could draw a throaty, pleasured sound from him and witness his composure unravel.

When I met his gaze, he slipped off his shirt but said nothing, which made me more frantic. I lifted my hips and added another finger, really getting into it, enjoying the sight of his flushed skin, his wet, reddened lips, his bright blue gaze burning like the hottest part of a flame.

I gasped, my muscles taut and coiled, my whole body tingling, so close—

"Don't come yet," he said, his gravelly warning sending shivers down my spine. "That's mine."

Pleasure rocked my body at that simple word, and I desperately wanted to echo it back.

Mine. I wanted him to be mine.

"I think of you when I do this," I admitted, not caring the secret tumbled off my tongue. "Please, give me what I can't stop thinking about. Give me all of you, babe."

I inhaled sharply. He'd spent months calling me silly names, but I'd never gone further than a joking James. I faltered at hearing the wildly inaccurate pet name fall from my lips, but he didn't.

Instead, he scraped his teeth over his bottom lip, his hands falling to his pants button. I filed this information away for later: *Bossy Pres likes appreciation. And maybe I'd had the upper hand this whole time.*

"Join me," I panted, patting the spot next to me. "Make me feel good. I don't want to wait anymore, baby."

"Fuck," he gritted out, exhaling hard.

"I need to feel you," I demanded. "All of you."

I sat up on my knees impatiently and placed a hand over his bare chest. His heart was *pounding* under my palm. Tracing where his heart rested, I touched myself with my other hand, and that's when whatever ounce of control he had snapped.

He lost the rest of his clothes, and we fell to the bed. We touched and teased, making out like never before, like this was the first time and the last time, like we had days, months, years to do this and no time at all.

I was pinned underneath him, and his lips covered my gasps as he roughly slipped two fingers inside me, taking over what I'd started.

"So wet," he murmured, pressing deeper and trailing his kisses lower, licking and nipping my skin. He lightly bit my nipples, soothing the sting with his tongue, until I could only moan his name and beg for more. "So good. I've been waiting for you, Rach. Waiting for so long."

A shiver ran through me, and I squeezed my eyes shut, reminding myself this was just sex talk as an undercurrent of unbridled, selfish desire pulsed inside me — *mine, mine, be mine.*

I shifted, hastily jerking open my bedside table, and tossed him a condom. He caught my hand before I closed the drawer.

"What's that?"

The blush that crossed my face burned.

"Um, my vibrator."

"Oh," he said, his eyes bright, "*yes.*"

In an instant, he was suited up and pulling me to the edge of the bed.

Standing between me, he slid his hand up my leg then

brought it to his mouth, following where his long fingers had traced. Without taking his lips off of me, he placed my ankle on his shoulder.

On my back, I gripped his muscled thigh, drinking in his tall, strong body as his hand became deliciously distracted by my breasts.

"Tell me you want it, Rach."

"Pres, *please.*"

I rocked against his hard length teasing my entrance as he leaned down, catching my earlobe between his teeth, his voice dark and low, "Hmm, not good enough."

"Are you *kidding*?" I said, rolling my hips, trying to get friction, deeper contact, anything. "Now is *not* the time to demand perfection."

He held my hip steady with one hand, the firm grip making me whimper, and nipped my throat, tracing the mark with his tongue.

"I want to know you've been thinking about this as much as me. Say it, Rach. Tell me how much you want my dick inside you."

"So much. So bad. Since we met, since we kissed. So much *right now*," I panted, my body vibrating with need, not even embarrassed by the desperate string of pleas spilling from my mouth.

The cocky expression that crossed his face was *almost* satisfying enough. But then he gently rocked against me, just barely teasing, and I couldn't take it anymore.

I huffed and lifted up on my elbows. "I swear, Pres St. Clair, if you don't fu—"

He entered me in one slow, deep motion.

Both of us groaned with satisfaction when he filled me completely.

Shivers scattered across my skin, and I demanded

more, more, more. He listened, thrusting solid, deliberate strokes. Then we were gasping each others' names, grabbing, kissing, biting, caressing, totally losing control.

It was hard, fast, and exactly what I wanted.

The weight of his strong chest pressed against mine paired with a steady pounding that matched our heartbeats. The exquisite feeling of lips and bodies and breaths connected, just him and me.

"Want you," I said through a sharp inhale, my fingers curling in his hair, gripping his shoulders and digging into his flesh, teetering on the edge of control. "You, you, baby, all of you."

He pressed his lips against my ear, a flutter of a kiss, a deeply gentle motion in direct contradiction to his otherwise demanding roughness. "You feel so good, Rach. You're everything I've always wanted."

I didn't really know what we were saying or what we were doing, what any of this meant, if any of this was real, and I didn't care. It felt so good, so hot, so right, exactly like what I'd been waiting for far too long.

Suddenly, like the excellent multitasker he was, my vibrator buzzed against my clit, sending shockwaves of bliss through every nerve, muscle, fiber of my being, as Pres thrusted inside me hard, his mouth never leaving mine.

I closed my eyes as another breathless shiver rocked my body. Then I was tumbling off the edge, a white-hot feeling of pleasure hitting me so hard, I nearly screamed, my release filled with desperate moans and murmurs.

"Fuck, yes, that's it, oh god, Rach, yes, *Rach*," he said, his voice breaking, losing his ability to stay calm and collected. His voice was loud, deep, and rumbly as he came, jerking with just a string of incoherent curse words and my name over and over.

We struggled to catch our breath, hearts racing, as I fell on my back, him on top of me, our skin hot and flushed.

After a moment, he lifted up on his palms to grin at me. He was disheveled, every part of him out of place, his gaze glassy, his hair a mess, his lips red and full. I was glad he was no longer resting on my chest so he wouldn't notice my heart skipping a beat.

"Sooo," I said breathlessly, "how's your ankle?"

"Fucking fantastic, I'd say."

We laughed as he rolled off of me.

"Ouch, what the—" He unearthed my laptop from under the covers, rubbing his shoulder where the corner had made contact. "What were you doing with this in bed? It's late, Rach."

I laughed. Leave it to Pres to have an incredible orgasm and immediately start correcting people before he even got his clothes back on.

I rolled my eyes and grinned as he carefully sat it on my bedside table and smoothed my sheets. "I'm not taking notes from you. If I were in your bed, I bet I'd find your tablet *and* phone."

"Ah, so it's a competition," he joked, smirking over his shoulder as he disappeared in the bathroom. After we'd switched places and I walked out, his pants were already on and he was buttoning his shirt.

"Well," I said, struggling to find the right words for *thanks for the best orgasm of my life.* "I appreciate your coming by tonight."

He laughed dryly. "Oh, you're welcome."

I pulled on a shirt and sat on the edge of my bed. He sat next to me, and he looked so serious and put-together, I had a hard time believing we'd just done what we'd done. Except my body still was kind of not over it.

We didn't do this sort of wrap-up after hooking up.

Usually, a phone would buzz, a team member would appear, a calendar reminder would pull us away. It was all laughs and jokes, a thrilling sneaking around feeling, fixing an errant tie in a closet, smoothing my hair in his office, silly, quick, light ways to tie the moment up neatly.

It made sense to keep it that way, our fling tidily bookmarked between when I was his real assistant and his fake girlfriend.

But here in my tiny apartment lit up by thrifted twinkle lights, I was unsure of my next move or what he wanted, and if it was close to what I wanted.

"Do you have to be somewhere early tomorrow?"

He smirked. "That question doesn't quite work when you manage my calendar."

I smiled wryly. "I guess I'll see you bright and early tomorrow morning at your place—"

"What were you doing on it?"

I cocked my head, confused.

"Your laptop. What were you working on this late?"

"Oh," I said, shaking my head. "Nothing. It's—"

"Personal?"

I laughed. "Well, it's not work-related."

He reached out, gently tracing lines against my thigh, his touch drawing a map only he'd know.

"I'm not here for work-related purposes."

He leaned down, his mouth picking up where he'd left off, and pushed up my shirt, his tongue skating over my ribcage, sending decadent and distracting shivers across my skin.

I exhaled a slow breath. "I was just playing around. Middletown University application stuff," I said with an uncontrolled laugh as he nipped and licked his way to my chest.

He moved lazily, like he had all the time in the world. Like out of everything he could be doing, this is where he wanted to be.

"I have three degrees." He said this nonchalantly, more focused on flicking his tongue against my skin.

"So it is a competition."

He laughed lightly, his mouth finding mine to kiss me deeply. "I could help you."

I shook my head as he ran his fingers through my hair, stroking my locks in a ridiculously soothing way. "That's not necessary. It's not real."

"Do you do that a lot?" he asked, his voice warm, destined to unlock something very serious from my heart. "Pretend you don't want something when you do?"

Why is now the right time? Who do you want to be? Maybe those college essays were more applicable than I'd thought.

"You want the truth?"

"Yeah, Rach. Truth," he said, like we were making another deal or adding another layer to Truth Chicken. No points, no skips, no backing out.

"Honestly, yeah," I said without thinking, "I do."

"You take care of everyone," he said, his breath skating over my chest, his gentle lips drawing a moan from my throat. "Who takes care of you, Rach?"

I didn't know how to answer, so I closed my eyes.

"You believe in everything and everyone," he continued. "But what about yourself?"

When I opened my eyes, he gave me a soft smile that hit me right then, right there, right in the heart.

This was the most intense, most erotic weirdly post-sex foreplay I'd ever experienced.

He was on top of me now, his mouth at my neck, his hands in my hair, our legs intertwined. I felt consumed by him, in far too deep, far too fast, and all I wanted to do was tell him everything. Then I wanted to know him inside and out, too, trace the lines of his body like he did to me, learn what made his heart beat hard, hear his secrets, spill all mine in return.

He pulled back, eyes bright and playful, tone serious.

"I must've missed the guest bedroom during the tour."

I laughed and laid facing him. This close, he looked happy and tired and like someone I could really get used to. He reached out, tracing delicate, small circles against my wrist, as I threaded my hand through his hair.

"Careful," I whispered, "we're getting very close to cuddling territory."

He smiled, soft and sweet, and moved his fingers up, gently taking off my shirt as my fingers went to his shirt buttons, both of us in sync, not needing jokes or games to move forward.

He kissed me first, or maybe I did, it was hard to keep the scales so carefully balanced all the time, and then we were down to our underwear, his arms around my waist, my arms around his shoulders, our legs tangled, just us under the covers, together.

CHAPTER TWENTY-THREE

I woke up with a start, knowing this was my one chance to seem composed, cool, and casual.

The morning after sex *and* staying over meant I needed to make the *exact right* impression.

Everything would hinge on these first few minutes.

I peeked over my shoulder.

Pres was fully awake, squinting at his phone and looking absolutely gorgeous, all chiseled and shirtless sexy angles. And, well, my phone charger had managed to get tangled in my hair.

"Oh, good, you're awake," he said as I struggled to discreetly pull the cord from my thick mane. "You were dead asleep for so long, I started to become concerned."

When he turned to place his phone to the side, I hastily yanked out a fairly sizable chunk of my hair with my cord. Quickly, I chucked both to the floor then sat up with a demure smile, hoping I looked prim, proper, and sexy, like someone out of the movies.

His face lit up, and he took my hand.

"I've been waiting to tell you something, Rach."

Oh wow, I was totally nailing this.

I *was* cool, calm, and collected.

Endless romantic notions popped into my head.

"Did you know that you snore?"

I opened then closed my mouth at a loss for words.

He actually looked *excited* about this discovery.

"Remember I'd guessed that in the grocery store?"

I covered my face with my hands. "Please tell me you're joking and just really bad at being funny."

He laughed. "I am bad at being funny. But I'm not joking. I couldn't believe it when it first happened. I've never heard such a sound."

"I am *mortified*." I threw off the covers, already planning my escape. "I'm leaving. Never coming back."

"This is your place, Rach."

"You can have it. I'll find a replacement assistant as soon as possible. I've got to assume a new identity in another town."

He laughed and reached for me before I could run away. "No, I liked it. It was like a white noise machine. I slept better than I have in years."

"*Pres*," I groaned. "These are not compliments."

He looked confused. "But I mean them positively."

"How has no one ever told me this before? Actually, don't answer, because it's definitely just that you're way too honest for your own good. I'll go ahead and add Snoregate on top of my Boobgate legacy."

He grinned and rolled his eyes. "I'm taking it as a sign that you slept well with me. Right? Isn't that how you view the world?"

"Did you wait for me to wake up just to tell me this awful fact? I'm starting to get the whole unlikable thing."

"No, I waited to give you this," he said, passing me my mug with a grumpy frog saying *I Toadally Need Coffee* on it. "I've attempted coffee."

I tried not to look too shocked. "You made me coffee?"

"Yes," he said somberly. "However, it is terrible."

"I'm sure that's not *toadally* true," I said just to make

him groan.

"You have a very strange collection of mugs and an alarming amount of Tupperware, which proved to be distracting," Pres grumbled. "I was unsettled."

"It can't be that bad."

"It really can."

I took a sip.

It was the worst cup of coffee I'd ever had in my life.

But I didn't care because it was also the kindest cup of coffee I'd ever received.

"It really is the thought that counts," I said with a smile I couldn't contain.

He frowned, but he only looked more adorable. Then he headed to my bathroom, saying he was using my shower because I owed him one — "two actually!" he called over his shoulder.

So I sat my awful coffee aside and introduced him to the wonders of my small shower, both of us elbowing each other, laughing, and groaning until we gave up and had a quickie against the sink.

Afterward, he slapped on a nicotine patch he kept in his wallet and slipped on his clothes from last night.

He grinned. "So if this wasn't a booty call then this isn't a walk of shame, right?"

I laughed. "I don't think it's possible to do a walk of shame in Hugo Boss. And don't you drive a Mercedes S-Class?"

He laughed, smoothed his wrinkled jacket, and kissed me. "I really should go."

"Right, you have a television appearance soon," I said, clearly recalling his calendar. I especially knew when he'd be on air so I could give his office a wide breadth.

"Yeah, and they normally go better when the person is

properly clothed."

I shrugged. "Not in my experience."

He laughed loudly. "I'll see you soon for our team meeting though."

"I'll bring the coffee."

"What would I do without you, pumpkin," he said with a grin, swiftly kissing me before leaving.

As he left, I was positive I'd never truly understand how we'd gotten here — or if I could even point out *here* on a map. It had started because I'd pretended to be someone at an event I didn't belong, and as I watched him walk away, back to business, back to reality, I couldn't help but wonder if it could ever be different.

...

One time could have been chalked up to a mistake.

Two times could have been a coincidence.

But by the third time Pres stayed over at my place, it was looking like a pattern.

After whatever PR thing we'd have — slipping on our boyfriend-girlfriend personas with ease — we'd end up back at my place, stripping off suits and dresses as he led us to my bed, teasing me until I was begging for more. It was all fun and games, an easy way to blow off steam.

We both understood we had to get our fill before this ended, and I was happy to play a symbiotic role in the future mayor's dirty thoughts and demanding sex drive.

And on the mornings after, he'd slip out early to get started on work or go on a run. By the time I'd wake for the day, the only sign it had even happened was a to-go coffee from around the corner replacing where the box of condoms had rested the night before.

It was all so casual, such a simple decision we'd made so effortlessly that I wondered if all flings worked like this. If by already knowing the end, you were free to enjoy yourself. If you were in total control of the outcome — such a Pres-way of thinking about it, I realized — you could just have fun playing the game.

Fake dates, real sex, who knew.

But then I'd walk into my bathroom and see a toothbrush next to mine. It was nothing, I reminded myself, just a piece of plastic and some bristles, something he'd probably picked up at the same corner store he got his nicotine patches.

I knew it didn't mean anything.

If I'd bothered to ask Pres about it, posed the question as serious as a college application essay — *What does a guy leaving his toothbrush behind mean?* — he would have asked how else was he supposed to brush his teeth. It was as rational as his reading glasses perched on my bedside table, his phone charger near my couch, a packet of nicotine gum resting next to my coffee pot.

I would have nodded, gotten that it was meaningless.

Of course, it all made logical sense.

It was as convenient as sleeping with your real assistant and fake girlfriend.

My head understood.

But my heart wouldn't listen.

Because the toothbrush felt momentous, deliberately, delicately balanced on my sink like it was meant to be.

So casual. Right.

...

Olivia actually looked frightened, and Jamar was confused. Ethan was the only one who didn't seem fazed because he was too busy scowling.

"You didn't get these, Rach?" Jamar asked, nodding to

the doughnuts and bagels invitingly spread out on the dining table. "You don't know what they're for?"

When we had all arrived, they had already been here. And everyone stood far away as if they were delicious explosives.

"No, I have no clue," I said, scrambling to pull up Pres' calendar. He'd left my place early, per usual, but he wasn't in the penthouse, which just added to everyone's confusion. "There's nothing on here about a meeting. I don't know—"

Ethan scoffed. "Isn't your whole job to know his schedule? Is it really that hard?"

"Yes, and I do," I said evenly, holding back from informing him that Pres had literally been inside me like eight hours ago — and yeah, it really had been *that* hard. "Nothing on his calendar means nothing is scheduled."

But it didn't explain the doughnuts and bagels.

"Are we allowed to eat them? Are they for a photo shoot? They look really good," Olivia said longingly.

"No, they're probably some sort of test," Jamar said hurriedly. "Pres wants to see which ones we choose—"

"Okay, that's a little out there," I said with a laugh although part of me could imagine it. "Let me track him down, and I'll ask what their purpose is—"

The elevator door opened, and we all rushed to see Pres step out, carrying a coffee carafe.

"Oh," he said, startled. "Is something wrong?"

"Did I forget something?" I asked, taking the coffee from him. "I don't have any morning meetings on my calendar. There wasn't anything in your inbox—"

"What do we need to be prepared for?" Ethan interrupted. "Who's coming?"

Pres looked even more confused. "What?"

"The food in the dining room. None of us brought it."

"Oh, yeah." He shrugged, walking past us toward his office. "I picked it up. Enjoy."

"What's the angle?" Ethan demanded. "We already have a meeting with the small business owners' association. Are you trying to win one of them over in advance? Personally, I think that vegan one covered in tattoos and piercings is going to be a problem."

"Nope, no angle," Pres said over his shoulder and shut his office door without another word.

We all stared at each other, not sure what we'd just experienced.

"He brought us food … to be nice," Olivia said slowly, still confused. "Is he okay? Yesterday, he said I was doing a really great job. I'd assumed he was being sarcastic."

"Me too! He said he appreciated all my hard work," Jamar said. "He said he should've been saying that for a long time now."

Ethan turned to me, shaking his head.

"Unacceptable. Just because you're playing around like his girlfriend doesn't mean you can slack off like one. *He's* not supposed to be running *errands*. If you can't even pick up doughnuts, what *can* you do?"

I rolled my eyes. "Oh my gosh, please shut up."

"You can't talk to me like that," Ethan warned.

I shrugged. "Consider it one of the few things I *can* do. If you'll excuse me, I'm going to set out this coffee."

He was so shocked that he actually did manage to stop talking. I helped myself to a bagel and coffee, and after a moment, Olivia followed me, laughing as she sat down.

"Someone really needed to say that."

Jamar trickled in after. "That was, and this is," he said, holding up a doughnut, "incredible. Thank you, Rach."

I shook my head. "I promise, I wasn't behind this. This was all Pres."

Jamar gave me a knowing look. "Exactly. The 'thank you' still stands."

I looked down at my coffee, hoping my cheeks weren't as red as they felt. Thankfully, my VIP inbox pinged, distracting me from having this conversation.

Need you. Office? -p

My cheeks not being red was definitely out of the question now. I quickly grabbed my things and ignored what seemed like Jamar and Olivia exchanging a look.

When I walked into Pres' office, Ethan was wrapping up a conversation on a policy talking point, so I busied myself with organizing his mail.

"Oh, how did that Middletown University networking dinner go? Your assistant neglected to tell me about it, so I apologize I wasn't there to support."

"I ditched it and made out with Rach on the steps instead," Pres said flatly. I turned to the window, holding back a laugh, as Ethan chuckled at the idea.

"Well, let me know if I should follow up with anyone you met. I'd love to get some time on your calendar to discuss Phase Two campaign items. We need to think big strategy, see how we can better leverage your father. I'd be honored to get one-on-one time with him—"

"If you need to be on my schedule," Pres said, facing his computer, his go-to signal that he was done with the conversation, "Rach is the one you ask. And if you'd like to speak to my father, you can contact his assistant. Thanks, Ethan."

When the door closed, I burst into laughter.

"I can't believe you told him we made out! What if he'd believed you?"

"People believe what they want to believe. Ethan is incapable of seeing me as anyone other than an extension of Senator St. Clair. And no one wants to envision my father making out with anyone," Pres added with a shudder.

I laughed and handed him a bagel. "So what's up with the food?"

He shrugged. "I was hungry. Smoking cessation causes an increased appetite."

I grinned skeptically at his formality. "Hungry enough for enough food to feed your team?"

"I'm an overachiever," he said dryly, such a secretly sweet prickly pear.

I laughed, and we moved to work. Most of what we went over was standard stuff until he said there was a birthday party he was obligated to throw.

"Sable mentioned it a while ago as a good PR thing. She believes it'll make me look more approachable and friendly. Nice guy hosts birthday party." He looked sheepish. "I kind of forgot about it."

"Kind of?"

"More accurately, I'd say entirely. I didn't think of it again until I saw the date, and … it's tomorrow."

I gasped. "Pres, you forgot you were supposed to throw someone a birthday party until the day before?"

"It's fine," he said calmly. "We can have it here, so no need to worry about a venue. There's barely anything else to do, right?"

I inhaled sharply. "Invites, decorations, servers, food, alcohol—"

"Oh, I already sent out the invites. This website lets you send electronic invites, so I uploaded the list," he said, pulling up the e-vite. "It'll save you time because they just RSVP directly here. That's helpful, right?"

I stared at the screen and then back at him.

"You sent this out?"

He looked at the invite, not seeing anything wrong.

Other than the address and time, all it said was, "*It's a birthday party.*"

It didn't even say who was being celebrated.

"You couldn't manage an exclamation point?"

"I added a color."

"Navy. You added a pop of *navy* on top of plain white. And it's in twelve-point Times New Roman."

"That's … the font you're supposed to use?" he said, genuinely confused. "I've literally never used a different font in my life."

I laughed. "Oh, Pres. You're adorable."

He frowned. "I was trying to be helpful. When we were at the university, you said you were busy."

I nodded, my heart melting even more. "Okay, I can take care of the rest. As long as you're not too married to any sort of theme or food selection."

He shrugged. "I couldn't care less. I trust you, Rach, so whatever you think needs to be done, do it. Don't stress about this, though. It's just for show. It's not important."

I nodded, almost feeling sorry for his friend. But knowing Pres, this probably wasn't even a real friend, just someone influential who needed to be impressed.

"Got it."

"Oh, and you can use this card," he said, pulling out his wallet to hand me an Amex black card.

My eyes widened.

This was an invite-only credit card, yet another reminder that Pres was lightyears out of my league.

"It has a higher limit than the one my assistants use,"

he said simply, distracted by a headline on the news.

I didn't move.

He looked back at me, confused by my hesitation.

Not a higher limit. No limit.

"I can't … take this."

"Yes, you can. You know I have a board meeting at PSC Healthcare all day tomorrow, so I won't need it."

I shook my head.

He squinted at me. "What am I missing about this situation?"

"It's just a big deal."

"No, it's not. It's like the matches. You had them, I didn't, I needed them, you gave them. That's why we're a power couple, snookie."

I rolled my eyes at his terrible pet name and the idea that a free book of matches I'd swiped from a hotel was equivalent to this. He reached it out again, slightly impatient, so I slowly took it.

The metal card felt much heavier in my palm than it really was because it weighed like unlimited possibilities and the amount of trust he had in me.

Holding this suddenly made things feel more real. But just as my heart fluttered, my stomach sank, wondering if he'd so casually hand this over if he knew the Rach he trusted was the daughter of a convict.

He turned back to his computer. "Oh, look, a couple people already said yes to my invite. That's fun."

I patted his shoulder. "Well, the invite was great."

He cut me a quick, unamused look.

I laughed. "Do you need anything else?"

"No, thank you," he said, catching my wrist as I stepped away. He pressed a quick kiss against my palm, making my heart feel tangled and confused, and then turned back to his computer.

I paused at the door, having one last thought.

"What kind of cake should I get for tomorrow?"

He looked at me like it had never occurred to him to consider a cake as an essential part of a birthday.

"Vanilla with vanilla icing?"

I made a face.

"What?"

"Are you sure? That's the most basic cake option. Shouldn't a birthday cake have more … pizzazz?"

"Well, what kind of cake do *you* like? Funfetti with extra sprinkles?" He rolled his eyes when my face lit up, but a hint of a smile appeared on his lips. "Okay. Sprinkles. Fun. That's fine." He turned back to his computer.

"Extra sprinkles?"

He sighed heavily, but it didn't quite cover up his smile. "Yes. All of the sprinkles."

I turned to walk out, figuring if he was going to make vanilla decisions, I really would just handle the rest.

"Oh. And, Rach," he cleared his throat, "would you be my date?"

If I hadn't spent so much time listening to him closely, mesmerized by his way, I wouldn't have noticed how his tone sounded slightly different.

Like he was really asking, a twinge of self-doubt in his voice, like there was a chance I'd say no.

I smiled, trying to think of a witty retort, something to keep it flirty and light, but instead I nodded and said honestly, "Yeah, I would love to be your date."

CHAPTER TWENTY-FOUR

I had exactly one hour to get ready for my real date with my fake boyfriend. Because planning a ritzy party for a stranger in 24 hours while simultaneously trying to impress my very particular, absent client actually took up a good portion of time.

Through a mixture of luck, the connections I'd made over the years, and a strategic dose of St. Clair name dropping, I'd managed to pull it off.

Subtle candles and fresh flowers dotted the penthouse with servers ready with appetizers and Champagne. The breakfast bar had been transformed into a full bar, and the terrace, which until recently only housed Pres' ashtray, was now lit up by bauble string lights, rented high top tables, and a smaller bar overlooking the city.

I'd even managed to get a waterfall balloon garland arch installed in navy, white, and gold because balloons were fun and apparently the theme of this birthday party was navy.

Even Ethan couldn't come up with something negative to say when he walked inside.

"Can you hold down the fort?" I asked, rushing to grab the elevator. "I'll be right back."

"Whoa, no," he said, slapping his hand to stop the door. "I'm not doing your job for you."

"I've done everything. I'll be back before the cake is

delivered. I just need to get ready. You don't have to do anything but stand here."

I was not about to show up to what felt like our first real date in worn jeans and a faded button-up.

"You want me to just … stand here?"

I was reminded of my first fake date when Ethan had said I'd be most useful by being a wallflower.

I could forgive, but I didn't forget.

So I said, "I think Pres would prefer if you stayed out of the way. If someone shows up, feel free to talk or network. Maybe mention how great he is. Your choice."

I smiled at my reflection as the elevator door closed on his stunned expression.

While I didn't have time to go back to my place to change, I'd thought I could buy a dress from a boutique on Pres' street. I was excited to wear something I actually owned and had chosen instead of thrifted or borrowed dresses and work clothes.

But it wasn't until I'd scoped out some price tags that I realized I was still very much out of my league.

"Anything I can help you with?" a sales associate asked, probably thinking I actually belonged here because I'd walked in with a ridiculous amount of now rapidly dwindling confidence.

"Just browsing," I said, scanning the store for the fastest exit route.

"Shopping for something in particular?"

"Just a party. And maybe a date. But we're not, like, together or anything," I added. "I mean, not *really*. Honestly, it's pretty complicated."

"We just got in some exquisite cocktail dresses," she said, guiding me from the exit to show me several little black dresses. Such little material for such big price tags.

"You'll definitely know if you're on a date or not after wearing this," she said, plucking out a sleek midi-length bodycon dress with a deep V-cut neckline.

I laughed and shook my head. I liked it. I really liked it. But it was more than what I made in a week.

"I think I need something more basic. Maybe a skirt? I can probably get by with the top I already have on."

She gave me a pitying look then pointed to the shop's corner. "Maybe the sales section is more your style."

I swallowed down the frustration forming a lump in my throat and made my way to the back.

Heat crawled up my neck as years' worth of shame built up tightly in my chest. Years of not fitting in and being judged for it, years of wishing things could be different, that I could be enough without needing the costumes, the status, the power, the money to feel like I could be a part of something.

It took all my willpower to not pull out my wallet and just do it — make a reckless mistake just to *prove* I was worth it.

I paused when I thought about what was in my wallet. Pres' Amex black card.

I could make this problem — this suffocating feeling that always lingered no matter how hard I pretended — go away with a flick of the wrist.

It was *right there*, and all I had to do was hand it over with a smile to get what I wanted. I had enough practice now that I knew I could do it effortlessly. To remove this woman's judgement, to wow Pres' guests, to make Pres truly believe I belonged, that I could be someone special with him for real.

He didn't even pay his own credit card bills. I handled that. He'd just sign off on whatever I'd tell him. I could buy multiple dresses if I wanted, have an outfit change just like he'd joked when we'd first met.

I could make *everything* a reality — renovate my apartment, buy a better coffee pot, get my own pair of Louboutins, tune up my car, maybe even figure out a way to sneak tuition fees or textbook costs if I applied to Middletown University. I could swipe this card bit by bit until I'd taken my fill. He'd never know. He trusted me.

A whole new life was *right here,* literally at my fingertips.

I could so easily picture it that I gasped and stepped back, dropping my wallet on the floor with a loud smack.

"Everything okay?" the sales associate asked.

I had to get out of here.

"Sorry," I said quickly, my heart racing at what I'd just thought. How easily it had come to me. Was this how my mom felt? Was this how it started? Was I destined to become her regardless of how hard I tried?

I rushed out of the store, struggling to breathe, and ran smack into Jamar and Olivia.

"Oh gosh, I'm so sorry!"

"Hey, are you okay?" Jamar asked, offering his hand.

"Can you tell Pres I can't make it? I need to go home. I don't belong here. I don't know what I'm doing—"

They exchanged worried glances. "Pres will move past firing and have us offed if we relay that message."

"Yeah, plus, you totally belong," Olivia said, confused. "Did something happen in that store?"

"I can't wear this outfit. I don't have anything to wear. You all look great, by the way," I said, forcing brightness in my voice. "You're going to have a great night."

"Let us help you," Olivia said, shaking her head at my attempt at a distraction. "Come on."

With a firmness I didn't know she possessed, she walked me back into the store with Jamar on my other side. The sales associate looked up, surprised.

"Hi, this is my friend, Rach, and she needs a dress," Olivia said unwaveringly. She glanced my way. "What's your budget?"

"I don't have a budget."

"And her budget is unlimited!" Olivia declared.

"Oh gosh, no, I meant I have virtually no money to spend on this," I whispered quickly.

"And her budget is limited, and we'd like to be directed to your best deals," Olivia corrected without batting an eye. "And do you offer student discounts?"

I glanced at Jamar, who looked just as shocked. Then, without meaning to, I cracked a smile. Suddenly, we were all laughing as Olivia dragged us to the sales section. Suddenly, this little corner didn't seem so sad now.

"Well, that was embarrassing," Olivia said through her giggles and shrugged. "Oh, this is cute."

She and Jamar flipped through the options seriously, conferring and debating like they were in a meeting.

"This plays up the boob factor."

"But Rach is also tall, so we can assume she has nice legs. This may accentuate those assets better."

"We literally have data on her boobs. That's what we should be optimizing for."

I covered my mouth, still laughing, truly grateful for these little nerds who'd become such a part of my world.

"Okay, I vote these two," Olivia said after a moment. Jamar nodded in agreement.

One was a long, form-fitting strapless black dress with a low-back and a thigh-high slit. The other was a short, silk black dress with a cowl neck, spaghetti straps, and a slightly fitted skirt.

They were being so nice, I couldn't bear to refuse to try them on even though I'd already determined the price was still too high to blow on a one-time thing. Just like the temporary man I was currently enjoying, it was fun, but unrealistic. Neither dress nor Pres would fit into my life after I faced facts and the ruse ended.

I studied myself in the mirror, soaking in how different I looked. How different things could have been.

Then I put my clothes back on, tied my hair into a sensible ponytail, and decided it was time to go home.

"Which did you like best?" Olivia asked.

"They were both nice. The short one, probably."

"Okay, get that one," Jamar said. "Our treat."

I shook my head. "No, I can't let you two—"

"We already decided," Olivia said firmly.

Jamar nodded. "We want to do something nice. You're nice all the time. You deserve a little bit in return."

"This is too much," I said in disbelief. "Just save me the next last doughnut or something."

"Rach, you saved my job," Olivia said, placing a hand on my shoulder. "Don't you remember? Pres was *pissed*. He basically fired me until you stepped in."

I shook my head. "He was just caught off guard. He wouldn't have meant it."

"He would've done it," she said with a short laugh. "I've seen him fire countless people. He's not someone who reverses a decision once he's made up his mind."

"Anyone would have stepped up to save your job."

"No, just you, Rach. You're the only one who did."

"I didn't do it to get a dress. I did it because it was the right thing to do. You don't owe me anything."

Jamar took the dresses, and I exhaled in relief.

But instead of returning them to the rack, he headed to the register, speaking over his shoulder.

"I've known Pres for four years, and I've heard him laugh more in the past three months than in all those years. Only one thing has changed. So yes," he said firmly, "we will help you. Because of that. Because you make a difference. Because you're kind without asking for anything in return. Because you're one of us. Because we're your friends. Not because we owe you."

The tears that appeared in my eyes surprised me, and I quickly smiled, choking out a quick thank you. It wasn't exactly how I expected to get a dress of my own, but I couldn't have been more grateful.

"Plus, it'll be fun to see Pres try to not check you out when he sees you in this," Olivia whispered as the sales associate rang us up with a tight smile. "He does a pretty good job pretending."

They both dissolved into laughter as they settled the transaction, whispering jokes about their boss that I didn't feel like I should really hear, so I ducked back into the dressing room to change.

I beamed in the mirror, looking at myself from all angles, wondering if it was at all possible this could be real.

...

"I can fix this," I rushed to say as soon as the elevator door opened in the lobby and Pres walked up.

Mostly everyone had already arrived upstairs when he'd texted that he was here. At the exact moment, it hit me that if Pres was the host of this shindig and if I were playing the role of girlfriend, I should probably know who the party was for.

And because I was his assistant and had put it all

together, I really probably shouldn't have *completely* forgotten to ask that very important detail until the cake was delivered.

It was massive, three towering tiers of funfetti and tons of sprinkles … and no name.

"I'm going to run out to the store to grab icing. I'm sure I can pipe a name, right? I've got strong wrists, you know, because of the knitting, so surely that'll translate into piping. I'll practice in your office first on a plate so no one will see me."

He stopped in his tracks when he saw me, blocking the elevator door.

"The cake," I hurriedly explained and tugged on my coat. "There's no name on it. I was so focused on pulling this off, I didn't even ask whose birthday it is. I guess the silver lining is if everyone leaves because this is the worst party in the world, at least we'll have a bunch of cake to ourselves." I inhaled sharply. "Oh no, was I supposed to get a gift on your behalf or was the party the gift?"

"Rach, stop," he said, guiding me back into the elevator. "I'm much more interested in your dress than whatever birthday fiasco may or may not occur."

"This is a big deal."

"No," he murmured, slowly slipping my coat off my shoulders and pressing his lips against my skin, "it's not."

"I've ruined someone's birthday."

His mouth made its way up to my neck, kissing me so softly that I had to close my eyes and tip my head back, giving him more access. "You really haven't."

"Yes," I half-groaned, half-moaned, trying to stay focused. "This is one of those instances where you're supposed to care. Be a good, likable person."

He laughed, crowding me against the wall. "I have no

interest in any of that when you're in this dress."

In addition to solving these problems, I now really had to find some time to exuberantly thank Jamar and Olivia.

"*Pres.*"

The elevator dinged. He groaned and stepped back, smoothing his jacket. I hadn't even noticed we'd gone back up.

"I don't care about cake. I don't care about a gift," he said, suddenly apprehensive. "And also I'm very sorry."

"Sorry?"

"When I realized you didn't realize, I should have been honest. But you already seemed stressed about doing this in a day, which was my fault. I didn't want to add to it. I may have miscalculated."

I opened my mouth to ask for clarification when the door slid open and everyone shouted at once—

"Happy birthday, Pres!"

CHAPTER TWENTY-FIVE

"It's not your birthday."

Our first real date and it was at a fake birthday.

Pres squinted at me then glanced at the crowd behind us. It had finally broken up enough so we could confer under the pretense of getting a drink.

"It appears that it is," he said solemnly.

"I'm your assistant. I buy your plane tickets. I know for a fact that it's not your birthday. I mean, you're so obviously a Capricorn, and we're in Sagittarius season."

He nodded slowly, not following that last part.

"The fact is, Rach, no one actually cares when my birthday is. To most people, the idea of celebrating when a planetary body completed its orbit around the Sun at the same time I was born is irrelevant."

"See, that's such a Capricorn thing to say!"

"I am sorry I didn't clarify with you though," he said seriously. "Once I realized you didn't know we were talking about *my* party, I figured you'd be more stressed if you knew. I was trying to be helpful in theory, but it's possible I'm not excellent at it in practice yet."

I shook my head. I wasn't mad — of course I wasn't, he was right, I would've totally freaked if I'd known I'd been planning *his* surprise birthday party, fake or not.

"But you do realize this is bizarre, right?" I said, glancing around the room. It was filled with people, and not one person seemed to know this wasn't real.

He sighed deeply. "Actually, yes. Sable was adamant throwing a birthday party would be a good PR boost before my announcement. Something about opening people up to my home and personal life," he said with an eye roll. "And my ridiculously distracting assistant has been telling me to be more open to my team's ideas. But I'm busy on my actual birthday, so here we are."

"So today is your birthday because of a scheduling conflict?" I said flatly, doing my best to hold back a laugh. "You've managed to find a way to literally control time?"

He laughed, a mix of delight and relief, loud enough to draw even more attention to himself.

He grinned. "I do owe you for pulling this off. It's better than I could've imagined. Let me get you a drink."

"I don't mind getting my own."

He shook his head, his voice firm. "No, you've done enough. Let's pretend you aren't my assistant tonight."

I smiled. "So I'm just your date, Just Rach?"

"Which means I'll do anything you ask, Just Rach," he whispered, his voice low and rumbly against my ear. "I want to get on my knees for you."

I shivered, steadying my flaming features as he turned and smoothly shook hands with an approaching guest.

Then he introduced me easily: "This is my girlfriend and host extraordinaire, Rach Montgomery."

I was used to him saying it — it'd been a practiced line between us for months, and we'd already agreed it meant nothing — but tonight, I allowed myself to feel the rush it gave me as if it were true.

In his penthouse, in the middle of an event I'd planned, in a dress that was all mine, where I knew every detail, including the guest of honor more than everyone else, I felt giddy, powerful, confident, and in control. For the first time, I felt like I belonged more than anyone.

And Pres just seemed to be enjoying whispering dirty things to me between talking politely to his guests. I wondered how he'd poll if the people of Middletown knew their future mayor was an absolute tease who got off on delayed gratification.

He definitely had my vote.

"You're ignoring everyone," I pointed out as he refreshed my drink in the kitchen. The room was closed off to guests, but he didn't care. Instead, he was focused on making a little dish of mini-quiches, smoked salmon crostinis, and baked brie with figs and pistachios off a tray waiting to be passed around.

Seeing Pres balance a tray and carefully arrange hors d'oeuvres for me did something funny in my chest. I suddenly had the urge to push him against the counter and kiss him until that silly suit of his was on the floor.

He rolled his eyes. "It's my birthday—"

"Not your birthday."

"—I can ignore whomever I'd like. Do you want to play a game? Truth," he paused dramatically, "or Dare."

I laughed. "Sure. I choose Truth."

"I *knew* you would," he said, sipping his drink triumphantly.

Pres had admitted in Truth Chicken that he avoided alcohol, especially red wine, because — in addition to being a control freak — it could trigger his migraines. But now, powered by vodka soda or maybe by an event where he was the center of attention without actually having to be present, he seemed lighter and much flirtier.

"You know me so well," I teased.

He laughed and examined me through his glass.

"Truth is easier, I think," he said, still musing, "when you trust the person you're telling it to."

I wondered which Rach he saw filtered through crystal and rainbow refractions, and if he liked her as much as I liked the guy in the kitchen holding the half-full glass.

"Okay, so Truth," he said, back to business, "would you ever let me pay for your schooling?"

I choked on my drink, more surprised by this than his soft sentiment on truth.

"Oh gosh," I said, trying to delicately clear my throat without sounding like a startled donkey. "Pres, that's… I'm not even applying. I mean, I'm still working on my essays, but there's no guarantee I'd get in … and even though that's generous, really so nice, I wouldn't feel comfortable … it's too much—"

He nodded. "That's what I'd predicted you'd say. Maybe with less coughing though. Now choose Dare."

"That's not how this game works."

He pulled a pouty face. "But it's my birthday."

I rolled my eyes, mocking his signature frown, but glad to move on from the topic. "Fine, Dare."

He peeked into the other room then faced me, eyes bright. "There's an older woman standing next to a potted plant, which I didn't know I owned, did you buy me plants? She's wearing a navy blazer and awful shoes."

"You want me to steal her shoes?"

He burst out laughing. "No, I dare you to talk to her. She's the Dean of Middletown University's Honors College."

I squinted at him, confused. "You … want me to set up a meeting with her for you?"

"Are you aware of the Jefferson Fellowship?"

"Yeah, it's the full-ride scholarship for the best and

brightest students. You …" I paused, but couldn't help but laugh. "You got it, Pres. You're still on their website. You were a *major* hottie in college."

He frowned, looking very concerned. "Am I not a major hottie now?"

I laughed at how serious and indignant he could sound even when saying "hottie."

"Seriously, Rach, meet with her, make a good impression, and apply for the fellowship."

"You really are so bossy."

He smiled. "Only when I know I'm right. The power of her positively associating your name as she reviews applications is significant. It increases your chances."

"My chances? I'm not a statistician, and I definitely don't understand probability—"

"Lucky for you, I am and I do," he said swiftly. "The probability of you getting into Middletown is unknown. The unknown is scary, but it's not impossible. But if you don't apply, it's guaranteed zero. And you deserve better than zero. You get to be in control of your own future. I don't know how to control fate, so I can only tell you the truth. You're smart enough, talented enough, all the enoughs, and more. I invited her hoping you'd meet. And I dare you to give yourself a chance."

I peeked at her. In this crowd, around these powerful, connected people, at a sort of event I'd done ten times over, she didn't seem so intimidating.

I turned back to Pres, stunned.

"You invited her to your birthday just in hopes I'd meet her?"

He shrugged, and I could have sworn he looked embarrassed. "It's not technically my birthday, so no."

I laughed, thinking this might possibly be the nicest

thing someone had ever tempted fate with for me.

"Okay." I nodded, glancing back at her. "I'll meet her. What's our play? The angle?"

I turned to look at him when he didn't answer.

He was watching me, a small smile on his face. "You don't need to play games to make a good impression, Rach. You should be yourself."

"Which version? One that polls the best?"

"You," he said, brushing his fingers over my cheek and pressing a small kiss against my forehead, "just you. You as yourself. The best version."

...

We first bonded over hors d'oeuvres then somehow naturally and elegantly segued to the university. When I'd mentioned I'd fallen in love with the campus when I'd toured it with Pres, the Dean perked up even more. After all these months of hobnobbing, this was almost *easy*.

Even when she recognized me from Boobgate, embarrassed immediately after she blurted it out. I reassured her it happened all the time, joking my boobs had the special power to bring people together.

It was at that exact moment Pres walked up.

"Well," he said seriously, his smile never breaking as he refreshed our Champagne flutes from a bottle I was certain he'd taken from a server just to do this, "I see you've appropriately met Rach."

He then spent a significant amount of time building me up. I watched him, amused, surprised, and flattered, realizing we'd switched roles.

He played the part of supportive boyfriend perfectly.

Throughout the night, we'd get separated, but people seemed to know who I was anyway. Boobgate preceded me, Pres' Instagram had introduced me, and he seemed to be mentioning me in his own separate conversations.

The facts that he'd share were not what I'd expected. He wasn't crafting the image of Perfect Girlfriend Rach.

Instead, I was someone who was astrology-obsessed, a crafty, excellent knitter, good at trivia, "hilarious" — *except the puns*, someone said, playfully mocking Pres' deadpan voice — down-to-earth, steadfast, passionate, and caring about others.

"He said I must meet you," said multiple people. "It almost felt like a directive."

And I found myself branching out, no longer at the fringes, becoming the sort of woman who could chat and laugh with strangers on her own right.

Pres would always find his way back to my side, switching between flirting, dissecting how my meeting with the Dean had gone, and strategizing how my follow-up email should be worded. He also took his self-imposed job of never letting my drink run out seriously.

So I'd become sufficiently buzzed by the time someone — I must have hired them with the cake — announced it was time to sing to the birthday boy.

Pres barely had time to smooth the prickly look that crossed his face before the massive, covered-in-*way*-too-many-multicolored-sprinkes funfetti cake was rolled out into the center of the room.

At some point, he'd slipped off his jacket and rolled up the sleeves of his button-up, but even that couldn't soften how serious he looked next to this ridiculous cake.

"I'm sorry," I mouthed across the room, barely holding back my fit of giggles. Everyone launched into singing, slightly sloshed off the free drinks, while he stood there, holding my gaze and smirking his secret, sexy smile.

"Make a wish!" someone called out.

"I wish this cake had more sprinkles," he said flatly, and I guffawed, not caring when everyone looked at me.

As the crowd thinned and the drinks ran low, I watched people stop him to shake his hand and chat.

He knew everyone, a mixture of college acquaintances, former colleagues, and clients, but I knew his body language to know this was Practiced, Perfect Pres.

My heart ached at the realization that he'd somehow built an entire life where he ended up lonely in a crowd.

Where he was surrounded by a room full of people to wish him a happy birthday, but no one close enough to know it wasn't real.

That he kept secrets hidden by sarcasm and small talk. That every part of his life looked poised and carefully curated, but he had confessions, too, pain points bigger than a quiet soccer field.

That maybe he and I weren't universes apart.

He caught my gaze from across the room, a warm smile appearing on his face.

I'd always wondered what it meant when someone kept their real smile hidden. Now I wondered what it meant if someone kept it reserved for just one person.

Because as I returned his smile, unable to pretend my heart wasn't pounding in my chest, I realized it was highly likely that I was falling in very real love with my fake boyfriend, my client, my date — everything that made up James Prescott St. Clair IV.

So I downed the rest of my drink, completely unsure of what to do with this information.

CHAPTER TWENTY-SIX

The clock struck midnight, the glittering Champagne glasses were packed away, and the crowd disappeared.

As the elevator closed on the final guests, I stood in Pres' living room, once again alone in a beautiful dress, uncertain of where I was headed.

But, for once, I knew exactly where I wanted to go.

"I thought I'd find you out here," I said as I stepped outside on the terrace. He was leaning against the railing, staring out into the sparkling landscape.

He turned and smiled, a soft, candy-sweet smile I felt all the way to my toes.

He had, much to my delight, ended up just as buzzed as me, his cheeks the absolute perfect shade of pink, his eyes just a little brighter, his laughs way too loud.

"It's over," he exhaled, pulling me into a tight hug. "Thank you so much, everyone is gone, it was wonderful, and I couldn't have done this without you."

I laughed, squeezing him back. "You really want to smoke, don't you?"

When he pulled back, his expression was grave. "I'd do anything for a cigarette."

"You could," I said with a shrug. "Just one, just once."

"It appears I'm quite terrible at one-time things," he said, turning to the moonlight. "Plus, you wouldn't."

"What do you mean?"

"You're the strongest person I know," he said, steadily meeting my gaze. A shiver ran through my body as he revealed yet another truth about myself I'd never considered. "You wouldn't give up or give in."

It wasn't an overly emotional statement, and it wasn't really a question either. Instead, he spoke like it was a fact, something he'd already decided, something proven.

Before I could respond, confusion crossed his face.

"Do I own those chairs?"

He nodded to where modern white patio furniture sat.

"Oh, I, uh, thought your place needed some … sprucing for guests."

"And the pillows on my couch and the patterned rug that is very pink…?"

"I also picked those up. And the blanket. That was actually free because I'd knitted it a while ago. And the plants were on sale at the store, and they looked so lonely. Your place is a little … bare. I felt it deserved a bit of life."

Amused, he smiled and took my hand, sinking down on the chair. I squeezed in next to him even though a perfectly acceptable matching chair sat next to his.

We were cramped, and without people and portable heaters, it was much too cold under the starry dark sky, our heated cheeks tingling against the frost. I never wanted to move.

"And the photos?"

I held my breath, positive I'd overstepped. Everything I'd done, from the pillows to the plants, had been as his assistant. But when I'd studied his place, decked out in ritzy decor and a few homey items for balance, I'd known something was missing. A little heart and soul.

So I'd had photos from his Instagram framed. To innocent onlookers, it sold our relationship. To Pres and his team, they were just pre-approved, staged photos that meant nothing.

Except the one he'd almost deleted.

The one of us in his kitchen, heads thrown back in laughter, hands brushing, bright smiles. I'd had a second copy made just for me, something to keep tucked away in my bedside table for when I wanted to warm my heart.

I'd hung up his copy on the fridge. It wasn't framed or carefully placed and adjusted for optimal viewing. It was innocent. A last-minute thought. Nothing but another piece in this game we were playing for others.

"I was just trying to make your place seem more like a … home. For other people," I added quickly. "You know, if they were looking, we'd seem even more…" I glanced at him, knowing he knew I wasn't being truthful.

"Rach, if you want to add blankets, plants, or even ten potholders to make this feel less like the place you come for work and more like a place you'd like to stay over sometimes, then that's what I want. Regardless, you can't take away my birthday gift. I'm keeping the photos."

I didn't even try to hold back my smile. "Yeah?"

"Yes, Rach, truth. Always truth." He wore a gentle expression, his features relaxed, his words less clipped, soft at the edges. "When's your birthday? Your real one."

I laughed, resting my cheek against his chest. "Are you going to plan me a party?"

"No." He laughed and wrapped his arms around me, his fingers playing with the ends of my hair. "But I can hire someone who isn't you well in advance."

I laughed and shook my head. "It's a long time away. Like eight months. So, you know, there's no obligation," I said with a light laugh that felt heavy in my chest.

The unspoken words between us lingered like

cigarette smoke.

By that time, Pres' campaign would be in full swing, and he'd be on the cusp of his first term as mayor. He definitely wouldn't be planning birthday parties, and I'd most likely be a memory.

"Well, I certainly have enough cake to last until then," he said with his own little laugh.

"You know, you already helped me have a pretty good birthday."

He pulled back to look at me, not understanding.

"The night we met," I admitted, the secret spilling out through Champagne-soaked words, "was my birthday. I hadn't had the best day, so, uh, it was nice to talk to you."

I told him about that day, how I'd volunteered for this job, thinking he'd be his dad, and the underwear fiasco.

"And I knew if I didn't get into the hotel to deliver that dress, I'd be toast. Then you appeared. You were the first person in a really long time who treated me…" I shrugged, choking on the sudden emotion in my throat. "Like you could see me. Like I mattered."

He'd been running a warm hand up and down my arm as he listened, tightening his grip at that part.

"Why did you pretend to be Ruth then?"

I shrugged, feeling shame creep up my cheeks. "It felt so nice to be someone else for a while. I know it's silly—"

"No, I get it. I didn't mean that negatively. Believe me, I get it. You weren't the only one pretending that night."

"What do you mean?"

He kind of laughed. "Rach, we were at a political whose-whose event, and you had no idea who I was. Do you know the odds of that?"

Knowing who he was and having seen him at similar events now where people crowded him, it really was so clear I hadn't belonged at that event.

"Why'd you help me in when I wasn't on the list?"

He shrugged. "The probability of you being a threat or, I don't know, a streaker was pretty low."

I grinned. "I think technically I am a streaker?"

He laughed loudly. "True. But that night, when you were standing up to the doorman, you said what we were all thinking. You made me laugh. Why wouldn't I have helped you? Maybe I'm not as unlikeable as people believe," he said with a scoffing laugh, a line of self-doubt crossing his brows.

I scooted closer as he rubbed his thumb against his index finger.

"For as long as I can remember, I've known being a St. Clair has always been more important than being Pres. When we met again outside, I could have clarified who I was. I *should* have. What I should have done was shake your hand, introduce myself properly, and, I don't know, ask for your business card."

I laughed. "Instead, you asked for a light."

He smiled, studying me and lingering on my lips. The question on his face if he should kiss me was so clear, I suddenly wondered if he overthought whatever was between us more than I'd given him credit for.

When he spoke, his voice was soft, "Instead, I had the strangest, most refreshing conversation of my life with an absolutely fascinating woman. And, yes, asked for a light because my since-fired assistant had booked me on the wrong flight so I was running late. When I'd stopped in my office to grab my lighter, I was distracted by an email introducing me to my new assistant. A woman named Rach Montgomery who yielded no Google results."

I laughed, shocked. "You Googled me then?"

"Rach, you know me, of course I did," he said, smirking. "It threw me off so much that I left without my lighter. When I saw you, I'd figured the chances of you having a light when you weren't smoking was slim. But I asked anyway. If you hadn't had those matches…"

"We would've never talked," I said softly. "You would have left to avoid small talk. Just gone back inside."

"But you would have probably still barged into my office, ruined my interview, gone viral—"

"And you would have fired me."

Because we'd talked that night, he'd recognized my face enough to stay calm and say I was his girlfriend. And my only saving grace had been because of how I'd seen his bright and easy smile that night, unable to believe he was completely ruthless.

He agreed. "I wouldn't have taken a chance on you. On the other hand, if you hadn't pretended to be Ruth, obviously, I would've realized who you really were."

"It would have ended before it started."

He nodded. "Funny how things work out, isn't it?"

"And if you'd taken me up on my offer that night…"

He laughed. "Your tour of my place would have been quite different. That's the thing. No matter how I evaluate the scenario, every aspect that was *likely*, predictable, should have occurred, didn't happen. It seems like how it worked out was…" he paused, unsure.

Meant to be, my heart begged to say.

I laughed. "You sure you don't believe in luck?"

He laughed, facing me. The way he looked at me was so uniquely Pres, with blue eyes that were so serious and so genuine, I'd always want him, even when this ended.

"How about I just believe in you, Rach."

I kissed him suddenly, hard and rough, needy with

desire. A low groan escaped his mouth, and I straddled his thighs as his talented tongue took over the kiss.

His mouth was hot against my chilled skin as he worked his way down my neck, his hands cupping my breasts, giving me all kinds of praise. I was almost certain his gratitude for Boobgate was mentioned at least once.

"Yes," I hissed, rocking against his hard length trapped in his suit pants — truly the best interpretation of business casual — as he pushed my dress up my hips. "Give me, Pres. Please, baby, all of you."

His skin was flushed, a shirt button had somehow popped off, and his eyes were bright, burning just for me.

"Say that again," he demanded. I almost didn't hear him, distracted by him unzipping his pants. But then his other hand trailed up my inner thigh, fingers pressing inside me without hesitation and filling me deeply.

"I want all of you, babe," I gasped, my breath hitching with each stroke. "All of you, Pres. Every single part. You make me feel so good."

I shimmied down his lap to where he was hard and waiting. He knew I didn't need instruction, but I loved how he ground out commands as I eagerly took him in my mouth until I was drawing out uncontrolled moans from him.

"Yes, that's it," he said, voice breaking. "Rach, Rac—"

He pulled me off of him with a start, breathing hard, and kissed me roughly as I wrapped my fingers around his dick. He matched my pace, massaging my clit with the pad of his thumb.

We were closer than ever, his free hand holding my hip as I rode his fingers, our chests flush, the smell of amber and oak mixing with peppermint shampoo, our heartbeats in sync, our breath nearly becoming one.

It was freezing out here, but we were on fire.

"Together," he breathed, and it sounded like how he'd said *truth*, desperate and demanding, out of control, raw and real. "Come with me, Rach."

His words pushed me over the edge, and we went off like a match, one stroke, one strike, one small sizzle bursting into something bright, burning, powerful.

When we pulled away, we were shivering, breathless.

"Incredible," he said with a laugh, a soft sound filled with exhilaration, Champagne, and happiness. "You're incredible. The chairs were an excellent purchase."

He adjusted my dress and himself, gently wiped my hand with a stray napkin, and smoothed my hair. My heart hitched as he delicately righted me into place, like someone worth treasuring.

"You're freezing," he said, rubbing my goose-bumped skin as his lust-drunk expression cleared. "You need to go inside. You're staying over, right?"

"In the guest room?"

His response was an annoyed, stern look.

I laughed and hopped off his lap, grinning. "I'm teasing. I'm not exactly sure of the rules of fake birthdays, but I think we can do whatever you want."

He looked at me seriously.

Then he said words I'd never thought I'd hear.

"I want to clean the kitchen."

"Are you being for real?" I said, already laughing because I knew he was.

"Of course," he said in his no-nonsense voice. "I won't be able to sleep knowing everything is a mess. Also, we need to be hydrating. Let me get you a water."

Once we'd slipped inside, he wrapped me up in his suit jacket and handed me a glass of water.

We talked about everything and nothing, laughing and sparring, trading secrets and stories. I kept him company, eating another piece of cake barefoot in my dress and his jacket, as he moved around in a suit, scrubbing a few dishes, wiping down his counters, and putting everything back in its rightful place.

It was the weirdest first date I'd ever been on.

It was the best first date I'd ever been on.

CHAPTER TWENTY-SEVEN

"Did you choose this seat?"

I opened my eyes to see an annoyed Ethan trying to convince himself that sitting next to me wasn't the worst thing that could happen on a plane.

"Nope, just fate bringing us together."

"Great," he grumbled. "The middle seat, really?"

"It could be worse," I said with a smile. "You could be on the wing."

Ethan glared, unamused by my little joke.

He sighed heavily and shoved his bag under his seat, elbowing me in the side. The man in the aisle seat was asleep, completely unconscious, and the way Ethan was jostling me, I was getting close to that state, too.

We were headed to DC for a jam-packed, two-day stint. Pres' client meetings, a television appearance where he was on a pundit panel to commentate on gubernatorial races, and a meeting with Sable for his campaign, oh my.

It'd been a busy time since his faux birthday. Everyone pulled late nights to finalize reports, plans, and polls.

I'd also been busier, fielding and researching a flood of end-of-year donation requests Pres received, coordinating holiday cards and clients gifts, and building numerous slide decks for his presentations.

The good thing was, when Pres came over to my place after a long day, bearing takeout and sexual favors, I had ample opportunity to make "deck" puns.

"I hope I can concentrate to get everything done before we land," Ethan snapped. "That personal day you made Pres take really threw me off."

I laughed. "Yeah, me too. You can't even imagine."

He ignored me, so I slipped on my headphones and turned to the window, cranking up the volume on a meditation guide.

Just as I'd finally gotten into it, he jostled me again, tapping my shoulder.

"Could you please leave me al—*ello*, how are you?" I fumbled as Pres gave me a strange look. "I'm just trying out a British accent. What are you doing here?"

"I switched. My seat was uncomfortable."

"Your business class seat was uncomfortable?"

He shrugged. "The company was less than desirable. Plus, the coffee was terrible."

The plane lurched forward, and I tightened my grip on the armrest, totally keeping my grimace at bay.

"You don't like flying?"

"You mean being in a tin box catapulting in the sky? No, I love experiencing the wonders of science firsthand," I said, my laugh only coming out a little maniacal.

"Ah, so you're scared of flying."

"I didn't say that. I might love flying."

He studied me for a moment, his eyes flashing, then leaned forward with a concerned expression.

"Oh no, do you hear that?"

I gasped and whipped my head to the window. "What? Oh gosh, is it pre-crashing?"

He laughed loudly, and that's when I realized he wasn't unlikable — he was actually diabolical.

"What is *pre*-crashing?" he said with another laugh. I narrowed my eyes, but his smile was undeterred. "But thanks for proving my point. You don't have to pretend things are good all the time. You can be honest with me."

"Will I get fired and thrown off the plane if I tell you to shut up? Because I think I've found my silver lining."

He grinned. "Have you ever flown before?"

Last night, I'd ridden his face. So I guess I could be honest *to* his face.

"I've never had the chance. But now I'm thinking, 'wow, buses are underrated.'"

"I could tell you the likelihood of a plane crash versus a bus crash," he paused, "actually, never mind, I won't."

As a flight attendant spouted off safety information, I reminded myself I just had to get through a few hours of this. Then we'd be in DC, go to a ton of meetings, stay a night, and we'd be back. Easy seats-function-as-rafts-in-case-of-a-water-landing-oh-gosh-were-we-even-*near*-water peasy.

My whole body tensed as the plane started to move.

Pres leaned in, his lips close to my ear. "We could make out."

I gasped and turned to him with wide eyes.

"We're in public."

"Lucky for us, the public thinks we're together."

"On a plane barreling toward the sun?"

"You're right, we should go to the bathroom. Have you ever considered joining the Mile High Club?"

"They said we can't take off our seat belts!"

He placed a steady, solid hand on my thigh as the plane made a thumping sound and I held back a gasp.

"What do you think about me touching you here?"

I didn't think my eyes could get wider.

And well, my body sparked awake at the thought.

"No way."

He shrugged, his eyes flashing mischievously. "You could take off your jacket, drape it over your lap, and let me get you off."

I bit my lip, my stomach flip-flopping at the idea.

"It's probably the only good thing about being this far back on a plane," he added dryly.

Then he leaned closer, whispering in my ear *exactly* what he wanted to do and how he wanted to do it. His fingers skimmed up and down my thigh, sending the smallest of thrills over my skin.

I closed my eyes, listening to the deep timbre of his voice, inhaling and exhaling as if he were actually doing what he was describing. I didn't care about anything but the reality he was creating, shifting in my seat, wishing it could just be true.

"Once you're really begging for it," he said, dark, delicious, and hushed, "you come so hard that you hit the call button. And the flight attendant brings you a glass of Champagne."

I exhaled slowly and laughed, meeting his sparkling eyes. "I don't think that's the kind of publicity you want."

He shrugged, glancing out the window.

"Oh, look at that," he said pleasantly. "It's beautiful."

I looked at him, a little dazed, but he just smiled, pulled out a thick report from his bag, and slipped on his reading glasses. Then I turned to the sky, shocked to see how far we'd come, amazed by the shimmering clouds below us, a kaleidoscope of rosy pinks and brilliant blues, the warm sun streaming magically, golden streaks more beautiful than anything that could be bought, and blinked rapidly at what should have been impossible.

...

I'd had a bad habit of playing a game with my mom

when I was a kid.

It had started after I'd come to a startling realization after Doughnuts With Dad Day in second grade. I hadn't minded sitting alone — my mom hadn't been able to get off work — thinking more doughnuts for me anyway.

My mom had always told me that I'd been a gift from the universe, just for her, so there was no need for me to worry about my dad.

When I'd excitedly shared this with Sydnee C. and Staci M., they'd laughed, making sure I understood over powdered sugar and sprinkles that *everyone* had a dad, mine just hadn't wanted *me*.

After that, if my mom and I were out in public, I'd suddenly stop, stand completely silent and still, and wait to see if she'd notice I wasn't next to her.

Sometimes, we'd be in the library, and she'd be headed to the self-help aisle to find *the book* that would make a difference this time. I'd stand with my feet firmly planted on scratchy carpet, somewhere between geography and history, reading and rereading the titles until I didn't feel lost or alone anymore.

Sometimes in the grocery store, I'd stop in the aisle with the frozen microwavable meals after she'd scoop up some for dinner, skin pinpricking with goosebumps and wait on her to notice and return.

I'd count the seconds then minutes until I'd start to wonder if maybe she wasn't coming back, that she was done with this one-sided game, that maybe she'd finally realized it was easier to be without me.

I'd wonder if she'd looked over her shoulder, realized I was gone and shrugged, thinking good riddance, Rach wasn't worth it anyway.

What if this whole time, this game I'd been playing

had been a reprieve for her. What if instead of trying to find me, to choose me, pick me, want me, let me be the prize, she'd been counting down the seconds, too, leaning against a grocery display or thumbing through a book, relieved to be rid of me for just a while.

As I'd struggle to breathe, losing count of the seconds, I'd stare at the lobsters the store kept in glass tanks. I'd hold my breath and feel just like them, surrounded by so much that was unattainable, swimming around and around in a circle and never getting anywhere.

I'd squeeze my eyes shut until she'd come back, wrapping her arms around me, saying she was sorry, she'd never let me out of her sight again.

When she was sentenced, I'd visited her before she was transferred. She'd told me visiting would just bring us down and pitched letters instead. Seeing each other was too sad, she'd said, it would only create bad juju.

"Let's only write when we have good things to say," she'd suggested with a bright smile. "Let's keep things positive. You focus on bettering yourself. Making good out of life. In no time, it'll be fun. It'll be happy mail."

I'd agreed because I'd been 18, wanted to respect her wishes, and couldn't realistically afford to visit her so far away anyway.

So I'd moved to Middletown, hoping I could fix my life without her, and wrote letters. I'd told her about my basement apartment — *it's sooo cozy* — the tips I made as a server — *the money really starts to correlate to the amount you smile!* — meeting JD — *he loves to tease me, I think he really likes me* — and landing the assistant to personal assistant's job — *so much access to coffee!*

And now, as I sat in my hotel room alone in between organizing meeting notes from today, I tried to think of how to word what was happening with Pres, who he was, and what we were doing.

Because it was possible that in an effort to explain what should have been considered a fake relationship based on a lie with an extra sprinkle of casual sex tacked on, I was realizing that maybe all my past letters had been filled with only half-truths.

I tried blunt honesty:

Mom, I met a guy. I really like him. Honestly, it's more than that—

A video call on my laptop interrupted me.

It was late evening, but between Pres' client meetings and Sable's hectic schedule, this was the only time everyone was available. I'd managed to snag alone time because I'd offered to grab everyone's dinners on my way to get Pres' suit steamed for his meetings tomorrow.

As the team trickled in the conference room, I smiled at where Pres sat at the head of the table.

"Pres, are you drinking coffee? It's pretty late."

"Don't worry, it's barely drinkable anyway."

"Geez, thanks," Sable grumbled.

"Why don't you get yourself some tea?"

"No, I need my assistant," he said, his voice light and casual, a grin quirking at his lips. "Could you bring me some after this meeting?"

"Sure thing, boss," I said brightly.

"Gosh, Pres, you can't even get your own tea in your own hotel room?" Sable said with a head shake. "Do you ever give her a night off?"

"Huh, no, I don't think I do," he said with a short laugh that, to outsiders, might have sounded wicked.

Sable sighed. "Well, sorry, Rach, I tried. Are we ready to get this meeting started?"

Everyone detailed how the campaign build-up was going: donors were pledging their support, Pres was being invited to even more community events, and his social media presence was popping.

"I've already had several media inquiries," Sable continued. "Photos of you and Rach have appeared in those society magazines that no one really cares about except the people who are in those magazines—"

"Those people vote," Ethan interrupted.

"Thank you for explaining that to me," she said with an eye roll. "Anyway, reporters are wondering why a St. Clair is suddenly showing up all over Middletown as an election approaches."

"We ran another poll," Jamar added. "Your likability has increased by a significant value. People see you as compassionate about the community and friendly in general."

"I think the words we're looking for are, 'Sable was right,'" Sable said. "The numbers don't lie, having a significant other has softened you, made you more approachable, and generally more likable. Sucks for us single people but—"

"So you'd recommend keeping things as they are," Pres said in a way where it was unclear if he was asking a question or giving a command.

"Well, we're ready to transition into the next phase of the campaign plan," Sable said. "We've planted the seed, now we need to start talking in absolutes. I can get people speculating about a run. We'll announce immediately after the new year."

"We'll run oppo-research," Ethan said. "Olivia has already spent a significant portion seeing what she could find about you, Pres."

"Sorry, what's oppo-research?" I asked, looking up from my notes and ignoring Ethan's eye roll.

"Opposition research," Pres clarified. "Information about me an opponent could gather to discredit me or hurt my campaign. Dirt against me, basically. We do it internally first to see what they could come up with so we're prepared to address it."

"I've had trouble finding anything substantial," Olivia chimed in. "Have you ever done anything risky before?"

"I've been in the public eye my whole life," Pres said with a dry laugh. "I've missed out on a lot of fun."

"The worst thing was Boobgate, but that ended up being a positive," Sable added.

Pres glanced at me and smiled. I was glad my connection was blurry so no one could see my blush.

"Yeah, it looks like you got a few speeding tickets as a teenager," Olivia said with a shrug. "And there's a video of you in undergrad shouting after your team lost a soccer game. You were pretty upset."

"Relatable and passionate," Ethan said with a wave of his hand. "Neither will take down a campaign."

Pres nodded. "Sable, let's practice interview questions tomorrow and prep for teasing the announcement. Jamar, send Rach that poll so she can get me a hardcopy. Olivia, forward me your research, please. Thanks, all. Rach, let's connect after this. I have a few personal requests for you."

Sable reached out, stopping him from standing. "We have to discuss Rach."

We glanced at each other, confused.

"How she fits into this next phase," Sable said slowly.

"She's served her purpose," Ethan said. "The numbers are up—"

"We don't want to risk fluctuations," Pres interrupted,

rubbing his temple. "We should keep things as they are, if Rach agrees."

I smiled. "I'll never turn down a fancy dinner."

Pres laughed. "Right, so we'll just keep things as is."

"Rach, do you understand what this means?" Sable asked. "Boobgate blew over because basically everyone had to take down the naked videos of you and silly viral stuff like that fades out. By the time we revealed who you were, no one really cared anymore."

"That's a little harsh," Pres said with a frown.

Sable looked at him, confused. "Um, sorry ... But, Rach, if we fold you into this campaign when things go public, you're opening yourself up to total exposure. So far we've been pretty low-key, low-visibility so what Pres is doing in the community comes across as authentic—"

"It *is* authentic," I corrected. "He does care."

"Sure. Okay. But when we do a full media campaign to finally announce James Prescott *St. Clair*, the son of the Senate Majority Leader, is running for the same office that started his father's career, this isn't a tiny column in the back of the paper or a simple tweet. This is big news."

"We'll have to do oppo-research on you, too," Ethan sighed. "If you have any skeletons, anything that would open you up to criticism, we'll find it. And Pres' opponent will use it against him."

I glanced down at the letter in my lap to my mom.

My stomach plummeted.

I was so foolish.

I'd known we'd never work — but I'd never thought that in order for Pres to win, I'd have to lose.

"I passed a background check for Prestige Staffing, so I don't really think there's much else to cover, right?"

"Well, obviously, if you'd been a felon, we wouldn't

have hired you," Ethan scoffed.

I glanced at Pres. His face was guarded and impassive. I'd seen this expression before when he watched the news, taking in information to analyze later.

"A background check barely scratches the surface. People aren't looking at if you've committed a crime. They care about *who you are*. Who Pres chooses to associate with matters," Ethan continued. "I've seen politicians' campaigns tank because of something stupid their kid posted online. Pres can speak to that in full. He's been in the spotlight his whole life because of his father. You think just because he doesn't have a record, he can do whatever he wants without someone checking or caring?"

I bit my lip, having no idea what to say.

"Your argument isn't sound," Pres said flatly. "It's hardly based in reality. Rach doesn't have social media."

"That's odd in itself," Ethan pushed back. "What are you hiding, Rach? People want to know."

"Why does anyone care about my life?" I asked, a lump rising in my throat. "Pres is the important one. He's the one who matters."

"Rach," Pres said, his voice firm and stern, "you're important. You matter."

Off camera, my hand tensed against my chest, my heart way too invested in this conversation.

"I do think it complicates things," Sable said slowly.

I knew this was serious because it was the first time she'd ever agreed with Ethan.

"We also can't risk people finding out you two are faking being together once this gets real," she said, glancing between us. "In my professional opinion, it's best to move Rach out of the spotlight."

"And what about your personal opinion?" Pres said,

his tone clipped.

Sable blinked a few times. "My professional opinion isn't swayed by my personal opinion. Just like you, Pres."

"You all agree with removing Rach from the plan?" he asked, looking around at his always agreeable team. "After all she's done, just get rid of her?"

They didn't speak, uncertainty hanging in the air.

"Pres," I said softly. Everyone's eyes were on me as I sat pixelated in my room alone, a half-written letter to my mom about a guy I'd never have — had never really had in the first place, no matter how hard I'd believed it to be true. "It's okay. They're right. We had an agreement. I knew this was coming."

"Of course," he said swiftly. "Yes, I understand."

"We should discuss how we'll phase her out," Sable said. "The holidays are right around the corner, so people are distracted. It'll be easy to use busy schedules as a reason for why she isn't around. Then, right after the new year, you'll announce. That news will bury that you two have broken up amicably. No one will notice," Sable said brightly. "It's a perfect plan."

I forced myself to keep a smile on my face, trying not to feel like I was equivalent to a drooping plant, an outdated pair of pants, or an expiring vegetable.

"We can talk about this later," Pres said, rubbing his forehead with his thumb, and stood. "I have a headache."

"Headache?" Ethan repeated. "What does that mean?"

"Is that code?" Jamar whispered to Olivia.

"I can get you a water," Sable offered, but he was already out of the room. She sighed and turned back to us. "Well, he's actually left. Should we continue?"

"Let's figure this out, and we can present our plans to him once we have it solved," Ethan said. "He's too busy to be concerned with something this trivial anyway."

I cleared my throat and forced another smile. "Hey, do you all need me for this?"

"Nope," Ethan replied, barely glancing my way.

I hung up while they strategized the best way to make me disappear, having absolutely no idea how to feel, and started a new letter to my mom.

Mom, I'm about to get a new job. New job, new life, right?

CHAPTER TWENTY-EIGHT

"Ethan, my text was clear, I'm exhausted—" Pres stopped when he'd opened his hotel door. "Oh."

His shirt was unbuttoned, and my mind went blank.

He placed his hand on the doorway, waiting. Standing like that, nearly shirtless — his abs and chest startling proof that his obsessive tendencies definitely had some positives — and shifting nicotine gum in his mouth, his pouty lips wet and sensual, I could only stare.

"Did you need something, Rach?"

"Right, I just wanted to, uh, give you this," I said, nearly shoving the piece of paper in his hand. "And you know, no hard feelings or anything."

His naturally cold blue eyes scanned the words I'd hastily written after the team meeting. Then he looked at me and frowned.

"What is this?"

"My resignation letter. Like, my two weeks' notice."

He squinted at it again, and I briefly wondered if I'd messed up the template I'd found online.

"Where did you print this?"

Out of all the questions, I hadn't expected that one.

"The business center. Downstairs."

His frown deepened. "I don't know what that is. There's a center specifically for business in this hotel? What sort of business?"

I laughed and shook my head. "It's like a tiny room

near the lobby with computers and ... never mind. Not important. I just wanted you to know, I understand, you know, what your team was saying—"

"I don't typically find myself concerned with what my team thinks."

I kind of laughed at his blunt honesty and glanced down at the hallway carpet, unable to meet his eyes.

"Maybe we should stop before this gets too..." I let my sentence fade, feeling silly at saying *real*.

"Okay." He said it so simply my gaze instantly snapped to his. "It's too much. I understand."

I wanted to say the right thing — that he shouldn't be so understanding, that he shouldn't so readily accept someone didn't want to be with him or that he was unlikeable — but I couldn't bring myself to be honest.

Because if I was honest about that, I'd have to tell him about my mom. And then he'd never like me the way I liked him. I was too much of a risk, and the stakes were too high for me to win in the end.

"Pres, honestly, it's not about you."

"So it's not me, it's you." He laughed shortly. "That's a good one."

"That's not what I meant. But this is the right choice. It's the proper thing to do."

He nodded, an agreeable smile on his face. "Okay."

"Oh. Okay, good, great," I said, unsure if I felt relieved or offended by how little he was disagreeing. "I'll help find and train a suitable replacement. Hopefully, you and I can stay friends—"

"Sure. I'm going to go to bed," he said, stepping back from the doorway. "Have a good night, buddy."

And then he shut the door.

One second passed.

Good, I thought, *exactly how I wanted that to go.*
Two seconds passed.
It *literally* couldn't have gone better.
As the third long, painful second passed, I held up my fist to knock right as he opened the door.
"Buddy?" I said indignantly, pushing the door open.
"I know, so fucking stupid," he said and pulled me inside.

...

I wasn't quite sure how post-breakup conversations from a fake relationship were supposed to go, but making out against a hotel door as soon as we burst into his room wouldn't have been my first guess.

We were frantic and tangled, refusing to break apart until we were breathless. When we pulled away, we quickly assessed what the other was thinking.

What we both wanted.

What we both couldn't have.

How this was going to end.

And what we were going to do anyway.

"Couch," he instructed quickly, and I pushed the papers he'd been reading off the cushion.

"Rach," he said on a sharp inhale. "I had those organized a certain way."

"Do you think I don't know how to reorganize them? Get over here."

He looked amused by my bossy impatience, but he sat anyway so I could straddle his lap. Our lips found each other again, and he gripped my hips, tugging me down.

"I want all of you," I gasped. "More, Pres."

If this was an experience with an expiration date, I was going to take as much as I could as quickly as possible.

"No," he mumbled as his mouth made its way down

my neck.

"Yes," I whined.

"We can't. I don't have condoms."

"Done," I said, hopping off him to unzip a small pouch in his leather carry-on bag.

"Did you pack me condoms?" he asked, bewildered. "On a work trip?"

"Well, I packed the rest of your luggage," I said with a laugh, holding up the shiny wrapper like a prize. "And I choose to be an optimist."

He laughed, shaking his head like he still wasn't exactly sure how I'd ended up in his life, let alone his lap.

"Is it considered a sign if you pre-planned this?"

I laughed at his teasing mocking tone and shrugged. "Best of both worlds. Now can we do it?"

His voice was rough and demanding, his blue eyes an icy fire, when he unzipped his pants and told me to ride him. A searing, desperate bolt of arousal shot through me when I realized he wasn't going to completely undress or waste time to reveal any more than what was necessary.

I opened the wrapper as his teeth scraped against my skin and his tongue soothed his bites, the wet, hot feeling deliciously distracting.

In my haste, my nerves got the best of me.

I dropped it.

On the floor.

A limp latex disappointment.

I gasped.

We both paused and looked where it was flopped and misshapen on the carpet next to a floor lamp.

"Oh noooo," I groaned, reaching down to pick it up. "Do you think it's still okay?"

He looked horrified. "I am not using something that

was on the *floor*. I don't know the last time this carpet was cleaned. Oh my god."

"I thought you weren't a germaphobe."

When I shifted closer, he jerked back and hastily zipped his pants. "Do *not* touch me with that."

"Wow, romantic. Don't be such a dick-tator—"

He groaned.

"—Condoms protect from STIs and stuff," I teased. "You probably won't catch anything from the carpet."

"Can you please throw it away? There's *lint* on it."

His whole body was tense underneath me ... except for the one part that really needed to be hard.

I held back a laugh. "Pres, seriously?"

"I can't help it," he choked out.

I bit my lip, but my laugh squeaked out anyway.

He narrowed his eyes, refusing to give into the laughter bouncing in his eyes. "This is *not* funny."

"Do you want me to see if the gift shop has condoms?"

"You only packed one?" he said dryly.

I burst out laughing. "Well, I'm not *that* much of an optimist. This *is* a work trip after all."

His dramatic look of misery was almost convincing. "I refuse to let this be a sign."

I laughed and shook my head. It was late. I was tired, and he had a headache. We had to get up early tomorrow. We were in a hotel. He was my fake boyfriend. He was my actual client. This was ending soon; his team was literally planning our breakup right now. Technically, I think I'd just tried and failed to quit my job.

Once again, a hundred signs said this was a bad idea.

But then he smiled, tossed me my clothes, and grabbed his wallet. "Come on, show me this gift shop. Do they also sell candy?"

And that's how we ended up raiding the small shop's sweet section. We were quick, acting like we were on a mission, racing down the hall together, slipping in and out of the elevators undetected.

Pres grabbed gift shop sunglasses, deadpanning it was vital he be in character, as I tried to suppress laughter. Then he pulled a baseball hat over my head emblazoned with the White House.

"Perfect," he said with a bright laugh as I posed. "Beautiful. I've genuinely never been more interested in the White House than in this moment."

I laughed, thrilled by this covert operation as he filled my arms with my favorite candies.

"We probably need salty to balance this out."

I grinned, wrapping an arm around his shoulders. "Babe, I have you for that."

He paused, blinked at me, and then burst into laughter, filling the small space with a strong, easy laugh.

Who cared about covert when this was the alternative?

As we waited for the total, I glanced at the newspapers at the checkout.

"Oh wow, that's your…" I trailed off, glancing at the clerk checking us out.

Pres sighed, pulling off his sunglasses and smoothing a hand through his hair. Instantly, he appeared poised, like a thread as heavy and long as his lineage had been pulled in his spine. "Yeah."

The clerk glanced at the photo below the headline — *Sen. St. Clair places Congress in 'paralysis'*— and rolled her eyes. "Senator Asshole is more like it. I don't get why everyone likes him so much."

"Maybe he's not so bad," I offered gently as Pres seemed to visibly relax. She didn't recognize him even if his namesake did look quite like him. "I think I've heard his son is pretty cool."

"You aren't from around here, are you?"

"She's from Kansas," Pres said with a laugh. "Come on, Dorothy."

He scooped up the candy, took my hand, and snuck us back into his room, dumping our haul onto his bed.

Then he picked me up and tossed me on the bed too, covering me with his strong body and kissing me through our laughter.

"Oh." He pulled back suddenly. "We forgot condoms."

I burst out laughing as he dropped his head on my shoulder and groaned. "What does this *mean*?"

"I'll be right back," I said, hopping up. "Stay, I'll go."

"Use my personal Amex," he called after me. "I doubt this is considered a business expense."

I nodded. "And when I come back, be naked."

He made a face. "I can't sit on this duvet waiting in the nude. I've read they aren't cleaned every time—"

I laughed and raced out, thinking this was probably the best fake breakup a woman could ask for.

CHAPTER TWENTY-NINE

"You strike me as a guy who likes chess," I said with a dramatic flourish and handed him the tiny travel set I'd found on the bottom of a dusty shelf. "They were also out of condoms."

"Why do you possibly think chess is a substitute for sex?" Pres asked dryly.

I shrugged and joined him where he sat on the bed. "How about lots of different positions you can play?"

"And the queen is more powerful," he added, lighting up when he opened the box. "Yeah, let's play."

It was official.

I'd fallen for a nerd.

A sexy nerd, but still.

We battled it out on his bed, laughing through trying to figure out how to turn it into Strip Chess before giving up and agreeing to just play.

"Is chess another skill JD and I share?"

I snorted at the plain jealousy in his voice and shook my head. "He doesn't even know I can play."

Pres nodded, seeming way too satisfied by that fact, as I tried to decide my next move.

"We'd always use a shiny black rock for this piece," I said, the memory slipping through as I slid the Knight forward. "I called it my lucky rock."

Pres looked at me, not understanding.

I laughed, shaking my head. "I mean, my mom taught

me how to play. She got a set at a yard sale, but it was missing a few pieces. We'd make do with pieces from real life. A rock for the Knight, a salt shaker for the Bishop, a lucky penny for the Queen, a matchbook for the King. Sometimes, we'd spend just as much time trying to find the perfect piece than actually playing. She said both were life skills to give me a leg up," I said with a light laugh.

He took his turn, thinking about this.

"Do you two still play?"

"No, I don't see her."

The secret was out of my mouth before I'd had a chance to stop it. I'd managed to get this far without really mentioning her, allowing simple facts — Barnum statements — to build the sort of person he'd probably like to imagine as my mom.

Pres always said people believed what they wanted to believe. If he liked me by believing I was the daughter of someone even remotely close to what he imagined, why should I burst that bubble when we only had a few weeks left together?

"I don't really see my mother much either. She lives in New York, so we get lunch about once a year. It's hard to sync up our schedules. Do you have the same problem?"

"Something like that. Hey, by the way, I'm sorry about the woman in the gift shop."

He shrugged. "In some ways she's correct, they did get his name wrong. People always forget to add the third."

I laughed at his wry response as he closely watched me take my turn.

"I'm sure it still hurts to hear the mean things people say about your dad. Do you see him often? Ethan was surprised you didn't ask me to set up a lunch with him since we're here."

Pres' tone was flat, "My father is focused on a singular goal to be the most powerful man in politics. He doesn't have time for lunches." He glanced up from the King in his hand to me. "What does your mom do again? I'm sure you've told me, but for some reason I can't recall."

"Oh, she stays busy," I said with a shrug, having effectively dodged this question at countless events by now. "You know how it is."

He laughed. "Right, is she a consultant, too?"

I had to change the subject, the conversation getting much too close to the truth. Moving my Queen, I asked, "Did your parents teach you to play chess?"

He looked genuinely amused by the idea. "They know how. But if I'd asked, they would have sent me to chess camp or hired a chess tutor when I was in boarding school."

We both studied the board.

"So how do you know how to do this?"

"I taught myself."

"Who did you play with then?"

He paused.

Just as I was about to say we could stop playing, end it early so we weren't both losers, he looked up from the board, his eyes serious and so blue I could *feel* the color against my heart.

"Myself." He smiled then, and I felt his warmth at my core. "You may have had a broken chess board, but at least you had someone to play with. So I win."

I nodded at the pieces in front of us. "Looks like we both lost."

"No," he said softly, leaning over to kiss me, "it's a draw."

...

It was a sight I'd never thought I'd see.

Pres was asleep next to me.

I'd accidentally woken up before my alarm when a discarded King rolled on my face. Which meant for the first time ever, I'd woken up before him.

And I was being aggressively cuddled.

He was fully on my side of the hotel bed, his leg tossed over mine, arm slung around my waist, holding me so close his face was buried under my hair. At some point in the night, he'd even managed to wedge an arm under my head so his chest was flush to my back.

This wasn't just a cuddle.

This was a power snug.

And I realized this felt familiar.

"Pres," I whispered.

He made a sleepy sound and frowned. "What?"

"Do you hold me like this every night?"

"I don't stay over at your place every night," he grumbled, burying deeper into my hair.

For once he was incorrect.

"Actually, you do."

"Oh," he said, tightening his grip on me.

Then he whispered, so soft and sweet, if I'd please shut up because this was the coziest he'd ever felt, and if I didn't like him staying over so much maybe I should stay at his place then, like those were the only two options, making me smile and fall back asleep in his arms.

Once I woke up for real, the day breaking on a packed schedule, he was already awake, adjusting his tie in the full-length hotel mirror.

"Would you—" he paused, considering his next words carefully. "Is it silly if I asked to take a photo together?"

I laughed, adjusting the baseball hat I'd thrown over

my hair and glancing at my sweatpants.

"Never mind," he said quickly. "Sable would advise against it."

"Ethan would say it's bad for your campaign."

"And we're on the verge of a break up, so it doesn't make sense."

"Yeah," I said, standing next to him.

Our reflections locked eyes.

I handed him his phone.

"I don't have to post it," he said, opening his camera. "I haven't posted on my Instagram in years. I probably don't even remember how."

I laughed and nodded. "Yeah, totally. It's silly."

He put his arm around me, the Pres in the mirror pulling my reflection close, a woman who was equally too much and not enough. But we were smiling so brightly, and he dropped a kiss on the top of my head as I leaned against his chest. His calm and heavy heartbeat thumped against my cheek, a close, tangible feeling from his body to mine. In the background, a scattered chess set rested next to a ripped up resignation letter and an unmade bed out of frame. Both of us looked tired and happy and smiling and laughing and click, posted, uploaded, captioned: *checkmate*.

...

By the time we'd landed in Middletown, we were all exhausted.

"Great work, team," Pres had said cheerfully, making them shift, confused and uncertain. "Or rather, keep up the good work. Don't let me down. Your career rides on my success," he snapped, and everyone nodded, feeling the universe tilt back on its axis.

When he stayed over at my place, I hadn't thought

much about it. But when I woke up early, I hadn't expected for him to still be here. And certainly not in my kitchen, scowling at his phone in reading glasses.

My counter was covered in shopping bags.

"Are you ... lost?" I laughed. "What's all this?"

"Typically, you sleep two hours later than me, so I figured I'd have plenty of time to solve this problem."

"What problem? My phase out? I think Ethan just sent over his ideas. Say what you want about him, he does move quickly."

"No, I'd had the idea to make breakfast. But the grocery store is overwhelming," he said, exhaling a frustrated breath and rubbing his temple. "I thought I could easily replicate when we'd gone together. But clearly, I miscalculated. Tell me, how does one possibly choose from the various packs of chicken? They all look the same, and the pricing system didn't seem to indicate any sort of quality metric."

I stifled a laugh, trying to keep a neutral expression as Pres became more flustered. His lips were set in a perfect pout, and his trademark frown wasn't going anywhere.

"The eggs and bacon aren't even near each other," he said as gravely as he delivered political commentary.

I moved to unpack the groceries, but Pres blocked me.

"No, I'm doing this. I'm being nice," he basically growled, thumping down items on my counter.

"Finding ingredients for *pancakes* shouldn't be hard. I spent five minutes looking for syrup. Is it a condiment or a baking ingredient? Who knows! No one knows!"

He sighed deeply, leaned against the counter, and closed his eyes. "I never should have quit smoking. My head is killing me."

I laughed. "At least you got whipped cream. Fancy."

"That's not for the pancakes," he said evenly, suddenly looking way less flustered and way more secret-sexy-smirk smiley.

I grinned, asking if he wanted to skip to that part, but he frowned and told me this was "very serious business" and required "all his focus."

I nodded, amused by how closely he studied the recipe and carefully worked his way through my kitchen.

"We should probably talk about the phase-out plan," I said, holding up my phone. "Ethan asked for time on your calendar to discuss it. Sable also emailed about your Instagram post, saying she feels it may be possible your content strategy is misaligned against her value propo—"

"Rach," Pres said, rubbing his temple again. "Could you not be my assistant for the next two hours? Could I not be James Prescott St. Clair the fourth for two hours?"

I paused, surprised. "Who would you like to be then?"

"Could I just be a guy trying to make you breakfast?" He smiled, smirky and hopeful. "And you can be a woman who is immensely impressed by my skills. Preferably one who has never dated a chef before. And maybe also has never had pancakes before."

I laughed, agreeing, and while he got organized, I read our horoscopes.

"My domestic environment may be volatile, well, that seems pretty self-explanatory," I said, nodding at my messy counters as Pres shot me a look. "I may experience clashes between family members, but should focus on the positive to bring normalcy and harmony. That's easy peasy. Professionally, it says a colleague may create a negative atmosphere."

Pres scoffed. "Well, that's really any job, isn't it?"

"Yours says you may face adversities on your property

and family fronts."

"That's every day. I work in politics," he said with a shrug, examining an egg to determine the best entry point to crack it. "Oh, I was wondering, who is in that photo?"

I glanced up from my horoscope app. "What photo?"

"The one in your drawer," he said casually. "You and a woman. I noticed it when I grabbed a condom last night."

I was grateful he was distracted by hesitantly tapping the egg on a bowl and scowling at its impenetrable shell.

Because even though I hadn't looked at the photo in months, I could see it clearly. Our arms around each other after I'd graduated high school in brand-new dresses with big smiles. We both looked happy, excited for the future. She was sentenced weeks later.

"That's my mom."

"You keep your vibrator, a very personal item, on your bedside table, and a photo of you with your mother, arguably something for display, in your drawer?"

The great thing about Pres was, he paid attention.

The terrible thing about Pres was, he paid attention.

I laughed. "Well, there is an argument here for easy access to my vibrator. You weren't too bothered by my organization skills last night."

He smirked, but quickly turned back to being analytical. "Yes, but having it in a drawer defeats the purpose of having it framed then, doesn't it? Oh *shit*—" His egg suddenly burst, and he stepped back startled, disgust flashing across his face at his yolky hand.

"It's nice, though, right?" I said with a light laugh. "Less clutter. You should appreciate that."

"Putting one frame away isn't going to solve your clutter problem," he deadpanned as he washed his hands.

"Are you sure you don't need help?"

"I am perfectly capable," he said firmly. "I bought extra. I calculated for a margin of error."

I laughed, ready to jump on the subject change, when he asked, "She looks like you. Are you similar?"

He glanced at me, waiting on what should have been such a simple answer.

I exhaled a deep breath, trying to force my body to not give me away under his sudden focus.

"Yes. Kind of. I don't know."

He made an understanding sound. "Try having the same name, too. It's a hard balance to honor where you came from while forging your own path. It's not easy."

"Yeah." I scratched a nail over my chipped green tile counters, having a hard time meeting his heartbreaking, honest blue eyes. "Does that ever scare you? That you're going to get it all wrong? Make the same mistakes?"

I expected him to say of course not, come on, Rach, get serious, but instead he walked over to me, tucked my hair behind my ear, and gently tipped my chin up until our gazes locked.

"Absolutely. The amount of pressure I put on myself to get it right, the feeling of constantly trying to avoid making mistakes, the weight of knowing who I am and who I don't want to be is because of the same person ... it's exhausting," he said honestly with a small laugh.

My heart tugged in my chest at the possibility that maybe he really did get it. I needed to tell him.

"Actually, it's egg-hausting," he said, laughing loudly at his own joke. I couldn't believe it.

He grinned, cupping my face to give me a deep, hard, impatient kind of kiss that shot sparks down my spine. I turned to lean against the counter and promptly knocked over a bottle of syrup. He quickly righted it, laughing, and moved to randomly punching buttons on my oven.

"You know, breakfast is a very personal matter, James St. Clair."

He smiled, the one I'd fallen in love with. "Then it's a very good thing you're my personal assistant."

It was then I decided I'd eat burned lumpy pancakes and undercooked bacon every morning if it meant I could be with him like this. Him in reading glasses, a Middletown University soccer sweatshirt, and joggers, barefoot in my kitchen as I sat on my counter drinking terrible coffee — since he still hadn't figured out how to use my machine — and watching the most powerful man I knew attempt to make me breakfast just because. Both of us getting closer and closer to the truth, to becoming the people we so desperately wanted to be.

Then he promised he'd clean my kitchen better than he'd cook in it, kissing and kissing me, syrupy sweet, until we fell to my bed.

It was slow and easy, teasing and full of laughter, a soft kiss blooming into a sort of gentle lovemaking that felt different, pure, our hearts beating against each other as he murmured my name, the dewey morning light washing over his skin.

He let me take control, so I slowly caressed his skin, memorizing the lines of his body, pausing on faint scars on his ribcage, the fine lines next to his smiling eyes, and raked my hands through that perfect hair of his, making him laugh.

I almost told him then, whispered in his ear to share yet another secret — that I loved him. Instead, I dropped my lips to his, inhaling his exhales, his breath mine, *mine, mine, mine*, as we came together.

"Tell me about yourself," he said softly afterward as

his fingers flitted through my hair.

"This isn't the usual game we play."

"I don't want to play games anymore, Rach."

"What do you want to know?" I whispered, trying to find the words to tell him all my truths.

He shrugged, his eyes never leaving mine. "Anything. Everything. Who are you? I don't know nearly enough."

I was so tired of faking it. Faking everything.

I wanted to tell him about my mom.

I wanted to tell him I was in love with him.

And I wanted to truly believe that the person I was could be enough.

Instead, I kissed him again to desperately buy myself more time in this perfect moment.

Just this once. Just one more one-time thing.

When we finally got out of bed, he gathered his things, put on a suit, and styled his hair until he transformed, poised and perfect — a hidden nicotine patch under his sleeve the only proof he was the same guy.

"Do you need this?" I asked, grabbing a binder he'd left on my coffee table.

"Oh, no, that's for you. I had some free time to put it together," he said, double-checking his reflection. He frowned and walked back into my bathroom to do something to his hair.

"When in the world did you have free time?" I called after him, but he just laughed.

As I waited, I leaned against my spotless kitchen counter to flip through the binder.

It was the Very Important Person binder we used for our event prep.

Except inside was every resource I could've imagined for Middletown University: a list of classes I could test out of with highlighted deadlines, countless grants and scholarship opportunities for adult learners from campus and the community, numerous essay examples for the Jefferson Fellowship, and a list of personal connections he had to the school with networking ideas sketched out.

I covered my mouth, overwhelmed by a feeling I didn't quite know what to do with, when I read the lone sticky note on the final page: *I've always had the jaded mindset that people believe whatever you want them to believe. But the world doesn't need more people who think like that. The world needs more people like you. You make people believe in themselves, in something better, in something so purely good that you're certain it can't be real. That's power. That's you, Rach. I believe in you as much as you believe in the world. So when you decide who you want to be and where you want to go, I'll be there. -jps*

CHAPTER THIRTY

"We need to talk."

Pres and I stepped back from where we'd been laughing in his elevator, startled by Ethan.

Pres' smile disappeared. "Good morning to you too."

"Hi, Ethan, how are you?" I said cheerfully.

Ignoring me, he frowned at Pres. "Where have you been? I've been waiting."

"That's really none of your business," he responded flatly. "My schedule isn't any of your concern."

"I got here early so we could talk before—" Ethan cut himself off, glancing at me. "Pres, I need to discuss something with you in *private*. Now."

"Do I need to remind you that I'm your boss," Pres snapped. "I don't take orders from you."

"Don't worry, I can take a hint, Ethan," I said with a laugh and stepped away to hang up our coats. "Pres, I'll bring you a coffee in just a moment."

He thanked me and headed to his office, ignoring Ethan on his heels.

"Morning," Olivia said brightly as I walked into the kitchen and the guys disappeared down the hall. "Heads up, Ethan's been on a tirade."

"I've noticed. What's his deal?"

She shrugged. "He's been worse than usual. He totally took over my oppo-research even though Pres actually *complimented* me on it so far. Can you believe it?"

I turned away from the coffee machine, confused. "What do you mean?"

"Pres said I was doing great work. He said he was actually impressed, and I should keep it up—"

"That's great, Olivia. He really does value you. But I meant Ethan. What oppo-research? I thought you all were finished? Isn't that what you presented in DC?"

She shook her head. "No, we'd just started. We really dig in, you know? It's kind of fun, honestly. We're like investigative reporters. Did you know that Pres was in a car accident right after high school?"

"How did you know that? That's not on Google."

"Google has nothing on us," she said with a laugh. "It's pretty typical to talk to people close to the candidate. So I interviewed his former roommate—"

"Roe?"

She shook her head. "No, the other one, Derek. The one Pres says is the loudest person he's ever met?"

I nodded. "Why would Pres' car accident come up?"

"Derek's brother was a victim of the car crash. We had to vet that there weren't issues with the family of the deceased or anything. Like, make sure Derek wouldn't suddenly start saying Pres was somehow to blame. He was taken to a St. Clair-owned hospital, so maybe there's a small possibility it could have been an issue? Speaking of, did you know that Pres' parents never visited him in the hospital?" she said, lowering her voice. "Apparently, the senator was too busy campaigning for reelection."

"The public needs to know that?"

"No, but someone might ask about his icy relationship with his father, and it's important to know what's out there. Sable is already working on statements and answers for those sort of questions. If we want to win, we have to anticipate *everything*."

Suddenly, it hit me.

"Oh my gosh," I gasped.

Maybe I should have seen the signs earlier.

In my defense, I'd been a little distracted.

"What's wrong?"

"I'm sorry, but I need your coffee," I said and grabbed her cup, unable to wait on Pres' to finish. "Excuse me."

I rushed off, pausing at his closed office door to catch my breath. Low murmurs came through the door, but I couldn't catch anything specific.

I knocked and opened it, holding up the coffee as my excuse for entering, and tried to remain calm. Pres was used to me coming in and out to do my job, so he just smiled and looked back at Ethan who had clammed up.

"Everything okay?" I asked, sitting down the cup at the edge of the desk.

"Yes, thanks," Pres said and reached for the mug.

I scooted it away. "Need anything else?"

"No, just the coffee," he said, reaching for it again.

I moved it back and smiled at Ethan. "You peachy?"

Ethan scowled at me but remained silent.

I knew that look.

I'd seen a similar look my whole life.

When the person people believed me to be was shattered.

He knew.

"Rach, could I please have my coffee?"

"It's, uh, actually not yours…"

"Then whose is it, and why is it in my office?"

"Uh," I said, trying to scope out the scene to figure out what had already been revealed. I subtly craned my neck to his computer for a clue, but he was blocking me. "…I don't know."

"You don't know whose coffee you have? I'm not sure I get this joke."

"Actually, could you come show me how you take it?"

"What?" Pres said, somewhere between skeptical and confused. "No, I'm sorry, I don't have time to do that. Ethan and I are in a meeting. It's fine, I'll drink that—"

He reached for it at the same time I tried to move it, our hands colliding. The coffee crashed to the floor.

I gasped, and Pres cursed.

"My *carpet*," he said in disbelief at the splattered mess. "Can you call someone to take care of this? Do I have a carpet person?"

"Sorry, sorry," I said hastily. "I'll grab a towel—"

"Pres, this is wildly unprofessional," Ethan said angrily. "This is exactly what I was trying to say—"

"Enough," Pres snapped before facing me. "Rach, Ethan and I are trying to have a discussion. Could you please come back later?"

I pulled the only card I had.

"It's a mess. It'll stain and ruin. I have to stay."

Ethan groaned.

Pres looked at me then the coffee puddle, weighing the options as he pressed his fingers against his temple.

"Fine," he said after a moment. "Please handle this. Ethan, what were you saying?"

I ran out of the office to grab a towel, trying to think of any way to stop this, to let this good thing we had going last a little bit longer, and came back just as Ethan was saying, "…felon."

I stood at the door, barely breathing, holding a towel in front of myself. It was like Boobgate all over again, except way more than my body had been revealed.

Pres looked up from his desk to meet my eyes.

"Oh."

"Pres," I said, my voice breaking as the towel slipped from my fingers. "I didn't know how to tell you."

"Your mother is a felon," he said, and it wasn't a question, but a statement, a hard, indisputable fact.

...

"You deserve to know the truth," Ethan said to Pres, not acknowledging me. "She's clearly determined to ruin this whole campaign. Where did she come from? Have you considered she's from the other team?"

Pres shook his head. "No, that's not possible."

"Anything is possible."

"Well that's just not true," Pres said flatly.

"I've been trying to tell you since the beginning that she's more risk than reward. She manipulated you to change your plan, and she's manipulating you now. What does she want from you?"

Pres held up his hand to stop him and nodded at his other desk chair. "You need to sit, Rach."

"I don't want anything from you," I said quickly. "You know that. You can trust me."

Instead of responding to that, Pres said, "Ethan has informed me your mother is in federal prison for fraud."

"Identification fraud, credit card fraud, mail fraud, wire fraud, and financial institution fraud," Ethan chimed in, reading off a file folder where all my secrets were spelled out in black and white.

"Is this true?" Pres asked me.

I wanted to make a joke or to point out a silver lining. Instead, I nodded.

"She'd worked her whole life to try to give me more

than what she had, and she made a mistake—"

"A mistake is not realizing that your cashier gave you extra change," Ethan snapped. "She did this to three different families."

He faced Pres, reading off the folder.

"She cleaned their houses, so she had access to their accounts, credit card offers in the mail, all of it." He cut a glance at me. "The apple doesn't fall far from the tree."

He continued, "She saw the chance to hurt these people, and she did. Made fake accounts, spent money that wasn't hers, and ruined people's credit. Ripped away the security that these families worked so hard to build. Thankfully, she'll be locked away for years."

Pres was excellent on television. Aside from Boobgate, he'd never had a gaffe, never misspoke, never struggled for a thought. He'd told me that his family required media training, and he'd started when he was eleven. He'd spent countless hours after school learning exactly how to keep his cool, to remain impassive, to be the best version of himself, regardless of what he was thinking.

And now, that training was coming into perfect use.

"Okay," Pres said with a simple nod. "Rach?"

"I didn't know she was doing it."

Ethan scoffed. "She's your mother. How would you have not known or seen the signs?"

"I found out when I was denied an apartment application," I said steadily even though I'd never said this part out loud before. "I had a credit card I didn't know about under my name. She would use it when she got behind on her payments. She used it to buy food, my school supplies, my clothes. She thought she could pay it off before I went to college because she was going to sell all these leggings. But you have to buy the leggings before you can sell them to other people—"

I shook my head, envisioning the boxes and bags of leggings no one wanted that had filled our living room.

I'd spent so much of my life believing in her, I'd been blind to how bad of a problem it had become.

"She just … ran out of options. I was upset about the apartment, it was in Middletown, I was going to come here for school…" I choked on my words when I met Pres' studying gaze.

I guess I'd finally gotten rid of that point in Truth Chicken. Now he knew why I hadn't gone to Middletown University, why I wasn't a guidance counselor, and how I'd ended up as his assistant.

How this wasn't the life I'd chosen at all.

Funny, winning Truth Chicken didn't feel so great after all.

I'd spent years trying to untangle myself from the situation and to not carry the burden of my mother's greatest mistake even though I was the reason everything fell apart. My very existence was why we struggled. And trying to be different had led to her ruin.

"I told her to do the right thing and confess. She told the families that same day. I don't think either one of us realized the gravity of what she'd done, that it was a felony. She'd planned to pay it back or work it off. She really thought she could. She thought someone would understand. I truly believed someone would be on her side even though I knew what she'd done was wrong. I was so foolish."

I looked at Pres. His brows were furrowed, working this over in his head, his thumb rubbing his index finger — his sign that he wanted a cigarette — the only tell he was freaking out.

"This isn't how I would have told you," I said quietly, shame for my mom's mistakes and shame for who I was, who I'd let myself be — a fraud — washing over me.

Then I turned to Ethan. "You didn't have to do it this way. You could have asked me about it when you found out. You didn't have to go behind my back."

"It's politics," he said flippantly. "It's not personal."

I nodded, gutted, having nothing else to say.

"I told you we didn't know her," Ethan said to Pres. He was smiling. He was *gloating*. "I said she was bad news from the start. I told you she was going to ruin your campaign. I told you so."

Pres stood. "Get out of my office."

I stood.

"Not you," he said sternly. He faced Ethan. "You."

"Excuse me?"

"Was I not clear? How about, get the *fuck* out of my office?" Pres snapped. "Is that clearer?"

The smugness drained from Ethan's face and he stood, shaking his head. "No, wait, I did this for the campaign. For you. We want to win. We need to know what we're up against."

"I never asked you to do this."

"You told me that you wanted to explore continuing with Rach past your announcement—"

I looked up at Pres, surprised. He clenched his jaw and shook his head, focused on Ethan.

"I did not tell you to do this," he said, holding up the file angrily. "I asked you to tell me if it was feasible. I asked if there was a way Rach and I could keep our relationsh-our arrangement in tact without significant public interest or media coverage. I asked you if there was a way I could do this without interrupting her life."

"That doesn't make any sense!"

Even in my shocked state, I almost laughed. Because even though he'd managed to discover all this, he still hadn't come to the conclusion Pres and I were together.

"There was no way to answer that question without knowing who she is," Ethan said, exasperated. "You asking that of me was concerning in itself. You know, I went back and checked the list from the night she just *appeared* outside Hotel Chanceux. She wasn't on it. Why was she talking to you that night? What did she want?"

"People can talk to him without wanting something, Ethan," I interjected. "He already knows I wasn't on the list. You could have asked me about it."

"Why, so you could lie?" he snapped before turning back to Pres. "You don't find that suspicious at all? Her just popping up, then bursting into your office to make Boobgate happen, and then worming her way into the plan? She went from a nobody to your girlfriend in *days*. And for what? Why would she want to be with you so badly?"

Pres' expression turned cold, which Ethan took as a sign that his argument was working.

"Why didn't you want to know what she was hiding? Why did you take your eyes off the goal? Don't you want to win?"

"I don't like to repeat myself," Pres said firmly. "You need to get out of my office."

"You can't be serious! I've studied all the St. Clair campaigns, and this is exactly the sort of thing your father would appreciate—"

"I am not my father."

"And you'll never be if you tie yourself to this," Ethan shouted, pointing at me and snatching up the file folder.

"You can't win with this associated with your name! You won't get lucky again like with Boobgate. If you approve of *her*, you're approving of her mother. You know how this will look! You condone stealing from people. How do you think taxpayers will feel about that? I never thought a *St. Clair* would be this foolish. You are—"

"You are not a team player. You are unprofessional. You are combative. You are insubordinate," Pres said, his voice icier, quieter, lower, and stronger than Ethan's outburst. "And you're *really* fucking unlikable. You are fired, Ethan."

Ethan stormed out and slammed the office door, leaving Pres and me in silence.

I struggled to find words, stunned that he'd so swiftly been on my side. "Thank you for that, thank you so—"

"Cancel all my meetings," he said, sitting down and rubbing his eyebrow. "I need you to clear my schedule."

"I'm so sorry. I can find a way—"

"Please stop talking," he said gravely.

"You have every right to be mad at me—"

"I'm having a migraine attack," he said, closing his eyes and leaning forward in his chair, his head in his hands.

I jumped to his side, but he brushed me off.

"Let me help you, Pres."

He stood, catching his balance with his fingers on his desk, and walked me to his door.

"You've done enough. Help me by letting me take a personal day, Rach."

Before I could respond, he shut the door in my face.

CHAPTER THIRTY-ONE

"Well, shit," Sable said as she walked up to where I was waiting at the airport. She tossed her hot pink designer luggage in my trunk, placed her hands on her hips, and cursed again.

"I'm … sorry?" I said slowly. "Is there something else I can do for you?"

"Now it all makes sense," she said, shaking her head. "You should really get a better webcam. You're even more gorgeous in person. God, how tall are you?"

"Like five ten?"

She sighed. "That'll do it. I knew something about that meeting in DC was weird. So you and Pres are sleeping around? That's what caused all this?"

"Oh, uh, well," I stumbled, "we're committed to the ruse and that can manifest in interesting ways."

She bit the straw of her iced coffee, not smearing her pearly pink lipstick at all, and laughed through her teeth.

"Geez, thanks for making my job even harder. Seriously, I like a challenge," she added. "I guess you do, too, huh? Nailing Pres. Mr. Untouchable."

I shook my head, unsure of what she knew or what I should say.

The past two days had been a flurry of chaos.

In the wake of Ethan's absence, Pres had closed himself in his bedroom, not saying a word to anyone.

Olivia and Jamar panicked and scrambled to help find a campaign manager replacement while I avoided questions about what had happened.

That night, I slept in my own bed, realizing just how lonely it felt without Pres taking up more than half of it.

When I arrived at his penthouse the next morning, he'd already run five miles, booked two interviews, and called Sable. I walked into his office with coffee, startled by the visual of him holding a can of Lysol in a suit.

"Should we talk?" I asked.

He held up the cleaner. "Does this work on desks?"

I nodded.

"I want a new carpet," he said, aggressively wiping down nonexistent dust. "Can you handle that? Sable is flying in this afternoon, so I'll need you to pick her up. Jamar has created a job posting, so if you can coordinate interviews on my calendar, that would be great. I've also emailed several people I know who may be interested. Please tell Olivia she can finish my announcement speech. Ethan was nearly done. I'll rewrite it once I have a draft to look at. I also need you to push all my client meetings and cancel everything else on my schedule. No holiday parties, no fake dates, whatever. Finding a new campaign manager has to be my priority."

"So that's a no on talking?"

"I can still see the coffee stain," he said, nodding toward the brown splotch on his otherwise pure white carpet. He sat down the Lysol with a hard thunk.

"I can take care of it. I'll find a carpet person. I'm sorry for spilling it in the first place."

He inhaled deeply and looked right at me.

"Were you ever going to tell me?"

"I hadn't found the right time just yet."

He nodded. "Well, yes, I suppose great timing isn't your forte. Boobgate being a prime example."

I winced. "Pres—"

"I'm kidding," he said, giving me a weak smile. "Sorry, bad at being funny, remember?" His expression grew serious. "We're going to be busy, Rach. If you need to take time off, now's the time to ask."

"No, I'm here."

"Okay." He stood, tall, strong, and guarded, and adjusted his jacket. "Then let's get to work."

I nodded, turning to walk away.

"Rach, wait," he said at the last second, making my heart jump. "Could I get my Amex back?"

My heart sank.

"Of course," I said, sliding the black metal card across his spotless desk.

"Thank you," he said, not looking at me as he slipped it back in his wallet.

I pointed at his door. "Do you want this open?"

He sat down, looking lost in thought even though he wasn't looking at anything. Then he inhaled deeply, once again impassive.

"No," he said shortly, "keep it closed."

"Okay, let's get this show on the road," Sable said after a car horn blared behind me, a most poignant reminder that I'd been parked too long in the airport pick-up area.

She settled into my car, much too glamorous and blonde to be folded carefully in my cracked seats and crumbly floorboards, and turned to study me.

"I looked you up right after Boobgate," she said, shaking the ice in her cup. "Nothing. I thought you were perfect. A total blank slate."

"I'm sure you were under pressure," I said gently.

"There was a media crisis happening. You probably didn't have time to do a lot of digging."

"No, I was right, you were perfect," she said with a shrug. "I mean, look at you now, being sympathetic when things are in shambles."

"Shambles feels like a harsh word. Would you be opposed to shenanigans or surprising shake-up?"

She laughed. "Rach, this isn't a thesaurus competition, it's a mayoral campaign. Anyway, I'm pretty much up to speed on the situation. Ethan has been fired and won't answer my calls, Pres refuses to tell me what the deep dark secret is, but it's not that he — my uptight, nearly perfect, almost electable boss — is having a fling, and we announce a St. Clair is running for mayor in two weeks. And somehow, you, the assistant no one knows, is in the middle of it all. I'd say shambles is an accurate descriptor. Do you have anything else you'd like to add?"

"He could've fired me. But he didn't. Twice."

"Is it bad or good things that happen in threes?"

"I'm still trying to figure that out."

She laughed and fiddled with my radio, settling on an '80s ballad before whipping out her phone to work.

We didn't speak until I parked on Pres' street. I glanced up at the penthouse, my heart aching at the thought of him still sitting in his office staring at nothing. I'd seen Pres in a lot of scenarios, but unsure of his next move had never been one of them.

"I went on a fake date years ago," Sable said, checking her reflection in my visor. Without a single smudge or hair out of place, she radiated beauty and power. She was also, I realized, slightly terrifying. "With Pres' former roommate, Derek, have you heard of him? He's really loud and kind of chaotic? His parents renewed their vows, and I guess his ex was going. He wouldn't really get into why he was so upset about it, but he asked me to go with him and pretend to be his girlfriend."

I smiled. "Hopefully it was kind of fun?"

She rolled her eyes. "He ditched me within the first hour to yell at his ex. Then he spent the whole night staring at her when she wasn't looking and scowling when she was. But I'd be lying if it didn't inspire some of my future client solutions."

I laughed. "So it wasn't so bad?"

She smiled. "Pres also attended. Without a date. He thought us pretending to be together was the stupidest idea he'd ever heard. He said something so disingenuous and dumb was destined to fail because liars never win."

I swallowed hard, feeling the sweet sting of her words against my cheeks.

"Okay," she said on a chipper exhale and opened her door. "Let's go. PR crises don't get solved in personal assistants' cars, do they? Nope, no, they don't."

Once inside, she beelined to his office and shut the door before I could even offer coffee or water.

After a day full of meetings, interviews, and disarray, we ended up pulling an all-nighter accompanied by cold pizza and leftover birthday wine.

"I can't believe this," Jamar said, a phrase he'd been repeating for hours, as he ran by with a box of mini-American flags. "We're so close to the press conference. Pres couldn't wait until after to blow this all up? I don't get this strategy."

"Maybe this is a good thing," Olivia offered from where she'd given up and was just laying on the floor.

Jamar groaned. "How so?"

Both of them looked at me.

I glanced up from my overwhelmed inbox. "What?"

"We're waiting for you to tell us how this is a good thing," Jamar said. "How it'll all work out in the end."

Before I could answer, Sable walked into the dining room, grabbed a wine bottle by the neck, drank directly from it, and pulled out her phone, furiously typing.

"What's happening?" Jamar whispered. "Why did he fire Ethan? Is this one of those plans that only makes sense to political geniuses?"

Before Sable could enlighten the group, Pres appeared.

Olivia shot up, and Jamar clumsily attempted to hide the wine behind the box of flags.

"It's fine," Pres sighed. He'd changed clothes, startlingly attractive in a windbreaker, running pants, and the baseball hat he'd bought me at the DC hotel gift shop. "No one said being in politics is easy."

He reached out his cup — my *Good Meowning* mug — to the bottle Sable hadn't commandeered. Jamar tipped wine in his cup, and we all glanced around, a silly little vibration in the air at our boss being one of us.

"Cheers," Pres said, holding up his cup in a salute before downing it in one drink. I reached out, brushing my hand against his. He glanced at me and smiled, a tired, sad smile that hit right in the most tender part of my heart. "I'm going on a run."

And then he left, the elevator chiming his departure before we could react.

I stared at where he'd just stood, noticing he'd carelessly placed his mug on a draft of his announcement speech. A half-moon of red wine stained the pages where he'd say this had been always been his dream.

"Sable," I said. "Could I get a meeting with you?"

She looked up from her phone, raising one perfectly

manicured eyebrow. "Professionally or personally?"

"Professionally," I said, my heart sinking. "Definitely professional."

. . .

He came back late, sweaty, breathless, and smelling like cigarettes, surprised to see Sable and me waiting on his couch.

"Hey," he said, giving us a strange look. "Sable, why are you still here?"

"I'm here for purely professional purposes," she said, glancing up from her phone and raising her fingers in a Boy Scout's promise. "Rach asked me to be here."

The confusion on his face deepened.

"Have you been smoking?" I asked, worried between that, red wine, and stress, he'd trigger another migraine.

He looked at me coolly. "Would you like me to lie?"

"Can we go to your office?" I asked, standing when he didn't move.

"No," he said, frowning. "No, we cannot. I'm not working right now. You aren't my assistant right now."

"Well, I'm working," Sable said, standing between us. "Pres, there's no easy way to do this—"

"Why is my PR person attending what sounds like the beginning of a bad breakup?" he interrupted with a dry laugh. "Get out, Sable. I'm going to bed."

"You're being dumped, Pres!" she called after him.

He rolled his eyes before turning down his hallway.

I whirled around to face her. "*Why* did you say it like that?"

"You have to rip it off like a bandage. Surely this isn't the first time he's been dumped." Her eyes widened. "Oh shit, I bet this is the first time he's been dumped."

I sighed, ignoring her, and followed him into his

bedroom where he was taking off his pullover.

"Could you put your shirt back on? We need to have a serious discussion."

He shook his head and headed into his bathroom. "No, I don't think so."

"What? Yes. Pres, please let's go to your office."

"No," he said, reaching into his shower to turn on the water.

Okay, so we were doing this here.

It seemed fitting.

This had all started because of his shower anyway.

I cleared my throat and pulled up the email I'd just sent him. "Dear James Prescott St. Clair the fourth, I am writing this letter to notify you that I am formally resigning—"

He scoffed, pausing from slipping off his running pants. "We've been through this before, haven't we?"

"This time is different. I'm being serious."

"Why, because I slipped up once and smoked? I'm quitting. I have quit. People make mistakes. I needed to clear my head."

"Of course not. We had a deal. I pretend to be your girlfriend and when it's over, I quit. I think it's fair to say it's over now."

"I don't agree."

"That was the agreement."

"Well, I don't agree to it anymore."

"It's not up to you!"

He reeled back, stunned by my raised voice.

"It's not up to you," I repeated, lowering my voice. "You can't control this, okay? We can't be together, Pres."

I had known this would happen.

I hadn't needed a sign to predict the end. We'd known

the rules of the game the whole time.

I'd practiced this scenario over and over, thinking my heart would be ready.

I just hadn't realized how much it would really hurt.

When I'd explained the situation to Sable earlier, I'd asked her for blunt honesty.

A douse of cold reality.

"No one will vote for him if this gets out. Ethan will take this to the other side. We'll never find a campaign manager who would advocate to keep you around. And Pres is refusing to even poll it," she'd said. "If he won't poll it, it's because he already knows the truth."

"The truth being?"

"You'll ruin his campaign. And he's going to let you."

I'd winced then, knowing that despite the world seeing Pres as cold and distant, my grumpy Capricorn was loyal. And I couldn't let his loyalty to the wrong person — me — jeopardize his dream.

There was no silver lining here.

There was no positive spin.

The truth was, sometimes bad things had to happen for the greater good. Tonight, I had to be that bad thing.

With my heart breaking in perfect pieces that only Pres would be able to reorganize in a future that wasn't for us, I'd made a choice.

Now, with the thundering shower steaming behind us, Pres stared at me with the familiar expression where he didn't seem sure how I'd ended up in his life.

"Is this really how you feel?"

"This isn't about feelings," I said evenly. "This is about facts."

He scoffed. "Well these certainly aren't fun facts."

I crossed my arms over my chest, trying to muster all

my strength. Because in a strange twist of fate, winning meant losing the most stubborn man I'd ever met.

"I thought I'd been clear when I'd said this couldn't last. I've been saying it this whole time. I've tried to be respectful of your feelings."

He looked at me incredulously. "Respectful of my *feelings*? Which part was that, the lying or the stringing me along for weeks?"

"Whoa," Sable said, jumping back from where she'd barged through the door. "Do you two ever keep your shirts on? Holy shit this could be misconstrued ten ways to Sunday. Is this consensual? Are we all okay with this clothing situation?"

"Yes," we both snapped in her direction.

She nodded and pulled out her phone. "Okay, I'm just jotting this down for my records. Also, Pres, sidebar, but would you be open to me leaking a few innocent shirtless photos of you? I think they could resonate with several demographics."

"Please leave!" we said in unison. She held up her hands innocently and backed out, saying she really wasn't paid enough for this much partial nudity.

I shook my head and refocused on my email, "… resigning from my position as your personal assistant, effective immediately—-"

"Are you joking? Stop it," Pres snapped. "Stop reading that email."

I raised my voice over his. "—I appreciate the opportunity for professional growth you provided during my time—"

"Did any of this mean anything to you?"

When I met his gaze, it was a look I'd seen a few times before — when I'd asked him why he thought he was special enough to win an election, when I'd asked in the grocery store if he'd believed we were meant to meet, when I hadn't answered why I was his assistant or what I wanted to do with my life, when I'd told him trivia was just a game, when I'd asked who I should be at his birthday party.

A look where he wanted to say something but was stopping himself. And that was the problem. He didn't live in a world where he could be honest and win.

I looked back down at the email, the words suddenly watery and blurry.

"…While I've enjoyed my employment, it is now time for me to move on to other opportunities. I wish you and your team the best."

I cleared my throat and locked my phone. I stared at the floor, trying to let the choking, overwhelming emotion in my chest pass. I had to stay strong.

My mom had ruined her future because she'd wanted the best for me. Because she'd been blinded by silver linings, hopeful endings, unfounded fortunes, and love.

I couldn't let Pres do the same.

"It was all fun and games, but this is serious now, Pres. I don't want to do it anymore. We have to stop before it gets too real. It isn't real," I said stoically. "It'd never been real."

His eyes were icy burning blue when I met his gaze.

"Well, I'm sorry I miscalculated the gravity of what we were doing," he said over the roar of the shower. "I'm particularly sorry I ever gave you a chance."

I shook my head, my heart veering unpredictably close to how I really felt: "You wouldn't have if you'd known."

"Well we don't know that now, do we?" he snapped. "I can't suppose what I would have done in the past, and

I didn't get the chance, did I?"

"How could I tell you?" I asked, suddenly angry.

At the universe. At him for being him.

And mostly, at myself.

"I couldn't just say, 'Hi, these are my boobs, my mom is a felon, and I have a lot of baggage, but please keep me around if you need coffee or a fake date so people will like you.' Please, I didn't need to be a pollster to know the probability of that working out was zero. You know you would have fired me the second you found out. I needed this job, Pres, and you were my only option."

A flash of hurt crossed his face, quickly followed by a scowl. Then he took a breath and steadied his features, his emotions shuttering, composing himself so tightly that he was almost unrecognizable.

"I should have never expected more from you," he said evenly. "You've just been using me. I guess you've been pretty honest about who you are the whole time, haven't you, *Ruth*?"

I was stunned by the harshness in his tone.

He narrowed his eyes, his words dripping with scorn, every syllable enunciated perfectly, each cold word hitting me right in the heart, "You're a liar. You're a mess. And you're a fake."

"And I guess there is some truth to you being unlikable," I snapped. "I'm not your girlfriend. I was never your girlfriend. I quit, Pres."

CHAPTER THIRTY-TWO

When my mom used to say life was a circle, I hadn't thought she'd meant delivering coffees to assistants.

"Hazel-nilla latte with extra foam, here you go."

"I said vanilla-nut," Kelsey said without looking up from her computer.

"Well, I'm not a very good assistant, and I'm sure you'll find a way to get over it," I said cheerfully and kept walking.

It had been one week.

One long week of coffee runs, errands no one else wanted, personal questions, side glances filled with suspicion, curiosity, or jealousy — sometimes all three if I was lucky — and a general sense of being so over it.

One week since I'd run out of Pres' bathroom. He'd slammed the door behind me so hard that his new assistant would definitely be replacing his office carpet *and* bathroom lock.

One week since I'd rushed to his elevator, hitting the call button repeatedly as hot, sad, angry tears fought for their release.

"Oh my god," Sable had said. "I didn't realize you two were in…to each other that much. That was *brutal*."

I'd wiped the back of my hand over my eyes, jabbing the button even harder. "Can you do me a favor?"

"Yeah, of course, anything."

"If you ask Pres, he says he takes his coffee black. He wouldn't even believe you if you told him otherwise," I'd said quickly, fighting every instinct to go back to him and pretend this would all work out in the name of love. "But the secret is, he actually likes it with a splash of honey and a dash of cinnamon. He doesn't realize that. So could you tell his new assistant for me? Please?"

She'd nodded, shocked. "Yeah, sure, is that all?"

One week since his elevator had opened, and I'd raced inside, covering my face with my hands, not wanting to see the Rach looking back at me.

One week since I'd stopping thinking things would just work out if I believed hard enough.

When I arrived back at my work desk — a tiny one between the bathroom and a trash can I'd never noticed was truly awful before — I tried to think of all the positives.

I squeezed my eyes closed and really, really tried.

My phone ringing interrupted the moment.

"Hi, Ms. Montgomery? This is James St. Clair's assistant. Are you available for a meeting this evening? We can send a car."

"Um," I said eloquently.

"Great," she said cheerfully. "I've texted you the details. The Senator looks forward to meeting you."

...

James St. Clair III's mansion was brimming with life.

Pecunia seemed like a quaint, cute town, straight out of a book of postcards. But that charm disappeared once the car twisted and turned up a series of hills until we were above the whole city.

When we'd passed through a golden gate, drove down a long cobblestone driveway, and circled a fountain, I had thought we were entering a neighborhood. It wasn't until the car parked and a man opened my door to welcome me to "the estate" that I realized this was his *house*.

I stood dumbfounded in the marble foyer while a 40-foot Christmas tree was being disassembled by a team of workers. The whole place was bustling, people cleaning, some directing, some swapping out holiday decorations with regular decor. Several smartly dressed people just seemed to be here to look busy and important, and an actual butler asked if I'd like still or sparkling water. I numbly shook my head.

"Ms. Montgomery," a delighted voice boomed out from the top of a marble staircase with a crushed velvet runner. It was literally a red carpet. "Welcome, welcome, please come in. Make yourself at home!"

I looked up to see a ghost.

Or at the very least, a man whose face dominated the news and looked like a strikingly similar older version of the guy I'd just dumped.

As he descended the stairs, a trail of people followed, taking my coat and slipping my phone out of my hands.

"Hi," I said, offering my hand, thankful for all the events I'd attended to be prepared for this. "I'm honored to meet you, Senator St. Clair."

He clasped both my hands with his big, warm, soft ones and beamed, a stunningly perfect smile splitting his handsome face.

His assistant — whose name I still didn't know — had suggested I dress business casual. I was in a blazer, slacks, and a silky shirt, suddenly wondering if business casual meant something different in this world. The senator oozed comfort and casualness in soft-looking jeans, a cozy sweater, and a navy *puffy* vest.

"It's so nice to meet you," he said, sounding like he really meant it. "Please, call me James, of course. I'm just like you, darling, I don't need any of those fancy titles."

I was guided through several corridors dripping in stately art pieces until we reached thick, ornately carved wooden doors.

"Oh wow," I said, stunned by his massive office. It was all velvets and warm woods, accented by golds and marble. "You have a fireplace."

He laughed loudly, the jovial sound making me jump, and pulled out a plush wingback chair for me.

"That's where we file all the negative press, isn't that right, team?" he said good-naturedly with another charming laugh. "I'm just teasing, of course. I'm sure you understand, don't you, dear? I've seen you've been hit pretty hard with it before, too. All that nonsense with your … well, I apologize, darling, I'm struggling to think of a neutral word…"

He looked to his entourage for assistance.

"Unmentionables."

"Mammary glands."

"Bosom."

He snapped his fingers and nodded. "Yes, great work, everyone. Please, Ms. Montgomery, sit. We can't have you uncomfortable, now can we? What sort of water are we getting you? Do we have someone working on that?"

"Yes, of course," a woman in a blue blazer said. "We have someone on it."

He sank down in a well-worn leather chair, smiling appreciatively at his team. "Great. Speed that up, would you? We can't have our guest parched. Are you parched?"

I opened and closed my mouth. Then realized it looked like I was actually *miming* being parched.

"I'm fine," I said quickly. "I had water today."

"She's already had water," he said to his team where they stood behind me. "Did anyone ask her about this?"

"We'll cancel the water," said a different woman in a black blazer. "We're taking care of it."

"Oh, you don't have to cancel it. Sorry," I said, running my hands through my thick hair nervously.

A man in a navy blazer strode in, brandishing a crystal pitcher of water and a matching glass on a silver tray.

"Now I thought we'd solved this water problem," the senator said to a different person in a different blazer. "I was told it had been taken care of."

"I love water," I said, jumping up to grab the pitcher before someone asked how I liked it poured. The fireplace was roaring, and I was definitely aggressively sweating. "I can drink it like a fish. Do fish drink water?"

He flicked his eyes to his staff. "Can someone please find that out for us?"

"Already on it," a woman said and dashed out.

"Alrighty then. Thanks so much, folks. Once again, great work," he said graciously and settled back in his chair. His team filtered out until it was just us. "What a bunch of fucking idiots, don't you think?"

"Oh, uh," I stammered.

He winked, like we'd shared an inside joke, and laughed again with a wave of his hand. "I'm kidding. They're great. You aren't used to playing around, are you? My son isn't big on jokes, is he?"

"Um," I said.

"I'm not usually in town, but with the holidays and the legislative recess, I try to pop over. It's kismet, don't you think, dear, that I'm here right when things are going downhill for you?"

He flipped open a file folder and popped on reading glasses, his voice silky smooth, "Rach Montgomery, twenty-four years old, associates degree in general studies—" he glanced up at me, the crook of his charming smile poised to share another inside joke "—well, that's just a big bunch of nothing, is it? Dismal credit, concerning apartment, dead-end job, unknown father, and a mother in prison. This was quite an interesting read. Now why don't you have a middle name?"

I was so shocked that all I could do was answer.

"My mom thought Rach was good enough. She didn't see the point if I already had a first name, I guess?"

He nodded, a huge smile breaking over his barely worn face. The only significant signs of weathering on his skin were *smile* lines.

His eyes were also different from Pres', less icy blue and more navy, warm and deep like the sky before a storm.

"Tell that to my son, why don't you?" He laughed, slapping his hand over the file folder to accentuate how funny it was. "But I see you, darling, I see that you've worked really hard and it's been tough on you. You can't seem to catch a break. It seems unfair, wouldn't you say?"

"Everyone has bad days."

"And you've had a whole bunch, haven't you?" he said with a warm, sympathetic smile.

I looked down at my hands, very taken aback by this incredibly nice, magnetic man dripping with charisma.

"Now I don't like to make promises," he said, rolling on as if I'd agreed with what he'd said instead of just sitting here looking stupid. "Instead, I like to make things happen. I'm not big on discussing theory. My son, sure, he can talk all day about what politicians *should* do and how public servants *should* act, but I have a whole staff tirelessly dedicated to telling me what I want to know. I can't spend all my time theorizing and number crunching and hoping and wishing, don't you think?"

I shrugged, unsure if he was really asking my opinion.

All of his words were at odds with each other, but when they were strung together, it felt like they did make a lot of sense.

He smiled pleasantly, waiting on my answer.

"I guess you are right," I said slowly.

"You're right," he echoed. "You're absolutely correct, Ms. Montgomery."

"Oh, thanks? I mean, thank you," I said, clearing my throat.

He nodded and pointed to the water, so I took a drink.

"I have to be honest with you. My son being in politics gives me kind of a headache," he said, his fingers barely grazing his temple. "I don't know if you noticed, but he's been going on and on about how I'm not the best. How James the fourth is different. I've seen the numbers. With this, he could go far. He doesn't stop at mayor, does he? I worry the kid might be gunning for my job," he said with a laugh. "People like this messaging. It's a really great strategy. My son is a genius. I wish I'd thought of it myself," he said with another deep laugh. "But mixing personal with politics can get messy, don't you think?"

I did agree. He was right.

"Exactly," he said, and I was almost convinced Pres' father could read minds. "My son never wants me around and never wants to talk to me because I'm involved in politics. He doesn't like to share, does he?"

I tried to think back on all the things Pres had said about his dad … was it possible he'd misconstrued the facts? Surrounded by this warmth, luxury, and a father figure so clearly concerned ... was it really that bad or was Pres just being negative?

"He doesn't really get it, does he?" James continued. I covered my mouth with my hand, checking to make sure I hadn't said all that out loud. "You seem like you've spent a lot of time with him. And now that it's all said and done, I'm curious, what did you get out of it?"

I wasn't about to tell him Pres had promised to leverage himself in a letter of recommendation to wherever I wanted. He probably already knew. And it didn't matter because I was never getting that letter now.

And I certainly wasn't going to admit that all I'd really gotten was a parcel delivered at my door a few days ago filled with things I'd left behind. I didn't recognize the handwriting on the box, so this — like all the other things he didn't want to deal with or felt weren't worth his time — had been delegated to his assistant.

I'd dug through a potholder, blanket, toothbrush, two bras, my cat mug, and more, searching for something, anything, that said maybe we could at least be friends.

All I'd found buried at the bottom was the photo of us in his kitchen, the corner ripped from where it'd hung on his fridge.

He hadn't needed a note. His message was clear.

There was no going back.

I was a user. A liar. A mess. And a fake.

It was over.

I tried to smile, but it felt tight and forced. "It was a learning experience."

"Do learning experiences pay bills?" James asked, deep concern etched on his face. "Did all that learning get you closer to..." He glanced down at the file folder. There was a lot to choose from. "...Any of your goals?"

I took another drink and glanced at the fireplace, wondering if his staff had slipped more wood in it.

"I didn't think so either," he said gently. "Don't you think it's time for a change? Aren't you tired?"

Without even thinking, I nodded.

"Your mother was tired, too. She made mistakes. She didn't have anyone, did she? But you've done well since you've been all alone. It just doesn't seem right that this is the end of your story. And my son, my *wonderful* son, ends up with everything. Is that fair?"

I gulped my water. "Technically?"

He shook his head. "You don't feel like it's fair, do you? I'm curious, Ms. Montgomery, what do you want? What can your senator do for you?"

"What do I want?" I repeated.

"I can help you," he said, fanning the pages from my file folder with his thumb. The air felt cool on my flushed face, and I closed my eyes, letting his next words sink in, "You can have what you want with a flick of your wrist. You can *be* anyone. Doesn't that sound nice?"

I nodded, the same feeling I'd had in the dress shop on Pres' faux birthday wash over me. An intense desire to take. To fulfill all my wishes easily. Before, it had been wrong to consider using his Amex.

But this ... this was fair game.

"I know a lot of people, maybe we could find someone interested in helping get your mother out early?"

"Is that possible?"

He smiled. "Anything is possible."

I was stunned.

"Wouldn't it be fun if you had an assistant? A job here where you aren't the lowest on the totem pole?" He swept his hands out, and, somehow, the room seemed even grander and more lavish. "You can have anything, Rach. All you have to do is tell me, and I can make it happen."

"What do I have to do in exchange?" I asked slowly.

He shrugged, like all he'd ask for was a light.

"You tell the truth. All I want is for you to be honest."

"Okay...?"

"A news interview," he said simply. "You've already mastered the element of surprise on national television, so an easy one-on-one on the local news would be like the little leagues to you, isn't that right?"

"I don't really do media appearances. No one really knows who I am..."

"That's a shame. More people should know who you are. You could be really special, Rach."

I closed my eyes. I had been *so close* to getting what I'd wanted. A good job. A future. Proof I wasn't all bad luck. I'd come so far just to end up right back where I'd started.

What had been the point of any of it?

I opened my eyes to see James smiling at me.

"Just an interview?"

He nodded, his eyes crinkling at the corners. He must have smiled like this all the time. "You just answer simple questions. Things you already have the answers to."

"Nothing negative about Pres, though, right?"

James looked concerned by the idea. "I can only ask you to tell the truth. I can't control how it comes out of your mouth, can I, dear?"

I opened my mouth and closed it. Then I nodded.

"If you want to go back to the life you're living right now," he said, holding up the file folder, "that's fine, too. But this could be life-changing."

I should have never expected more from you.

You're a liar. You're a mess. And you're a fake.

If the only person who'd ever really believed in me and saw me for me thought that, I didn't really have anywhere to go but up, right?

I nodded. "Okay."

"Excellent. Let's get it all arranged." As if on cue, the doors opened and his staff returned. "We'll get you set up on the news the day before. My team will make sure the local feeds into the national, so no worries there. We took some liberties with the facts when we briefed the reporter, but they're close enough so that the interview will feel natural. The truth always sounds a little better when it's spruced up. People love to *feel* facts, Rach, you get this, of course. Just stick to the talking points, and everything else falls into place."

"I'm a little confused," I said, feeling like I only had enough time to ask one question before the chaos fully surrounded me. "The day before what?"

"Fish don't drink water," a woman said, kneeling next to me. "They breathe it. It's like their air."

"Excellent," James said, his exuberant voice filling the space. Everyone beamed at me. "I'm so glad we found that out! Great work, everyone. Now let's get Rach booked. When is my son's announcement again?"

"January eighth."

"Book her for January seventh."

I glanced down at the talking points that had appeared on my lap: *Hi, I'm Rach Montgomery, the woman behind Boobgate … and I'm excited to tell you my truths.*

"Rach," James said with a smile. It was the warmest, nicest smile I'd ever seen. I was suddenly parched, my heart pounding. "I hope you're ready for your luck to change."

CHAPTER THIRTY-THREE

Something Pres had never told me, never complained about, never even acted like was an issue, was how hot studio lights were.

I'd watched countless clips of him, and he'd never broken a sweat. He always looked comfortable in a suit.

And here I was, in a tiny scrap of a dress, melting.

"Wow, these can get you cooking," I said with a laugh as the cameraman adjusted the lights next to me. "Do you have a tool in case I melt to the leather?"

Penelope Rose — *Middletown's favorite reporter* was how she'd introduced herself — laughed across from me.

"You should save those jokes for the camera, Rach."

I smiled and nervously adjusted my hair to fall in front of my chest.

We were at one of the local news stations, empty anchor desks steps away and the meteorologist's screen just beyond that. I'd never been in a studio before, always shying away from cameras and Pres had never minded.

So I was surprised to see how big it was and that it all took place in one large, darkish, industrial room with strategically placed lights to tell me where to look.

We were off to the side in two facing armchairs next to a remarkably realistic potted plant. It wasn't until I touched its hard waxy leaves that I realized it was fake. The coffee cup they'd given me was empty, but they told me to hold it and sip it sometimes if I felt the urge to shift.

I glanced at one of the senator's assistants who held actual steaming hot coffee. I guess there really were some perks assistants had over their clients.

A makeup artist stepped forward and gently moved my hair back behind my shoulders.

"I'm sorry," I said, trying to shift away from the heated lights. "I don't mean to insult anyone's work or ideas, but this dress you asked me to wear seems a little ... tight?"

They'd also redone my makeup, slathering products I'd never heard of on my face until I barely recognized myself in the mirror.

"You look great. The camera always makes things look different."

"Like ... bigger? Or looser? I know I'm known for my boobs, but this seems like—"

"You look great," she repeated and looked over at the assistant. "This is the dress you wanted, right?"

She nodded. "Senator St. Clair insisted."

"He did?" I twisted to face her, mortified my thighs squeaked against my seat with each movement. How was I always the least clothed and most embarrassed every single time? "He insisted I wear a dress where my boobs spill out like two melting icebergs on TV? You're certain?"

She smiled. "Wow, you *are* funny."

I gave up. It didn't matter. What was another dress that wasn't mine for another event where I didn't belong?

If Pres and I were on speaking terms, I would've loved to ask if people dictated his clothes. I couldn't imagine someone telling him to unbutton more buttons. And I certainly couldn't imagine him being basically shirtless on television.

But I hadn't heard from him since I'd emailed him

Happy New Year and asked if maybe one day we could grab a drink as friends.

My heart had jumped when I'd received an immediate response — *You too! Thank you so much, Rachel. Mr. St Clair is currently out of the office and unable to respond to messages. I'll be certain to pass along yours should it require a response. Best, Carolyn, EA to James Prescott St. Clair IV*

That had been six days ago, so I'd gotten the message clearly. The last words he'd ever speak to me still rang in my ears: *You're a liar. You're a mess. And you're a fake.*

"This isn't live, right?" I asked. "Because I really don't feel comfortable with live television."

Penelope looked up from her notes and nodded. "Correct. It's a pre-recorded spot, so we'll be able to add in b-roll and voiceovers after. Work in a couple other interviews. It'll run during primetime."

I nodded, glancing down at my talking points. I'd memorized everything, and it had been so simple. It was literally a one-pager about myself, peppered with the sort of easy questions I could expect: about my childhood, relationships, and employment.

Ironically, these were questions Sable had prepped me with when Pres and I had first started our agreement.

"Okay, let's begin," Penelope said once the lights were fully melting my skin and I'd been miked up. At least the microphone provided some additional coverage near my cleavage. She counted down and on a silent three, I was suddenly aware of the massive camera pointed at me.

I took a deep breath.

I just had to get through this, and I could move on.

The senator had promised I'd be compensated well. He'd painted the future so brightly. And if all I had to do was wear an uncomfortable, borrowed dress for the last time in my life and answer questions about my boring self, I could handle it.

I didn't have anything else to lose.

Because I was a liar, a mess, and a fake.

"Rach, you made quite a name for yourself after going viral several months ago when you stumbled onto Pres St. Clair's broadcast on CNN. Was that really unplanned?"

I laughed and nodded. "Yeah, I promise, I was just as startled as the entire viewership, too."

"Pres was your boss at the time, right? You two had an interesting relationship … you were his assistant *and* girlfriend?"

I glanced over Penelope's shoulder to the senator's assistant, but she just nodded for me to continue.

"Uh, sorry, can we pause?" I glanced at the camera, not sure exactly how this worked. "I can't talk about my relationship with Pres."

Penelope titled her head. "Why's that?"

"I have an NDA and, uh, what we had was private."

"He made you sign an NDA?" She leaned forward. "Was this before or after the relationship started?"

I looked at the assistant for help, but she said nothing.

"I told the senator I couldn't talk about his son."

"Interesting," Penelope said slowly. "Okay, let's move on. How did your friends and family react when you went viral?"

I smiled. "My ex-boyfriend couldn't believe it, but he was a good sport about it. He thought it was funny. I told my mom in the most delicate way possible, and she was speechless."

Penelope squinted at me, looking displeased.

"Your mother was speechless?"

"Yep, she probably couldn't believe it. But honestly,

being a part of Boobgate was kind of great. I think I reached a lot of people who maybe wouldn't be interested in politics otherwise," I said with a practiced laugh.

When this ended, I had to write Sable a thank-you note. She'd unintentionally prepared me so well for this.

"Pres knew you weren't very involved in politics before you got together, correct? It's interesting he pursued a romantic relationship with his assistant despite your background. How do you feel about that now considering you two have since broken up?"

I blinked a couple times, wondering if I'd missed the lights turn up because I was fully sweating at this point. I was going to look so weird on camera.

"Um, my background?"

"Some might say he realized you had no other choice given where you'd come from. Some might say he took advan—"

"Wait, how did you know we're broken up?"

"The senator's team briefed me," she said, like it was obvious. "Speaking of, there are rumors your mother is in federal prison for multiple counts of fraud. How do you respond to that?"

I shook my head. "No, I'm sorry, it's not my place to discuss my mother. Cause … you know, I'm not her so…" I shrugged and laughed, hoping these questions were just us working out the kinks. "Will this be edited out?"

The assistant cleared her throat. "Rach, you should try being honest."

"I am being honest?" I said, looking back at Penelope. "I'm feeling a little confused because this isn't really going how I'd thought. Maybe I should stop?"

"No, it's fine," she said quickly. "It takes a while to feel comfortable. Rach, we just want to tell *your* story. Let's continue."

"Can I get some water first?" I asked, standing up and accidentally knocking into a light. Penelope gasped and moved to catch the wobbling light, dropping her notes.

"Oh my gosh," I groaned, rubbing my head. "Sorry. I just need a sec because I'm having trouble breathing. I think it's the lights or maybe, uh, the lack of water? These cups are empty, you know? Not that I don't appreciate everything everyone is doing—"

"Sure, take a beat. It's not always easy to tell the truth. Let's get her a minute so she isn't so spooked."

This had to be the weirdest interview ever.

I paused my mini-freakout when I saw her notes and what appeared to be suggested headlines:

Scorned assistant speaks out amid St. Clair rumored mayoral run

Daughter of felon tells all about St. Clair son

Oh.

My.

Fudge Nuggets.

Other notes jumped out at me:

Mother in federal prison. Rach: Willing accomplice or victim of yet another broken home? With no other options ... Rach was taken advantage by her boss. (No other choice but to date Pres?) This assistant tells all in our primetime exclusive...

Pres has a history of firing people ... We'll take a look at what former employees have to say.

Is this the sort of mayor we should have? Why some are concerned another St. Clair in politics could be a bad sign.

Keeping my face neutral, I stepped back.

"What other interviews did you say you're doing with this piece?" I asked, eyeing the exits. All the doors blended into the black walls, and I realized this was it, this was the moment, I'd finally experienced hell on earth.

She scooped up her notes. "Grace Turner, Ethan Janson, and Emma Bower. Are you ready? We need to keep rolling."

"Emma Bower?" I repeated. "I used to work with her. She was let go because she was terrible at her job— wait, *Ethan Ethan*? Who is Grace?"

"She says she was fired unfairly because she wouldn't change her cleaning products," Penelope said with a shrug. "Maybe you can weigh in on that since you were privy to that sort of information as Pres' assistant?"

I sank down in my chair, ignoring my pounding forehead, and tried to catch my breath. Cool, calm, collected. Isn't that what they all wanted?

I was a positive person.

But I wasn't stupid.

I could do this.

And at the very least, if things got too bad, I could just take off my shirt to end it.

"All set?" Penelope asked.

"The cleaning product stuff is because he gets migraines. Certain smells trigger them. When she refused to switch, he couldn't keep her on."

Penelope's face fell. "Oh. Really? Migraines?"

I nodded, hoping that wasn't part of the NDA.

Surely my ex wouldn't go as far as *suing* me, right?

"Let's try a different approach. Rach, I want you to tell me whatever you'd like to say. The senator's team said you had a unique perspective, and I know our viewers would love to hear directly from you."

I'd been so foolish and desperate for change that I'd become completely blind to the signs.

Pres had been right — People believed what they

wanted to believe. And I'd *really* wanted to believe in a deal that was way too good to be true.

I'd somehow allowed myself to agree to tear Pres down to get what I wanted?

… And the senator believed I would?

"Right," I said and cleared my throat, wondering how in the world Pres did this all the time. "Okay, I'd love to be honest. I'd love to tell my side of the story, actually."

The senator's assistant perked up, and the rest of the crew listened closer.

"I think you interview people who seem to have it all put together, so you believe them without question. And I just want to be honest that I'm not like that. I don't have it all together. There's pretty good evidence out there to prove it actually."

Penelope laughed. "Like Boobgate?"

"Right, Boobgate. Or every event where I've worn the wrong shoes or outdated dresses or smudged makeup. Every time I've said the wrong thing or made a stupid joke or fell over when I was trying to look cool. Every time I've tried to be someone else. I can't do it anymore. And that's why you should trust me. Because I don't have it all together. But I believe in myself, and I've never met a problem I didn't work my way through or around. And *this* problem that you're all trying to *create*? No. Just no. A huge, resounding no," I said, punctuating my syllables by banging my fist on the armrest.

"Yeah, Pres is a scary boss, but sometimes bosses are scary. They have to, like, tell people what to do and everyone kind of hates them no matter what? But they're also the sort of people who stay up all night to work tirelessly for others, balance boring budgets, and fight for your city. I've never met someone who cares more about a town's future than Pres. He reads reports for fun. *For fun.* Like, before bed, he puts on reading glasses and reads studies on the criteria needed to get more crosswalks or affordable housing. Once, I asked if he wanted to fool around, and he asked if we could wait until after PBS' *Frontline* ended. He wasn't even joking."

"Whoa, Rach, that's not—"

"No, please don't interrupt me," I said, frowning at Penelope. "I'm not *finished*. Do you want my side of the story or not?"

She glanced at the senator's assistant.

"No, don't look at her," I demanded. "It's *my* interview, right? I'm the one with all the power, right? All the secrets? That's why the senator basically bribed me to blackmail his son? And you want to focus on *my mother*? Because even though what she did was wrong, at least she owned up to it. Honestly, I think it kind of sucks that everyone is making her mistakes my own. I've made *plenty* of my own, so we can focus on those—"

I took a deep breath, officially unhinged, "I worked at a job where no one appreciated me because I didn't think I was worth more. No one even knew my *name*. And I just blindly accepted being treated like a nobody. That was a mistake. I asked Pres to sleep with me the first night I met him. That was definitely a mistake. Super embarrassing, but I'm glad I did it because, *wow*, it paid off later. When Boobgate happened, he could've thrown me under the bus and ruined my life. Instead, we came together as a team. Was that a mistake? Sure, yeah, maybe it was reckless and cost me my heart, but I wouldn't change a thing. I'm so grateful that I got to know who Pres really is and fall in love with him because he made me realize something I knew all along."

Penelope was leaning so far forward in her chair I was certain she was about to fall off.

"I'm not my mother's mistakes. I'm not a daughter of a felon. I'm not a poor girl from a no-nothing town. I'm not a wallflower. I'm not just somebody's girlfriend. I'm not my past, and I'm not my future either. I'm a messy live-in-the-moment person who is just trying to figure it out. I am not your list of facts and figures that all add up to a version of myself that the world can judge and decide I don't belong. People believe what they want to believe. And if that's true, then I'll just believe in myself, okay? I don't need this. I don't need this interview, the blackmail, or whatever other lies people are trying to tell. The truth is, I'm in love with Pres St. Clair, and he's the best thing that's ever happened to me. And he could be the best thing that's happened to this town, too. He's not his father. He's not whatever you're trying to make him out to be. And he's not whatever a bunch of faceless polls say either. He's a *real* person. He's a compassionate, flawed, beautiful man who just wants to be better than who he came from and what he knows. And I hope he wins. This town would be lucky if he was the mayor."

I stood, trying to rip the microphone off my dress, officially over this, but instead got tangled in the wires.

"Baaaah," I groaned. "*Please* edit this part out."

Before she answered, a door behind us slammed open.

"What the *hell*? No, absolutely not, shut this down—"

Sable skidded in next. "Pres, no, don't—"

And there he was.

Tall, powerful, angry, and covered in … trash?

. . .

"No comment," Sable shouted as Pres made his way to us. "We actually have no comment."

"He can't be here," the assistant interrupted. "We specifically required a closed studio."

"Mr. St. Clair," Penelope said, jumping up and motioning for the cameraman to swivel, "what a surprise! How do you respond to the rumors that you're planning to announce your mayoral run tomorrow?"

He stood in front of me, blocking me from the camera and Penelope. "What the hell do you have her wearing?"

"His first question is *not* in fact about her appearance nor does he feel like he does or should control her clothes," Sable interjected, holding up her phone, clearly recording. "But we do wonder if Rach is chilly. It is winter, and that dress is pretty revealing."

Pres was also strangely dressed, wearing navy suit pants, a Middletown Soccer t-shirt, a clashing, ill-fitting black jacket with a dirt patch on the shoulder, and tennis shoes. His hair was disheveled, and a literal banana peel clung to his muscular thigh.

"No one would let me in this building," he seethed at Penelope, "so I doubt I'll be offering any commentary outside of the back doors near the dumpsters can easily be opened."

"What we're seeing here is an impassioned plea for the overall safety of your staff in regards to your feeble security brought up by a concerned citizen who just left his suit fitting and nothing more," Sable translated loudly.

"What happened?" he asked, reaching out to grasp me like I'd been injured. He skated his hands down my bare arms, running his fingers through my hair, and narrowed his icy fire eyes at my banged forehead. "Are you hurt?"

I shook my head. "No, I said a lot of embarrassing things and may need to go into hiding for a while but—"

"What did you ask her?" he demanded over his

shoulder at Penelope while he wrapped his jacket around my shoulders. "She doesn't owe you any answers. She doesn't owe you *anything*, and you don't get to use whatever bullshit my father dug up to hurt her."

"What my client is saying is, his strained relationship with his father can be attributed to … the overall climate of the media and political agendas unrelated to … this whole thing," Sable scrambled. "Actually, no comment."

I was basically swaddled in his jacket, but Pres didn't notice, tightening his grip on the lapels at my neck even more as he turned back to Penelope.

"You had the audacity to ask my PR person how I respond to the allegations that my ex-girlfriend and employee said I was manipulative and shouldn't run for mayor? Are you joking?"

He whirled around to the senator's assistant. "And *you*. How dare my father—"

"Pres, Pres," I said, pushing away his death grip on the jacket, "you're slowly killing me and also, um, maybe stop if you don't want people to think you're … intense."

"This set is supposed to be closed," the assistant repeated. "The senator did not agree to *any* of this. The deal is off."

"Well then why don't you tell my father to fuck off?" Pres snapped.

Everyone gasped, and the cameraman nearly knocked me over to frame the shot.

"You can't talk to me like that," the assistant shot back. "See, this is what we're talking about! He's a bad person. Are you getting this? Make sure you're getting him being an asshole—"

"Whoa, *you* can't talk to *him* like that," I snapped, pushing Pres out of the way to give her a piece of my mind. "I'm all about assistants sticking together, but you can't just twist the truth—"

It happened so quickly that I wasn't even sure all the recordings would accurately pick up the series of events.

Me, in borrowed heels that didn't fit, pushing Pres aside, and promptly slipping on an actual banana peel.

"Noooo," I groaned in slo-mo, unable to believe this was actually happening. I tried to catch my balance, grabbing something solid. A human arm. An assistant's arm that had been holding hot coffee—

"Oh my fuc—" Pres shouted, suddenly groaning in pain as he was doused in coffee. "Oh, it's so hot—"

"Take off your shirt," Sable shouted frantically. "Just rip it off—"

By the time I'd righted myself, my ankle throbbing and bare leg coated in gross banana slime, Pres was standing in the middle of the studio shirtless.

To console myself after our breakup, I'd listened to Taylor Swift and sprayed whipped cream directly from the can into my mouth.

Pres had clearly spent all his time doing crunches.

"And *you*."

He faced me with a stormy expression.

The scolding coffee hadn't slowed him down at all.

"You continue to be the most unpredictable woman I've ever met. And if this is what running for mayor is like, if we can't be together, if it asks this of you and makes you feel like you have to give away pieces of yourself, then I'm not doing it. Because winning doesn't matter if it's not with you."

I opened my mouth to interrupt, but he wouldn't stop, everything he'd ever held back coming out.

"It's not your job to be selfless so others can be selfish,

Rach. I think you dumped me because that's what you thought *I* wanted. If that's true, then you couldn't have gotten it more wrong. I don't want to be mayor, or a St. Clair, or any other variation of those things if I have to do it without you. It's not my dream. *You* are. Because who I want to be most is *yours*. Your teammate. Your plus-one. Your boyfriend. Your partner. All yours."

He sounded completely unrehearsed, each word hurried and full of emotion, as if he didn't say this now, he never would.

"Because it's you, Rach. You're the person I was supposed to meet. You're the most special person in my world. And I stopped pretending a long time ago. Because I fell for *you*, Rach. It'll always be you. You're meant to be, exactly as you are. And maybe you could be you, and I could be me, and we could figure this out together. Because I think … I hope … I believe that *we're* meant to be. And I love you. You in your entirety."

I was stunned.

He looked around the speechless studio, wincing when he noticed all the cameras. He tried to smooth his hair and grabbed his coffee-soaked shirt from the floor, looking unsure if he should put it on.

Meanwhile, my heart was pounding at an alarming rate.

"And if you don't love me back, then that's okay, too, it's your choice," he said quickly. "I can, um, still be a reference for your next job, if you need. My new assistant can set up a neutral meeting time—"

I covered my hand over my mouth, but it was too late.

I burst into laughter.

He narrowed his eyes. "You're laughing?"

"Oh my gosh," I gasped, tears filling my eyes and my

stomach clenching so hard from my laughter that I had to kneel over.

"No, this is the best day of my life, and…"

I inhaled sharply and literally snorted.

Pres' baffled expression was classic, still begging the question: How in the world did I end up in his life? How in the world did he fall in love with me? And yeah, we were going to be together forever, weren't we?

"I'm so lucky," I said with another laugh, "because now I'll have video proof of it forever. Also happy birthday, by the way. I think you win, yours was worse than mine."

He stared at me, his eyes so blue, mesmerization and amusement washing over his gorgeous face.

I reached out to offer my hand. He looked at it, unsure.

"Hi, I'm Rach Montgomery, mess extraordinaire. Would you want to go out on a real date sometime?

"Oh," he said, and his smile lit up my heart. "I'm Pres St. Clair, total loser, and I'd really like that, please."

He took my hand, pulling me to him. I laughed once more and threw my arms around him.

Then I whispered, though it was hardly a secret, "I love you, too, Pres. Of course I love you. I love everything about you. Even your prickly pear parts—"

"Please don't mention my prickly pear parts."

He glanced over his shoulder at the rest of the room. "I do need to do something about this though," he whispered. "But first, can I kiss you?"

I nodded, and he kissed me, deeply, real, and very un-mayor like.

EPILOGUE

"I've heard you've been insubordinate."

I perched on Pres' desk with my most innocent look.

He sighed and leaned back in his chair. "Rach, I know you work hard—"

"Really hard."

He smirked then cooled his features, back to being stern, his long, delicate fingers adjusting his tie. I resisted the urge to reach out, wrap it around my wrists, and pull him closer.

"If you can't figure out how to act appropriately," Pres said slowly, carefully considering his words, "then I guess I have to—"

"Please don't fire me," I gasped. "I'll do *anything*."

He leaned his head back against his chair and groaned. "This feels slightly wrong."

I held back a laugh. "Come on, you said you'd be into this. You literally said you'd be into role-play."

"I am," he huffed. To be fair, he was. We'd had lots of practice over the past 10 months. "But I also want to be clear I don't actually mean this. The power imbalance—"

I climbed onto his lap and covered his mouth with my hand. "Mr. Prescott—"

"Not my last name," he mumbled against my palm.

"You're really ruining my fantasy, so I need you to get on board before I take this to the bedroom alone. I'm in charge, and I'm demanding you be my stern boss."

"Right, okay," he said, cleared his throat, and refocused. "Maybe I could make an exception for you on one condition."

"Anything," I breathed.

He stood to unknot his tie. I shifted impatiently, loving when he made it painstakingly slow.

"You have to be quiet," he said, pressing his lips against my neck as his fingers trailed up my thigh. I shivered, nodding obediently. "We can't have anyone hear you get special treatment."

"We don't have much time," I groaned as he pushed up my dress. "Your schedule is so full."

I moaned deeply, scrambling to grip the desk's edge, and knocked over some reports and a framed photo of us once he was on his knees, his head between my legs.

"Pres," I cried out, thanking the universe for his talented tongue and double-bolted desk as I came with a blinding white hot, incredible high. "Yes, I'm so ready for you. Give me—"

He entered me in one deep, decadent motion, wrapping his arm around my waist to pull me closer as I cried out again.

"You're mine," I breathed.

With that sign, he knew I was getting close again. We all had our little quirks. Mine was staking claim to him right as I was about to come, saying *mine mine mine* over and over again.

His was my favorite, when he couldn't stay in control, his voice hurried and desperate and demanding, "Love you, Rach, god, I love you so much, fuck, Rach—"

Our lips met as our climaxes crashed over us. It was so good, so hot that fire alarm bells started blaring—

"Oh shit," Pres gasped, ditching the condom and quickly zipping his pants. "The oven—"

I blinked, still catching my breath, but he'd already shot out of the room.

What he lacked in cooking ability, he made up in soccer skills. Like dashing across the hallway and into the kitchen as smoke billowed out of the oven.

"What did you do?" I gasped as he futilely waved a potholder around the air.

"I was trying to be helpful," he said, randomly hitting oven buttons. "I'd thought we could have breakfast together before today's chaos. The box said to just pop them in the oven. I thought I set a timer, but maybe I hit broil? Is that a typo? How do you turn off the alarm?"

"Babe," I said slowly, climbing on the island and turning off the smoke alarm. "It's going to be okay."

He sighed heavily, dumping a melted box and charred bits of what may have been quiche or eclairs into the sink.

"At least we know the alarm works," he grumbled.

"That's the spirit," I laughed. "By the way, speaking of fun surprises, I'm visiting my mom this weekend."

"That's not a surprise. It's been on your calendar for weeks. You're still planning to use my car, right? It's so much more reliable, Rach, and if you're going to be driving that far consistently, I want you to be safe."

Shortly after getting back together, Pres and I'd had a long conversation about me visiting my mom in person. Not for advantageous or political reasons, he'd said, but because, the truth was, he thought I really missed her.

"Maybe it could be good for you," he'd suggested gently. "Either way, I support whatever you choose. I'm here for you."

When I'd come back after the first time, he'd been

waiting up with food — a terribly cooked homemade meal and back-up takeout in the fridge.

"It was a really good visit," I'd said, letting myself cry for the first time in years as he wrapped me in his arms. "I miss her so much, and I think by keeping it all to myself, I'd somehow kept all those emotions locked away, too. I hadn't really had a chance to be real with her, to show her the ups and downs of my life because I was worried she'd feel bad or like she was missing out. We had one of the first honest conversations we'd had in years. I told her we needed to cut the bullshit."

He'd raised an eyebrow. "You cursed?"

I'd laughed, nodding. "I was trying to be firm and serious. I thought, what would Pres do? Then I did a modified version of that. But I think she really just wants to be my mom, no matter what. Talk about boys, gossip about our coworkers or, in her case, inmates, you know. Our situation is just a little different, but that doesn't mean she's not my mom."

He'd smiled softly. "That's great, Rach."

"I think Ethan using her against me was the final straw. Like, why distance myself from her, spend time being ashamed, and try to pretend everything is okay, if it's going to end up how it did regardless? So in a way, it was a good thing, I think."

That had been a few months ago, and my mom and I were working on rebuilding our relationship — even if it looked a little less than traditional. I was kind of a pro at going about relationships nontraditionally anyway.

"Yes, I'm still planning to use your car," I said now as Pres tossed the wet, melted box in the trash. "But I was thinking, what if you drove?"

"I really don't like driving," he said, focused on

rinsing the sink. "I could get you a driver if you're uncomfortable using my car."

"Um, okay, but what if you still came with me?"

He knelt down to look under the sink for a sponge, glancing at me with a confused frown. "Rach, I don't need to supervise you with a driver. I'm not that worried about my vehicle."

I groaned. "I'm asking if you'd like to meet my mom."

He blinked at me and then dropped the sponge on the floor, stunned. Even though things were getting pretty serious between us, maybe this was *too* serious. Meeting the parents was a big deal, and I'd bombed the first and only time I'd met his father, so maybe meeting my mom was just too much—

"I'd be honored," he said, standing and meeting my gaze seriously. "But what if she doesn't like me?"

I laughed, relieved. "You'll be fine. It's probable you'll even be charming."

He looked utterly unconvinced. "It's your *mom*. She made you, and you're fantastic. And I've yet to prove success with parental interactions."

I burst out laughing. "If it helps, the last time I visited, she said you're clearly a Capricorn. So she's prepared."

He shook his head. "I still don't really know what that means."

"It's mostly a compliment," I said with a grin. "Just be yourself, Pres. She'll love you, I promise. Just like I do."

He still looked apprehensive, but kissed me anyway.

I hopped away before we got too carried away. Since his team had grown and now worked out of a satellite office, the penthouse had become a very distracting playhouse.

"I'm trying to be responsible," I laughed when he

pouted. "And your schedule is packed. We have to go. Want to pick up breakfast burritos on the way?"

"Breakfast burritos," he agreed solemnly. "Then we vote."

...

"Pecgate is trending again," Sable said tiredly once I met her in Hotel Chanceux's ballroom while Pres did get-out-the-vote things with his group of volunteers. "I told my interns to stop sending me screenshots of Pres' bare chest, but they seem committed to the task."

I peeked over her shoulder and tried to hold back a smile. Of course, I failed.

In exchange for Penelope to change her story angle, Pres offered her an exclusive sit-down to give her what the media had been asking him for years ... what he really thought about his father. He outlined all the ways Senator St. Clair had let down Middletown and the state in general.

What was supposed to be his greatest weakness — his dad's shady deals and broken promises — somehow became his biggest strength.

What we hadn't planned for was, right after it aired, the makeup artist posting Pres' shirtless declaration of love on Instagram. Even after Pecgate stopped trending online, one thing had become clear.

People really liked a politician who didn't hold back on how he felt. Truthful trumped unlikeable any day.

And the poll where people thought he was too dull, too cold, too stuck-up, and too stiff ... that was a concern of the past.

"You have to run," I'd said, holding up the latest batch of emails from fans, activists, and political organizers. "They want *you*, Pres."

He'd looked up from where he'd been lounging on my couch struggling to knit a potholder — a newfound obsession to keep his hands busy as he worked on quitting smoking — and frowned.

"I already said I wasn't running. It's not worth it."

"You said you wouldn't if it hurt me. But we're a team. And if you want this, I do, too. Because your passion and drive for this is part of why I love you. So let's figure it out. Together, Pres."

He'd paused for a very long time then inhaled slowly, nodding. "I only have one condition."

The next morning, just like we'd agreed, he was in a suit and evaluating countless campaign managers, and I was applying to Middletown University.

He carried his boldly truthful, no-nonsense strategy into everything. He snapped sarcastic retorts and straight facts in debates, didn't hold back in interviews, and even went live online consistently under the header of "what everyone's telling you, and what's actually real."

When the prison story finally broke, most voters on his side knew him — and me — well enough that it didn't have a scientifically significant impact.

"Sometimes pollsters get things wrong," Pres had said with a shrug, unable to stop laughing at his team's shocked faces.

Sure, he had haters. That was just the reality of the game. And Pres was always great at playing games.

He also had a lot of fans.

And those fans were translated to the map I stood in front of now. Middletown was spread out on a massive screen on the stage, district by district filling with colors that would determine our future.

As the night continued and the map started to fill, the

room did as well. It was an incredible mix of all walks of life, business people, volunteers, parents, community members, activists, students, and more. Everyone was enjoying the open bar and the spread from local restaurants. We'd even booked a local band and the community center's children's dancing troop.

"I thought of a silver lining if I lose," Pres whispered when he appeared, wrapping his arms around my waist. "I won't have to fire you."

I laughed and rested my head back against his chest. "Gosh, you're so romantic."

After we'd gotten back together, we'd been cuddling in bed when he'd asked if I had interest in coming back.

"Because Olivia and Jamar really miss you," he'd said as casually as he could possibly manage.

"What's wrong with your current assistant?"

"Other than that she keeps watering the fake plants Olivia has in the dining room, asked how to put Hugo Boss on my calendar, didn't think the purple carpet installed in my office was a mistake, sent my car to the wrong location four times, and put a recurring 'covfefe time' on all our calendars and we're still unsure if that was a joke? And I just noticed several of my emails have been stuck in my outbox for weeks. Look, my letter of recommendation for you never sent."

"You wrote me one?" I'd gasped.

He'd rolled his eyes. "Of course I did. I said I would. I'll send it to you now—"

"So what does it mean if my former client who is asking me to return to my former job just sent me a glowing letter of recommendation?"

"Clearly, a demand for you exists. You have leverage. You could separate from your agency and come in full-time. Negotiate a higher salary, ask for a flexible schedule, determine boundaries that make sense—"

I'd stopped him to clarify that he was, in fact, coaching me on how to negotiate against him. He'd grinned, and I told him I would put a meeting on his calendar to discuss it during work hours. Then I pulled him on top of me.

If he won, I'd transition to being just his personal assistant, and he'd have an executive assistant at the mayor's office.

And if he lost ... well, I'd have to renegotiate my schedule anyway because I had my own secret. I couldn't wait to tell him I'd just received an acceptance letter from Middletown University, congratulating me for being selected as a Jefferson Fellow.

But tonight was his night, and why wouldn't I try to have two days of celebrations?

"No matter what happens," I said, squeezing where he'd been rubbing his thumb against his index finger, "you'll always be a winner in my heart."

"That's what people say to losers." He paused, considering. "But thank you. I do think it helps."

I just laughed.

Some things hadn't changed.

In the moments before it became clear how the election would go, Pres pulled something out from his pocket.

"I've heard this is good luck," he said. "But I think it's true only when it's in your hands."

He pressed it in my palm, his fingers brushing against my pulse racing in my wrist. It was the only thing I'd ever seen him hold on to.

A scrap of clutter, something seemingly insignificant.
Meaningless.

Just a worn matchbook with one match missing, used

almost a year ago in this same place, exchanged when we were strangers, lost and alone and pretending, on the cusp of the moment when we'd found the other.

"You don't need good luck anymore?"

"I have you." He pressed a kiss against my lips. "I'm forever indebted to you, Rach. With or without this matchbook. I owe you one, always."

The great thing about your former-boss-fake-ex-current-client-and-very-real-boyfriend running for mayor was that he was plastered everywhere — on yard signs, in headlines, on social media, even in ads following you online— and his face was really, truly, amazingly gorgeous.

The even better thing?

His smile when he won.

I had no idea what he said in his acceptance speech.

I had kind of blacked out after he'd asked me to share the moment with him on stage.

I wasn't even sure how I got off the stage after he praised me in front of everyone. Jamar and Olivia were screaming in my ear and hugging me, Derek and Roe had snuck in airhorns to cheer on their most serious friend, and several volunteers cried happy tears around us.

"Well," Sable said with a smile, her fingers flying on her phone screen. "We've gone viral again."

I barely heard her.

Because as soon as he was finished, he paused, smiled at the crowd — finally, a real smile for everyone — and then walked off the stage, right up to me, and kissed me.

Which was a good thing because the flashing cameras were pretty bright.

"You were right," I said, pulling back to say something I had been thinking for a while.

"Of course I was," he said immediately. He grinned, tracing his fingers over my smile. "About what?"

"We are meant to be. I love you, Pres."

The smile that appeared on his face was so genuine that I felt it, deeply and directly, in my heart.

Then, of course, he frowned, quick to correct.

"Well, I love you more."

I laughed. "It's not a competition."

"It's always a competition."

Then he kissed me.

It was a promising kind of kiss, a sign that this was certainly not going to be a one-time thing.

ABOUT THE AUTHOR

Amanda Gambill is a Top 40 Amazon bestselling contemporary romance author.

Check out her other works, *A Guy Like Him*, an opposites-attract romance, and *For The Record, I Hate You*, a frenemies-to-lovers romance.

—

Want a Pres and Rach sequel? A whole novel dedicated to Sable (hint, hint)? If you've read my other books, maybe you're curious about Roe? Come let me know on Bookstagram at @byamandagambill! I love interacting with readers.

Printed in Great Britain
by Amazon